Be Here Now

by
Julia Goda

Gill,
hope you enjoy Jason
& Loreley

Jul Goe

Jill.

Hope you enjoy Team
& Loretey

Jn Coe

Copyright

Dedication

To Andre,

my dear husband, my best friend, the only person that I take a
kick in the behind from without complaining (too much)—and
frequently do.

Thank you for supporting me on this amazing journey.

Like so many things in my life, I couldn't have done it without
you

One

PROLOGUE

LORELEY

Eight Years Earlier

The beginnings of Pearl Jam's *Given To Fly* woke me out of my deep slumber. Thinking it was my alarm, I fumbled for the snooze button knowing that I could push it at least three more times. I was a snooze button girl and always set my alarm to wake me a good twenty minutes before I actually had to get up.

I hated mornings. I didn't do mornings. And since it was Saturday and I didn't have any early classes, my alarm should not be going off at this hour. I must have forgotten to turn it off last night.

I hit the snooze button.

Nothing happened.

I opened my eyes just enough so I could peek at the alarm

1

clock on my bedside table. It was 9:30 and the little red button next to the words *Alarm On* was not lit, which meant it wasn't the alarm that was making the noise. It was my phone. The ringing stopped, then immediately started up again. I ignored it and pulled the blanket over my head. Whoever called me at this hour on the weekend knew better and could leave a message. It stopped again and thankfully, stayed silent. I rolled over, snuggling deep under the blanket and into the pillow, and went back to sleep.

What seemed like only seconds later, I was woken up again. This time, someone was knocking on my door.

"Go away, Chris!"

Silence for a second, then the knocking started up again.

Arrgh!

I opened my eyes. He had got to be kidding me.

I grabbed the blanket, shoved it back angrily, and stomped to the door as I ranted.

"Since when do your hook-ups kick you out this early? You better have coffee if you expect me to—"

I opened the door and froze mid-sentence.

It wasn't Chris, my ex-boyfriend now best friend, who was standing in front of me.

It was Jason Sanders.

Jason Sanders, the extremely good-looking singer and guitarist of the Indie rock band I had seen at the bar the night before. He was also one of the most notorious players on campus, which was why I had blown him off when he approached me after the gig at first. But against my better judgement, I had ended up talking to him and had been surprised at how easy and comfortable it was and how much we had in common. We had talked for so long that I hadn't realized how late it had been, so he had walked me to my dorm in the early morning hours, but I hadn't let him into my room when he asked to talk some more. I wasn't that kind of girl. I also wasn't stupid.

"I'm sorry to disappoint. I'm not Chris and I hope to God that Chris isn't your boyfriend. Though judging by your little rant, I doubt it, since I don't think you're the kind of girl who would be okay with her boyfriend hooking up with other girls. Or at least I hope so. On the bright side, however, I did bring you coffee." He held up one of the to-go coffee cups he was holding.

I stayed frozen, too surprised and shocked to do anything but stare at him.

Jason chuckled.

"You're not a morning person, are you?"

I shook my head slowly.

Jason chuckled again. "Then I'm glad I brought you coffee. You gonna let me in?" That took me out of my shock. I looked down at myself. I was wearing my short pajama pants—they were so short they were just long enough to cover my ass cheeks— and a tight tank top with nothing underneath. I felt my cheeks redden with embarrassment as I looked back at him.

"Uhm, I'm still in my pajamas." Jason's eyes looked me down, oh so slowly, before they met my eyes again. The instant heat in them made me gasp. Jason smiled a knowing smile.

"Believe me. That fact wasn't lost on me." I blushed. His smile turned into a grin.

I tried to shake myself out of the daze he had put me in to ask a very important question. "What are you doing here?" I asked, still a little breathless.

"I said I'd call you today, which I did, but you didn't pick up, so I decided to come over."

"I'm not usually up this early on the weekends."

3

"Neither am I," he said in a low voice. My eyes got wide at the meaning behind those words.

"How about this," he said as he handed me one of the coffees. "I'll wait outside while you get ready and then I'll take you out for breakfast." He changed his voice back to normal, taking pity on my sorry state. I was grateful. Still, I had my doubts as to where he was going with that invitation or what he would expect in return.

I took the coffee but kept looking at him. "Why?" We both seemed to know that my question was about more than the reason why he wanted to take me to breakfast. Jason stepped closer to me, invading my personal space. He dipped his head down so he could keep holding my eyes.

"I like you. More than I've ever liked a girl. You intrigue me and I'm never intrigued. I want to spend time with you, get to know you."

I narrowed my eyes at him. "I told you last night, Jason, I'm not one of those girls who swoon over and fall for pretty boys and their pretty words. You won't get into my pants."

He gave me another grin.

"I realize that and it's strangely refreshing. That's one of the things I like about you: your honesty, your no-bullshit attitude. This is not some trap or play. I really want to get to know you better. Though I do hope to change your mind about the no sex thing eventually."

I raised my eyebrows and thought about what he was saying.

"Come on, Loreley. Let me take you to breakfast. Let me prove to you that I'm serious."

And that's what he did.

Over the next few weeks, he proved to me that he was serious about getting to know me; then he proved to me that he was serious about a lot of other things.

We fell head over heels in love.

Or so I thought.

Two Years Later

"Congratulations, Lore. I know this means a lot to you." Chris said as he hugged me tightly.

"Thanks, Chris. It does. I never thought I would get in with a label that big. I didn't think I stood a chance."

"This just proves even more that you're awesome. You just wait and see. They're gonna love you so much, they'll offer you a job before your internship is over."

I laughed.

That was highly unlikely. Though, I loved that Chris had that much faith in me.

"I doubt that. All I'll probably do all summer is grab coffees and hope I get the lunch orders right. But still, it's a foot in the door that I can't pass up."

Chris chuckled. "Well, then you'll be the best coffee fetcher and lunch girl in all of L.A." He pulled back and looked at me. "When are you leaving?"

"In two days."

Chris' eyebrows shot up. "Two days? Poor Jason."

I sighed. "I know. He's not gonna be happy. Heck, I'm not happy that I won't see him all summer, but I can't say no to this. He'll understand."

Chris said nothing, just looked at me with skepticism in his eyes.

"He will, Chris. He knows I want this and he wants me to be happy. And it's a step closer to the future we both want."

"Yeah, it is. But I think you underestimate how much that

man needs to be close to you. He can hardly go a day without seeing you. Now he's gonna have to adjust from thinking you'd be with him during his first real tour to not only not having you with him, but you being in a city like L.A. on your own."

"I can take care of myself."

"I'm well aware of that. So is Jason. That doesn't change the fact that he's not gonna like it."

I sighed again.

Chris was somewhat right. I knew that Jason would be upset about the fact that I wouldn't be able to go with him and his band on their first tour. It's all we'd been talking about for the past few months. A scout had approached them after they played a gig at one of Austin's bigger bars earlier that year and had set up a meeting with a manager, who had taken them under her wing and had organized a summer tour across half the country where *The Crowes* would play at bars and small festivals all summer. I was supposed to go with them and once the tour was over and was hopefully successful, we'd move to L.A. together, where I would try my luck to get a foot in with a label somewhere as an intern or personal assistant to get some experience under my belt while he kept working with his band and hopefully got some studio time.

That had been the plan. And me accepting an internship for the summer that started in less than a week meant it couldn't happen that way.

He would be disappointed. *I* was disappointed that I wouldn't see him for three whole months. But I was also excited. Excited to get this chance, to get some experience and be able to learn from some of the best people in the music business, which was a dream come true. And I was eager to get an early start on our future together.

Yes, Jason would be disappointed, but he loved me and

would be happy for me, for us, once the initial blow had worn off.

I was absolutely, no doubt about it, certain of that.

A few hours later I wasn't so certain anymore.

"You can't go, Loreley. I don't want you to." Jason had not taken my news well at all. Worse than I thought, he wasn't just disappointed. He was mad as hell. And that was starting to piss me off.

"Yes, I can, Jason. This is my career, my future we're talking about. I have to go. It's what I want."

"*Your* future? I thought it was *our* future. All this time it has always been *our* future. Now you get one lousy offer for a shitty internship and everything else isn't important anymore? I thought you weren't one of those selfish bitches. Guess I was wrong."

I flinched and gasped as hurt hit my chest at hearing his hateful words. He had never talked to me that way, had never said anything remotely negative about me or *to* me, had always been loving and supportive and gentle with me. Sure, we'd had fights, but they'd never turned dirty or ugly. Not like this.

I stood there, completely stunned. But he didn't take back those hurtful words. Nor did he apologize. Not even when tears started to fill my eyes and silently run down my cheeks. He didn't say anything. Didn't do anything but stand there and glare at me. I turned around as if in a trance without saying another word and walked out of his apartment.

He didn't try to stop me, nor did he come after me.

The next morning, I stood in Chris' apartment, sipping my coffee as I stared silently out the window. I was lost in thought, still trying to wrap my mind around what had happened last night.

"He didn't mean it, Lore." Chris was sitting at the kitchen

7

table behind me, drinking his own coffee. The night had been long, filled with lots of tears on my side and lots of talking on Chris' side. Neither of us had gotten much sleep.

"So you've said."

"And I'll say it again. I'll say it a million times if that's what you need to hear. He didn't mean it."

"Then why hasn't he called? Why hasn't he come after me?"

That shut Chris up.

I turned around and looked at him. He was shaking his head. "I don't know, Lore. But I'm sure there's an explanation. Maybe he needed to cool off first or maybe he is too embarrassed. Who knows, he could be sitting in front of your dorm room door waiting for you to come home. What I *do* know is that he didn't mean what he said last night. He's scared of losing you, scared of being without you for three months. Being scared makes men do stupid shit, stupid shit we almost always regret the minute it happens."

I wanted to believe him so desperately. It hurt thinking that the man I was in love with and had imagined and planned my future with more than once could say those hurtful words he said last night and not regret them.

"Go to him. Talk to him. You'll regret it if you don't."

I nodded. He was right. I would regret if I left without at least trying to talk to him.

I went to my dorm room first to take a shower and change into fresh clothes. My whole way there, I was hoping and praying that Chris was right and I would find Jason sitting in front of my room waiting for me to come home so he could apologize.

He didn't.

The hall was empty when I turned the corner and there was

no note on my door or any sign that he had been there. But I powered through the disappointment and told myself that he was probably still sleeping. Or maybe he was just waiting for a decent time to come to me. It was early. He knew better than anyone that I hated being woken up early in the mornings. Instead of waiting, I would take Chris' advice and go to him.

Less than thirty minutes later, I wished I hadn't as I stared at the blonde who was standing in front of me.

The second she opened the door for me, I knew.

She was wearing nothing but a towel, her hair wet and uncombed, her skin still covered in water droplets as if she had jumped out of the shower just seconds ago.

She didn't have to say anything for me to know that Jason didn't need to cool off last night or had been too embarrassed to come after me or try to call me. No, none of what Chris had said was true.

Jason had been too busy screwing this blond groupie whore to do any of that.

I didn't need her to say anything, but her words still confirmed it. "He's still in the shower. You can come in and wait I guess."

No, I absolutely did not want to come in and wait.

I worked hard to keep the overwhelming hurt and devastation off my face. I wouldn't give either of them the satisfaction. But I knew I wouldn't be strong enough to keep my voice neutral. So for the second time in less than twenty-four hours, I turned around and walked away from Jason without saying another word.

"You want me to tell him you came by?"

I shook my head but said nothing and kept walking without turning around. The door clicked shut.

Not even five minutes later, my phone started ringing. I

9

ignored it, just like I did the next three calls and five text messages that came in. They were all from Jason.

Not a single tear left my eyes until I got to my room and buried myself under the blankets. Then the floodgates opened and I cried and cried until I couldn't cry anymore and fell into a fitful sleep.

It was the next day before I checked my phone. I deleted all of Jason's calls and voice mails as well as text messages without listening to them or reading them and then called Chris.

He came over and helped me pack.

The day after that I boarded a plane to L.A.

Two

LORELEY

I looked over the crowd as I finished drawing another beer and closed the tap. Rock music blared through the speakers and the noises of a bar fuller than it should be wafted over me. Saturday night at Coopers was always busy, but with summer coming, our quaint little small town in the Rocky Mountains was starting to fill up with tourists, which meant that the bar was just as crowded. Every single table was taken and the bar was full, some people double-parking at the bar, because there weren't any stools left to sit on. Cindy and Ashley were running their butts off out there. Their tips would be great tonight, but I'd have to talk to Chris about hiring another bartender and at least two more waitresses to get us through the season.

I looked down the bar counter and saw Rick Summers sitting at the end, looking sullen, like he had done so often in the past few months. His head was bowed to the glass in front of him—whiskey neat it looked like—elbows to the bar, the fingers of his right hand holding the glass loosely, swirling the whiskey. I decided to ignore the orders being shouted at me for the moment and headed over to him.

He didn't hear or see me approach, which was unusual for

11

him. Rick was a cop, a detective, and would normally see everything that was going on around him. He was a laid back guy, but intense and always alert. That had changed last Thanksgiving when his already stupid sister Gina did something even more stupid and helped a guy kidnap my friend Ivey. The guy had been Ivey's ex. He had beaten her badly when they had been together, so badly that she had ended up in the hospital for almost a week. She had pressed charges, so he had ended up in jail and was looking for revenge. Gina had helped him because she was petty and jealous. Ivey and Cal had just gotten together a few weeks earlier. Gina had always had a crush on Cal and for some fucked up reason thought she had a claim on him. So she helped Ivey's ex teach Ivey a lesson and was now paying for her stupidity by being locked up in a penitentiary for conspiracy to commit kidnapping. I hadn't been a big fan of her before that, nobody in town had, but now I was even less of one.

But I *did* feel bad for Rick.

He didn't deserve this.

He has always been a good guy. I knew him from when he used to hang out with Cal in high school; I actually had a small crush on him back then. He was tall, dark, and handsome, had intense dark blue eyes with a shimmer of green to them, had an easy smile he used often, and never minded when I followed him and Cal around; never treated me like his best friend's unwanted little sister; never teased me or tried to get rid of me. I think he had known that I had a crush on him and had found it very amusing. Still, he never teased me about it. He became one of my good friends when I grew up and grew out of that crush.

"Hey, Rick. You okay?" I asked as I made it to him. I leaned my elbows on the bar across from him, getting close enough to talk quietly without anyone overhearing.

His head shot up and his sad eyes warmed as they saw me.

He gave me a small smile that was nowhere near the easy smile he used to have. "Hey, Loreley."

His non-answer was answer enough. He wasn't okay and probably wouldn't be until he found a way to forgive himself for not having protected his sister, or figure out that it wasn't his fault his sister was a total idiot and vindictive whacko bitch in the first place.

"Went to see Gina today. She's not doing so well." His eyes went back down to his drink.

I was torn. On the one hand, I didn't want Gina to do well in jail. She deserved to be locked up. Ivey could have been killed and Gina had had a hand in that because she couldn't get over the fact that Cal didn't want her skanky ass in his and his son's life. How she could have ever dreamed he would want her, I had no idea. As I said, she was a whacko bitch, totally delusional. Nobody in town blamed Rick, not even Ivey. There was nothing that Rick could have done to prevent what had happened. Gina had always been a bitch. Even as a kid she had made other kids' lives a living hell. She was the queen bee in high school and had kept on living her life like that after she graduated. It had only been a matter of time until she got what she deserved. Nobody would have thought that she was capable of going to such extremes, but there you go. You couldn't foresee what people did, especially crazy people, so Rick wasn't to blame for any of it.

Not knowing what to say, I put my hand on top of his. His eyes came back to mine. They were still sad, but also still warm.

"I know you never liked her and think she got what she deserved. You're right. Hell, I didn't like her most of the time. She did wrong and had to be punished for what she did; trying to get Ivey hurt; thinking she could get away with it. I get all that and I agree with it. Wholeheartedly. But she's still my little sister

13

and seeing her like that…I can't help it. I want her out of there."

"I know, Rick. And I understand. You wouldn't be the man you are if you didn't feel that way about your sister. You feel responsible for her, want to protect her. You're a good man for still feeling that way after what she's done."

"A good man, huh? A stupid one I'd say."

"Rick, you are not stupid," I said in a firm voice. "You're a good man and you feel guilty. I keep telling you, you don't have to feel that way. It wasn't your fault. Nobody could have seen that coming."

"You taking your own advice on that?" He shot back at me. His eyes were serious now. He had me there. I gave him a small sad smile. "I'm working on it, Rick. I'm getting there. And so should you."

His eyes stayed locked to mine as he studied me. Then he nodded slowly. "I can see it, Loreley. You're doing better. You're stronger. You're finding your way back to you." He took a deep breath before he shook his head and chuckled bitterly. "I'm sorry. I came to the bar tonight to get my head straight and check on you and here I am, brooding. Trying to pull you down with me. I'm an asshole."

"Oh, shut it, Rick. You are not," I snapped at him while I slapped his hand and straightened.

"Spunky. I always liked that about you," Rick murmured through a smile. His easy smile was back. I grinned at him in relief until I saw a mischievous sparkle in his eyes.

"You think I'm a good man, why is it you haven't agreed to go out with me?"

My smile died. "I'm not ready, Rick. I've told you that."

"And how long are you gonna keep using that excuse?"

I glared at him, not sure how to answer that. It was an excuse of course. I was as ready as I was ever gonna get. As

14

Chris would say, it was time to get back in the saddle.

I opened my mouth when I heard my name called and turned my head to see who was yelling at me.

"Hey, Loreley. You gonna get to work or you gonna chit chat all night?" That was Chris, giving me the get-a-move-on glare while he was handing out beers.

I turned my head back to face Rick again, seeing his head was turned to glare at Chris. It came back to me when I started speaking.

"I'm sorry, Rick. I gotta get to work." Rick's eyes narrowed on me a second, then he gave me a chin lift. I moved away from him and started taking orders and handing out drinks.

For the next hour or so, I didn't have much time to think about anything other than making and handing out drinks and exchanging the occasional joke or sarcastic comment with patrons. We usually had a band playing on Saturdays and I had been pretty ticked off that they had cancelled at the last minute, but right now I was glad they had. It was hard enough keeping up without having the crowd the band would have brought.

When the crowd finally started to thin a little, Chris and I took a little breather as we leaned against the back of the bar.

"You know, it's calmed down some. I think the worst is over. You should go up there and have some fun." He lifted his chin towards the stage. "Give it a nice farewell. It deserves to go out with a bang, don't you think?"

I agreed. It definitely deserved to go out with a bang.

We were getting a new stage. The contractor was coming tomorrow. Our old lady would be replaced by a bigger and better one.

I grinned at Chris.

He returned my grin then lifted his chin in the direction of the stage again, telling me I should get my behind up there and

15

play already.

My grin got bigger and I rolled up on my toes to give him a kiss on the cheek.

"You good behind the bar by yourself for a little while?" I asked.

"I can handle it. Now get your butt up there."

I gave him another peck on the cheek before I went to the back room to get my guitar.

The stage was on the left side of the room when you entered through the front door. There were a few wooden booths along the window front as well as round dark brown wooden tables that could seat four in the open space in front of the stage. For bigger events, like the band playing next weekend, we had to move most of the tables to the other side of the room, but when it was just me and my guitar, or we had an open mike night, we left the tables where they were, so that people could enjoy the music while sitting down with their drinks. By tomorrow night, there would be more tables and chairs where the stage was now, and the new bigger stage would start to take shape on the other side of the room against the far wall.

When I stepped onto the dimly lit stage, I heard shouts and hollers throughout the bar, making me smile in anticipation. I grabbed a bar stool from the corner of the stage and moved it in front of the microphone, hopped onto it, and looked out to my audience. From where I was sitting, I could see the whole place. Being on a stage about to perform was exhilarating, always had been. I had been told before that my voice would get me places, but I wasn't much for being in the lime light or playing in big places. My dream had been to work in the background and write music, but then life happened and changed my priorities. But every now and then—in a small setting like this—I enjoyed sharing my music and my voice. It was one of the most intimate things I could imagine, sharing yourself and your emotions like that with an audience.

I started strumming my guitar randomly, not really playing anything specific, just running my fingers across the strings softly and playfully, letting my fingertips feel the roughness of the metal strings. As I looked out over the people watching me expectantly, I noticed that I knew probably only half of them. It looked like tourist season really was starting early this year.

I kept strumming quietly when I addressed my audience.

"A lot of you know that Cooper's has been jonesing for a new stage for some time now. Well, our wish has been granted, and starting tomorrow, this old lady will be replaced by a bigger and better one." I looked down at my hands on the guitar as I kept strumming then looked back up. "But I wanted to give her one last farewell. She's seen some good times throughout the years and deserves one last hurrah."

Loud hollers and hoots echoed through the room.

I grinned. "I see you guys agree."

The hoots and shouts got louder. My grin got bigger.

"Well, for everyone who doesn't know me, my name is Loreley Cooper, and I'll be playing a few of my favourite songs for you tonight. If you'd like me to play *your* favourite song, feel free to shout it out and I'll see what I can do."

I stopped strumming and laid my hands flat on the strings, stopping the sound.

"The first song I am going to play is one of the saddest and most beautiful songs out there. I dedicate it to the people in my life I have lost, people who were and still are close to my heart and who I think about and miss every day."

I looked down to my hands as I started playing the opening notes of Eric Clapton's *Tears in Heaven* unplugged version. The audience was quietly watching and listening as I played the quiet

17

and sad notes of the song's intro. When I started singing, asking if he'd know my name, I lifted my eyes back to the people watching me. But instead of seeing their eyes on me, I saw the eyes of the people I had lost. They were watching me, smiling at me, encouraging me.

Losing two of the most important people in my life, people I had loved with all my heart, had almost destroyed me, and I had struggled for the past year to come to terms with it and move on with my life. When I got to the part of the song about being strong and carrying on, tears started to pool in my eyes. I remembered how hard it was sometimes, how painful, to get up every day, knowing they were no longer a part of this world. But like Rick had said earlier, I was in a better place now; I was stronger. As I sang, my mind went through all the good and happy memories it had stored, and I felt a kind of peacefulness wash over me that I hadn't felt in a long time. It almost took my breath away. I kept on singing and closed my eyes, giving myself over to the song, feeling it, breathing it, letting its words heal me.

Because that was what it did.

It healed me.

It helped me say goodbye. Eric Clapton's beautiful and devastating song about love and loss helped me let go.

My eyes stayed closed throughout the whole song, throughout the whole almost five minutes of it as I watched those peaceful and happy eyes I could see behind my eyelids as they watched me, and I let go of the pain. I could practically feel it leave my body and be replaced with acceptance, a sad acceptance, but acceptance nonetheless. Acceptance they were gone from this world but would live on in my heart and soul, would forever be a part of me; and because of that, would never be lost to me. I carried them with me every hour, every minute, every second of every day, and the thought of them being with me made me unbelievably grateful and happy.

As the song came to an end and I played its final notes, I opened my eyes again and saw some of the feelings I was feeling reflected on the people's faces in front of me. It was a powerful song, and I wasn't surprised that people felt deep listening to it. And seeing as half of the people here had known me since I was born, they knew about the loss I had endured and had watched me go through it.

I ended the song on a smile, finally feeling at complete peace with myself. I caught Chris's eyes behind the bar. They were worried and concerned as they took me in. My smile grew bigger and brighter, reassuring him and myself that I was okay. His eyes warmed on me and his face split into a big and proud grin as he started hollering and clapping, breaking the silence that had come over the room since I finished the song. Every person in the room followed his lead and started clapping and shouting. I let that wash over me, too, as I pulled myself together.

"Thank you," I said into the microphone when the noise died down.

"I promise that was the only sad song I will play tonight. Now, I heard there is a birthday celebration going on tonight, so let's party and play some rock 'n roll!"

The cheers and shouting and clapping picked up again as I started the next song and continued for the next hour. I played mostly classic rock songs, but mixed them with the occasional newer hit and requests that were shouted at me.

I had a blast.

And judging by the smiles and laughs and singing and general rocking out, I was guessing, so did everyone else in the bar.

"All right everyone," I said as I got up from my stool and

took the guitar strap off my shoulder. "That's it for tonight. Make sure to stop by next Saturday when *Breaking Habit* is christening the new stage!"

I made my way to the side of the stage to hop off it when I a loud voice stopped me in my tracks. "Wait! I've got one more request!"

I looked out over the people to try and pinpoint whose voice that had been. There were so many people I didn't know that I had no clue. A lot of them were turning around to look at the shadows in the back, like me, trying to figure out who was speaking.

"Please," I heard, "Just one more," the voice begged. It sounded strangely familiar, but for the life of me, I couldn't figure out whom it belonged to.

Giving in to the request, I walked back to the stool and sat down. "All right, I'll play one more. What'll it be?"

"*Angel* by Sarah McLachlan," I heard the voice say and my body went solid, my mind finally making the connection as to whose voice I was hearing.

It was Jason Sanders' voice.

Jason fucking Sanders.

I had forgotten. Forgotten what that voice used to do to me; how his voice could affect me.

But it all came crushing back now.

Memories flooded my brain, the good and the bad: his voice singing to me while we were in bed, both naked after making love, me lying back, watching him, while he sat cross legged with his guitar in his lap, his eyes lovingly on me, singing the very song to me he was now asking me to sing; his growly voice as he was saying my name while moving inside me; his soft voice as he said he loved me.

And his angry voice filled with accusation as he told me I

20

was being selfish for wanting to chase my dream of becoming a song-writer and go to L.A. without him.

And finally, his half-naked whore's voice after she opened the door to his apartment, telling me Jason was in the shower.

All those memories ran through my mind within seconds and I squinted my eyes, trying to find him in the shadows.

That bastard.

He knew of course that *Angel* was my all-time favourite song. I loved Sarah McLachlan, and this song in particular was so beautiful, it had always threatened to bring me to tears. Jason knew this. Back then, I sang this song to him more than once, just as he had to me.

And now that motherfucking bastard was in my bar after almost six years, asking me to sing it for him again.

I closed my eyes in an effort to get control over all the feelings that were rushing through me. When I had stood on that doorstep, looking at the whore he cheated on me with, my world had turned from not-being-able-to-wait-for-the-future-to-start to a world of hurt and betrayal and disbelief. When a few months later, he refused to even talk to me on the phone and I had gone to one of his concerts to talk to him, my world had turned from hurt and betrayal and disbelief to one of anger and hate.

That. Mother. Fucking. *Bastard.*

I opened my eyes again and now I could see him standing at the back of the room.

God!

He looked just as good as I remembered in his jeans and t-shirt, his tattooed arms hanging at his side. It made me hate him even more. His hazel eyes seemed almost black they were so dark and they were locked on me.

They were serious.

And determined.

21

And remorseful.

Yeah, right.

He had no business showing up at my bar out of the blue, asking me to sing to him. Looking at me like that. Looking at me like he was asking for forgiveness. He had no business being anywhere near me!

There would be no forgiveness from me.

He had broken my heart, obliterated it, made me turn into a person I didn't recognize, sent me through hell and back twice.

He didn't deserve my forgiveness.

He didn't deserve shit from me.

But I would play the song.

I'd had one hour of acceptance and peace, one hour where I felt like I could be happy again at some point in my life. And I wouldn't let him take that from me. He had taken enough.

So I would play that damn song.

I would play it and show him that I didn't care, that neither he nor the significance of the song had any power over me.

That I was over him.

That I had moved on and he meant nothing.

His eyes were still boring into mine as I pulled the guitar strap back around my shoulder and settled in.

"Sorry, guys. I know I promised you I wouldn't play another sad song tonight, but since it's someone else's request you can't blame me. So here it goes."

I kept my eyes on him, making sure to have a look of indifference on my face that told him his presence didn't touch me, that he didn't affect me. I could see his eyes flare and his jaw clench and I smiled a cold smile I didn't know I had in me. Then I started playing the song, my eyes fixed on his the whole time, never wavering. It almost felt like we were locked together, fighting a silent battle. A battle in which we could read each other's thoughts and emotions: I was telling him that he wasn't welcome here, that I had no idea why he would come back after all this time, not caring that he did, not wanting him back in my life, while he was telling me that he was determined and that nothing would make him change his mind, that he would do what he came here to do. What that was exactly, I had no clue, but I could tell that his resolve was solid.

That he wouldn't waver.

That he would fight.

I narrowed my eyes at him as the song ended and people all around us were breaking out into loud applause and cheers. I didn't hear any of it as I broke our eye contact, got up, and hopped off the stage, the guitar still hanging on my shoulder as I headed for the back hall and my office.

I needed a minute.

But I didn't make it that far.

I was halfway into the hall when a strong hand on my arm made me stop and turned me around.

And then I was standing not two feet away from the man who had ripped me to shreds twice.

And he looked good enough to eat.

I had to clench my teeth so as not to remember the things I would feel when he touched me, when he explored my body, when he whispered sweet nothings into my ear, when he kissed me. My body instantly reacted to him as if it was conditioned to his closeness, his smell, his aura. My heart rate picked up, my breaths came in shallow pants, my belly dropped, and my whole body was about to shiver.

But I'd rather die than let him see any of that. So I locked it down, clenched my teeth harder to the point it hurt, and glared at him.

Jason was watching me, trying to read my reaction while at

the same time I could see his body reacting to mine the same way mine had reacted to his. I could see the signs: his eyes had melted, his face was soft, his body was leaning into mine as his hand on my arm tensed in preparation to pull me towards him.

Oh no. That was not going to happen.

With a vicious twist I tore my arm free from his grasp and took two steps back.

"Loreley—" he started to say in his soft voice, but I interrupted him.

"What do you want, Jason? What could you possibly want from me?" I asked, my voice harsh and cold.

He flinched, then straightened and narrowed his eyes on me.

"I came here to talk to you."

"You and I have not one thing to talk about," I hissed.

He crossed his arms on his chest.

"Oh yes, we do. More than one thing actually, but we'll start with this: I came here to apologize. I know it's about six years too late, but here I am. I was a dick, a dick and an idiot for letting you walk away from me over some stupid fight, for not fighting harder for you, for not fighting for us. I said things I shouldn't have said. I didn't mean them and I have regretted every word every day for the past six years."

My body locked.

Oh. My. God.

He had to be shitting me.

He came to my town, to my bar, after he threw me away like we meant nothing, and thought he could make it all better with a lame ass confession and half-assed apology?

What an asshole.

I mimicked his stance and crossed my arms on my chest.

"You can't be serious!" My voice was still a hiss.

His eyes narrowed on me. "Yeah, Loreley, I'm serious. I miss you."

At that I burst out laughing, head thrown back, full on belly-shaking laughing. He had missed me.

Fucking hilarious.

My laughter turned to chuckles as I looked back at him. His face was set in hard lines and his eyes had turned angry.

"You think that's funny?" He asked through clenched teeth.

"Oh yeah, I think that's hilarious. Let me refresh your memory: *you* threw *me* away. *You* threw away what we had by being an asshole."

"Like I said, I know I behaved like a dick, but you didn't fight for us either, Loreley. You just walked away without looking back. I called. I left messages. You wouldn't talk to me."

Wow. If I hadn't already known he was an asshole of the highest order, that comment would have told me.

"Oh, forgive me for not wanting to talk to the cheating asshole that fucked the first whore that came along," I hissed sarcastically.

Jason's head jerked back as if I had slapped him. "Cheating... What the fuck are you talking about?"

He could not be believed. Did he really think I didn't know?

"I'm talking about you sticking your dick into the first pussy that came along only hours after we had a fight!"

"You think I cheated on you?" He asked incredulously.

"I don't think. I *know*."

"Loreley—" Jason said as he took a step towards me, but I put my hand up, making him stop.

"Don't, Jason. You said what you had to say, now go. And don't come back." I lifted my chin, indicating the back exit door.

He ignored me.

"I never fucking cheated on you, Loreley." His voice was

25

low and very, very angry.

I shook my head at his audacity. That lying cheating asshole.

"Leave!" I leaned in and yelled in his face.

He advanced on me, his hands going up in preparation to hold on to me, to get close. I backed up until my back hit the office door, giving him the opening he needed to move into me. His hands cupped my face and lifted it to his, his nose almost touching mine.

"Listen to me," he said on a soft but serious shake of my head, his voice low and growly.

"Let her go, Sanders," I heard a different voice growled from behind Jason. I looked over his shoulder at Chris, whose face was set in an angry scowl.

"I'm talking to Loreley. This is none of your business," Jason replied, not letting me go, not even taking his eyes from me.

"Loreley *is* my business. She asked you to go, you need to go. Now."

Jason studied my face, his eyes serious and searching. I didn't waver and glared back at him. Then he whispered, "I swear to God, Loreley, I never cheated on you. I'm gonna go, but I'm not leaving. We need to talk." Then he let me go, turned and walked out the back door, slamming it.

I looked at the door for several moments, trying to come to terms with what had just happened.

"What the fuck was that?" Chris asked. I looked at him to see his eyes still on the door as well. His body was rigid and his voice was strained.

I shook my head at him. "I have no clue."

He kept looking at the door.

His eyes came to me, assessing. "You okay?"

I nodded. "I'm okay."

"Good. Go cover for me. I'm gonna make sure he's gone." He said as he walked to and out the door, his movements pissed but controlled.

I closed my eyes for a second and took a deep breath. Then I left my guitar in the office and went to pour drinks, determined to forget the last fifteen minutes ever happened.

Chris came back inside only a few minutes later. I didn't ask but assumed that meant Jason had left. Chris didn't say anything, but he still looked livid as he came marching back around the corner and started taking orders. Throughout the rest of the night I caught him looking at me several times. The first time I assured him I was okay; the second time I glared at him, telling him to stop. When he still didn't stop, I ignored him all together. I just kept on serving drinks, trying not to let my mind wander as to why Jason was here in my town and what his unwanted reappearance in my life meant.

Of course, I failed at this.

I was livid.

How dare that asshole come into my bar, hide in the shadows while I play, make me sing that song, and then lie to my face about never having cheated on me.

What a total bastard.

If that was why he was here, to lie to me, to pretend I got it all wrong, then he better slink back under the rock he crawled out from.

No. Scratch that.

No matter why he was here, he better slink back under the rock he crawled out from.

He shouldn't be here, had no business showing his face, had no right to talk to me, to get close, to touch me.

Seeing him again, being close to him, feeling his eyes on me, feeling his touch, it all brought back what I had worked so hard to forget. I despised my body for its traitorous reaction to being within touching distance of him. You'd think that after the pain and disappointment and heartbreak that man caused me, my body would see through the attraction and instantly repulse him.

But no such luck.

Seemed like when it came to Jason Sanders, my body was a slut.

I had no respect for sluts.

In fact, I hated them.

Just like I hated Jason fucking Sanders.

I almost broke the glass as I slammed Rick's beer down on the bar in front of him, making it slosh over the sides and onto my hands.

"Goddamnit!" I hissed. I shook the excess beer off, grabbed a cloth, dried my hand, and then threw the cloth back behind the bar, all this time mumbling and grumbling profanities under my breath.

My head shot up when I heard Rick chuckle.

"You're hotter than usual when you're pissed off and I enjoy the view, but what's crawled up your ass? Not twenty minutes ago you had a blast on that stage. What happened?"

I narrowed my eyes on him and did what every woman did when she was mad but didn't want to talk about it. I said, "Nothing. I'm fine," in the way that every man knew there was not one thing that was fine and he better back off and take cover if he didn't want to get injured in the crossfire.

But Rick didn't back off. Instead, he chuckled again, longer this time. Then, "Right. We both know that's bullshit, but I can see you don't want to share, so I'll leave it alone for now." Then he leaned in and his voice dropped, so that only I could hear him. "But Loreley, you know you can talk to me. I get why you don't want to go out with me. I don't agree with it and I can't promise you I won't keep trying, but I get it. Doesn't mean I won't still be your friend. I'll leave you be for now, but I want you to know that if you want to talk, I'm here."

I was still glaring at Rick, but we both knew I didn't mean it. I wasn't mad at him.

I was mad at Jason Jackass Sanders.

And I was mad at myself for letting him get to me like that.

Rick was a good man, probably one of the best men out there, and I wished I could feel more for him than friendship. He would make some lucky woman real happy someday. He would not be the kind of man who declared his love to a woman and then cheat on her, ripping her heart out, destroying her; nor would he leave that woman in the dust when she needed him. No, Rick wouldn't do any of that. He didn't have a bastardly bone in his body.

I hung my head for a second and breathed in a calming breath, then looked back up at Rick and told him what was wrong with me. "You're right. I'm pissed. I'm pissed, because someone who screwed me over years ago just showed up out of the blue and got in my face. And I'm pissed at myself for letting someone who means nothing get to me like that."

Rick studied me. "Can I ask who that someone is?"

I shook my head and clenched my teeth as I crossed my arms in an effort to ease the pain in my chest. The pain I had tried to let go of for the past six years. But since Rick was a detective, he didn't miss much, meaning he didn't miss this either.

"Who, Lore?"

I kept shaking my head at him as I answered, "It doesn't matter."

Rick's eyes narrowed into slits, then he said in a tight voice,

"Lore, I've known you for over twenty years, have been your friend for over twenty years, and have liked you more than a friend for a good chunk of that time. That look on your face and that pain in your eyes you are trying so hard to hide tell me that whoever that guy is, he means something to you. If he didn't, he wouldn't affect you like this. Tell me now, Lore, whose ass do I need to go and kick."

I smiled at him. "You're a cop, Rick. You can't just go and kick someone's ass."

"Watch me."

I studied him for a few seconds before I looked away from his knowing eyes over his shoulder towards the crowd behind him, which I realized gratefully, was not really a crowd anymore. I kept looking at the people who were mostly strangers to me, watching them, but not really seeing them, while I tried to decide if and what I should tell Rick.

I looked back at him and could see that his eyes hadn't moved from me and that his patience with me was running out. Before he could jump over the bar and shake the truth out of me—which I didn't doubt he would do—I blurted it out before I could change my mind.

"Jason, my college boyfriend. We dated for almost two years. We were serious, planned to move in together, talked about our future together. We had a fight right after graduation and I caught him cheating on me. I left him. Now he's back and I have no idea why."

Rick's jaw was clenched now as were his fists and his eyes were ablaze with anger.

"Your college boyfriend?"

I nodded. Rick knew what that meant. He understood.

"Fucking hell," he muttered under his breath as he shook his head. "What are you gonna do?"

I shrugged my shoulders. I hadn't gotten that far yet. "I don't know. Try to ignore him."

Rick's eyes were boring into mine. "You ever need me, I'm here, Lore. I hope you know that."

I did. "I know, Rick. Thank you."

"What are you gonna do?" Chris asked me the exact same question Rick had asked me when he was driving us home.

I shrugged my shoulders and gave him the same answer I had given Rick. "Ignore him."

"He seemed pretty determined, Lore. I'm not sure ignoring him is gonna work."

"You have a better idea?" I asked.

Silence, meaning he didn't.

"Maybe you should tell Cal. Between him and me, we can make sure Jason stays away from you." Yes, Cal would make sure Jason stayed away from me. He would also probably end up getting arrested in the process. And I wouldn't let that happen. He had a family to take care of, a new baby on the way. He didn't need this shit.

"Let's hope Jason leaves town before Cal gets wind of him being here, or I don't know what he'll do. It wouldn't be pretty if Rick had to arrest him."

Silence again. I could practically hear the wheels in his head turning.

"And the same goes for you, Chris. I don't want to visit either of you in prison."

Chris chuckled. "Don't be dramatic, Lore."

"I'm not. Jason is a famous rock star now. He's the frontman of one of the most popular rock bands out there. You don't think he would press charges if you beat the shit out of him?"

"I honestly don't care. But if he did, it would make him an

31

even lesser man than he already is."

"Promise me, Chris. Promise me you won't seek him out and get yourself in trouble." Chris sighed, but said nothing.

"Chris," I prompted, my voice angry now.

Another sigh. Then, "Fine. I promise I won't start a fight. But if he gets in your face again like he did tonight or gets in my face, I can't promise I won't punch that pretty face of his."

"And promise me you won't tell Cal."

"He's not gonna be happy you kept it from him, Lore. He's protective of you. And he'll find out eventually. This is a small town and people talk."

He was right. Cal would be mad when he found out. We had practically grown up together. Our dads had been co-workers and best buds and his mom had taken me under her wing when my mom had died when I was six. He was eight years older than me and mostly treated me like his annoying little sister. But no matter how annoying he thought I was still to this day, I had his love and protection in the brotherly way that was seriously awesome.

"Yes, he probably will. But hopefully, Jason will be gone by then."

"All right. But don't tell me I didn't warn you when his head explodes and he reams you out."

"Noted."

Neither of us talked as he drove us home the rest of the way.

Three

LORELEY

My classic rock mix sounded in my ears while I was running through the woods that started behind my house and skirted around town, leading me around in a big four-mile loop until I would come out down the hill at the other side of town. I had decided to run the big loop today. Running always made me feel better, always cleared my head. Since there was a lot going on up there today, I figured I needed a long and exhausting run to sort it.

Not only had I tossed and turned last night, trying to figure out against my better judgement how I was going to handle Jason being in town, but I had been worried of what today might bring.

This day last year had been a dark day to say the least.

It had been the day I lost Jesse.

For months, I had been in deep mourning. Holed up in my house after I came home one night, closed all the blinds, locked both doors, and gave myself over to a bottle of Tequila. I had wanted to be alone, not see anyone, not talk to anyone, not think about anyone, not feel anything. The bottle of Tequila had been empty before dawn, and I had passed out not long after that. I

33

had woken up in the hospital, with my dad and Chris sitting beside my bed.

My dad had tears in his eyes that started to roll down his cheeks when he saw me open my eyes.

"Honey," he whispered brokenly before he closed his eyes and rested his forehead on the hand that was holding mine in a tight grip. His shoulders were shaking with silent sobs.

"Daddy," I whispered. My own tears were wetting my cheeks at seeing my big strong father in a state like this. I lifted my other hand to the top of his head, running my fingers through the hair that was just like mine. His head came up and he looked into my eyes. The devastation mingled with fear I saw in them scared the shit out of me. My dad was the strongest person I knew. And he never showed fear.

"Daddy," I whispered again.

"My precious girl, my baby, I'm so sorry, so goddamn sorry—" he started sobbing again; big body heaving sobs. I sobbed with him.

"You could have...you almost..."

"I'm okay, dad. I'll be all right," I tried to soothe him through my own tears.

At my words, I felt a wave of rage come at me from the other side of the bed. I turned my head and froze. Chris was sitting in a chair, his elbows to his knees, his red and swollen eyes on me, fury in them.

"Chris—" I started, but he didn't let me finish.

"Shut your trap, Lore. I don't want to hear the bullshit I know will come out of it," he said in a very low, very angry, very hurt voice. I snapped my mouth shut and stared at him. He had never talked to me like that.

"Boy—"

"No, Roy. You know as well as I do that it's bullshit. Lore is *not* okay and she will *not* be all right. You wanna know why you're here, Lore? You wanna know what I walked into this morning?" He asked, but didn't let me answer. "You drank yourself unconscious! Found you passed out on the floor, thought you were dead. They had to pump your stomach, Lore, rushed you to the hospital to pump your fucking stomach! You stopped breathing in the ambulance on your way here! You almost died! Does that sound *okay* to you?"

"Chris—" I tried again. Chris jumped out of his chair, and a second later his face was in mine.

"Not one word, Lore. Not one fucking word! Did you hear me? You almost fucking died!"

"I didn't mean to," I breathed.

"You didn't mean to? Well, guess what? Accidental suicide is still fucking suicide, the result of it you being DEAD! You want that? You wanna die, Lore?" Chris' face was still only an inch from mine, his voice low his eyes wide with fury. And fear.

"No," I whispered, but I wasn't sure if I was lying or not. I had decided on Tequila because it gets you drunk fast, and in doing that, numbs not only your whole body, but your brain as well. But it hadn't numbed my emotions, not one single bit. It had done the opposite, had made the sorrow and despair inside me hot like a branding iron, searing through my insides until I couldn't breathe. In that moment, just before I passed out, I had wanted to die. And Chris could see it in my eyes.

"Jesus, Lore, you do. You want to die," he said as his body jerked back from me as if I had slapped him, pain and hurt flashing through his eyes.

"Baby girl," I heard my dad's choked whisper and turned my head again to look at him. "Is that true? Did you try to kill yourself?" I shook my head, tears streaming down my face, my throat closing up.

35

"No...I...I didn't...I wouldn't...I'd never..." I stammered.

The door flew open before I could gather myself enough to give a coherent answer, and Cal stormed in. He stopped two feet into the room and glared at me.

"What the fuck, Loreley! Are you out of your ever-loving mind?" He roared at me. I flinched. He was as mad as I had ever seen him. And scared. His eyes were haunted.

"You know. You of all people know what it's like to lose someone precious to you, to lose someone you love with all your heart. Look at your dad, look at him!" he shouted when I didn't look at my dad.

I looked at my dad.

Hunched over, his hand still holding mine, his red-rimmed eyes were bleak with sorrow and desperation. The same eyes that have been staring back at me through my mirror for the past few months.

I started sobbing again, which made the tears in my dad's eyes spill over.

"Yeah, Loreley, take a good look. *You* did that to him. You want him to feel like that? You want him to lose you?"

"I..." was all I could get out. No, I didn't want my dad to feel like he did now. I didn't want him to look like he had lost all that was precious to him. He had already lost my mom, the love of his life. I didn't want him to go through losing his only child.

"I'm sorry," I sobbed, "I'm so sorry, daddy." My dad grabbed me behind the neck and pulled me into his chest where he held me while I wept. This lasted a long time. When my sobs quieted, my dad pulled me out of his chest and locked his eyes with mine. His were still haunted, but now they were also serious. Determined.

I braced.

Then he laid it out for me.

"When your mother died, I thought my whole world had died with her. I know what it feels like to not be able to breathe because the pain and loss are consuming everything you are. But you know what, honey? My world didn't die. I still had you, my precious baby girl. You to take care of; you to love; you to cherish. You've lost one of the most precious things a person can lose and my heart breaks for you, honey. If I could take away the pain, take the burden from you, I would, darling. You are the most important person in my life, and watching you endure that kind of pain breaks my heart for you every single day. But you are not alone. Your world did not die with Jesse. You've got me, you've got Betty and Pete, you've got Cal and Tommy, and you've got Chris. We all love you and we all need you. And we're all here for you, honey. Please, promise me, let us help you get through this. Please, baby," my father begged.

I closed my eyes and rested my forehead against his.

"I promise, daddy," I whispered. His hand at my neck gave me a squeeze.

"Good," he whispered back, then kissed my forehead as he gave my neck one more squeeze and sat back in his chair, keeping my hand in his. I looked back to Chris and Cal who were both standing in the middle of the room, watching us.

"I'm sorry," I said.

"You gonna let us help?" Chris asked. I nodded. "Good," he said, "that means we're gonna find someone for you to talk to and you're gonna go and do it. No arguing. You need professional help, we'll find a professional to help you. You're also on suicide watch from now on. That means I'm moving in and staying as long as it takes for you to get back on your feet. You won't be alone again until you're healthy and solid."

I nodded again. "Okay."

Chris exhaled in relief and returned my nod. "Okay."

I looked to Cal. He hadn't said anything since he had barged into the room and reamed me out. His eyes were locked on me. They were still furious.

"Cal?" I called.

"I'm still fucking mad at you, Loreley. You're like a sister to me, have been for over twenty years, which means I'm your big brother and it's my job to protect you. I couldn't protect you from the pain you had to endure these past few months, but I sure as hell can protect you from yourself and I'm gonna do that. And you're gonna let me. No matter what it takes, you'll get your shit together. I swear to God, Loreley, I don't care if I have to spank your ass until it's raw."

"Okay," I replied instantly.

He was right. They all were. I had fucked up. Fucked up huge and scared the hell out of all of them and myself in the process. Made them go through something that nobody should have to go through: coming close to losing someone they love.

I watched as Cal took a deep breath through his nose and then kept watching as his body slowly relaxed.

"Everyone is out in the waiting room. My mom is crying and mad as hell at you, dad is broken-hearted, and Tommy is freaked. In a minute, they're gonna come in here to see you and you're gonna do your damndest to make amends for putting them through that. I mean it, Loreley, you're getting your shit together and won't scare us like that ever again."

"I promise, Cal," I whispered. I felt ashamed. Everyone was even more worried about me now than they already had been. My dad; Betty and Pete, who were like parents to me; Cal, my surrogate big brother; Chris, my best friend, who had done everything he could to get me through all of this; and Tommy, my sweet Tommy, Cal's son, which made him my bona fide nephew; he was only ten years old but he had an old soul and was an Alpha male in training, which meant he had been even more protective of me since Jesse died, just like his dad had been.

"Good," he replied, then came close and just like my dad had, he hooked me at the back of my neck and pulled me up while he leaned in to kiss my forehead before he turned on his heel and left the room without saying another word.

That had been the lowest point of my life.

Since then, I have been seeing a therapist, at first three times a week, then twice a week, now I was down to once a month. Talking about my feelings with an uninvolved stranger had helped immensely. I could just let fly and talk about whatever I was feeling without needing to have a mind to the person listening, or thinking I felt sorry for myself. During the first few months of sessions, there was a lot of crying, which turned into a lot of anger, which slowly turned into settling into who I was now. I had learned to deal and focus on the good, remember all the beautiful and fun moments while accepting that there would always be pain connected to those memories, but not letting them swallow me up. Now, a year after I lost Jesse, I was much better. It was still hard and sometimes thinking about him hurt more than others, but I was dealing and I was living my life and moving forward.

I made it to the other side of town and ended my run at the town's grocery store to get a bottle of water. I hated running with having to hold one, so I always stopped at the store after my run and drank the water as I walked through town back to my house.

I did the same today.

When I came out of the store, turning on the sidewalk, my head bent back, taking big gulps of water, I stopped to admire the black Challenger parked at the curb. Challengers were sweet. Not as sweet as my 1965 Ford Mustang Shelby GT500, but still, they were nothing to sneeze at. They were pretty unusual in Cedar Creek. Especially at this time of year. It was early summer and camping season was starting, so the town was usually filled with big SUVs that could pull trailers, not sexy sports cars. The driver's door opened and my heart stopped for a second before it restarted and beat in overtime as I saw the person emerging.

It was Jason.

He threw the door shut and leaned against the side of the car, his arms crossed on his chest and his sunglass-covered eyes fixed on me as if he expected me to come to him.

Great.

Jason was not someone I wanted to deal with this morning or today or ever.

I looked away from him and drank some more water as I started walking past him, initiating my strategy to ignore he existed like I had told Chris and Rick last night I would.

But Jason didn't let me.

He walked towards me and started right where he had left off last night: lying to me.

"Where did you get the idea I cheated on you?"

I kept walking without answering him. I wouldn't let him rile me up again.

"Where, Loreley?"

I took another drink of water and carried on towards my house when just like last night, a hand on my arm stopped me.

"Don't touch me, Jason. Go away. I don't want to talk to you." I snapped.

He let me go immediately. What he didn't do was leave. Instead, he moved closer, and I had to force myself not to take a step back.

"Fine. I won't touch you, but you gotta talk to me. I swear to God I never cheated on you. If someone told you I did, they were lying—" His boldness of approaching me and confronting me as if he had a right to infuriated me. Chris had been right. Jason wouldn't let me ignore him. So I broke my promise and got riled up.

"Tell me, Jason." I interrupted him, "What is it you are trying to accomplish here? Why are you here in my town, tracking me down, following me, lying to me? What is it you want from me?"

"I told you last night. I wanted to apologize. I was a dick and an asshole and lost you because of it. I've regretted saying those words to you every single day, Loreley, I've missed you every single day."

"That's it? That's what you came here to do? Apologize and tell me you missed me? All right. Consider your mission accomplished. You can leave now." I started to turn away from him again, but he stepped around me and blocked my way.

"That's not all I wanted to say."

"Then what is it? Spit it out so we can get this charade over with and I can forget about you again and get back to living my life!"

Jason ground his teeth and clenched his fists. Then he moved in even closer and said through his clenched teeth, "I love you and I want you back. I have wanted you back since the moment you walked away from me six years ago. I get now why you didn't answer any of my calls that day if you thought I fucked someone else. But I swear, Loreley, I never did. I never cheated on you. I loved you too much to hurt you like that. I still do. I want you back."

I couldn't believe his audacity. This time, it was me who was moving closer towards him until our noses almost touched. "Tell

41

me, how is it, living in La-La-Land? Is it as nice and wondrous as you hoped it would be?" I asked in a cold voice.

Jason glared at me. "Don't be a sarcastic bitch. I'm being serious."

I narrowed my eyes at him. "There you go again, calling me a bitch. Guess your apologies aren't worth shit. And you're not being serious; you're delusional. I have long since moved on from you." At my words, Jason ground his teeth so hard I saw the muscle in his cheek jump.

"Tell me who told you I cheated on you," he went back to his original topic.

"Nobody told me."

"Then why——"

"I saw her, Jason. I saw her at your apartment when she opened your front door, wrapped in a towel, still wet from the shower, and I heard her loud and clear when she told me you were still *in* the shower."

Jason's body locked at my words. "You came to my apartment and saw her?"

I said nothing as I kept glaring at him.

"Shit. Now it all makes sense." He whispered as if talking to himself.

Yeah. It did. He got it now. He got it that I caught him, that there was no way he could deny it now. "See, Jason, you can stop playing your game now. There is no way I will ever forgive you for what you've done."

"No. You don't understand. That girl——"

I couldn't believe he wouldn't let it go, that even after he knew I had seen her at his apartment, he was still going to lie to me about it. At the end of my patience, I stepped back from him and shook my head in resignation. Why was I even arguing with him? No matter what I said, there would always be another excuse, another lie.

I was done.

"It doesn't matter what you're going to say, Jason. None of it matters," I said, resigned.

"Of course it matters."

"It doesn't. And you know why. So you can stop this cruel game of yours and leave me alone."

"Loreley—"

"No, Jason," I said with steel in my voice. He knew that voice. I could tell by the look in his eyes that he remembered.

Good. At least he remembered something.

This time when I turned around and walked away from him, he let me. I didn't look back at him, so I missed the fact that he kept his eyes locked on me until I turned the corner. Just like I missed the look of complete and honest confusion on his face.

JASON

For the second time in his life, Jason stared after Loreley as she walked away from him without looking back. The difference was that last time he was mad and disappointed.

And scared.

Scared of her moving to L.A. without him, of her chasing her dreams without him, of not seeing her for three months. God, he had been so fucking scared he would lose her and had acted like a dick because of it.

Every day since then, every single day since she walked away, while he was on tour with his band, playing in small bars; the day they were discovered during a gig; the day they signed their record deal; the day they made it big. Every single day since he let her walk away from him, he wished she was with him; every single day he missed her, missed her to the point that he couldn't think straight, got drunk, and fucked the first available pussy.

And every single day his wounded ego had kept him from following his heart and going after her, of begging her for forgiveness and winning her back.

Until something happened that made him realize that he was tired of all the fakeness he was constantly surrounded with; that apart from his band, being with and loving Loreley had been the only real and true and good thing he had ever had in his life. That day he had made the decision to go after her and get her back.

He hadn't expected it to be easy. He had hurt her, he knew that, but he hadn't expected to be faced with hatred coming from Loreley.

There was a hardness to her that hadn't been there six years ago. A hardness that had blindsided him last night and just now. She had always had a no-bullshit attitude, had never had any patience for games and lies. That combined with her passion and pureness and big dreams had made him fall in love with her almost from the very beginning. Back then, she would always stand her ground, would always stand up for herself and her beliefs; she could get mad and did on occasion, but she would never be bitter or nasty about it. Sassy and spunky? Yes. But never bitter.

The fact that she wouldn't even let him talk, wouldn't give him even the slightest chance to explain what had really happened that night, was something that was so very unlike the Loreley he knew.

And what had she meant when she said he knew why it didn't matter if he cheated on her or not? Of course it mattered! If she believed he didn't cheat on her, then there was no reason for her hating him. Did she hold him responsible for her dream of being a songwriter not coming true? Jason had been surprised that, as the years passed, he never heard anything about Loreley in the music world. She had been an amazing songwriter when they were together. In fact, she had co-written some of their songs with him back then, songs that were now number one hits.

Was that it?

No, that didn't make any sense.

He had no idea what she meant. But he could tell by the tone in her voice that she had no intention of talking to him. He was not going to get through to her.

Jason closed his eyes in frustration as he lost sight of Loreley when she turned the corner.

He had promised himself that this time, he would not let her walk away, that he would do whatever was needed to get her back. So far, he had been extremely unsuccessful. But he wouldn't give up. He would fight for what he wanted, for what he needed.

But in order to do that, he needed answers. And he didn't care what he had to do. He would move heaven and earth to get them.

He would also need proof he hadn't cheated on Loreley if he wanted her to give him a chance.

So his first order of business would be to get in touch with Murphy.

Then he'd talk to Chris. Judging by his reaction to seeing him last night, that could be painful. Chris had looked ready to rip his head off. But if he wanted answers, there was no one else who knew more about Loreley than Chris.

Or Cal.

But talking to Loreley's overprotective big brother would be a last resort.

45

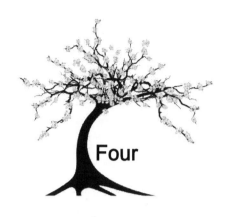

Four

LORELEY

I was stepping out of the shower when my phone rang. Grabbing a towel and wrapping it around me, I walked into the living room where I had left my phone on the table and put it to my ear.

It was Chris.

"Hey," I answered the phone.

"Hey back. You forget something?"

"I don't think so. Why?"

"Because there is a certain someone here ready to measure and discuss your plans for the new stage."

Oh shit. I had completely forgotten that Cal was coming to the bar. With everything that had happened last night and this morning, that had completely slipped my mind.

He was gonna be pissed I stood him up.

"Shit, Chris. I totally forgot. How mad is he?" I asked while I ran to the bedroom, tripping over my clothes on the way, and headed to the closet to find clean clothes to wear.

"His face hasn't turned red yet, but he's seriously unhappy," Chris said.

"Shit. Do me a favour. Tell him where we want the new

46

stage to go and what we need it to look like. I'll be there in ten minutes tops."

"Already on it. He's measuring as we speak, but he still wants to talk to you, so get your ass in gear," Chris ordered right before he gave me dead air.

I rushed through brushing my teeth, dried off my hair with a towel half-heartedly, fixed it in a loose bun on top of my head, got dressed in a clean pair of jeans and a t-shirt, and was on the road only minutes after Chris called me.

I pulled into the parking lot behind Cooper's only five minutes later.

Cooper's had been in the family for thirty-five years. My dad had opened it when he was only twenty-three years old, had used up all his savings to buy the building that didn't look much better than a shack back then.

Now, I was running the bar with him—was a co-owner actually— and it felt good to continue the family legacy. Even though I had grown up helping my dad out and had taken over doing the books for him by the time I was sixteen, owning a bar had never been my dream job. But life happened and I was happy here. My dad and I were a good team. He was still the hard worker he always had been and took his shifts, not as often as he used to—which would mean every night—but he was behind the bar probably two to three times a week. He had a great head for business and had expanded the bar and added the stage to have live music at least once a week over the years. He didn't always stay on top of things with the paperwork, but it didn't matter since I didn't mind doing it.

When I opened the back door, I could hear male voices talking and chuckling over rock music softly playing in the background.

A good sign.

Cal couldn't be too mad if he was chuckling.

I walked through the back hall and turned the corner by the restrooms into the main part of the bar. Cal and Chris were standing at the wall to my right past the bar, looking down at some sheets of paper, Cal drawing and explaining, Chris' eyes glued to the paper, his head nodding.

"See this side? The stairs can go right here closer to the wall so the bands don't have to wade through the crowd to get up and down the stage like they have to now. Easier for them, less hassle for you. Put a guy by the stairs if you have some bigger band play and you don't have to worry about people trying to get up there." Cal explained.

"Sounds good, man. That would definitely make it easier to handle the crowds when it gets busy," Chris agreed.

"Hey guys," I called out when I got closer to them. Both their heads shot up at hearing my voice. Chris took in my appearance and gave me an amused smile while Cal's eyes took me in and his eyebrows shot up mockingly as he said, "Well, look who is gracing us with her slightly dishevelled appearance. If it isn't the squirt herself."

I rolled my eyes at him. "I'm twenty-nine years old, Cal. Long past being anyone's squirt," I snapped. His lips twitched slightly before he turned back to Chris and said, "All right, we'll do it the way we discussed. I'll order the material today, send two of my guys to start tomorrow morning, you'll have a new stage by the end of the day. You got a band booked for the weekend?"

"Yeah. Our regulars from Boulder. *Breaking Habit.* Place is always packed when they're playing. Having the new stage done by then would help a lot. Plus, it's Lore's birthday this week, so we've got lots to celebrate."

I rolled my eyes at that, but neither of them noticed. I didn't like making a big deal out of my birthday and could only imagine what Chris had planned to get me in the mood to celebrate.

"It'll be done. Talk to you later," Cal said as he shook Chris' hand, then he collected all his papers as well as his measuring tape and pencil and headed towards the front door.

"Uh, Cal?" I called.

"Yeah?" He asked, turning his head to look at me over his shoulder but not stopping.

"I thought you wanted to talk to me?"

"No need," he answered as he reached the front door and opened it.

"Then why did I hustle my ass here?" He looked at me again and gave me his shit-eating grin, telling me without words that that was his revenge for standing him up.

"You're an ass, Cal," I snapped at him, mad at myself that I fell for his play. I should have known better. His grin widened.

"Mom and dad are coming over for dinner tonight. Bring Roy and Chris. Ivey is making some fancy chocolate dessert."

Ivey was making dessert. And it had chocolate in it. Pretty much anything Ivey cooked or baked up in her kitchen was flippin' fantastic, but Cal knew I wouldn't be able to say no to the chocolate. Yeah, it was a cliché, but chocolate always got to me, mellowed me out instantly. Cal knew this and had used it frequently over the years when he did something that pissed me off.

"Sure," I said, shrugging my shoulders, trying to be aloof about it. Cal chuckled.

"All right, squirt, see you at six," he said as he turned and disappeared out the door.

"I am not a squirt!" I shouted after him and heard another deep chuckle before the door closed behind him.

49

Ass, I thought.

"You know he's only calling you that to get a rise out of you, right? And you play into it every time he does it," Chris said.

I knew this. Still, I couldn't *not* react. It was probably childish and immature, but I didn't care. I hated it when Cal called me a squirt. I wasn't a squirt. I wasn't even short. Or small. Yes, I had been a skinny little thing as a child when he had come up with that ridiculous nickname, but I wasn't a skinny kid or a gangly teenager anymore. I had filled out and had some nice curves in the right places, long legs. I looked the opposite of a squirt. It was annoying.

I scowled at Chris before I changed the subject.

"So you two got the new stage all figured out?"

"Yup. It's all good."

"It's gonna look the way we talked about, right? At this side of the bar, at least double the size, two feet higher up," I asked him suspiciously. Chris looked at me.

"Yes, boss. It's gonna look almost exactly like what we discussed. Cal came up with a better idea of where the stairs should be, but that's it. Don't worry. What? You don't trust us to do the job?"

I sighed. Of course I trusted them to do the job right and give the bar exactly what it needed. I was still pissed off from dealing with Jason earlier.

"What's up, Lore? You're not usually this grouchy after a run."

I sighed again. "I ran into Jason this morning and we had words."

"Did he corner you again?" Chris was instantly alert and looked like he was ready to hunt Jason down.

God, I loved him.

Chris was one of the few people who had seen me at my

worst, who had done whatever it took to help me out of that deep dark hole that had swallowed me up last year. We had been best friends since college, had even dated for a short time when we first met until we realized we were better as friends. We were tight. He had quit his job and moved to Cedar Creek for me, to help me get back on my feet and never left.

Without him, I didn't know where I'd be today.

I owed him my life. Literally.

"No, he didn't. It was outside the grocery store on the sidewalk so he didn't have much of a chance." Chris relaxed slightly when I told him what had happened and what Jason had said.

"You're joking. He wants you back?"

"Apparently."

"I don't get it. It doesn't make sense."

"No, it doesn't." Chris said nothing. His face was contemplative. And worried.

"I'm fine, Chris. You'll see, he'll leave soon enough and everything will get back to normal. Let's stop talking about him. This day is hard enough as it is without me having to worry about what he's up to."

Chris' eyes grew tender and sad. He pulled me into a hug and kissed the top of my head. "Of course, Lore. I'll drop it." He held me for a few moments in silence before he said, "I can stay over for longer than just tonight if you need me to."

I lifted my head from his chest and looked up at him. "I appreciate the offer and I'm very grateful that you're staying with me tonight. But I'll be okay. You need to stop babying me."

"What if the reason for me wanting to stay with you is purely selfish?"

I wouldn't believe it for a second. "What do you mean?"

"I mean staying with you for a few nights would prevent me

from sticking my dick in any pussy offering. Might do me some good."

I laughed silently. "Trouble in bachelor paradise?"

Chris' return grin died. "Not really. Sometimes I just get tired of it, you know?"

"Tired of being one of the hottest guys in town and having your pick of the litter?" I asked him incredulously.

"Yeah," he answered to my astonishment. "I don't know. Sometimes I just want more than the emptiness of a casual fuck. You know the last time I've been on an actual date?"

I thought about it for a second. Then I thought about it some more. For the life of me, I couldn't remember Chris ever taking a girl out on more than one date. Not since he had come to Cedar Creek last year. And not at college. He saw a lot of action, always had, but they were all one-night stands with barflies who didn't mean anything to him. Easy girls. Always pretty, not always nice, but always pretty and easy. Maybe too easy.

"Yeah. That's right. Neither do I, it's been so long," he said when I didn't speak.

"I thought that's how you wanted it. I don't remember you ever taking anyone out on more than once. Well, other than me, that is," I said, frowning.

He smiled at me.

"Yeah, other than you I haven't been dating. Actually, *since* you I haven't been dating."

Uh oh. I didn't like the sound of that. He wasn't... No. That was impossible. I would know if he had feelings other than best friend love for me. We were too close and spent too much time together for him to be able to hide anything like that.

I was still standing in the loose hold of his arms, so I felt it when Chris' body shook with silent laughter.

"Lore, babe, you should see your face."

"What?"

"You're panicking. Don't worry. I'm not holding a torch for you," he answered my unasked question, proving that he could read my exact thoughts on my face. "We are great as friends. The best. We didn't work as a couple. Doesn't mean that I don't miss being part of a couple."

"Where is this coming from? Have you met someone and she isn't falling for your charms?"

He shook his head. "No, haven't met anyone. And I won't if I keep chasing tail the way I've been doing. At least not the kind I want. I want something real, something good. I won't find that if all I do is hook up with convenient pussy."

"So what you're saying is you want to use me and sleep in my bed so you won't end up in anyone else's."

"Kinda," he said on a smirk. I shook my head and smiled at him.

"You know you can't bullshit me, Chris."

He gave me a final squeeze before he let me go. "But I can try. Go to Lola's and get us some coffee and muffins. I'm starving," he said as he headed back towards the bar. "Then you can help me restock before we go for lunch and head to Boulder."

"You're coming to Boulder with me?"

"Yeah. Mark is coming to hold down the fort until tonight."

"All right. You want the usual?" I asked.

"Yeah. Make it a large. And a lemon poppy seed muffin." His head was already disappearing into one of the large beer coolers behind the bar to check what needed to be restocked.

"Okay. Be back! Me paying for breakfast means lunch is on you. I want a milkshake from Tom's with whatever is on special today!" I called across the expanse of the room as I walked

53

towards the front door to get us both breakfast from the only coffee shop in town, which was just down the street from Cooper's and was owned and run by the town sage Betty, who was also Cal's mother, which in turn made her my surrogate mom.

"Right," I heard him shout back and I smiled to myself.

When I walked into Lola's, Betty's eyes zeroed in on me like a hawk's. She was reading my mood, worried about me. I had expected it. Betty loved me like her own daughter and I loved her like a mother, but I didn't want her to worry.

I gave her a reassuring smile as I approached the counter. Her eyes stayed locked on mine, reading me, looking into my soul it felt like. She could do that, look into your soul. And she would tell you what she found there. No matter if you wanted to hear it or not.

Before she could open her mouth and do exactly that, I cut to the chase. "I know you're worried about me and I love it that you are because it says something beautiful, but I also hate it that you think you have to worry, because it says that I gave you reason to do so. I made a promise and I'm going to keep it. I'm much stronger than I was a year ago, Betty. And Chris is staying with me for a few days so I am not alone. I know I'm not alone and never was. I've got all of you, an amazing family who loves me, and I won't disappoint you again."

Betty leaned over the counter and put her hand to my cheek while still looking deep into my eyes. "My beautiful girl. Yes, you are much stronger than you were a year ago. Doesn't mean I'm not still going to worry about you. I'll always worry about you. It's what a mother does. My blood or not, you're like a daughter to me, and parents never like to see their children suffer."

Like always, Betty's words were beautiful and felt great.

She kept talking. "I'm glad Chris is staying with you to hold

54

you up and keep you strong. It's no shame needing and accepting the help of people you love and who love you, sweetheart. It's the opposite. It's what family and friends are for. We stick together, we lean on each other, we help each other be strong. Now, know this: you need me or Pete or Cal or Ivey in any way, you call. No matter what time of day or night, you feel like you can't deal, you call."

God, she was killing me.

Tears stung my eyes and I had to swallow them down before I could say anything. I nodded.

"I will, Betty. I promise."

"Good, sweetheart. That's what I want to hear," she said with love and pride and compassion in her voice.

"Now, what can I get you?" She asked as her hand left my cheek, she leaned back to standing straight again and walked towards her fancy Italian commercial coffee machine, her pride and joy. She should be proud. It made the best coffee in town.

"I need two large lattes and two lemon poppy seed muffins."

"All right, dear. Coming right up."

Pete came out from the back carrying a big tray of baked goodies. You wouldn't think it by looking at him, but Pete was the one who did all the baking for the coffee shop. And all of it was freaking amazing. I was a chocolate kind of gal, not much into cakes and cookies and pastries and stuff, but even I would kill for one of Pete's baked anything, they were that good.

"Hey, there, sweetheart. How you doin'?" He asked when he saw me.

I gave him a smile and said, "I'm doing okay, Pete, thanks."

"Hear you're joinin' us for dinner at Cal and Ivey's tonight."

"Yeah, Cal wanted to butter me up with the lure of Ivey's chocolate dessert. I got mad at him because he played me this

55

morning. Told me he needed to talk to me about the new stage
he's building for me, made me haul my behind out of the shower
for nothing."

Pete gave me a look then he said in a low voice full of
meaning, "That's not why he asked you to come for dinner,
sweetheart. And he didn't play you."

I frowned in confusion.

Then it came to me. I was such an idiot. Cal made me come
into the bar this morning not because he was upset I had stood
him up and wanted payback, but because he wanted to check on
me, make sure I was okay. And inviting me over for dinner
tonight was more of the same: surrounding me with family and
love on the day that he knew would be hard for me. They were
probably all in on it.

My face got soft with that realization and I had to swallow
my tears for the third time this morning.

"That's right, darlin'," Pete whispered when he saw that I
understood.

I swallowed again before I said quietly, "I love you all."

"And we love you right back."

I smiled a shaky smile at him and he returned it with a
bright one of his own.

"Here you go, Lola Girl. Two lattes and two lemon poppy
seed muffins." I heard Betty say and turned back to facing her. I
loved it when she called me Lola Girl. The only other person in
my life who had ever done that was my mom.

Betty and my mom had been best friends since
Kindergarten. Both their families were Cedar Creek natives,
going back a few generations. They had been closer than sisters,
always together, always looking out for each other. It just so
happened that they ended up dating and falling in love with two
best friends, which made the four of them like family. Betty and

my mom opened *Lola's* after college. And yes, it's named after me. My mother had been pregnant with me when they first opened the coffee shop and they decided to make me the namesake. Technically, half of *Lola's* was mine. My mother had left it to me when she died. Betty and Pete have been running it ever since. It was theirs, at least in my head. I knew they deposited half of the monthly profits into an account that had my name on it, but I have never touched it. Never even considered it. Not even when money was tight right after college.

Betty calling me Lola Girl always reminded me of my mother.

And I loved that.

"Lore," I heard my name called from across the table. I had been sipping my chocolate cherry milkshake, lost in thoughts, my mind filled with Jesse and, to my chagrin, Jason. Chris and I were at Tom's eating lunch. I looked up and saw Chris's concerned eyes on me.

"You haven't heard a single word I've said, have you?" I shook my head slowly.

"I just miss him, Chris. I miss him so bad." My voice was filled with sadness. I felt Chris' hand take mine and opened my eyes.

"Of course you do, babe. There's a lot to miss," he said on a squeeze of my hand. He leaned his upper body across the table without taking his eyes from mine, holding my hand tightly in his.

"You loved him with all that is you. You still do and you always will. Jesse was a part of you and when he died, that part was ripped out of you and left a hole that nobody else can ever fill. It's his and you won't ever get it back. It burns, it hurts, and it always will to some degree. It will get better over time, but it will never go away completely, Lore."

57

I nodded. We had talked about this often over the past year. Chris knew what he was talking about. He understood. He knew what it felt like to lose someone who is a part of you. Our sophomore year in college, shortly after we broke up, he lost his younger brother to leukemia. They had all known that it was coming, but that didn't make it any easier or any less painful. He'd been devastated, had felt powerless because he couldn't protect his little brother, couldn't save him.

It wasn't the same, but still, he knew the meaning of survivor's guilt.

He also knew that even after therapy, I was still blaming myself for Jesse's death to some degree. The accident hadn't been my fault, but it was still me who had been driving the car when we got hit and went off the road. Whereas I had walked away with only a few scratches and bruises, Jesse had been declared dead on scene.

"Lore," Chris again took me out of my thoughts. "Blaming yourself is not gonna bring him back. All it does is make you miserable. It leads nowhere. Jesse wouldn't want that for you. He loved you and would want you to be happy. Hold on to the good things. All the fun you guys had. What a great person he was. He wouldn't want you sad."

I nodded. "You're right. He wouldn't want that. He always tried to make me laugh. And he did more often than not with all his antics. I smiled again thinking about that.

Chris smiled back at me.

Our food arrived.

"We taking your car to go to Boulder, or mine?"

"Let's take mine. I'll let you drive."

That earned me a grin. "Of course you will."

I grinned back at him.

Half an hour later we were leaving the diner. Boulder was

58

an hour away and my appointment was in an hour and a half. We were walking down the sidewalk heading towards my place to get my car. Chris had thrown his arm over my shoulder, pulling me in close. My arm was wrapped around his waist and my head was resting on his shoulder so we were walking holding each other.

My head shot up from his shoulder and I whipped it around when I heard the loud angry growl of an engine from across the street.

The Challenger.

"Nice ride," Chris muttered admiringly as his head followed the car when it passed us. "Not as sweet as yours, but still nice." I would have smiled at Chris saying almost exactly what I had thought when I saw the car for the first time a few hours ago.

"Yeah, it's nice. Would be nicer if it wasn't Jason's."

Chris stopped us and looked at me.

"That's Jason's?" I nodded. "What? Is he stalking you now?" I shrugged and started us walking again.

"I know I promised you I wouldn't seek him out and kick his ass, but I don't like that he seems to be following you. First, he waits for you and confronts you after your run this morning and now, here he is again."

I sighed but stayed silent. There was nothing I could say. I knew that if Jason didn't let up and left me alone, there would be nothing I could do to keep Chris from going after him to tell him off or worse.

59

Five

LORELEY

I was staring at the bright blue sky that I could see through the tree branches. My back was to the ground while I was lying flat out on the grass between the two graves. My right hand was playing with the grass on top of one of them while my left was resting on my belly.

I watched as a small flock of ravens landed in the cherry tree above me. They seemed to have come just for me, or at least that's what I told myself; as if they knew I would need that sign. I visited Jesse's grave every week. Most of the time, there were at least one or two ravens sitting in the tree above, or even on one or both gravestones, watching over them or waiting for me, I didn't know. But for some reason they were always around.

Jesse had loved birds, had been fascinated by all types of them, but especially, to my dismay, ravens. I had two ravens tattooed on my back in his honor, one of them flying, one of them sitting on the branches of the cherry tree I was lying under that also decorated my back. Today had been my last appointment to get the tattoo finished. It had been cathartic to have the last bit completed on the anniversary of Jesse's death.

When Jesse had died, I had wanted him to be buried right

here, next to my mom. She had never met him, but I had no doubt in my mind that she would have fallen head over heels in love with him at first sight, just like I had. In my mind, I was giving him to my mom to watch over him, to take care of him. I had never been scared of cemeteries, actually, I thought of them more as peaceful and quiet parks where people went to remember the ones they lost. My mom had loved them as well, had taken me for long walks here on a regular basis, said it filled her with a sense of peace and contentment, being so close to her departed family. Sometimes, we would even bring a picnic and have lunch under exactly this tree. She didn't think it as disrespectful, but more as us sharing a meal in the company of the departed. Most people might find this freaky and abhorrent, but it never creeped me out in any way. When my mother had been buried, this tree was further away from all the other graves than it was now. She had died twenty-four years ago, and the new graves were moving closer and closer every year. But even though it was removed from all the other graves back then, my father had insisted on her being buried in exactly this spot, under our favourite tree. It had helped me grieve for her, knowing she was in her favourite spot, and it had helped me grieve for Jesse.

I still came and visited them every week. And I always came alone. Chris had driven me here, but he didn't come to the graves with me. I knew he visited Jesse occasionally, but we never went together. I needed this time with them by myself and Chris respected that.

As I lay on my back, staring up at the sky, I talked to them out loud like I always did.

"A year ago today, my love. A year ago today since I last kissed you, since I last ruffled your hair, since I last heard your laughter, since I touched you and held you in my arms. I miss you. Every day I miss you. I miss our Friday night movies, our

61

walks through the woods, our cooking dinner together. I miss everything about you." I smiled, remembering all that had been Jesse.

"I went and got the last bird tattooed on my back today. It looks like it's taking off from sitting on a branch. It's beautiful. You both would have loved it. Even you would have, mom."

I took a deep breath and said nothing for a while, just enjoyed the moment of being close to them.

"All right you two. I gotta go. I have to check in on the bar before I head over to Cal's for dinner. Ivey is making some fancy schmancy chocolate dessert that I absolutely have to have. I'll come visit again soon, I promise." I finished my visit with our tradition, a tradition my mom had started. Every night when she tucked me into bed, we would play the "I love you" game, where we would come up with hilarious ways of telling each other how much we loved each other.

Then I got up and kissed both their gravestones.

"Miss you, guys, " I whispered, then turned around and headed for the parking lot where Chris was waiting for me.

He was leaning against the driver's side of my Shelby. I gave him a reassuring smile as I came closer and didn't stop when I reached him but let him wrap me in his arms.

"How was that?" He asked against the top of my hair.

"Good. Very good," I murmured against his chest.

"Good. I'm glad. Let's go," he said as he kissed my forehead and let me go. I went around the back of the car and got in on the passenger's side, buckled up, and leaned back against the seat, resting my head against the headrest, so I could look up into the sky.

I was so absorbed in that—and I guess Chris was so busy worrying about me—that neither of us saw the Challenger parked down the street from the cemetery parking lot, nor did we see it as it pulled out and followed us back into town at a safe distance.

"Hi, baby!" I cooed at the dog attacking me as soon as I walked into Cal and Ivey's house.

Cal had bought Stella for Ivey when they had started dating, before they started dating actually. Before Cal had made her his, Ivey had lived in the house they were living in now all by herself. The house wasn't in town. It was up the mountain, about a ten-minute drive from the town centre. Cal had convinced Ivey that she needed a dog to watch over her, which Ivey had denied, but he had bought her one anyway. By the time Cal had gotten Stella from the breeder two weeks later, they had been a couple. Yeah, Cal worked fast when he knew what he wanted. So, technically, she didn't need a dog anymore, because she had Cal to watch over her. But getting her one had been a smart move on Cal's side. Because, what woman didn't fall in love with a man that bought her a cute little puppy to cuddle and love and to protect her?

Stella was now almost a year old and the most beautiful dog I had ever seen. Purebred chocolate lab with beautiful green eyes, big floppy ears, slender and fit built. She was gorgeous. And she knew it.

"Down, Stella," I heard Cal grumble as he closed the front door behind Chris and I.

Staying bent over, I only turned my head to look at Cal. "It's okay, Cal. She's just happy to see me."

"She can be happy to see you with all four paws on the floor, or better yet, sitting down."

I glared at him. "She's only a puppy!"

"Yeah, she's only a puppy. Her jumping you won't be so much fun when she's all grown up, which means she needs to be trained now. And the only reason you're giving me that look you're giving me right now is because you know I'm right."

I knew that of course, but I wasn't going to tell him. Instead, I turned my attention back to Stella, who was now sitting patiently waiting beside me, and scratched her behind her ears.

"Come on, sweet girl. We'll find a ball and play some fetch in the backyard. Far away from your mean, grouchy daddy." Stella was only too happy to agree with me and followed me towards the back of the house.

Before I reached the kitchen, I heard Cal ask Chris quietly, "How is she doing?"

"She's doing good, Cal," Chris answered him just as quietly.

"Good. Thanks, man."

"No need. She's my best friend. I love her."

My heart melted at the seriousness and love in his voice. God, I loved that man. Too bad it hadn't worked out between us. It would have saved both of us a lot of pain and confusion. But then again, I wouldn't have had Jesse. And that wasn't worth thinking about.

I entered the kitchen and immediately felt at home. I loved their old little farmhouse—well, not so little anymore since Cal put an addition onto the house. My favourite place was the kitchen. I loved to cook, and Ivey's kitchen was not only any cook's dream, it screamed warmth and family with its light colored cabinets, big windows and huge farmhouse table in the middle of it. It really was the heart of this home.

Both Ivey and Betty were bustling about, chopping lettuce and potatoes and turning the meat in the marinade.

"Hey, guys," I greeted as I entered, moving in close to each of them for a hug.

"Hey, Loreley," Ivey said, grinning.

"Lola Girl," Betty whispered in my ear when I moved in for a hug, then she put her hand to my cheek and looked deep into my eyes. Satisfied with what she saw, she gave me a proud grin and a quick nod before she turned her focus back on chopping the lettuce. My eyes went to Ivey, and she gave me her own proud smile. I smiled back at her.

"Anything I can help with?" I asked.

"We're as good as done. There is beer in the fridge. Help yourself. Take some out to the guys as well if you don't mind," Ivey told me.

"Okey dokey," I said on my way to the fridge. "I'll take Stella out with me, play some fetch."

"Sure. Tommy has taught her some new tricks. You should ask him to show you."

I leaned down to Stella and cupped her cute face with my hands. "You know some new tricks, pretty girl?" Stella smiled at me, tongue hanging out the side of her mouth, panting. "Well, let's go see! Go get your ball!" I ordered. While Stella went in search of her ball, I grabbed a few beers out of the fridge, then she followed me out the back door excitedly.

I put the beers on the table and expertly opened them—hey, I *did* co-own a bar— passed them around to muttered "Thanks" from Cal, Chris, and Pete, and my dad, and took a pull of my own.

"Where's mine?" Tommy asked teasingly.

"You want a beer?" I asked in faked shock.

"Yeah." Tommy's eyes were sparkling.

"Ivey lets you drink beer now, does she?"

"Sure. She says I'm responsible for an almost twelve-year-old. I can handle it."

"That's probably true. Have at it then," I said as I held my bottle of beer out to him.

His eyes got big and he started reaching for it when, just as he was about to touch it, I yanked it back and took another pull.

The men chuckled.

"I can't believe you fell for that one, bud," Cal said. Tommy shrugged. "Can't blame a man for trying," he muttered.

"Bud, you've got a few more years of being a kid. Don't rush it," Pete said.

"You have a girlfriend yet?" Chris asked him.

Tommy's ears turned red, probably with embarrassment, as his eyes moved to the ground. Then he straightened his shoulders and looked at Chris.

"Nope," he said.

"He's got three," Cal said at the same time.

Tommy's eyes shot to his father. "I do not, dad!"

"At least three different girls called this past week asking for you."

"Doesn't mean they're my girlfriends."

Cal's eyebrows shot up. "It doesn't?"

"No, dad."

"Don't let Ivey hear that you're stringing along three different girls at once. Or your grandma for that matter. They're gonna tan your hide, bud," Pete said through his chuckle.

"I'm not stringing along anyone. They aren't my girlfriends."

"Do they know that?" Chris asked, grinning.

"Yeah, they do. They just like me because I'm nice and don't tease them all the time like the other boys in school do."

"That would do it," I murmured, "I bet they're all head over heels in love with you. I would be." Tommy narrowed his eyes on me. "I'm not teasing you, Tommy. I'm sure all the girls love you. I know I would have."

"What do you mean?"

"I mean keep doing what you're doing. Be the good kid you are, don't tease the girls, don't be mean, be a gentleman and you'll end up with a good woman like Ivey."

Tommy's eyes were on me. "Or you," he said.

He was such a good kid. "Or me," I confirmed on a grin.

We were having dessert. Ivey sure as hell didn't mess around when it came to sweets. Her breakfasts were always killer and I haven't tried a single one of her desserts that didn't instantly make it to the top of my most-delicious-things-ever-eaten list. She was the master. Hands down. So I told her exactly that.

"You are the master, Ivey. The goddess of desserts. I'm so glad Cal finally got his head out of his ass and went after you," I told her reverently before I took the next bite and closed my eyes, moaning in bliss, savouring the smooth taste of dark chocolate with raspberries on my tongue.

Ivey chuckled. "Well, I am glad, too."

"Keep it up, squirt. Keep it up," Cal growled as he gave me a mock glare.

"I'd have to agree with Loreley, son. We're all glad you finally got your head out of your ass. And not just because Ivey makes fabulous desserts," Betty said as she looked at her son. He transferred his glare to her, and a knowing grin spread across her face. Pete chuckled.

Betty turned her grin to Chris and asked, "What about you, boy? Figured out what you want yet?"

Ivey's eyes went to her plate, a smile playing around her lips.

Pete's chuckle grew louder while Cal muttered, "Here we go," under his breath before he looked at Chris and said, "Advice, listen closely to what she's got to say and then go out and follow her instructions to the letter or you'll never live it down."

Chris' mouth opened to reply, but Betty got there first.

67

"He's not quite ready to listen yet," then her eyes went serious and searching as they were locked on Chris. "Soon, though."

"Fucking fantastic. Maybe you can focus on that instead of riding my ass," Cal kept growling. Ivey's shoulders started shaking with silent laughter. I joined her.

"Baby, I'm not finding anything funny." Ivey lifted her eyes to him. They were shining with amusement.

"Well, that's tough, honey, 'cause I do," she said through her laughter. And just like always, that was all it took for Cal to lose his annoyance as his face turned soft on his wife.

"You know, Betty, this should freak me out, but I'm actually looking forward to it," Chris said. He looked to Cal and Ivey who were still smiling at each other. "If you know how to get me what they have, I'm game."

"Oh, I do. But as I said, you're not quite there yet. And anyways, I believe it's Loreley's turn first." I whipped my head around, not sure I had heard her right.

"My turn?"

"Yeah, your turn."

I shook my head at her, saying, "That's not gonna happen."

For the third time today, Betty studied me with her searching and soulful eyes.

"Mark my words, baby girl, something is in the air, which is good, since you've been living under that dark cloud for too long. I can see it's lifting, but my girl deserves more than that. She deserves sunshine, pure and bright sunshine. And she'll get it. Soon," she said with a conviction that scared me. I was nowhere near ready to start a relationship with anyone. I had just found my way back to me, and it had been a long and hard fight, so being with someone was not going to happen anytime soon. I shook my head at her again then dropped my eyes to my plate and the dessert on it. My appetite had vanished.

"Loreley," I heard my name called from across the table. It was my dad. Slowly, I lifted my eyes to find his on me.

"I'm proud of you, sweetheart."

I swallowed. Then I nodded, knowing what he meant. "Thank you, dad." My dad had always been proud of me, no matter what I did, and had always showed me that he was. He was proud of me for being strong, for fighting my way out of the sorrow and finding my way back to me.

My dad returned the nod then continued to devour his dessert. I felt Chris squeeze my leg under the table, took a deep breath, and gave him a small smile.

We all ate our dessert in silence for a few moments before sweet Tommy tried to lighten the mood, but in doing so, created a tension so thick you could cut it with a knife.

"Ivey and I met a rock star yesterday," he said excitedly. I froze.

Oh shit. My eyes grew wide while my brain tried to come up with a distraction but failed miserably. I looked at Chris. His eyes on me, telling me "I told you so."

"How so?" Cal asked him.

"He's renting the house. Ivey and I went up to meet him and give him the keys."

Cal's head turned to look at his wife. "A rock star is renting our house?"

"Yup," she answered, "a true world famous rock star is renting our house. I was surprised myself when we met him. His assistant was the one filling out all the paperwork, so I didn't know it was him until we met him at the house."

"Well, he better not trash the place," Cal muttered.

"Don't worry, honey. I upped the deposit for that eventuality. It's substantial and he paid it without blinking. He

69

seemed like a nice guy when we met him, though. I don't think he'll be any trouble. Probably just wants some quiet time away from all the craziness of worldwide fame."

"Who is it?" Chris asked. I glared at him.

Tommy answered, still excited. "It's the front man of *The Crowes*. His name is Jason and Ivey is right. He was supercool and real nice. We listened to his album after we knew he was renting the house. His music is awesome. Ivey thinks so, too. Do you know him, Lore? You know all about music."

I didn't answer him.

I turned my head slowly as I felt the air grow tense.

"You have got to be shitting me." That was Cal's low growl. "That fucker is renting my house?"

I stared at Cal. He was beyond mad.

"Dad?" Tommy asked at the same time Ivey asked, "What's going on?"

He answered neither of them. His eyes were fixed on mine. And they were filled with rage.

"You don't seem surprised by this news, Loreley." Uh oh. He was calling me Loreley. That never boded well.

I swallowed and said, "I'm not."

"And may I ask why that is?"

I sighed, resigned to the fact that I wouldn't be able to come up with a plausible lie. So I told him. "I know he's in town. Have known it since yesterday. He came to the bar last night and tried to talk to me and then I ran into him again this morning."

"So not only have you known that asshole is in town, he has approached you, and you didn't think of telling me any of this?"

"No, I didn't. I didn't tell you because it doesn't matter, Cal. *He* doesn't matter."

"I'm guessing you knew, too?" He asked Chris without looking at him.

"I did. I was there last night when he got in Lore's face." I narrowed my eyes at him once more. Chris was making this worse than it already was.

Traitor.

"He got in your face?" Cal exploded. He got up and marched towards the front door. "I'll teach that motherfucker a lesson he won't soon forget." I was up and out of my chair and running after Cal.

"No, Cal. Stop. He's not worth it."

"He's not, but you are. He's got no right to come here and get in your face. But I'm glad he did. Gives me a chance to finally kick his ass." I got to him and planted myself in his way, forcing him to stop.

"I don't want you to do that."

"I don't care."

I glared at him. He glared back at me.

"Chris, dad, help me out here," I called without taking my eyes from Cal's.

Nothing. Great.

It was Betty who came to my rescue. "Sit your butt down, son." He didn't. "Cal," she urged him again when he didn't move.

"He puts one finger on you or gets in your face for whatever reason or even so much as talks to you when you don't want him to, I am up on that mountain and I will kick his ass, Loreley. You hear me?"

I nodded.

Cal turned and went back to sit in his chair.

"Would someone mind telling what is going on?" Ivey asked. Her voice had gone from sweet to angry and suspicious.

"Remember I told you about that asshole that cheated on Loreley and broke her heart in college?" Ivey's eyes narrowed

71

with understanding. "Yeah, Jason fucking Sanders is the asshole that did that to her. And now he's living in our fucking house."

"Is he the one that—"

"Yeah."

"I'll call him right now and tell him he needs to find alternate accommodation," she said as she was starting to get up. Cal's hand on her arm stopped her.

"I'd rather you didn't. Don't get me wrong, I hate that that prick is staying in our house, but I'd rather know where he is when I need to find him." Ivey's eyes flashed, then she nodded and grinned knowingly.

"Works for me," she said.

All the men at the table chuckled. All but Tommy.

I heard a weird sound coming from the direction where Tommy was sitting and my eyes found him. He had his head bowed and his fists clenched on the table.

"Tommy," I whispered. He shouldn't have heard any of this.

He looked at me with the same rage I had seen minutes earlier on his dad's face. Then before I could say or do anything, he trained his eyes on Ivey and said, "He sucks. And so does his music," before he pushed his chair back, got up, and left the room. A few moments later, we heard the door to his room slammed shut.

I started to get up from my chair to go after him when Cal said, "Leave him. He needs a moment." I nodded but didn't sit back down. It was time to go.

"Loreley," Cal called. I turned back to him and saw that Chris had gotten up and was coming towards me. I looked at Cal. He was worried. Looking around at the people that were my family I saw concern in all their eyes.

"I'm okay. I told you he doesn't mean anything."

"I know that's what you said, Loreley, and I know that's what you want to believe, but I'm your brother and I'm gonna find out why he is here and give him a good reason why he should stay out of your life," Cal told me.

"Don't, Cal. Don't give him reason to believe he has any importance in my life. He doesn't."

"I see you want to believe that, too. You do what you gotta do to protect yourself, I'll do what I gotta do to protect my sister from more pain."

I stared at Cal and Cal stared back at me. The look of determination on his face and the rigid stance of his body told me that I had no chance of changing his mind. This was something he needed to do for me as much as he needed it for himself.

"I'm not gonna be able to talk you out of it, am I?" Cal shook his head, his jaw clenched. I sighed.

When Chris made it to me he grabbed my hand and pulled me towards the door. "I've got her. Don't worry. Cal, you go see him, you give me a call. I've got a score to settle with that fucker, too. I'll let you know if he shows up again," he said over his shoulder. He opened the door and guided me through. Just before it closed, I heard Cal's growled, "You got it."

73

Six

LORELEY

"Really, Chris. I appreciate what you and Cal are trying to do, but I think we should just ignore him." We were in my Mustang on our way to Cooper's. Chris was driving. We had both been silently brooding until now.

"He's confronted you twice in two days and it looks to me like he's following you around. I think the only reason why he didn't approach you earlier today, is because he knows I won't let him near you. He's trying to get to you when you're on your own. Cal and I will make sure that he stays away from you. And, Lore, we gotta do this, so you'll let us."

"You know, having protective Alpha males in my life is getting really old." I sounded like a petulant child even to my own ears.

"I care. Cal cares. Every man in your life cares and wants to know the whys so we can kick his ass and he leaves town. The way Tommy reacted, I bet even *he* wants to go kick his ass." I sighed. Yes, Tommy's reaction indicated exactly that. He was way too observant for his age and was protective of the people he cared about. Just like his dad.

We were both silent as Chris drove into town.

74

"You know, I could never wrap my head around him cheating on you. It wasn't like him at all. I didn't get it then and I still don't get it now. And don't get me wrong. He's an asshole for doing that to you. What he did to you makes him the lowest of the low. But before that, he'd always been a decent guy, loved you to distraction, was protective of you, would have thrown himself in front of a bus for you. I never got it."

I was looking out the passenger window but turned my head at Chris' words. "What does it matter how he used to be? He did what he did and that's that. Nothing can change that, Chris."

"I know, Lore. I'm not trying to make excuses for him. I'm just trying to understand."

"I told you, Chris. I. Don't. Care. Whose side are you on?" Chris grabbed my hand and looked at me. "Yours, Lore. Always. Never doubt that." His voice was sincere and so were his eyes. I believed him. Of course I did. He was on my side. He always had been and always would be.

I nodded and took a deep breath to let go of the annoyance that had started to rise within me. His hand gave mine a quick squeeze before he put it back on the steering wheel and he faced the windshield again.

Both of us stayed quiet for the rest of the drive.

The music was blaring and the sounds of a really busy bar welcomed us as we walked into Cooper's. We looked at each other. I shrugged my shoulders at Chris' eyebrows that were raised in question. We walked through the crowd to the bar. Mark spotted us when we were five feet away, relief showing on his face.

"What's going on, man?" Chris asked him.

"No clue. A big group came in about an hour ago and it kept going from there. I was about to call you to come in early."

"Well, you're in luck. You got both of us. I'll just stow my

75

stuff and be right out." I went into the back hall that led towards the office, so I could stow my jacket and my purse. Chris was right behind me.

"Looks like the summer season is starting earlier this year. I meant to talk to you about that last night. We need to put an ad out and hire at least two more waitresses and one more bartender."

"I'll take care of it tomorrow. You want in on the interviews?"

I shook my head. "Nah, you can handle it. Or call my dad. You know he's good at reading people." Chris nodded.

"I call dibs on the bar," I said. I pulled my keys to the office out of my pocket and unlocked the door.

"We'll send Mark out on the floor. Give him a break from the bar," Chris suggested. I chuckled. Apart from the waitresses who were hired to do just that, none of us bartenders liked working the floor. I would usually give in and wait a few tables or at least clear empties to help keep up, but I wasn't in the mood today. Chris never waited tables. He hated it. And being my second in command, he had the authority to send Mark out to do the dirty work.

Mark realized that as soon as we made it back and joined him behind the bar. "Shit," he grumbled, gave Chris and me a glare that made me chuckle again, and stomped out towards Cindy to divvy up tables. I took the far side of the bar while Chris started taking orders on his side.

"Hey Lore!" I looked down the bar and saw Macy and Larry sitting at the far end. Macy was waving at me, her face split into a grin, which made me smile as I walked towards them.

"Hey guys! What brings you to Cooper's on a Sunday night?"

"I needed a break from the rugrats, but didn't want to go

too far just in case. I finally stopped nursing, so I begged Larry to take me out for drinks."

I raised my eyebrows at Larry. "She begged you, huh?" Larry grinned at me. Macy was known for being a little crazy. She was sweet, but she could be quite the ballbuster if you crossed her or hurt the people she cared about. What she was not known for, was begging.

"She'll be begging me for way more than a drink before the night is over."

I started laughing when Macy slapped her husband's arm. "Larry!" Larry looked at his wife.

"Am I not right?" He asked. Macy rolled her eyes.

"So, tell me what's new in your life? The baby kept me so busy I'm completely out of the loop. It feels like we haven't talked in ages."

Macy was one of my newer friends. She was a townie like me but was a few years older, so we didn't have the same circle of friends. I had always liked her. There was a lot to like: she was open and caring and loyal and crazy in a funny way. But it wasn't until Cal hooked up with Ivey that I got to know her better. Macy was Ivey's best friend, and since Ivey and I had become closer since last fall, I had also gotten closer to Macy. She was part of the package, so to speak. You know how when you meet some people and know almost from the second you talk to them that you'll get along great? That's what happened with Ivey and Macy and I.

Before I could answer her question, Rick sat down next to Larry. He looked much better than he had last night.

"Hey," I greeted him as I walked to the cooler to get him a beer.

"Hey, Lore. How you doin'?" He asked, his voice warm.

Rick had been one of the first ones on scene when Jesse and

77

I had been in the accident. He had been the one to hold me in his arms when Jesse was being worked on. He didn't say anything, knowing there was nothing to say, but had just held me silently, waiting, while I sobbed and cried and screamed. He had kept holding me when Jesse was pronounced dead on scene, when I had collapsed in his arms, too overwhelmed by the pain and sorrow and loss to stay on my feet. He had held me in his strong arms until my dad and Cal and then Pete got there.

He had also been one of the ones who had tried to help me through the loss, who had phoned me regularly, stopped by the bar just to check on me. In the beginning, I hadn't let him help me though, like I had let nobody help me back then. But he had never given up, had always made it clear that he was there for me. Just like he did now.

"Good. Okay," I answered him, my voice just as warm. "You're looking better."

"I am, thank you. Do me a favor, pour the four of us a shot. Tequila."

"I'll pour you three. You know I don't drink when I'm working," I said while I reached for the Tequila bottle and grabbed three shot glasses. I flipped them expertly and poured the drinks.

"You'll make an exception this time. We're toasting to Jesse." Rick told me in a quiet voice full with meaning. My head shot up from watching what I was doing to meet his. He gave me a quick and reassuring nod. I smiled a small and grateful smile, reached for another shot glass, filled it, and lifted it. Rick, Larry, and Macy followed my lead and lifted theirs.

"To Jesse," I whispered.

"To Jesse," they repeated. Then we all downed the shot together and slammed the glasses on the bar almost in synchronization when we were done.

That felt good.

I grinned at Rick. He grinned back at me. Then his eyes took on a teasing glint. "I'm on the top of my game tonight, so you better watch out," he said before he put the bottle of beer to his lips and took a swig.

I laughed and shook my head at him.

"You still haven't talked her into going out with you, Rick? You're losing your touch," Macy said mockingly.

"I'm working on it. I'm a patient man."

"I'd say," Macy mumbled. Larry chuckled. I just kept shaking my head. "Throw the man a bone, Lore. He deserves a reward for being so persistent."

I looked from Macy to Larry and back to Rick, who was watching me intently.

Then I heard my name shouted from Chris' end of the bar. Only Chris wasn't there. "Hey, Loreley, you think you can stop flirting with the detective for long enough to get a paying customer another drink or what?" My good mood instantly disappeared as I saw who it was.

Brad. He was a complete and total asshole and he had tried to bring trouble to the bar on more than one occasion. I had to give it to him, he was extremely good looking— about ten years ago. Now, you could see that the glorious days of the former high school hotshot quarterback were long gone. He went to school with Cal and Rick, so I've seen him play back then. He could have been something great. Got a full ride to UCLA, but got kicked off the team when he was busted at a party and arrested for possession during junior year. Stupid. So very stupid. But he wasn't only that. He was also a total douchebag.

One look at him now and I could see he was in rare form. Apparently, so could Rick. Out of the corner of my eye I saw that he was getting up from his stool. His eyes were fixed on

Brad and he did not look happy. Not happy as in *seriously* not happy and ready to rip into Brad.

I put a hand on his arm to get his attention, shaking my head at him when I had it. "Don't worry, I've got it. Not the first time I've had to deal with a jerk."

I could tell he didn't like that, but he sat down nevertheless, letting me do what I needed to do in my place of business.

I strode over to Brad, making sure I put some extra swagger into it while I had my narrowed eyes fixed on his face. It was both a challenge and a warning at the same time, to let him know I wouldn't take any of his bullshit. When I reached him, I leaned my hands on the bar and moved close to him. His eyes went to my cleavage and I had to stop myself from gagging.

"Warning, Brad. Don't push me," I told him in a low voice.

His eyes came back to my face and I must have not done a very good job of hiding my disgust, since his jaw clenched and his face turned into a sneer.

"Looks like our fancy big city detective is finally going to get lucky tonight."

God, he was such an asshole.

I leaned in closer, threateningly, and hissed under my breath, "Listen, asshole, I get that you're unhappy with your life, but don't come to my bar and take it out on me. You want a beer? I'll get you a beer. And it even comes with some free advice: if you hate your life so much, maybe you should try and be a little friendlier and nicer to people instead of being a complete douchebag all the time."

At that, Brad's right hand shot out and he grabbed my left wrist, pulling me in closer across the bar that separated us until I could smell the beer and cigarettes on his breath.

Disgusting.

"You think I should be friendlier? I'll show you exactly how friendly I can be," he whispered as he leered at my cleavage again.

Gross.

I didn't deign to reply and tried to pull my wrist from his grip. "Let go," I said when he didn't. His grip tightened to the point of pain and he pulled me in closer. "Let go, Brad," I told him again but stopped pulling since that would only make it hurt more.

"No," he said and before I could react, he pressed his lips roughly to mine. I reared my head back and swung up my right arm, using the heel of my hand to hit the bottom of his nose with the upward motion. Brad let go of me and stumbled back, his hand going to his now bleeding nose.

"You fucking bitch! You broke my nose!"

I glared at him while I rubbed my left wrist with my right hand and cradled it against my chest. I was going to have a bruise there.

"Get out of my bar, Brad."

"Fuck you!" He yelled. He made as if to advance on me but was stopped by, I was shocked to see, Jason, who was now standing in front of him with a hand on Brad's chest, pushing him back. Chris was right there with him, glaring at Brad, his hands clenched into tight fists at his side. And so were Rick and Larry.

"Out," Jason growled.

My initial shock at seeing Jason coming to my rescue turned into irritation at seeing him here. "Go away, Jason. I can handle it. I don't need you to rescue me."

He didn't turn his eyes from Brad as he answered me. "I saw that. Doesn't mean I'm not gonna teach this asshole a lesson for putting his hands on you." His voice was low and growly with rage.

81

"Thanks, but I don't need or want your help. As you can see, I have more than enough friends who'll do that for me. You can leave now."

Brad stumbled backwards when Jason gave him another push in the direction of the front door, but caught himself and tried to push past the four men, showing again how very stupid he was.

"I think you're forgetting that I'm a cop, Brad. A cop who saw you touch a woman against her will. You gotta be very careful right now," Rick warned him.

"*I* gotta be careful? She assaulted me! That fucking bitch broke my nose!"

"Yeah, and she had every right to since you wouldn't let her go when she asked you to. Now, let's go outside before I have to arrest you." Brad threw me another glare before he turned around and stalked out the door, followed by not only Rick, but Chris, Jason, and Larry as well.

Great.

I hoped I wouldn't have to deal with the police now and press charges or something like that, because Rick was involved.

"You're covered in blood, honey," I heard Macy say. She was standing next to me behind the bar.

I looked down at myself. There were blood splatters all over the front of my shirt.

Great. Blood was a bitch to get out.

"Shit," I said, "thanks to that asshole, one of my favourite shirts is now ruined."

Then I lifted my right hand, the one I'd hit Brad with, and saw that it was also covered in blood; my left hand was fine, but my wrist had red welts all around it. I flinched when I turned it. It stung.

"You need to put ice on that." Macy walked me over to the

ice chest, grabbed a towel, wrapped some ice in it and pressed it gently to my wrist. I flinched again.

"There you go. That's a mean right hook you've got there. Think you can teach me that?"

I smiled at her. "Sure."

She smiled back at me. "Who was that Jason guy? I've never seen him around town before," she asked as she started to dab at the blood on my shirt.

I sighed. "That's a long story."

Macy studied me for a few long moments before she went back to dabbing and said, "Soon, you, me, and Ivey. Girls' night. No arguing." As if I would.

"Ivey is gonna hate the fact that she won't be able to drink," I said through a snicker. Macy shrugged, but I could see her smiling. "It's her turn. I've been benched three times. It's payback time."

JASON

Jason was sitting in the far corner of the bar at a table. It was crowded enough that Loreley wouldn't see him but he could watch her. It looked like she was having a good time with her friends. He watched as she laughed and smiled and shared a drink, as they toasted to something he was too far away to hear.

Seeing her smile and have fun with her friends like that made his chest burn with jealousy. He wanted to be the one who made her smile like that, happy like that, the one she would look at with her beautifully warm and sparkling eyes. It took everything in him to stay in his seat as he witnessed the familiarity between her and the guy who was sitting closest to her. He could tell by the looks they were exchanging that they were close, that they liked each other. He could also tell that the guy wanted in her pants.

"Hi, my name is Ashley. What can I get you tonight?" He heard a smooth and silky voice ask him. He turned his head and saw a waitress was standing next to him. When he didn't answer, she leaned in closer, showing him her cleavage. Jason ignored the boobs that were practically in his face and grunted, "Beer. Heineken. Bottle. No glass." Then his eyes went back to the bar, to Loreley, dismissing the waitress.

Less than a minute later, he felt eyes on him. Glancing down the bar, he saw the waitress leaning across the counter, both her and Chris' eyes were on him. The waitress' were miffed. Chris' were furious.

Shit.

His plan had been to find a quiet moment to talk to Chris, maybe when he went in the back or after they closed. But it looked like he wasn't going to get that. Chris said something to the waitress without taking his eyes off him then he lifted the partition, strode around the bar, and marched towards him, his eyes heated with fury, his face set in a mask of rage.

"You've got balls, I give you that," he seethed as he arrived at his table.

Jason knew he had to play this a certain way if he wanted the answers from Chris he so desperately needed. He couldn't antagonize him. He needed his help. So instead of meeting Chris' anger with his own as he usually would, he schooled his face into a neutral mask and said, "Like I told Loreley last night, I'm not leaving until she talks to me."

Chris' chuckle was cold. "You wanna talk to her, you gotta go through me."

"That's why I'm here." Chris stopped short, surprised by Jason's words.

"You're here to talk to me?"

"I am," Jason said.

Chris smirked at him. "All right. Let's go outside. We'll talk." Jason could tell by the way he said the word *talk* that talking was not what they'd be doing outside. Chris was itching for a fight. Jason wouldn't normally shy away from a challenge like that, but again, he needed Chris on his side. He couldn't risk getting into a physical fight with him and lose his maybe only chance of finding out what the hell was going on.

"I'm not here to fight you, Chris."

"Oh, I heard what you're here for. I'll save you the time and energy. She's never going to forgive you for what you've done."

Jason was getting frustrated and impatient, not only with the conversation, but also with the accusation. His low and growly voice communicated this as he said, "I did not cheat on her, Chris. You know I would've never done that. No way would I have hurt her like that. I loved her, was completely committed to her and our future. No other woman existed for me. She owned me. She still does. You really think that would change and I would fuck the next pussy that was offered because of some stupid fight? You knew me better than that. Yeah, I know I was a complete dick that night for yelling at her and calling her a selfish bitch for wanting to pursue her dreams. I get that. I've hated myself for it for the past six years. But you know, man. You know I was going to ask her to marry me. Fuck, you helped me pick the ring."

Chris hesitated. The fire in his eyes changed and turned contemplative. There had been no mistaking the sincerity in Jason's voice. He meant everything he had said.

Jason tried to push his advantage. "You gotta help me out here, Chris. You're right. Loreley won't talk to me. She won't believe that I didn't cheat on her. She hates me too much to even listen to me, to let me explain, and I have no idea why. I'm missing something here. Something important. And I need you

85

to tell me what that is so I can fix it. You know her better than anyone. Please, man, give me something to go on. Help me out," Jason implored. He was not too proud to beg for his old friend's help.

Before Chris had a chance to answer him, a commotion at the bar had Jason's eyes swing that way and grow big and panicked at seeing some slimy guy's hands and mouth on his Loreley.

"Motherfucker," he swore and he was off.

"Thanks, but I don't want your help. As you can see, I have more than enough friends who'll do that for me. You can leave now." Jason ground his teeth together. He had the urge to growl and throw her over his shoulder like a caveman, to carry her off and make her listen to him. But dealing with this asshole was more important right now. He had touched his woman against her will, had put his filthy mouth on her against her will. A red haze of rage covered Jason's eyes as he gave that asshole another push and made him stumble.

Finding out that Rick was a cop pleased him, but at the same time, it annoyed him immensely. It pleased him, because that meant Rick could make this guy's life really unpleasant if he didn't smarten up. But it annoyed him, because that meant he couldn't punch Rick in the face for wanting in Loreley's pants.

All the men followed that asshole outside. There were four of them: Chris, Rick, himself, and some guy he hadn't noticed had come to Loreley's rescue as well. When he took a closer look, Jason realized it was the guy who had sat at the bar with Loreley's other friends.

"What? That bitch sending all her boyfriends after me now?"

Jason and Chris advanced at the same time but were stopped when Rick spoke. "You need to shut up and get out of here, Brad, before I find more reason to arrest you. And you better hope Loreley doesn't press charges. Would be difficult to get out of that with the whole bar and a detective as witnesses." Rick's voice was low and lethal.

"Press charges? What for? That bitch provoked me!"

Jason felt himself growling. He took a threatening step towards Brad but was held back by a hand on his shoulder.

"Did you not hear what I just said? You need to shut your mouth and get out of here. I mean it, Brad, one more word and I'm getting my handcuffs out."

Brad glared at Rick, his eyes blazing, but he kept his mouth shut, then turned around and stalked away. Jason's body relaxed with every step that increased the distance between them.

"So you're Jason," Rick was now talking to him, his voice a little less lethal and menacing, but not by much. Rick had heard about him. He knew who he was and didn't like him much. Not surprising.

Jason sliced his eyes from watching Brad's retreating back to Rick. "Yeah, I'm Jason."

"Heard you got in Loreley's face yesterday." Jason didn't respond. He didn't owe this guy an explanation. Rick kept speaking. "You need to stay away from her. You've hurt her enough and she doesn't want you here."

"Sorry, detective, but what I do or don't do is none of your business."

"You're right. It's not. But Loreley is my friend, which makes her my business."

"No. It doesn't." Jason replied and he could tell that Rick got his meaning.

Good.

They went into stare-down, glowering at each other for long moments. The urge to punch the cop intensified, but Jason

87

couldn't afford getting arrested. So far, the media hadn't discovered where he was, but that would change within in the hour if he got taken in. The press would have a field day with the mug shots alone. To Jason's satisfaction, Rick was the one who broke contact when his eyes went to Chris. "I'm gonna follow Brad, make sure he goes home and doesn't start more trouble. You got this?" He asked, gesturing to Jason with a chin lift.

Chris nodded. "I got this."

"Make sure she gets home safe."

"Always."

Rick nodded and started walking towards what Jason assumed was his car, but not before he gave Jason one more threatening glare.

"I'm gonna go in, make sure Macy isn't taking punching lessons from Loreley," the guy that had come outside with them called to Chris as he was heading back into the bar. Chris gave him a low chuckle as he said, "Good luck, man."

When the door closed behind him, Chris turned his attention to Jason.

"Now that we're alone, let's get back to our earlier conversation."

Jason waited.

"You're right, I thought I knew you. Thought I could trust you. Just like she did. That turned to shit when she knocked on my door for the second time in less than twenty-four hours, heartbroken and destroyed. Because she met the skank pussy you fucked."

"Goddammit! I didn't fuck anyone!" Jason yelled, the control he had on his anger finally snapping.

"Cut the bullshit, Sanders! Lore went to your place to talk to you the next morning, to figure stuff out, to find a compromise to make things work for both of you! She didn't want to lose you. I knew you overreacted, that you said shit you didn't mean. We talked about it all night. Then she went back to you only to find a woman fresh out of the shower wrapped in a fucking towel telling her you couldn't come to the door 'cause you were still *in* the shower! You broke her heart, Sanders, and I've waited six years to kick your ass for it!" Chris advanced on him. Jason didn't retreat. If Chris were going to come at him he would meet him head on. He advanced right back on Chris and got in his face.

"Fuck! Fucking listen to me, Chris! I didn't fuck that girl! Murphy did!"

"Of course, how convenient. Blame the guy who screws around so much he can't remember every girl he's fucked, let alone the girl's name the next morning."

"I'm telling you the truth! They crashed at my place that night because it was closest to the bar we played at. I wasn't even there. I stayed behind and got drunk. Ask Nathan. He was with me."

Jason watched as Chris's body went solid. Not with rage this time, but with surprise and shock.

"I would never cheat on Loreley, Chris, you know that," Jason repeated his earlier words, a little calmer now that he saw that what he was saying was sinking in.

"That girl at your door was with Murphy?" Chris asked.

Jason nodded. "Yeah."

"You weren't even home?"

Jason shook his head. "Not until early the next morning. I took a shower and then crashed."

"You didn't cheat on her?"

"No, man." Jason shook his head.

Chris closed his eyes and hung his head as if defeated.

89

"Fuck! Fucking shit!" He swore under his breath. "Are you telling me she went through all that pain and heartbreak because of some fucking misunderstanding?"

"It would seem so," Jason nodded again. Chris went quiet as he watched him with thoughtful eyes for a few tense moments. Then he started talking again, and in doing so, confused the shit out of Jason.

"What about a few months later when she tried to get a hold of you?" Now it was Jason's body that locked. "What do you mean, she tried to get a hold of me?"

"A few months later when she… She tried to get in touch with you, left you messages, wrote you emails, even went to one of your gigs to talk to you."

Silence, as Jason shook his head, confused as to what Chris was talking about.

"I didn't see her," he murmured as if talking to himself.

"No, you didn't. But she sure as hell saw you." Jason's head snapped up at those words. "What do you mean?" He asked with dread in his voice. When he had realized that he wouldn't hear from Loreley, that he had lost her, he had fallen off the wagon and head resumed to his old ways of screwing around, of having meaningless sex with meaningless women in order to try and forget about the woman he loved with all his heart.

"Yeah," was all Chris said. He didn't need to say any more.

"She saw me with another woman," Jason whispered in horror. Chris nodded.

Jason ran his hands through his hair in desperation and anguish. "Shit! I…I was…I missed her so much…I wanted to…I tried…" He tried to explain, but failed to formulate a full sentence.

"Yeah, I'm a guy, so I get it. But seeing you with her own eyes, drunk and all over some other woman, was the last straw

90

for her, man. It pushed her over the edge from being heartbroken to hating you, and she swore to never talk to you again."

Jason's eyes were wide with despair. Then his brain kicked in and went over what Chris had said. "You said she tried to get a hold of me, that she left messages. I never got those." He kept thinking. "You didn't tell me *why* she tried to get in touch me. What was so important that she wanted to talk to me even though she thought I cheated on her?"

Jason saw it when Chris locked his jaw. "You gotta tell me, Chris. I've got nothing to go on if you don't."

Chris sighed and hung his head once more. Then he gave Jason his eyes. Jason froze solid at what he saw.

Pain. Soul destroying pain and misery.

"Chris," Jason growled through clenched teeth, knowing that he was about to hear something that had the potential to crush him.

"She...Fuck, Sanders. She has endured so much...I can't..."

"Chris, fucking *tell me!*"

Chris shook his head. "I can't, man. I can't tell you. We thought you knew and...I can't tell you. It's her secret to share. But shit, man. She has been in so much pain. You have no idea..." He took a deep breath, then let it out and said in a low voice, his eyes serious on Jason, "We almost lost her."

Jason's body again went rock solid. Almost lost her? What the fuck was that supposed to mean?

"What does that mean, you almost lost her?" He whispered brokenly.

Chris took another deep breath. Then he gave it to him. Not all of it, not nearly enough, but he gave him something.

"I can't tell you why, Sanders. But I can tell you this: when

91

she thought you cheated on her, her whole world fell apart. She went to L.A. the next day, but she wasn't herself. She was heartbroken, devastated. Then, when she tried to contact you, and she thought you turned your back on her when she needed you most, when she saw you with that other woman.... She got back on her feet, but then...a year ago... Fuck! Something happened a year ago that made her lose it. She lost herself, drowned in her sorrow and pain and despair. It almost killed her, Sanders. That's what I meant when I said we almost lost her. She almost killed herself. I don't think it was intentional, but it was a fucking close call. I think if she had had you to help her through it... Fuck, it doesn't matter now. But you need to know that too much has happened for her to listen to you. She has closed that part of herself off, has closed *you* off, and she won't give you the slightest chance to talk to her."

There was a lot there, but not nearly enough to give Jason any idea of what was going on. His heart hurt. His mind was racing. He couldn't believe what he was hearing, that Loreley had almost died, had almost *killed herself.* What in the hell had happened? His beautiful and energetic, always happy and eager for life Loreley would never consider suicide. Not even as a last resort. Not ever. Not for anything.

"I don't believe you. Loreley would never do anything like that."

"Believe it, man. It was bad, still is and always will be, but she's much better now. What I'm saying is, she won't let you in. No fucking way. She won't listen to a single word you have to say."

"I'll make her listen."

"No," Chris said, shaking his head, "No, we need to somehow finesse this. I have no idea how, but I'll figure something out. I'll talk to her. You need to back off and give me a few days—"

"Just fucking tell me what happened, Chris!" Jason exploded, only to see Chris shake his head again.

"I can't, Sanders. I can't betray her like that. And that's what she would see it as if she found out I talked to you. As a betrayal. As me choosing your side. I can't do that to her." Jason clenched his teeth, frustrated that he didn't know what was going on, that after everything Chris had said, he still had nothing to go on.

"Fine. But I can't wait that long, Chris. Especially not now. And I'm not gonna back off. I can't. From what I gather from the little you have actually told me, everything that happened could have been avoided if I had fought harder, if I hadn't let her walk away, if I hadn't let her shut me out six years ago. I'm not gonna do that again. I came here to fight for her and now that I know that me losing her was based on a fucking misunderstanding, I'm gonna fight even harder for her. And I'm gonna win her back."

"Sanders—"

"No, Chris. No. I get you think you can't tell me what happened. But I'm not backing off. I can't."

They stared at each other for a few minutes. Then Chris sighed and gave in. "Shit! How long you think you can give me?"

"Tonight. It takes everything I have in me not to walk in there right now, throw her over my shoulder, and make her listen to me." Jason meant it. If Chris didn't agree, that's exactly what he would do.

Chris gave him a chin lift, agreeing, though Jason could tell that it wasn't easy for him. "One more thing, Sanders. When you find out, it's gonna be a blow. It's gonna hurt like fuck and you're gonna be furious with her for not telling you sooner.

93

Promise me you won't take it out on Lore. She's dealt with everything the best way she could."

Jason locked his jaw, then gave Chris a chin lift, giving him his word. He couldn't imagine he would blame Loreley, no matter what happened.

"There a way you can get Murphy or Nathan here? It would help if they both corroborated your story."

Jason nodded. That was a good idea. He had tried to call Murphy earlier today after what Loreley had said, but the call had gone to voice mail. "I'll try. I'll give them a call, see how soon they can get here." Thinking they were done, he turned to leave to get on that shit when Chris spoke again, making him stop.

"And something else. Expect Cal to show up at the house."

"What house?" Fuck. Cal, Loreley's quasi brother. He didn't know if he had it in him tonight to deal with another one of Loreley's protectors, who thought he was a cheating asshole. Chris was a hard man when he needed to be, but Cal was a badass and would beat the shit out of him. No doubt.

"The house you're renting. It's Cal's house."

"What?"

"Yeah, Cal hooked up with a woman, got married last Christmas. They're living in her house, renting out his. You're the renter."

Jason sighed and hung his head. There was no way Cal wouldn't show up at his doorstep. "Fuck!"

"Yeah," Chris agreed, his lips twitching. "I'll give him a call, try to talk to him. He trusts me to take care of his sister, but I suspect he's still gonna show up."

"No doubt," Jason muttered. "You still got the same number?"

"Yeah."

"Good. I'll text you mine." Chris jerked up his chin, then muttered, "Later," and headed back into the bar. Jason stayed where he was, thinking.

He was furious.

Six years.

Six *fucking* years he and Loreley had lost because of him being a total jackass. They would be married by now, have children. Live a happy life somewhere at a beach, or even here in the Rocky Mountains, away from all the drama that was L.A. No matter where they would have settled, the point was that they would have settled by now and made a family or were about to.

Fuck!

He should have kept his shit together when Loreley told him about the internship instead of starting a fight that night. He should have gone after her right then and there instead of playing the gig. He should have tried harder to get to her before she left for L.A. He shouldn't have let her shut him out.

If he had done any of those things, they would have never been apart. Neither of them would have been heartbroken, Loreley would not have fallen apart and almost killed herself.

"Fuck!" Jason exploded.

Six years of heartbreak and pain for both of them because of him and his wounded ego. That misunderstanding he could do nothing about now. It happened and he would show Loreley the proof that he wasn't lying, that it really *had* been a misunderstanding. Murphy and Nathan would help him. They were his brothers. And they had reamed his ass more than once in the last few years whenever he was brooding or wrote another song about losing Loreley. So that was the easy part. But he also wanted to know what had happened to the messages and emails Chris said Loreley had left for him. Someone had to have gotten

95

them. Jason doubted it would be easy to get to the bottom of that, but still, he would try. And if someone was responsible for it, that someone was going to pay.

Jason looked back at the bar's back door as he ran his hands through his hair in frustration. Every cell in his body urged him to go inside and go to her. But he had given Chris his word that he would give him tonight. Then tomorrow, he would go to her and talk to her.

And then they would work it out, be together, and finally fucking be happy.

Seven

LORELEY

I was showered and in my pajamas as I came out of the bathroom, ready to fall into bed and go to sleep. It had been a long day. I heard Chris' voice speaking low as I closed the bathroom door behind me. He was in the living room, what sounded like talking on his phone.

He hadn't said much after he came back into the bar after the Brad incident other than telling me to take a load off and keep the ice on my wrist, after he'd inspected it with anger clear on his face. But there had been something else on his face, too, something I couldn't quite pinpoint. He was deep in thought, as if contemplating something important, something he needed to figure out, but didn't know how. And then there was shock and consternation on his face, confusion, as if he was dumbfounded, shell-shocked even. Mixed in with all that were sadness and melancholy and dread and worry. Normally, I would have asked him what was wrong, but the day as a whole had been rough and, honestly, I couldn't take any more drama. I was too exhausted. And somehow I knew that it had something to do with why it had taken Chris so long to come back inside after Larry told me that Brad had left, that Chris had been talking to

97

Julia Goda

Jason. There weren't any bruises on his face and his knuckles weren't swollen from punching someone, all evidence that he hadn't beat Jason up and vice versa. That was a relief. I had seen and touched enough blood for one night.

I was proven right about Chris being lost in thoughts and the general reason for it on our way home.

"I talked to Jason tonight," Chris had said, his voice careful.

"Chris—" I tried to tell him that I didn't want to talk anymore about Jason tonight.

"Hear me out, Lore," he was almost begging me. I didn't reply and went quiet as I waited for him to go on. I knew that once he had made up his mind about something, I wouldn't be able to stop him from telling me what that was anyways. It was easier to just let him get it off his chest. And I was too tired to fight with him.

"I believe him." My body locked and my tiredness disappeared instantly at his words.

"What?" I hissed, stunned and shocked.

"Don't get upset. Just listen." His voice was firmer now, and unyielding, telling me exactly what I had thought: that he would tell me what was on his mind, whether I wanted him to or not. Since we were in the car and the car was moving, I had no way to escape, so I heaved a big sigh and remained silent.

"I believe he didn't cheat on you."

"This is unbelievable," I muttered under my breath as I shook my head with incredulity.

"It isn't, Lore. I talked to him about it in length, explained everything to him—"

I whipped my head around. "You explained everything to him?" I almost screeched.

"No, Lore, not that. I meant about that morning after you fought, what you saw, what made you think he had cheated."

98

Chris swallowed. Then, "And I told him about how later you tried to get in touch with him, about how you saw him drunk and with another woman." I hung my head. I hadn't wanted Jason to know about that. Chris wasn't done. "And I told him about how we almost lost you." *That* was definitely something I hadn't wanted Jason to know. It was none of his business.

"You did what?" I shouted at him. Chris flinched.

"I didn't tell him why. I told him that was your secret to share—"

"I can't believe you did that, Chris. Why? Why did you talk to him at all?" I interrupted him. I felt betrayed.

"I didn't want to at first, was ready to beat the shit out of him when I saw him sitting at a table, watching you. But then he got in my face about the cheating, said he could have never hurt you like that, that you owned him, that no other woman existed for him and he would have never thrown that away, I couldn't *not* talk to him. He was sincerely shocked and appalled by the whole idea."

"You forget that I saw the skank he cheated on me with, Chris. Saw her standing on his doorstep in nothing but a towel, still wet from the shower she had taken with him."

"He says he wasn't with her. That Murphy was. That they crashed at his place that night while he stayed at the bar and got drunk."

Pfft. I almost laughed. "How convenient," I said sarcastically.

Chris smiled a small smile. "I said the same thing. How very convenient to blame the guy who won't remember who he fucked that night and will back him up simply because they're like brothers and that's what brothers do."

I didn't say anything, just harrumphed in agreement.

"He also said Nathan stayed with him until he went home.

99

He told me to ask him." I shook my head in annoyance. So what? Nathan would corroborate his story just like any other of his band members would. That didn't prove anything. And anyways, cheating on me wasn't the worst Jason had done.

"I'm done talking about this, Chris." I said as I stared out the passenger side window.

"Lore—"

"No, Chris. I've listened and now I'm done. Please. I'm too tired to fight."

We pulled into my driveway and I got out of the car and walked to the front door. I was half-way through the door when Chris said from behind me, "We need to talk about this, Lore. If he didn't cheat on you then—"

"It doesn't matter, Chris. I said I'm done talking about it." I threw my purse on the couch and went straight to the bathroom. "I'm going to take a shower and then go to bed."

Chris sighed in frustration, but I ignored it. "Fine. I'll leave you be for tonight." That was all I heard before I closed the bathroom door behind me. I turned around and stared at myself in the mirror. I looked as exhausted as I felt, maybe even more so. I longed to take a nice hot bath and try to relax and get my thoughts organized, but I desperately needed this day to be over.

I heard Chris' voice speaking low as I closed the bathroom door behind me.

"Yeah, man, she's okay. Jason and Rick dealt with Brad. She's in the shower." Pause then, "Yeah, he did, showed up at the bar tonight. But listen, Cal, before you lose your shit on him we need to talk. He doesn't—" Another pause while Chris listened to Cal on the other end. "No, Cal, don't go up there before we talk. He didn't cheat on her and he doesn't know, man."

Chris was getting agitated. I could hear him pace in the

living room. I couldn't listen to this. I couldn't listen to Chris trying to justify Jason's behaviour. He was supposed to be on my side, not defend the person who shattered my heart into a million pieces.

I turned around to go to my bedroom. I needed to sleep and not think about anything. I didn't have the strength for anything else tonight. I could still hear Chris talking, but didn't listen to it, didn't let it penetrate.

"That's not what I mean. I mean he doesn't know about—" I closed the door firmly but quietly behind me, shutting out his words. I leaned against the door, where I closed my eyes and took a deep breath in an effort to clear my head. But there were too many thoughts fighting for attention in my head. Frustrated, I shoved them all aside and walked over to my bed, turned off the bedside lamp and crawled under the covers.

I woke up the next morning and felt strong arms holding me as well as a hot and hard body spooning me. Chris. I turned around slowly so as not to wake him and looked at him. He was breathing deeply and evenly, still fast asleep. I might be upset with him, might not understand him right now, but I was still glad that he had crawled into bed with me last night. I had needed that. Carefully, I lifted his arm and slid out from underneath it, then rolled to the edge of the bed and into a sitting position. When I got up, I looked over my shoulder to check once again. He hadn't moved. I smiled to myself. Chris was a deep sleeper. Once he was out, he was out, and nothing short of a train running through the room would wake him. He needed three alarms set for different times, turned up to full volume, so he would wake up.

I went to the bathroom, did my business, brushed my teeth, and washed my face, then headed to the kitchen to get the coffee started, and then got ready for my morning run. I decided to run the big loop again today. I needed it to clear my head. I was worried that Chris was not going to give up and would try and make me talk to him about Jason when I came back. I had seen the determined look in his eyes last night. I knew that look. Chris was an understanding, supportive, and kind man, but when he was convinced of something and had made up his mind about you needing to agree with him, he could get pushy and bossy and not so gentle. Even though he had given me a reprieve last night, I knew that that reprieve was over, and I wasn't looking forward to the argument I knew was going to happen, since I was not planning on backing down on this.

About to leave him a note telling him I was out running and that the coffee was ready, Chris' voice sounded from behind me and made me jump.

"You're up early."

"Jeez, Chris, you scared the crap out of me." I put a hand over my beating heart. Chris smirked at me. "Sorry, didn't mean to scare you." He took me in then said, surprised and unhappy, "You're going for a run?"

"Yeah, I need to clear my head."

"Lore, we need to talk. I need to talk to you about what happened last night, about what Jason said—"

I whirled around and snapped, "I told you, Chris. I don't want to talk about what that asshole told you or what he wants. I don't care and neither should you." I dropped the pen and paper I still had in my hand on the counter and headed to the front door.

I heard Chris' footsteps as he followed me. "I heard you last night, Lore, but you have to listen to me. You have to know what he told me and you need to talk to him."

I stopped in my tracks and stilled.

What the fuck? Now he not only wanted me to talk *about*

102

Jason, he wanted me to actually talk *to* him? He could not be serious. He went from hating that man almost more than I did to defending him in less than twelve hours.

"Are you serious, Chris?" I was disappointed and angry now. Disappointed that Chris wouldn't not only let it go, but actually take Jason's side, disappointed that he was siding with the enemy against me. Or at least that's what it felt like. Like a betrayal.

Chris' eyes were on me and they were sad and compassionate. He lifted his arms as if to hug me, but I stepped around him and headed to the front door.

"Lore? Don't leave like this. Shit, Lore, I'm sorry." He followed me, his voice pleading. But it wasn't enough. I was too angry and, frankly, too hurt to forgive him right away.

"I'm leaving. I can't talk to you right now, Chris. Maybe you should go home."

His voice was firm when he answered. "I'm not going anywhere. I'll wait for you right here and we'll talk some more when you get back."

I sighed. I had known he wouldn't leave me even before I suggested it, but right now, for the first time in my life, I had to get away from him.

I opened the door and walked through it as I said, "Fine. Stay." Then I shut the door behind me and went on my run.

As I started running down the street and into the woods, my mind stayed on my best friend. Ever since we met, I could always trust Chris to have my best interests at heart and do anything in his power to make things easier for me. He was my best friend, my confidant, the one friend I could always come to and know he wouldn't hesitate to help, who kicked my ass if I was stubborn, and made sure I took care of myself. He was always there for me, no matter what, no matter how.

And now, that best friend wouldn't stop trying to talk to me about the man who had broken my heart, had shattered it into a million pieces. Chris had turned on me. He believed Jason. After six years of hating him for what he had done to me, it had taken Jason all of ten minutes to talk my best friend around, and that was something I couldn't grasp. He knew how hurt I had been by Jason's betrayal. He knew. And still, he insisted I hear him out. No, I wouldn't. I loved Chris but I was not going to cave on this. I couldn't.

For the rest of the run, I focused on clearing my mind. I focused on my breathing, and bit by bit, I was able to push the anger and disappointment aside for the moment and enjoy my run, let the adrenalin take over as I exhausted myself.

It was unfortunate that feeling didn't last long.

I was about to make the turn into my driveway when I saw the car that was parked on the street in front of my house.

It was a Challenger.

A Challenger just like Jason's.

What. The. Fuck.

I made the turn and stopped short at what I saw.

Chris was standing in the door.

And he was talking to Jason.

JASON

Jason was strung tight with anticipation as he drove into town. He was going to Loreley's house. In just a few minutes, he would find out what the fuck was going on.

When he got home last night after talking to Chris, he had made some phone calls. Murphy hadn't answered his phone so he had left a message to call him back asap. So far, he hadn't heard back from him. And Jason worried he wouldn't any time soon. *The Crowes* were on break after a long tour, which meant Murphy would be incommunicado for at least a few weeks. His phone would be off and he wouldn't check his emails. Last he heard, he had holed himself up somewhere in the Carribean with his latest squeeze. So he had called Nathan, their bassist. If there were one person who knew how to get a hold of Murphy it would be Nathan. The two of them were complete opposites but they were tight, had grown up together. They were like brothers. Nathan was also the glue that had been keeping the band together for the past few years. Jason was hoping that Nathan would be willing to corroborate his story about the night Lore and he had had their fight. Out of all his band members, Lore had been closest to Nathan. She had liked him and trusted him, so he hoped that if Nathan backed up Jason's story, she would believe him. Nathan remembered that night only too clearly, because according to him, it had been the night when Jason lost his muse and turned into an asshole. He had called him a "stupid shit" on more than one occasion over the years because of it. He had been right of course, but Jason never admitted it out loud. Though, he did last night when he called Nathan and told him what he'd learned from talking to Chris.

"Told you, man. Letting her get away was the biggest mistake you've ever made. You lost her because of your stupid wounded ego and you know it. You've been a miserable ass for almost six years now, man, and it's taken a toll on all of us."

"I know, Nathan. Don't need the lecture. What I need is to get in touch with Murphy so he can tell Loreley it wasn't me fucking that girl that night," Jason had been impatient and angry.

"Relax, man. I doubt he's gonna get back to you. We've been on the road for months and had to live with your sorry ass 24/7. He won't call you. But I'll try to talk to him. If he doesn't want to help or doesn't remember—which is very likely, since you weren't the only person that was trashed that night—I'll come out to Colorado and talk to Loreley. Scratch that, I'll come down no matter what Murphy says. I'll book a flight right now. You're not the only one who has missed our girl, and someone's gotta make sure you don't fuck it up again."

Jason had sighed in relief. "Thanks, man. I owe you."

"Oh, you owe me all right. You have no idea how much. But I'd do pretty much anything if that means you'll get out of that funk." Nathan had hung up and Jason was hoping he would get a call back soon, telling him that he either tracked down Murphy or that he was on his way down here.

Then he tried to get some information on how to retrieve old emails and text messages. Apparently, it wasn't that easy, since they were more than two years old and he had changed his phone number and email addresses multiple times in the past six years. He had made a few calls and was expecting to hear back.

But instead, it was Cal who phoned him and Jason had nothing to show him yet. He knew that if he wanted Cal to let him live, he would need definite proof that he hadn't cheated on his sister.

To his surprise, Cal had sounded only slightly enraged when he answered the phone.

"I was half-way out the door last night to beat the shit out of you for screwing Loreley over when I got a call from Chris," he had said. Jason had closed his eyes in relief and gratitude. Apparently, Chris was coming through for him and would be his ally in this.

"Yeah?"

"Yeah. Told me you said you didn't cheat on her. Said he believed you."

"He can. I didn't." Jason's voice was firm.

106

"He also told me you never got her messages. That true?"

"Yeah, that's true. I had no idea she was trying to get a hold of me. I still don't know why she did."

Silence for a few seconds, then Cal asked, "So it's true you don't know?" Jason lost it in that moment, frustrated with everyone hinting at something, but no one telling him anything. That's why he snarled at Cal, "No, Cal, I have no fucking clue. I have no clue why Loreley called me, or what happened that made her almost kill herself. What I *do* know is that it must have been something big if she tried to talk to me even though she thought I had cheated on her. But I *don't* know what the fuck that was, since nobody is fucking telling me shit!"

"We're just trying to protect her, Jace. This is gonna be a blow for her and we don't want her to lose it again. You weren't here. You didn't see how bad it was."

"Well, I'm here now, Cal, and I'm here to stay. I'm not letting her leave me ever again. She is mine, which makes it *my* job to catch her if she loses it. But I can't fucking do that if I don't know what the fuck is going on!"

Silence, then, "Fuck, man. Lore is stubborn and hurt. She won't talk to you."

"I experienced that yesterday and the night before," Jason growled in a low voice. "I gave Chris last night to talk to her. I'm headed over there this morning. I would like not to go in blind." He heard Cal swear again under his breath. Then, "Ivey is gonna kick my ass if I interfere," he said as if he was talking to himself. He assumed Ivey was the wife Chris had mentioned last night, but Jason didn't ask, he just waited for Cal's decision.

"Fuck," he heard Cal swear on the other end. Then nothing.

Jason kept waiting.

"I think you need to hear the story from her, but I'll come to

107

Loreley's house and help if I can. But you gotta know, that no matter what, Loreley is my first priority, and I will kick your ass if you make this worse for her than it already is. So I need your word. I need your word that you're not gonna bolt, that you're gonna stick around and fight for her even if it's her you have to fight, and that you're gonna take care of her once you've got her back." Cal's request told him that he would have a fight on his hands but that he believed he would eventually get what he wanted if he didn't give up. Cal was giving him a chance. And Jason was going to take it. Not that he needed Cal's blessing, but it was better to have it than to fight a war on two fronts.

"You've got it." Again, Jason's voice was firm. Like steel.

Cal sighed. "All right. I'll meet you in an hour. But you better be telling the truth, Jason, or I swear to God, I will make it so you wish we'd never met. You get me?"

"Yeah, I get you." Then he lowered his voice and said, relieved, "Thank you, man."

"Don't thank me." Then Cal had hung up.

So Cal would be at Loreley's house, too.

Jason parked his Challenger in front of the driveway. He got out and knocked on her front door. Chris opened it. His eyes grew wide with panic when he saw Jason.

"Shit, man, you're too early. I haven't been able to talk to her about everything. She's mad as hell at me for even mentioning—"

"I gave you last night, man," Jason interrupted. "I told you I wouldn't wait any longer."

"No, Jason. You can't. You don't understand—"

"That's exactly why I won't wait any longer, Chris. Because I don't understand, because I don't know what the fuck is going on."

"Fuck!"

"What the fuck are you doing at my house?" Both Chris and Jason turned when they heard Loreley's lethal voice.

"He's here to talk to you, Lore." She threw Chris such a menacing glare full of heat, it would bring even the best man to his knees. Out of the corner of his eyes, Jason saw Chris wince. He didn't blame him.

"I cannot believe you," she hissed at Chris. Then she turned that glare on Jason. "Go away. I told you last night and the night before: you're not wanted here."

Jason took a step towards her. He was close enough to touch her, but he didn't, no matter how much his hand ached to.

"We need to talk," he said firmly but pleadingly. He hated to beg, but there was nothing he wouldn't do to finally make her listen to him. His Loreley was stubborn, always had been. Back when they were together, he had gotten off on her stubbornness, fuck, he still did. But right now, he would give a lot for her to be more compliant.

"There is nothing to talk about. Nothing you could say that I want to hear." She was as angry as he'd ever seen her. Angry and hurt. He could see it in her eyes, just like he had yesterday on the sidewalk.

"Lore—" Chris started, but Jason interrupted him.

"I don't agree. There is a lot we need to talk about, starting with that shit about me cheating on you." Loreley's body didn't flinch, but her eyes did, telling Jason that the hurt and betrayal ran deep.

Fuck.

He couldn't take it.

He had to touch her, had to try and soothe her somehow. So he went for it. He raised his hand and put it to her cheek, sliding his fingers into her hair while cupping the side of her face with his palm.

"Baby," he whispered in a rough whisper.

The fire that had disappeared for a split second was back in an instant, and Loreley jerked her head away from him. "Don't touch me. Don't you dare touch me! Get in your car and leave!"

Jason shook his head. His eyes remained on Loreley when he said, "I'd do almost anything you asked if that meant you'd talk to me. But I can't do that. I'm not leaving."

"Why?" Loreley asked. "Why, after all these years do you all of a sudden have to talk to me? I don't get it!"

His face softened a little as he answered, "Because I missed you, baby. I've missed you every single day for six years."

She uncrossed her arms and pointed a finger in his face when she leaned into him and spat, "That is fucking bullshit! You're the one who threw me away! You're the one who couldn't keep his dick in his pants! Don't you dare give me that bullshit about missing me!"

Jason leaned closer into Loreley, so she had to put her hand down if she didn't want to poke his eye out. "I keep telling you. I didn't fucking cheat on you, Loreley. It wasn't me with that woman. It was Murphy."

Fuck! He wasn't getting through to her.

"Bullshit!" Loreley spat again.

"It's not bullshit! It's the fucking truth! I loved you. I still love you. Why in the fuck would I cheat on you?"

"Oh, I don't know! Because you're a selfish jerk who didn't get his own way?" She yelled sarcastically.

Jason looked to the sky, seeking patience.

Fucking hell this woman was so fucking stubborn!

Before he could figure out a way to get through to her though, she spoke again, not yelling this time. No, it was worse, the way her voice sounded was so much worse than yelling.

It was broken.

Crushed.

And resigned.

"You know what? It doesn't even matter."

Jason's head snapped back down and he narrowed his eyes on her. "Of course it matters. You shut me out because you thought I cheated on you. We would still be together if—"

"Oh, no. We wouldn't be." She sounded sure about that. Definite. Her voice was low and full of something else...hatred? Jason flinched.

"Even if you didn't cheat on me, how long exactly did it take you before you forgot about me and moved on?" Jason clamped his mouth shut. He knew what she was referring to.

"Yeah, I thought so. But that doesn't matter either."

There it was again: the hint at something. The hint at the secret that everyone seemed too scared to tell him.

"Would you fucking stop talking in riddles? Spit it out! What made you hate me so much that you can hardly bear to look at me? Why, Loreley? Why are you so sure we wouldn't be together right now?"

"You know. Stop pretending you don't."

"I don't know or I wouldn't fucking ask."

"Lore—" Chris tried to mediate, but neither of them paid him any attention.

"Stop playing this game, Jason. Stop it and leave."

"I'm not playing a game, Loreley. I have no fucking clue what is going on."

The hate in her eyes intensified as they stared at each other silently.

"Lore, I think—"

"No, Chris. He wants to do this? We'll do it. He wants me to say it? I'll say it. Maybe then he'll leave." She didn't take his eyes from his. "You abandoned me. You turned your back on

111

me when I needed you and abandoned us."

"I didn't. Those messages—"

"So you *do* remember the messages."

I shook my head. "I don't. Chris told me about them last night—"

"Lore!" They both heard shouted from across the street in a familiar boom. It was Cal.

Fucking finally.

He jogged towards them and stopped close, his eyes on his sister.

"You both need to calm down and take this inside."

"What?" Loreley snapped as her eyebrows shot up in disbelief.

"We need to go inside and talk," Cal repeated. His gaze swung to Jason and he studied him for a second before he turned it back on Loreley.

"Cal is right, Lore, let's go inside and talk about this calmly," Chris said soothingly and beseechingly.

"No way. He—"

"He doesn't know, Lore. You can't just throw it in his face like that." Cal again.

"Watch me."

Cal leaned in closer to his sister. "You're not hearing what I'm saying to you, Loreley. Jason doesn't know anything about Jesse."

Jesse? Who was Jesse?

Before he could ask, Loreley spoke again. "I'm aware of that, Cal, since I never talked to him again after I saw him screwing around and realized he really didn't give a shit about his child."

Wait. What?

"What are you talking about? Who is Jesse?" But Jason

112

didn't need anyone to answer his question. Before he was even done asking, all the pieces fell into place. Everything made sense now. Why Loreley had tried to get in touch with him a few months after she had left; why she had come to one of his gigs to talk to him even though she still thought he had cheated on her. It was obvious now, and Jason wanted to kick his own ass for not having figured it out sooner.

Loreley had been pregnant.

She glared at him.

"Lore—" Cal tried again, but she ignored him, and with what she said next, pulled the ground from under Jason's feet.

"Jesse was your son you didn't give one shit about. But don't worry. He's dead now."

Jason heard Cal swear under his breath beside him and Chris pull in a shocked breath. He heard them both talk, to him or Loreley, he didn't know. He couldn't comprehend anything while his mind was trying to make sense of what Loreley had just said.

He had a son.

A son who Loreley had kept from him.

A son who had died.

The thought made him sick.

Sick with hurt.

Sick with loss.

Sick with disappointment.

Sick with anger.

He came back out of his thoughts and turned his heat filled glare on Loreley. She was watching him with an expression on her face that he didn't want to interpret. It was remorse, remorse and shock and sorrow. But Jason didn't want to see any of that coming from her right now.

All he was interested in was to somehow get rid of that

113

strangling feeling he had in his throat, the weight that was sitting on his chest and was threatening to choke him.

And he did that by lashing out at her.

"Tell me you didn't keep my son from me." He didn't recognize his own voice. It was cold but hot with anger at the same time.

Loreley flinched.

Good.

Jason stepped closer to her and leaned into her face until their noses almost touched and repeated his words on a hiss, "Tell me you didn't fucking keep my son from me." It was a threat as much as it was a plea.

"I didn't. I called you, left messages. Emailed you."

"I obviously never got those messages, Loreley. I would have never ignored you, would have never abandoned you and our child. And you should have known that, Loreley. You knew me. You knew everything about me. You knew me down to my soul. You should have known that there was no way I would have ignored those messages."

He watched as Loreley's eyes filled with panic.

"I thought you cheated on me. You——"

"No, Loreley. You also should have known that I would never cheat on you. I can be an asshole and say things I don't mean, but we were committed to each other and I would have never hurt you like that. We were going to get married and spend the rest of our lives together. We talked about our future all the time. What? You think I would throw all that away for some groupie pussy?"

Loreley didn't say anything, but Jason could see it in her eyes. That's exactly what she had thought. She had been convinced that he had thrown them away to get himself some. After everything they had talked about, after all the times he had told her that she was the one for him, the one who made him happy, the one he wanted to spend the rest of his life with, the one he couldn't imagine living without. After all that, all it took was one misunderstanding and she had stopped believing in him, had stopped believing in *them*, and as a consequence, had kept his son from him, a son who he would never have a chance to meet now.

And that hurt.

It hurt like a motherfucker.

Jason let her see just how much as he kept staring into her eyes. Tears welled up in hers as she stared right back at him. She made as if to move into him but Jason stepped away from her. She froze.

"Jason—"

"You should have told me. You should have done everything in your power to talk to me," he interrupted her. He wasn't interested in her apology. It was too late for that.

He turned his head and locked his eyes first with Cal's then with Chris'.

Cal stayed silent, just watched him carefully and apologetically. Chris did the same.

He didn't want their apologies either.

This time it was him, who without another look, turned on his heel and walked to his car, got in, and drove off.

Eight

LORELEY

"What have I done?" I whispered in horror as I watched Jason drive away. Silent tears were running down my cheeks.

How the tables had turned.

Less than five minutes ago, I had been the one who had been betrayed by the love of her life, who had been hurt, whose heart had been shredded.

Now, it was Jason who was experiencing the pain of betrayal.

But it was so much worse.

Not only had he just found out that the love of his life had stopped believing in him because of some misunderstanding that she was too blind to see as such, but he had also just learned that that same woman hadn't tried real hard to get a hold of him when she learned she was carrying their child, and as a result of that, he would never get the chance to get to know his own son.

And that woman was me.

I had done that to him.

To us.

To Jesse.

Jason was right.

116

I should have known that he would have never cheated on me. If I had really loved him the way I said I did, I would have tried to get to the bottom of it instead of running away.

He was absolutely right.

Had I not run away and shut him out, we would have still been together when I found out I was pregnant.

We would have been a family together.

Or if I had tried harder to get in touch with him when I did find out.

Even if he *had* cheated on me and we were over, I should have known he wasn't the kind of man to turn his back on his own child.

But instead, I had wanted to believe that Jason Sanders was a jerk who didn't deserve to be a part of Jesse's and my life.

It was all my fault.

A mistake I would have to live with now for the rest of my life.

"What have I done?" I whispered again, my voice conveying exactly how broken and empty I was feeling inside.

Strong arms went around me and pulled me into a hard chest. I felt Cal's chin rest on the top of my head as he squeezed me tight.

I closed my eyes, hoping this had all just been a bad dream even though I knew it wasn't.

I had been a bitch and had wanted to hurt Jason. I had been so wrapped up in my own head and too blind to see that he had not been playing a game, that he really hadn't known what I was talking about.

I had been a bitch and had said ugly things with the sole intention of hurting him.

And boy had I succeeded.

I lifted my head out of Cal's chest and leaned back so I

could see his face. He tipped his chin down to see mine.

"I behaved like a bitch."

Cal clenched his teeth in what I took as confirmation that yes, he agreed that I had indeed behaved like a bitch and he was disappointed in me.

"Yes, Lore, you did. But it's understandable why you did it."

I shook my head. "No, Cal, it isn't. The things I said to him, *how* I said them to him, it was ugly. Nobody deserves that. Nobody deserves to find out about the death of their son like that, no matter what they have done."

Cal looked at me with serious eyes, not saying anything, which again I took as agreement. I felt my lower lip start to tremble.

"What am I gonna do, Cal? How am I gonna make this right?"

"I don't know, Lore. I don't know." He pulled me back against his chest and rubbed my back soothingly as silent tears ran down my cheeks. I was in complete shock. Everything I had believed for the past six years had been a lie. The look of absolute horror and shock and then pain and betrayal that had flitted over Jason's face had told me everything I needed to know.

He didn't cheat on me.

He hadn't known I was pregnant.

He loved me and would have never left us.

But I took his chance of being part of our family away from him by keeping the existence of our son from him.

I betrayed him, betrayed both of us, and betrayed Jesse by wanting to believe the worst of his father.

I couldn't blame him if he hated me now and would never want to see me again.

Because what I had done was truly unforgivable.

Cal held me like that for a few minutes before he turned us and walked us into my house. I looked at Chris then. He had wanted to talk to me that morning, had said it was important, had urged me to talk to Jason. He had known that Jason wasn't to blame for what happened. He had known and wanted to tell me. And instead of trusting my best friend that he had my best interests at heart and listening to him, I had gotten my feelings hurt and got mad at him for choosing Jason's side.

I was an even bigger bitch than I thought I was.

The silent tears turned into not so silent sobs.

"He's right Chris. I should have known. I should have—"

"No, Lore," Chris interrupted me. He came to sit next to me on the couch and took my hand. "There was no way for you to know that that woman wasn't with Jason that morning. And there was no way for you to know that he didn't get your messages, that he didn't know you were pregnant."

I shook my head at him. "I gave up on him—"

"No, Lore," he interrupted me again. "You couldn't have known. Don't blame yourself for what happened. It was a misunderstanding. And it's not like *he* hunted you down to talk to you. He gave up on you just like you gave up on him. Worse, because you actually thought you had a reason. He was a jerk to you that night, but you still went back to talk to him. You didn't know Murphy was staying at Jason's place, so how would you know that woman was with Murphy and not with him?"

He made sense of course, but in that moment, all I could think about was the look on Jason's face when I told him about Jesse being dead. "That doesn't excuse what I did, Chris."

"If you mean what you did today, you're probably right. It doesn't." I flinched and felt my bottom lip start to tremble again. Chris put one hand to my cheek and wiped the tears that were again falling away with his thumb. "But it's understandable, Lore. You've been in so much pain for such a long time. I'm not surprised that you lashed out to let go of some of it."

"Chris is right, Loreley. Your reaction was harsh, but it was understandable. You couldn't have known any of that. You acted on what you thought you knew. Yeah, it was ugly and it hurt, but nobody can blame you for lashing out at the person you thought was the cause for a big portion of the hurt you've been carrying for six years," Cal stated.

"Jason is going to blame me. And he's got every right to."

"He'll come around, Lore. If he is the man I know him to be, he'll come around once you've talked to him, once you've explained everything to him. He told me last night that he hasn't stopped loving you for all these years, so he'll come around." Chris assured me.

I hoped he was right. "He said that?" I asked. Chris nodded.

"And I know that you never stopped loving him either. If you had, you wouldn't have still been so hurt and angry after all this time." I closed my eyes and touched my forehead to his.

"I should have listened to you this morning."

"Yeah, you should have. But I didn't try very hard either. I didn't want to cause you more pain. And I was scared you'd be mad at me."

"I probably wouldn't have believed you. I'm such a stubborn bitch."

Chris chuckled. "You're stubborn and you can be a bitch when provoked, but you're not a bitch normally."

I took a few deep breaths in an effort to calm down. "Thank you, Chris."

"You're welcome. Now, get your shit together. You've got a phone call to make."

Grateful, I smiled at him.

Then I got my shit together so I could make a phone call.

I made that phone call and a couple more within the next few hours.

Jason never picked up.

The first two times, I left messages for him, apologizing and asking him to call me back so we could talk. He never did. I doubted he even listened to the messages.

Chris and Cal had both still been at my house during the first call. It had rung a few times before it went to voice mail. My phone number was still the same it had been six years ago, so I was pretty sure Jason knew it was me who was calling him.

My heart was beating in overtime as I listened to the phone ringing and sunk when the call went to voice mail.

Both Cal and Chris had thunderous expressions on their faces when I hung up—well, Cal's was definitely thunderous. Chris' was more sad than angry, but the glint in his eyes couldn't be mistaken for anything but anger.

"Give him some time, Lore. He'll come around," Chris repeated his words from earlier.

The next time I called a few hours later, it didn't ring. It went straight to voice mail.

The message was clear.

Jason didn't want to talk to me.

I understood why, but still, I didn't give up. I called him once more with the same result and then decided to go up to the rental and talk to him face to face.

When I drove up to Cal's A-Frame, the Challenger was nowhere in sight. Still, I went to the front door and knocked and peeked through the windows when nobody answered. The house looked and felt empty. He wasn't home. Determined to talk to him today, I waited on the front porch. I waited for over two hours until I gave up and decided to go to the cemetery.

I would come back and try again later.

Jason wasn't the only person I owed an apology.

I owed my son one as well.

I had never talked to Jesse about his dad, never even so much as mentioned his name. It had been too painful to remember. And what was I supposed to tell him? That his father had abandoned us? That he didn't want anything to do with us? That he was off enjoying his rock star career and probably didn't even think about us? Those weren't things a son should think about his father. So I had put it off and placated him when he asked why he didn't have a father or where his father was or if his father would ever come to see him.

Now, I realized that that had been one of my biggest mistakes. Jesse deserved to have a father, and I had withheld that option from him even in spirit. I shouldn't have done that. I should have lied to him, come up with a reasonable story about why his father wasn't with us. Or even tell him the truth. Or at least the truth that was fit for a five-year-old's ears. The truth about his parents falling in love with each other, but things not working out between us; that we both loved him very much, but that his dad lived too far away for him to visit.

I couldn't turn back time but I could sure as hell try and make up for it now.

So kneeling in front of his grave, I told my son about his father.

"The first time we met I didn't really want to talk to your father, but he was resilient and sat down next to me and started talking until I couldn't help but listen. He made me laugh. He had so many crazy stories to tell and was such a good storyteller. That's something the two of you had in common: make me laugh even when I don't feel like it, because your stories are so crazy and over the top that I can't help but laugh. You would have loved him. And he would have loved you. No doubt about it."

I swallowed as tears stung my eyes and my throat closed up.

"I owe you an apology, Jesse. An apology for keeping your father from you. I am so sorry," I choked as the enormity of what I had done overwhelmed me. Tears streamed down my face yet again as I sobbed at my son's grave for the first time in months. "There is no excuse for keeping him from you. I should have told you about him, should have told you how much in love we were when we made you. I am so sorry." I cried some more.

"He never knew about me?" I turned around and saw Jason standing behind me. His face was set in an angry mask that did nothing to hide the pain and anguish in his eyes.

I wiped the tears away, but it was no use. Seeing him like that and knowing I was responsible for it, broke my heart yet again.

"I'm sorry, Jason. I'm so sorry," I whispered brokenly through my tears.

"You being sorry is not gonna turn back time, is it? It's not gonna let me meet and get to know my son, is it?"

I shook my head. "No, it isn't. And I take full responsibility for that. You're right. I should have tried harder, I should have done anything in my power to talk to you. This is all my fault." I looked up at Jason's face. I was literally on my knees in front of him, apologizing, begging him to forgive me. His face softened a fraction but not enough to chase away the anger. He moved his eyes from mine and gazed at his son's headstone.

He stared at his son's name and date of birth and death for long minutes:

Jesse Cooper

123

January 15, 2007
†*June 22, 2012*
Your beautiful spirit will forever
leave a smile in our hearts.

His angry mask dropped and was replaced with an expression so tortured it would have brought me to my knees if I hadn't already been kneeling. I sobbed again when I saw tears pooling in his eyes. I got up and slowly moved towards him until I stood beside him. I reached out a hand and touched his. He let this happen for a few short moments, and I was immensely relieved, until he took a step away from me and my touch.

"I can't do this, yet, Loreley. I'm still too mad at you. Too hurt. I can't understand how you could ever think so little of me. I don't have it in me to forgive you right now, maybe with time, but not now."

"Okay," I said brokenly. I nodded as I wiped away a new set of tears. Jason watched me do this and his face softened another fraction.

"I'll want to know about him, see pictures of him." His voice sounded sad and heartbroken.

I nodded again, a little more enthusiastically, and repeated, "Okay."

"Okay," he whispered back. Then he swallowed and said, "I'm not ready, yet, but I'll call you."

Another whispered, "Okay" from me before he gazed at the grave one more time and turned around to walk away.

I stayed at the cemetery for a long time after that, talking to Jesse and my mother, telling them both about Jason, begging their forgiveness again and again. I cried until there were no more tears left in me. When I could finally make myself leave, I got up and softly touched Jesse's headstone as I whispered one of his favourite "I love you so much"-phrases. "I love you so much I want to eat all the chocolate cake in the world until I'm as round as the Willy Wonka Blueberry Girl and you'll chase me when I roll down the hill and roll and roll until I can't roll any more, that's how much I love you." I kissed my fingers and pressed those fingers against the hard and cold stone. Then I went home.

When I pulled into the driveway, Chris was waiting for me at the front door.

"You okay?" He was worried about me. His eyes roamed over my face and grew even more worried when he saw my puffy-and-red-from-crying-for-hours eyes.

I shook my head and gave him a small smile that I knew didn't reach my eyes. "Not really."

He closed his arms around me and hugged me tightly. "You talk to Jason?"

I rested my cheek on his chest and closed my eyes. "I did," I said softly, my voice filled with sadness.

"And?" Chris prompted when I didn't say any more.

"He says he needs time, says that he can't forgive me right now, that he's still too mad and hurt." Chris arms tightened around me as he spoke into my hair. "He'll come around." I nodded into his chest but wasn't at all convinced that Chris was right. "He'll come around, you'll see," Chris repeated as if knowing my gloomy thoughts. We stood like that for long moments, him holding me and rocking me and softly stroking my back, me leaning into him, cheek to his chest, eyes closed.

"I have to go check on the bar. I know you're off tonight but I want you to come with me."

"I'll be okay, Chris. Don't worry."

"As if that could ever happen." He leaned back so he could look at my face. I did the same. "I'll always worry about you,

Lore. You're my best friend, my family. I hate seeing you this sad." I knew that. It was the same way I felt about him.

"Look at me, Chris. There's no way I can go into town the way I look. I'll scare off the customers," I half-heartedly tried to lighten the mood, but Chris wasn't fooled.

"You've got two options: you can either come with me and hide in the office and do some paperwork, or I can drop you off at Cal and Ivey's and you can stay there until I'm done. I'm not leaving you here alone in this state."

I sighed in defeat. I knew I didn't have a prayer winning this fight. "Fine. I'll come to the bar. Just let me go wash my face." I left Chris' embrace and headed to the bathroom.

By the time I fell into bed that night, I was so exhausted that I could hardly keep my eyes open as I waited for Chris to be done in the bathroom. Losing the fight, I closed my eyes and thought about Jesse and Jason like I had most of the day, thought about the smile they shared, their laugh, their beautiful eyes.

And then I saw him.

Jesse.

For the first time in a year, I saw my son as if he were lying beside me in bed. He was watching me with proud but sad eyes. He looked older now, as if wherever he was, he was growing and maturing as if he was still alive. He would be six years old now.

I felt his hand as he put it against my cheek like he had done so many times. I felt it as if it was real, as if Jesse was really here with me. I breathed a sigh of relief and smiled as I held his hand against my cheek with mine, then turned my head and kissed his palm.

"It'll be okay, mom. You'll be okay," I heard Jesse whisper.

Tears stung my eyes at hearing my son's beautiful voice for the first time in a year. I had missed it so much.

"Don't cry, mom. It'll all be okay. I promise," he whispered again.

The tears were running down my cheeks silently. "I miss you so much."

He smiled a sad smile. "I know. I miss you, too. But I'm always right here with you."

Yes, he was. He was always with me. I carried him with me wherever I went. "I know, baby. I know. It's just so hard."

He didn't say anything, just smiled his sad smile at me as he cupped my cheek in his small hand.

"I visited you today."

"I know."

"Did you hear me when I told you about your dad?"

"I know all about my dad. I've been watching him just as I've been watching you." My eyes grew big.

"You have?"

Jesse nodded. "Of course."

"I'm sorry I didn't tell you sooner."

"It's okay, mom, I understand. And so will dad." I sighed as relief washed through me. I stared at him for countless moments, drinking him in. Then I kissed his nose, his cheek, his forehead. I kissed him all over until he giggled and pushed me away playfully. I didn't care if this was real or if I was dreaming. I would enjoy this moment for as long as it lasted.

Then he looked at me and whispered, "I love you so much I'm gonna let you eat all the chocolate cake in the world until you are as round as the Willy Wonka Blueberry Girl and I'll chase you when you roll down the hill and roll and roll until you can't roll any more, that's how much I love you."

I thought I didn't have any tears left in me, but they started running freely and steadily again. He had heard me today at the cemetery. He had been there and he had heard me.

127

"I'll always hear you, mom. I'll always be there." He said as if he had listened to my thoughts.

Then, looking into my son's warm eyes, I drifted off and fell into a peaceful sleep, a sleep so peaceful I didn't wake up once, not even when Chris came to bed and pulled me into his body, not when he kissed the top of my head and murmured, "I'm so sorry this is causing you more pain."

Nine

LORELEY

The next day I hoped and prayed that Jason would call me. Every time the phone rang or someone was at the door, my heart skipped a beat, only to have the feeling of disappointment and emptiness inside me expand and my stomach drop when it wasn't him.

He didn't call that day.

Or the next day.

Or the two days after that.

I wanted to call him, wanted to talk to him, to apologize again, to tell him all about Jesse, about how much he had been like his dad. But he had told me he needed some time and I had to respect that.

The emotional pain I went through was like nothing I had ever experienced. Not that it was worse than watching my son die and burying him way before his time. It wasn't. It was just different.

It was indescribable.

And I couldn't escape it. It was all around me, in every memory, everywhere I looked. It was grief, it was sorrow, and the certainty that I had brought it on myself made me desperate.

Chris was still staying with me, but even so, my house felt empty. Jason had never lived here with us, had never even seen it before Monday, but I still missed his presence in it. Because I knew he would have been here with us, and that made the feeling of emptiness and loneliness that much harder to bear.

I felt numb almost all the time. I often caught myself staring blankly at nothing, even in the middle of doing something like mixing a drink or wiping the counter or putting up chairs. I tried to put on a brave face to reassure everyone that I was okay, but I knew that I wasn't fooling anyone. People were worried about me. Heck, I was worried about me. What was I going to do if Jason didn't forgive me? What would I do if he never wanted to talk to me again? But no, I couldn't let myself think that. He said he was going to call me. He needed time. That was all. I had to hold on to the hope or there would be nothing else left.

I developed a pattern: I woke up, went for a run, went to work, came home and stared at the TV, then cried myself to sleep while I waited for that phone call I was desperate to receive. I couldn't even escape the pain when I was sleeping, since Jason's tortured and pained expression at hearing that the son he didn't know about was dead followed me into my dreams.

There were only a few things that broke through that pattern.

On Wednesday night, Macy and Ivey came over armed with a bottle of Tequila.

"We're here so you can pour your heart out and know that you will be safe. No macho men here to try and protect you from reality or lose their shit when they realize they can't use their badass super powers to make everything right for you. It's just us girls. No judgement, no empty platitudes. Just an open ear and lots of alcohol." Macy had informed me upon marching into my kitchen to cut the lime and get some glasses.

130

"That's right," Ivey had said when she embraced me, "Just us girls and lots of alcohol for the two of you. In my experience, that's all you need when you don't know what's up or down: your friends and Tequila. And pizza of course."

So I had opened my heart and soul to my two best girlfriends.

I told them everything. From the moment I had met Jason to the moment I had seen him hook up with another woman at that gig and had sworn to never talk to him again. Then I told them how I wished I hadn't walked away that morning after our fight, how I wished I had pushed past that woman I thought he had cheated on me with and had confronted Jason. If I had done that, none of this would have happened. We would have been together and happy, and Jason would have known his son. Maybe Jesse would even still be alive.

"Stop right there, Lore. You can't put that on yourself. You can't blame yourself for Jesse's death. Believe me, it won't get you anywhere," Ivey had stopped me in a gentle but firm voice. Her eyes had been on me, soft but hard and reprimanding at the same time. "Believe me, Lore, I know all about survivor's guilt and blaming yourself for your baby's death. It took me a long time to figure out that life happens and there isn't much we can do about it. We make our choices based on what we know, and you couldn't have known that Jesse would die that day. You couldn't have known that when you got in your dad's truck that morning, that Jesse would not come out of that truck alive. You couldn't have known, just like I couldn't have known that my boyfriend would beat me half to death and kill my baby. Don't put that on yourself, Lore, or you might not find your way out of it." I had thrown myself into Ivey's arms at her words, had started crying big and ugly tears as she held me and comforted me. Ivey had been through a lot. She'd had an abusive

131

childhood in which her dad beat her and her mom for years, had escaped all that when she went to college, only to find herself entangled with another abusive man who beat her so bad that she lost her baby and had to stay in the hospital for almost a week. She hadn't really recovered from any of that until she and Cal had gotten together and he had made her go to therapy. So she knew what she was talking about.

"You also couldn't have known that Jason didn't cheat on you. Honestly, if I had been in your place, I would have thought the same thing. And I would have run away, just like you. He says you should have known. Well, I say he should have come after you. He should have known that you wouldn't leave him without looking back because of a fight you both say was stupid. You're both to blame, but at the same time, it's neither of your fault. Life happens and we can't change the past. What we *can* do and *need* to do is face the past and overcome it."

"Wow, Ivey. I think you've been hanging out with Betty too much," Macy had mumbled through her own tears.

We had talked and cried and talked some more until Chris came back and Cal showed to drive Macy and his wife home in the early morning hours.

On Thursday, something else and very unexpected broke through my fog of emptiness and regret: Nathan was in town.

Nathan, Jason's drummer and one of his closest friends, was in Cedar Creek. We had been good friends back then. He had been the band member I had bonded with and liked the most. The fact that he was here gave me hope. At least that meant that Jason was still in town and hadn't fled back to L.A.

He gave me the biggest hug when he walked into the bar on Thursday night and came straight behind the counter when he saw me standing there.

"God, it's so good to see you," he murmured into my hair as

he lifted me up and shook me back and forth jerkily. "I've missed you, beautiful."

"What are you doing here?" I asked when he released me.

"I came here to help out my buddy and beg you to give him another chance. But now I'm here to shake some sense into that stubborn little shit."

"So you know? He told you?"

His eyes grew sad and compassionate. "Yes, beautiful, I know. And I'm so very sorry for your loss." My lips trembled a little but I didn't cry.

"Thank you, Nathan," I said in a shaky voice. The emotional turmoil of the last week was taking its toll on me.

"That stubborn son of a bitch," he whispered darkly. "Come on, let's talk." He grabbed my hand and let me out from behind the bar and to a table in the corner where we could talk more or less privately.

"You know, he never deserved you. I've said it before and I stand by it. I haven't given up the dream that you'll someday run away with me," he teased after we sat down and Chris had brought us each a beer.

I gave him a small but sad smile. I knew he was trying to cheer me up, but I couldn't bring myself to let him.

Nathan sighed a heavy sigh, then started talking in earnest. "Jason is angry. And he's got a right to be." I tensed. Nathan kept laying it out. "He's angry and he's hurt, and we both know that he lashes out when he's like that. But it's always easier to blame other people for what happened, even though you know most of that anger is directed at yourself. It's easier to lash out at someone else, because it saves you from having to look at your own mistakes. Jason has hated himself for years for not going after you, for letting you slip through his fingers, and he's been a miserable fucker because of it. Now, he's got even more reason

133

to hate himself, for being a thick-headed asshole, because not only has it cost him you but his son. He won't ever get that back and he blames himself for it. But it's easier to blame someone else than to admit that you did it to yourself. Believe me when I say this, Loreley: he doesn't blame you. He might say he does, but he doesn't. Not really. And I'll tell you what I've told him: if he doesn't realize that soon and get his head out of his ass and talk to you, he won't just have to look forward to a royal ass kicking by Cal and Chris. I'll be right there to cheer them on and wait my turn."

That had been yesterday.

Nathan and I had talked some more before Chris had joined us. He had stayed for most of the night and had given me another tight hug and a "Chin up, girl" with a kiss on the cheek when he left.

Now, another day had passed and still, Jason hadn't called.

It was now Friday afternoon, day four of no contact, and I was getting restless and more and more anxious and resigned by the hour.

Maybe this was it.

Maybe there was no way he could ever forgive me.

Maybe he had gone back to L.A. and was done for good with me this time.

What Ivey and Nathan and Chris and everyone else had said to me in these past few days did penetrate to some degree, but that didn't mean that I didn't still blame myself.

The thought of never seeing him again, of never getting the chance to tell him about how great of a son Jesse had been and how much he had been like his dad in so many ways, made my breath hitch as a sharp pain pierced through my heart yet again.

This all reminded me of how I had failed to get in touch with Jason six years ago. But whereas then I had been hurt and

134

disappointed and bitter, now all I felt was a terrible sadness and emptiness that I couldn't seem to shake, that actually grew darker and emptier with every day I didn't hear from him.

JASON

Jason was sitting on the back porch strumming his guitar as he stared out to where the sun was slowly setting over the mountains. Apart from going to the cemetery every day to visit his son's grave, this was pretty much where he'd spent the past four days while he wallowed in self-pity and anger and confusion.

For the most part of those past four days, he had been too incensed to feel anything besides anger and loss. Or at least that's what he told himself. Though deep down inside he knew almost as soon as he had walked away from her at the cemetery that he couldn't really blame Loreley for anything that had happened. If he was honest with himself and put himself in her shoes, he couldn't blame her for one fucking thing that had happened. Not even for throwing his son's death in his face the way she had and completely gutting him. But in that moment, Jason hadn't wanted to be honest with himself or look any deeper than his anger. Because if he had, he would have had to face everything they had lost. And just like Nathan had said to him over and over again, it was always easier to blame someone else than face reality and take responsibility for your own actions.

But Jason hadn't been ready to listen to his friend's words and outbursts and lectures and pleas. He had clung to his anger and wrapped it around himself like a blanket. This blanket of anger made it possible for him to ignore Loreley's calls, Chris' calls, and Cal's calls without remorse.

135

Until he went to the cemetery again today and let go of the anger and finally cried.

Reading the inscription on Jesse's headstone over and over again had brought him to his knees. Literally. He had kneeled at his son's grave like Loreley had days before with tears streaming down his face as the reality of having lost his son without ever having met him crashed over him. He cursed at the unfairness of it all as he gave himself over to his grief. Slowly, his anger at Loreley for not telling him had faded away and made room for the truth that he had refused to see.

It wasn't Loreley's fault.

If anyone was to blame for anything, it was him, Jason, first for being a dick by saying things he didn't mean and making her leave, then for being too proud to go after her and bringing her back.

Not only was it his own fault that he hadn't known about his son, but he was also to blame for Loreley having lost Jesse without Jason being there with her. Without supporting her, without sharing the loss and the grief. Yes, she had her family and Chris to rely on and be there for her, but that wasn't the same as being able to share the agony the loss of your child brings with the other parent, your partner. It was like Chris had said that night. If he had been there, Loreley might not have gotten so lost in her anguish that she almost killed herself.

The thought of a world without his Loreley was still something he couldn't stomach.

So now it was time to man up and stop being an asshole.

He had to face her.

They had to talk about everything and see where they stood. Or more, Jason had to show Loreley how they would continue from here on out.

Which was together.

Neither of them functioned right without the other one in their life, so the only way this could go was for them to face life together as a unit.

With that decision made, the tightness he had carried in his heart for years slowly eased, and Jason felt like he could breathe free for the first time in a very long time. He felt peace and contentment when—without him even trying—the notes flew into his head and out through his fingers onto the guitar strings. He could hardly keep up with writing everything down as he created a new song. A song he was going to use to win his girl back. Music had always been the language they both understood best. It was how they had communicated their deepest feelings and darkest fears to each other. After watching Loreley sing at the bar the other night, he knew that that hadn't changed. He had been mesmerized by her voice just like he had always been. It had pulled him in and let him feel exactly what she was feeling as she was singing her soul out on that stage. And when he had made her sing their song, he had definitely felt everything she wanted him to feel. Even though he hadn't particularly liked what those feelings had been.

Just as he was putting the last finishing touches to the song, Jason heard cars coming up the driveway, then two doors being slammed, then footsteps first on the gravel, then on the front porch, then someone was banging against the front door.

Jason got up.

He realized it had gotten dark outside. He had to get to Loreley. He didn't have time for visitors.

Judging by the force he heard fists banging the door with, someone was here with an agenda. It could only be Cal or Chris. Nathan had a key and wouldn't announce his arrival like that. He would just rip into him as he had several times already. He had no idea where Nathan was. The last time he had seen him

137

was in the basement playing a video game before he left for the cemetery. He hadn't seen him since he got back.

Jason had been surprised that neither Cal nor Chris had shown up before now. They were so protective and possessive of Loreley that Jason had expected them to show up that first night. Yeah, both of them had called repeatedly, but neither had shown up and confronted him.

Obviously, they were done giving him time.

That was fine. Let them come. Jason had a few things to get off his chest as well.

This confrontation was long overdue.

Apparently, Cal felt the same way, since before he could reach the door Jason heard a key turn in the lock. A second later the door swung open and an incensed Cal stepped into the front hall and came right at Jason.

"You son of a bitch!"

Chris was right behind Cal, his face showing the same fury as his eyes zeroed in on Jason.

Jason held his ground and crossed his arms over his chest as he held Cal's glare with his own. What he didn't do was speak.

"You son of a bitch! I warned you, Jason. I warned you if you didn't follow through on your word and bolted again instead of fighting for her, I would make it so you wished you'd never met me."

Cal had stopped just inches from Jason's face, but still Jason didn't move, just met Cal glare for glare.

"You promised me. You promised me you wouldn't take it out on her once you found out." That was Chris. His voice, too, promised violence.

Jason clenched his teeth but didn't move.

"Are you done?" He asked both of them when neither said anything more.

"Fuck no, I'm not done," Cal growled into his face. "You're gonna get your ass down the mountain and talk to my sister. You're gonna make the guilt and anguish and hollowness disappear from her eyes. And you're gonna make her stop crying. I don't care what you have to do to make that happen. She has suffered enough. She doesn't deserve this."

"I agree," Jason concurred.

Surprise flashed in Cal's eyes.

"You agree?"

"Yeah, I agree. And you might have found that out if you hadn't stormed in here out for my blood."

Cal took a step back and relaxed his body into a more comfortable and non-threatening stance.

"Then why am I the one holding Lore while she cries herself to sleep every night?"

Jason's eyes moved to Chris. "She's crying herself to sleep?" he asked, concern and horror clear on his voice.

"Yeah. She's devastated, man. I haven't seen her like this since the day Jesse died. It's like she's not only lost you, but lost a part of Jesse all over again."

Fuck him. He had underestimated the situation. Loreley had sounded sad and regretful that day at the cemetery, but she had also agreed to give him time.

Fuck.

Hearing that she was suffering like that, made a sharp pain slice through his chest and his stomach drop.

"Fuck," he swore.

"She has convinced herself that everything is her fault, that she should have known you didn't cheat on her and would have never abandoned her. Or should I say you convinced her of that?"

"Fuck!" He swore again. "I told her I needed some time to

139

come to terms with everything. She agreed."

"Yeah. And you also told her that you weren't able to forgive her. You said you would call her and you haven't. What did you think she would do?"

"I thought she was giving me space. That we would talk once I was ready. That's what I told her."

"You need to fix this before things get out of hand and she loses it again." Cal's voice was borderline scared. He was worried that last year would repeat itself.

"That's not gonna happen," Jason rumbled as he strode to the back porch to retrieve his guitar.

"So you're gonna talk to her?"

"Oh yeah, I'm gonna talk to her. She at the bar?"

Chris nodded. The anger and concern melted away and his face split into a knowing grin as he saw Jason reappear in the room with his guitar in hand. Cal looked confused and a little impatient. "Let's go," he said. He started towards the door but stopped when he heard Jason speak.

"One thing." He focused all his attention on Chris who stiffened as he read Jason's intensity. "I get why seeing a half-naked woman opening my front door would make Loreley believe I cheated on her. I would have thought the same thing if a half-naked man had been in her room. So I get why she was hurt and took off. But you weren't ruled and blinded by your emotions, Chris. You should have kept a clear head and at least answer one of my many calls. And those messages…I don't even know what to say about that. Again, Loreley was blinded by her emotions and that's somewhat understandable, but you should have known that I would never in my life abandon my own child. You knew how much I loved her. You knew that she owned me down to my soul. That I wanted to build a life with her. You knew, because I told you about it. You knew, because you came with me when I went ring shopping. Did none of that ever cause the slightest doubt in your mind?"

Chris clenched his teeth as he held Jason's stare, but Jason didn't miss the guilt and remorse flash across his face. Neither of them spoke a word as understanding crossed between them, ending in a short nod from Chris and a chin lift from Jason.

Then without another word Jason strode out the door to his car.

It was time to get Loreley and him back on track.

Ten

LORELEY

The bar was packed. And Chris was nowhere to be found. He had left saying he had an errand to run and would be back soon. That was over an hour ago. Mark was behind the bar with me and two waitresses were on the floor, but it was so packed that they could make use of a third man pouring drinks.

We might have been okay with just Mark and I if I was on my game. But I was far from it. I kept getting orders wrong and dropped things constantly, making everything take twice as long. Mark had given me more than a few looks during the past hour, but thankfully, he hadn't asked any questions.

I didn't think I could take another person asking what was wrong with me, if I was okay, wanting me to confide in them. They all meant well and I appreciated their concern, but I was done hearing the same words, the same advice over and over again. Every single person that knew what happened had told me that nothing was my fault. That I should stop blaming myself, that it would get me nowhere, and if Jason was worth my love he would understand the situation I had been in and would come around.

Of course, they would say that. They loved me and were

142

partial to seeing things from my perspective. I knew they were concerned about me, but I wasn't in danger of drinking myself unconscious again because I couldn't stand the pain for another second. No, I was nowhere near that. I had done that last year to escape the pain, to be numb. Now, I didn't need the help of alcohol to feel numb.

Because I already felt dead inside.

There was no more pain, no more agony, no anger. I had shut all that down.

It had been four full days since I had last heard from him. I had resigned myself to the knowledge that I had lost Jason, that he had left me for good, that there was no way I would get the chance to try and fix things.

And with that knowledge, I had resigned myself to the fact that nothing would ever be right again.

Just a few days ago, I had thought I had found my way back to myself again, had been optimistic that I would somehow find some happiness.

Now, I knew that that part of my life was forever lost.

I would live my life, run this bar, play my music, hang out with friends, and remember and hold on to the happy memories I had of Jesse.

But my heart would never be full again.

I had accepted that.

Welcomed it, actually.

My head snapped up from the beer I was pouring to look at the front door. There was a commotion with lots of shouting, and I could see people shoving each other, but I couldn't see what exactly was going on.

I made eye contact with Mark and my eyebrows went up in question, asking him if he had any idea what was happening, but he shrugged his shoulders and went back to mixing drinks.

"Want me to go check it out?" I heard Nathan ask. He was sitting at the bar in front of me, had been sitting there for over an hour, keeping me company, chatting with me, watching me. It was like he had declared himself my personal watchdog.

I placed the beer in front of the customer who I thought had ordered it, took his money, and decided to go investigate.

"Thanks, Nathan. I'll go take care of it." I really couldn't deal with a brawl today. I could have sent Mark or Nathan, but no matter what mood I was in, I was still the owner of this bar and had to act accordingly if I wanted the patrons' respect.

When I got close to where the brouhaha was happening, I saw Chris step out of the crowd. He saw me and headed straight for me. Seeing as he had just been in the midst of the bustle and hadn't seen the need to do anything about it, I stopped and waited for him to get to me.

The expression on his face was one of anticipation mixed with determination. I had been so sure to see mostly worry on his face when he looked at me that the anticipation and determination I saw there instead confused me. He looked like he was up to something, but I had no idea what that could be. I knew he had something planned for my birthday tomorrow, even though he was well aware I hated surprises. But it was nowhere near midnight yet, so it couldn't be about that.

I narrowed my eyes at him as he reached me, suspicious. But instead of talking and telling me what was going on, he grinned at me, then took me by the elbow and steered me towards the newly finished stage.

What the hell?

We didn't have anyone playing tonight, so I was confused and a little irritated as to why he would want me to go onstage. There was no way I would be able to perform tonight.

"Chris, what the hell is going on?" I asked, resisting the pull

144

of his hand on my elbow and stopping about ten feet from the stage, planting myself in front of him.

No, I was not going up there tonight. No way.

But Chris didn't answer.

What he did instead was lift his chin to someone I couldn't see behind me then he grabbed my upper arms and turned me so that my body was facing the stage and he was standing behind me. He didn't let go of my arms.

What the hell?

I felt someone crowding me on my left and looked to see that Cal was standing close. He looked at me with warmth in his eyes. To my surprise, there was no worry there, but I could see the same determination and anticipation I had seen on Chris' face. Then I heard a "Fucking finally," grumbled on my other side and saw that Nathan had joined us. His arms were crossed on his chest and his grin was big and proud.

I opened my mouth to again ask what the hell was going on when I heard a guitar being strummed on the stage. Surprised, I whipped my head around and stilled when I saw who was sitting on the stool in front of the microphone.

It was Jason.

Chris' grip on me tightened and Cal moved in closer, but none of that registered with me. All I could do was stare at the man on stage, too overwhelmed and confused by what I was feeling to move. People all around me started cheering and shouting Jason's name as I stood there, frozen.

Then he started speaking into the microphone.

"All right everyone. Calm down for a second, so I can talk." Almost immediately, people started to calm down and waited for him to go on.

Which he did.

And what he said made my breath catch in my throat.

"I know this stage is supposed to be christened tomorrow, but there is something I need to say to someone that's important to me, something that couldn't wait another second." His eyes drifted over his audience while his fingers lazily strummed his guitar. Then his eyes found me and he zeroed in, holding me captive with his gaze as he kept speaking.

"You see, I've been in love with a very special girl for a very long time. I'm a man and men can be stupid, so you can probably guess that I fucked it up and made her leave me." Men were chuckling all around me in agreement. "Since then, everything I have done I did thinking about her, missing her, wanting, no, *needing* her to come back to me. Of course, she didn't. She was too hurt by what happened and I never heard from her again. It's been six years since I held her, six years since I touched her, kissed her, made her laugh, and pissed her off. Six very long and very lonely years." He stopped and kept strumming his guitar almost lovingly as he held my gaze with captivating intensity. "And when I finally got my head out of my ass and went after what I wanted, what I needed to feel whole again, I promised myself that this time, I wouldn't give up, that this time I would fight, even if the thing I had to fight was her, until she was mine again and then I would never let her go. But life's a bitch most of the time and things didn't turn out the way I had imagined. See, she had a secret, a secret she didn't think I deserved to know, a secret that, upon finding out, nearly destroyed me." His voice broke a little on those last words and I could feel tears well up in my eyes yet again. "Her words almost destroyed me and still, I couldn't leave. Even after everything that's happened, after we both said and did things to hurt each other, she is everything I want, everything I need. I realized during the past few days that no matter what, I will never be able to let her go." Goosebumps were covering my whole body at hearing his words and I shivered. Then he stopped talking to the crowd and addressed only me. "So I'm here to fight, baby. I'm here to fight and I won't give up until you take me back."

Then he played and sang the most beautiful song I had ever heard. He sang about love, about pain, about strength, and about forgiveness. He sang about the agony of losing the one person that makes you feel whole, about the ache in your chest when you know you lost the other half of your soul. And he sang about not giving up, about doing whatever it took, giving everything to deserve that love again.

And during the whole length of the song, not once did Jason's eyes move from mine.

He was talking to me through his music, was opening up his heart and soul to let me see the love and devotion he felt for me, let me see the promise, the vow that he would never let me go again, that he would never give up on us again, because I was the other half of his soul, and he couldn't live a day longer without feeling whole again.

His words were so beautiful they tore at my heart and filled it up with warmth, filled that emptiness inside me with the happiness and joy I had given up on ever feeling again. For the first time in a very long time, the tears that were running down my cheeks were happy tears.

Chris' hands, which had been holding me in place, had become arms that were wrapped around me from behind, supporting my weight as I was leaning back against him. My left hand was clasped in Cal's in a tight grip, my right hand was covering my mouth in an attempt to stop myself from sobbing.

The song ended.

Everything around me was quiet. Not a single person clapped or cheered or shouted. It was as if everyone could feel that something profound had happened, that as if they moved or talked or even breathed, the magic of the moment would break and it would be as if it never happened. I couldn't blame them. I felt exactly the same way. I was too scared to move, scared that if I did, I'd wake up from this dream only to feel alone and empty once more.

So I stayed frozen and kept staring as Jason slid off the stool, jumped down the stage, and came slowly towards me, his eyes burning while they still held mine captive. In that moment, nothing existed but him and me, nothing mattered but him walking towards me. I saw nothing but him.

Seconds later, he reached me and laid a hand against my cheek, his thumb sliding through the wetness there. I closed my eyes at the relief his touch brought me and leaned into his hand.

And then I was in his arms and he was kissing me.

He was kissing me with an abandon I had never experienced.

His arms were locked around me so tightly it felt like he wanted to pull me inside him.

His tongue was exploring my mouth, reacquainting itself with the feel of me just as mine was rediscovering the feel of him.

It was wild, it was deep, it was completely out of control.

And I didn't want it to end.

I could hear the cheers and hollers and clapping that had erupted as soon as our mouths touched, but I didn't heed them any attention. I was too absorbed in Jason and the feel of his arms around me, in the feel of his body pressed against mine, the feel of his mouth exploring to let anything else penetrate.

Then I was lifted and I wrapped my legs around Jason's waist as he carried me through the crowd and out the front door. The next things I knew, my back was pressed against what I assumed to be a car and we were making out heavily.

What could have been minutes or hours later, Jason

wrenched his mouth from mine and leaned his forehead against my shoulder where I could hear him take a few deep breaths. He was trying to get control of himself.

His head came up and he cupped my face with his hands, his eyes boring into mine. "I need you, baby. But not here against the car in the parking lot of your bar. I need you in a bed where I can take my time with you, where I can touch and kiss and lick and rediscover every inch of your body."

I nodded. I wanted that, too, but I was too lost in the haze of lust to say anything.

Jason groaned and kissed me again.

Then he stepped back, so I could slide down his body, grabbed my hand, opened the passenger side door of his Challenger, and guided me into the seat before he closed the door and got in on the other side.

I didn't know if it was the loss of his touch or the car door being slammed that made me snap out of the haze and start to think again. But as Jason pulled out of the parking lot and started driving down the street, I came back into myself. Jason must have felt it, because he took my hand and pulled it towards his face to kiss it gently. "You okay, baby?"

I bit my lip, not wanting to remind him of how mean I had been, but needing to get this out before we went any further.

"Baby? What's wrong?" He prompted when I didn't say anything.

"I...I am so sorry, Jason," I whispered. "I don't know how you can ever forgive me."

He pulled my hand to his mouth again to kiss it softly. "There's nothing to forgive, baby. You did what you thought you had to do and I don't blame you. How could I? The evidence against me was condemning."

"You were so mad when you found out about Jesse. The

look in your eyes…I thought you hated me." I was still whispering.

"No, Loreley, I could never hate you. I admit I was mad as hell at you for not telling me at first, but I couldn't hold on to it for long. I love you. I've never stopped loving you."

"But Jason, we—"

"No, baby, not now. I know we have to talk and we will. I promise you we'll talk later and figure all this out. But right now, all that matters is that I love you and won't ever let you go again. Okay?"

"Okay," I whispered.

We hardly made it through the front door before his mouth was hot on mine again and his hands started to roam all over my body as he started to undress me. My shirt went first, then his hands went to the button of my jeans and down they went until they were pooled around my feet. Jason lifted me out of them, and I clung to his body, needing to get as much contact as I could. The feel of my naked legs wrapped around his jeans clad hips made me groan. Jason gripped my ass with both hands in the back of my panties and ground his erection against me.

Oh yes, that was even better.

We both groaned with pleasure at the contact as we devoured each other's mouths.

"Bedroom," he said between kisses.

"Down the hall, last room on the left."

He started walking and two seconds later, I was thrown onto the bed. I watched, panting, as he lifted his shirt over his head and tossed it on the floor and I could see his glorious chest. It was covered in tattoos, as was his whole right arm and half of his left arm. He'd had tattoos back then, but this was something else. Then I kept watching as his hands went to his jeans and he started unbuttoning them. He pushed them down his long legs, taking his boxer briefs with them until he stood before me completely naked.

I couldn't help but lick my lips as I took in his hard cock, remembering what it felt like to have him inside me.

Jason's low groan brought my attention back to his face, and I shuddered in anticipation at what I saw there: pure and carnal lust mixed with love and longing.

"I've missed you," I whispered.

Jason closed his eyes for a second in what seemed to be relief. "Thank fuck." Then he lowered himself to his knees and, wrapping his hands around my ankles, he pulled my body towards the edge of the bed.

I shuddered, knowing what was about to come. Jason had always been good with his mouth between my legs, had always seemed to enjoy it, which made him that much better at it. Knowing I would get that from him again after not having had it for so long made my body shake with anticipation and arousal.

He ran his nose over my panties and groaned. "You smell so good, baby. So fucking good." Then he kissed me lightly while his fingers were softly running up and down the insides of my thighs.

I threw my head back and moaned.

"Look at me, baby. I know you like to watch. I want you to keep your eyes on me while I make you come with my mouth and fingers."

Then, in one smooth movement, he ripped my panties off and dove in.

JASON

Jason groaned at the taste of her. Nothing had ever tasted this sweet, this good. Nothing and nobody even came close. He

151

couldn't get enough, would never be able to get enough of her.

He used his thumbs to open her up to him as he licked along and in between her folds until his tongue found her clit. She started to groan and squirm as he flicked it over and over again, then increased the pressure and circled until he could hear her panting. He withdrew his tongue and blew onto her clit. His dick grew at the sight of her pussy. He was rock hard and ready to reclaim what was his. But Jason wanted to play a little longer, wanted to make his girl writhe and moan while he feasted on her juices, wanted to make her come against his mouth.

He added a finger and plunged it inside her, groaning against her at the feeling of her wet heat. He dove in again, teasing her, eating her, licking up all her juices and revelling in her reactions. He loved how damn responsive she was, had missed how he could make her body writhe and dance in ecstasy, in total and complete bliss. Everything about her was real. There was no over the top fake moaning and screaming, no exaggeration, no calculation. No, his Loreley had always given herself and her body over to him, had always let him play the way he wanted, trusting that he would take care of her and give her what she needed. He had always loved that about her and now that he had it back, he realized just how much he had missed it.

He couldn't wait much longer.

He had to sink into that wet heat. And he had to do it soon.

He added a second finger while he took her clit in his mouth and sucked gently, then released her nub to blow on it again before he went back to swirling and flicking and sucking, all while his fingers explored her from the inside. She moaned a deep moan and arched her back off the bed, pressing her pussy harder against his mouth. He could feel her moan in his dick. He had thought he couldn't get any harder than he already was, but the sound of her moans and the feel of her tightness around his fingers made him so hard he thought he was going to lose it before he even got inside her.

He let go of her clit with a pop and started flicking it again, over and over and over until he knew she couldn't take much more. Open the way he held her she would feel every sensation this much more intensely.

This was it. He needed her to come. He needed her to come, so he could plunge his cock inside her before he came at just the sight of her. No other woman had ever had this much power over him; no other woman had ever made him lose control like this, overwhelmed by the need to be inside her.

Without taking his tongue away, he looked up her body to see her watching him with lust-crazed eyes. "I need to be inside you so bad, baby. I need you to come, so I can slide into that wet heat of yours. Come for me, baby. Now!"

He kept plunging his fingers in and out as he again locked onto her clit and sucked until he could feel her tense up and then explode against his mouth. He didn't stop while she came, licking up all her juices, sucking every last shiver out of her.

When she relaxed into the mattress, he removed his fingers and kissed her pussy one last time before he moved her body up on the mattress and climbed on top of her. His hands were roaming the skin on her stomach, moving up towards her breasts, which were still covered by her bra.

That wouldn't do.

He quickly relieved her of the bra and then latched on to her nipple, sucking and licking and nipping just like he had done her clit, alternating between both breasts while his hands kept touching her skin everywhere.

Then he lowered his body onto her and spread her legs even

further with his knees, lining up his cock with her entrance. A delicious heat ran through his cock when he first connected with her pussy. It almost felt like an electrical shock running through him. He had to clench his teeth so the sensation wouldn't overwhelm him.

God, he wouldn't last long.

"I'm coming inside now, baby. I can't wait any longer."

"Please," she whispered hoarsely, almost making him come undone.

In one swift move, he plunged his rock hard cock inside her and they both cried out.

It was like coming home.

He felt her all around him with his naked skin to hers, her arms around him, their eyes locked, and his cock inside her.

The feeling was so overwhelming and all-consuming it almost brought him to tears. And judging by the look of absolute bliss and relief in Loreley's tear-rimmed eyes, she felt the same way.

He leaned down to rest his lips against hers. "This is it, baby. You and me. I'll never let you go again. I can't," he whispered hoarsely but firmly before he took her mouth in a searing and fierce kiss. Loreley opened for him and kissed him back just as fiercely.

God, she was tight. So tight and hot as she clamped down on him.

He tore his lips away and rested his forehead against hers for second in an effort to regain control.

But he was too far gone. The feeling of her hot and wet pussy constricting around him with little aftershocks threatened to shatter his control.

"I gotta move, baby. You're so hot and tight around me it's killing me. This one's gonna be fast and hard. You ready?"

At her instant nod and her whispered, "Yes, baby," he pulled out until only the head of his cock was inside her and rammed it back in, making them both scream again. A shiver ran through his body and he groaned. Over and over he drove into her, taking her fast and hard, the feeling so explicit his eyes rolled to the back of his head in bliss.

He couldn't hold out any longer. His spine started to tingle and his balls drew up. He was going to come. And it was going to be enormous.

Needing her to come with him, he pressed his thumb against her clit once more and started flicking and rolling. She lifted her hips in search for more friction as he kept pounding into her with everything he had until he felt the inside walls of her pussy clenching around him.

"That's it, baby. Come! Come with me!"

One, two, three more strokes and she exploded around him.

"Fuuuuuck!" With one last plunge, he planted himself inside her and stayed deep as the most intense orgasm he had ever experienced ran through his body, making him explode inside her, spilling himself deep inside her pussy as she kept clenching and pulsing, sucking him dry.

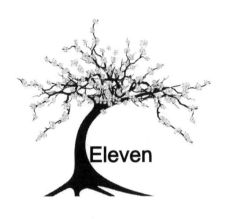

Eleven

LORELEY

I took his weight when Jason collapsed on top of me. We were both breathing hard, completely spent. The feel of him still inside me after so long was overwhelming; at the same time, it was beautiful and perfect.

I had missed him.

So much.

I still couldn't believe that he was here with me, in my bed, and that he had promised me he would never leave me again. That he loved me. I had desperately needed those words from him, had needed the assurance that this was real.

Still, there was so much we had to figure out. He had promised me we would talk, but I was worried that once I told him about Jesse, once I showed him pictures and videos of his son, that he would resent me and eventually hate me.

And that was something I wouldn't be able to live with.

I glided my hands up and down his back, trying to ease my anxiety with the contact as those thoughts ran through my head.

"Mmm. That feels good." Jason murmured as he nuzzled and kissed my neck. He kissed a line across my cheek to my mouth where he captured my lips in a slow and sensual kiss.

"Was it too rough?" he asked when he ended the kiss and looked down at me.

I shook my head. "No. Why would you think that?" Sex between us had always been passionate and could get rough sometimes, especially if we'd had an argument or hadn't seen each other for a while.

"I told myself I'd go easy and enjoy every single inch of you all night long, but being inside you again…I couldn't hold back."

I smiled at him, liking the fact that I made him lose control.

"If it wasn't too rough then what is it?"

"What do you mean?"

He studied me for a second as he ran his fingers softly along my cheekbone. "It might have been a while, Loreley, but you're still an open book for me. You're worried about something."

Uncomfortable, I tried to avert my eyes, but he caught my chin between his thumb and finger and turned my head back to him so I had no other choice but to look at him. His eyes were alert and assessing.

"Hey, what's wrong?"

I shrugged.

I didn't want to ruin the moment of our reunion even though I couldn't quite shake the anxiety. But Jason didn't let it go.

"Talk to me."

I shrugged again before I said, "I'm just a little worried."

"About what?"

"I'm worried that…when I tell you about…Jesse…I'm worried that you'll…" He stopped me with a kiss. Then he slid off me and out of me and pulled me into his arms so that we were both on our sides, facing each other.

"Listen to me, Loreley. I know there's a lot we need to talk

about. A lot we need to figure out. And yes, most of that talking
will be about our son. I want to know everything about him, look
at every single picture of him you have. I want to know what
food he liked, what his favourite color was, if he looked more like
me or more like you, if he had your passion and loyalty, if he
shared your fun for life, if it was easy for him to make friends, if
he was funny, if he was happy, if he was as perfect as I imagine
him."

"He was," I said in a broken whisper. "He was all of that
and more."

Jason gave me a sad but proud smile and touched his lips
softly to mine. "He was ours so there's no way he couldn't have
been perfect." He kissed me again.

"What I'm saying is, yes, I'm unbelievably sad and angry
that I never got to be a part of his life, but I'm not mad at you,
Loreley. How could I be? I'll admit I was furious with you when
I first found out, furious and hurt that you thought so little of
me. But then I realized that you didn't have any other choice but
to hate me. You thought I had cheated on you. You had no way
of knowing the girl in my house was with Murphy and not me.
Yes, you could have answered my calls, but I get why you didn't.
And Loreley, I should have tried harder to get you to talk to me
before you left for L.A. But I was too proud. I couldn't get past
my male ego, couldn't get over the fact that you would leave me
like that without looking back over a stupid fight we both knew
only happened because I was an insecure jerk. And baby, I
didn't know you thought I was cheating on you or I would have
moved heaven and earth to talk to you right then. I thought
you'd left me because of the things I'd said that night. I was too
proud to question it and look deeper, too proud to run after you.
I called you all day after that and the day after that. I called
Chris about ten times, but neither of you answered. It was clear

you didn't want to talk to me. So I stupidly left you be and hoped that you would come around and call me back. Only you didn't. And knowing what I know now I can't blame you for that."

"I wanted to call you, so many times. But I was too hurt. I was miserable. I hated L.A. without you, hated that I was alone and broken-hearted. I was so angry. But I never hated you. I told myself I did, but for some reason I never really could."

Another soft lip touch.

"I'm glad to hear that, honey. I could never hate you either. And I won't hate you even when you tell me all about Jesse. That's what this is about, isn't it? That's what you're worried about?"

I nodded.

Jason pulled me in closer and brushed his lips against my forehead. "I could never hate you, Loreley. It's just not possible. I love you way too much for that to be even imaginable."

"I love you, too. I never stopped," I whispered.

He sighed in relief as he tightened his arms around me. "Good. Then I need something from you."

I lifted my face out of his neck and looked up at him. "What's that?"

"A promise."

"What kind of promise?"

"I need you to promise me that you won't run. That whatever happens, you'll come to me and we'll talk. We've lived completely separate lives for the past six years and a lot has happened. Promise me that no matter what you hear or see about me, you'll come to me and we'll talk about it and work it out. And I'll promise you the same. I won't run and I won't let you go ever again."

I could only imagine what he meant by that. But he was

159

right. We'd lived completely separate lives. While he was off becoming a famous rock star and touring the world, I lived in the small town I grew up in near the Rocky Mountains, raising a child and running a bar. I didn't want to think too much about what I could hear or see that would make me run away from him again though. As long as we promised each other to talk about everything that might come up, I believed we could make it.

So I nodded and said, "I promise."

"Thank you, baby." He rolled back on top of me and took my mouth in a deep and fierce kiss. Then he explored every inch of me with his mouth and tongue and hands, kissing me, nibbling me, suckling me as he caressed and worshipped my body until he slowly sank back into me and we made slow and intense love.

I woke up the next morning curled into Jason's side. He was on his back with both arms around me, holding me close and tight even in his sleep. Carefully, I slipped out from underneath his arms and got up, snatched my robe from the chair in the corner and threw it on, and headed to the bathroom. After doing my morning business and brushing my teeth and hair, I walked back into the bedroom to see Jason hadn't moved. I decided to let him sleep a little longer while I made some coffee and got breakfast started.

My house was small but cozy. It was one of those cute little 1950s bungalow style houses we had a lot of here in Cedar Creek. Mine was one of many on a street that was lined with huge elm trees that gave great shade in the summer and looked absolutely beautiful in the fall. The front door led you right into the living room that was open to the kitchen at the end of the house. There was a cozy wood-burning fireplace with a comfy dark brown couch in front of it, filled with pillows. In my opinion, you could never have enough pillows. They were everywhere in my house, or at least everywhere where you would want to hang out and get comfortable, be it on the furniture or on the floor.

The kitchen was the only room I had remodelled after I moved in when Jesse was just barely a year old. It was now decorated in vintage chic. The cabinets were a mix of off-white and light blue and had that rustic and used look to them that made you feel at home as soon as you walked in the door. All my appliances were retro as well, except my oversized high-end Wolf oven, my pride and joy. I loved to cook and did it often for friends and family. Where Ivey was the queen of desserts, I was the queen of fancy and complicated meals. I loved to experiment and create new dishes and I always had enough people around to volunteer for a tasting. In the corner of the kitchen was a big enough table to seat eight people, ten at a squeeze, and it was regularly filled to capacity, with the usual suspects being everyone who was at Cal and Ivey's house last night.

My formal dining room to the right of the front door wasn't a formal dining room as such. I had it set up as a music room with my guitars and my piano, a big Laz-y-Boy chair and lots of—yes, you guessed right—pillows all over the floor. This was where Jesse and I would sit on the floor, where I would play and sing to him, where he had learned his first guitar grips. His little kid guitar was still standing in its holder in the corner of that room.

The bacon was sizzling in the pan, the toast was in the toaster waiting to be toasted, and the table was set with butter and jam. My first cup of coffee was half-consumed and in my hand as I stood in front of my kitchen window, holding the birthday card I was reading when I felt arms snake around my waist from behind and lips against the nape of my neck.

"Morning," Jason mumbled as he lightly kissed my cheek. I snuggled into him and whispered, "Morning," as he rested his chin on my shoulder.

"What's that?" He asked.

"It's a birthday card. The last one Jesse made for me."

He was quietly holding me as he studied the card. It was a hand-drawn picture of him and me with a big red heart on top and big block letters that spelled "Happy Birthday" and "I Love you mom" on the bottom. Jesse had died a few days before my birthday, but I had found the card in his nightstand a few months later and put it on the board that hung on the wall in the kitchen with all his other artwork, so I could look at it every day. I had since taken down everything else and put it away in a treasure box. But the card had stayed.

"He did a good job," Jason murmured.

"Yeah."

"Is it normal for a five-year-old to be able to draw like that?" I shook my head and laughed silently. You'd expect the picture to be drawn with crayons but Jesse had never had much patience with those and had said they were for babies. He had preferred pencil crayons because he could draw more details with them.

"No. It's not."

"He was very artistic."

"Yeah," I repeated, "Like his dad."

"I can't draw worth shit, honey." He said through a light chuckle. I snickered with him. "No, but you're an artist. You create beautiful music." His arms turned me around so I was facing him. "So do you." He kissed me. "So I guess he got that from both of us." He kissed me again. "Happy Birthday," he murmured against my lips.

I smiled. "Thank you."

162

"Any big plans for today?"

I shook my head. "Not until later. My dad's throwing a birthday barbeque for me this afternoon. And we have a band playing at the bar, so I'll have to go check on their set up and go in early tonight."

"Anyone I know?"

"I don't think so. It's an Indie band from Boulder. They mostly play at bars and small venues in the city, sometimes in Denver. They play at the bar about once a month. They're good."

"I guess I'll have to check them out then."

"Does that mean you're coming to the bar tonight?"

He smiled at me. "Of course I am. I'm also coming with you to your dad's this afternoon." I melted into him, liking that he was going to spend the day with me. "After breakfast, we'll head up to the rental and get my stuff."

My eyes shot to his. "Your stuff?"

"Yeah. My stuff. My clothes. I'm gonna stay with you while I'm in town." The reminder of him leaving eventually made me drop my eyes.

"How long can you stay?" I asked, my voice quiet.

Jason tilted my head up with a finger under my chin. "The band is taking a break for a few months. We just got back from a tour. So we'll have time. I might have to take a couple of trips back to L.A., but they won't be for longer than a day or two. And just saying, if you can swing it with the bar, I want you to come with me. But for now, let's take it one day at a time and enjoy being back in each other's lives. We'll figure out the logistics of where and how we're going to live later."

My eyebrows snapped together in puzzlement. "What do you mean we'll figure out where we're going to live later?"

"I mean exactly that. We'll figure out where we're gonna

163

live later."

I gave my head a small shake, still confused. "We're going to live together?"

Jason lifted both of his hands to cup my cheeks and he pulled me close to his face, his eyes boring into mine.

"You love me?" he asked.

I swallowed then said, "Yes."

"You wanna be with me?"

I nodded and repeated, "Yes."

"Don't you think we've wasted enough time?" I closed my eyes and leaned into him as I nodded again. He kissed my forehead and wrapped his arms back around me.

"Then it's decided. We're getting my stuff after breakfast and I'm staying here with you. I told you last night I would never be able to let you go again and I meant it. I'm here and I'm staying. Everything else we'll figure out later."

"Okay," I agreed.

"Okay," he said on a squeeze before he let me go. "Now, let's eat breakfast." I smiled as he turned and fixed himself some coffee. Then I got the bacon and toast and we sat down for breakfast.

I hadn't even taken the first bite of my toast before my phone started ringing.

It was Chris.

Seeing his name flash on the screen made me realize that he hadn't come home last night. I snatched up the phone and brought it to my ear.

"Chris?"

"Good morning, gorgeous. Happy Birthday!"

"Thanks," I replied. "You at your place?"

"Yeah. I figured you had someone else holding you last night." He said teasingly.

164

"Very funny."

"So have you guys talked yet?" He asked, his voice more serious now.

"Some. He said we would talk more later." Jason caught my eyes and his warmed as he gave me a reassuring smile before he took another bite of his bacon.

"He there now?"

"Yeah. And he says he's staying." Another reassuring smile.

"Staying in town or staying at your place?"

"Both. We're getting his stuff from Cal's house after breakfast."

"Good. I'm glad. Though I'm a little disappointed that I'm losing my own personal cock blocker," Chris went back to teasing.

"I'm sure you'll be strong enough to keep it in your pants without using me as a shield, Chris." Jason lifted his eyebrows in surprise and question at me. I smiled at him and shook my head, indicating I would tell him later.

"I hope you're right."

"I've got faith in you."

Chris chuckled. "At least that makes one of us. You still coming to the bar to watch the guys set up?"

I rolled my eyes, but said, "Of course."

"You bringing Jason?"

"Probably," I said as my gaze went back to Jason. He sat back in his chair while he sipped his coffee and watched me.

"That'll be interesting," Chris mumbled.

"Interesting? Why?" I asked.

"Nothing. I'll see you later then."

"All right, see you later. And Chris?"

"Yeah?"

"Thank you."

"Anything for you, Lore. Anytime. You know that." Then he hung up. I placed my phone back on the table and reached for my coffee.

"Chris needs your help keeping it in his pants?" Jason asked, amused.

I gave a short laugh. "I know. Who would have thought he would ever want to keep it in his pants. But apparently, he's tired of all the empty sex he's been getting and is looking for something real." The laughter left Jason's eyes as they went from me to the table and he took another sip of his coffee. I felt the smile leave my face as I guessed why he was avoiding my eyes now.

"I don't want to know," I said. And I didn't. I didn't think I would be able to stomach hearing about what he'd been up to. Just the thought of how many women he had slept with in the past six years made my stomach drop and pain slice through me.

"And I don't want to tell you. But we'll have to talk about it."

"No, we don't."

He gripped my hand and squeezed it. "Yeah, baby, we do. I know it's unpleasant and I'm not gonna share any details. I also don't wanna hear any details from you. But we gotta get this out of the way, because you'll eventually hear or read about it and I want you to hear it from me instead of someone else or finding out shit online when I'm not around to explain." I pulled my hand out of his and crossed my arms across my chest as I glared at him.

He sighed, but continued talking. "There were others, lots of others, but—"

I held up a hand to stop him. "I get the picture. I saw it firsthand that one time. I don't need any visuals. I mean it, Jason. I know you haven't been celibate. I get it. We weren't together. You don't owe me an explanation."

"I know I don't, but you still deserve one." His voice was determined.

"Let me rephrase then. I don't want one."

I got up from my chair and started to clear the table, but Jason snatched my hand with his and pulled me in his lap and wrapped his arms around me tightly, keeping me in place before I could even react.

"I need you to you listen to me, baby. Yes, there were lots of women, but none of them came even close to meaning anything to me. I know it makes me an asshole, but not one of them was more to me than a convenient fuck." I flinched, but he ignored it and went on being brutally honest with me. "I've fucked a lot of women, Loreley, too many to remember." I closed my eyes in an effort to block out his words and struggled to get out of his hold. Jason only gripped me tighter. "Look at me, baby. Look into my eyes." He shook me and my eyes snapped open again. "None of them meant anything to me. I did it because I was trying to forget you, because I missed you so goddamn much. You're the only woman I have ever loved, Loreley, the only woman I have ever felt anything for. It's always been you."

Okay, that made me feel slightly better. Yes, I was terribly jealous of all the women he had been with, but could I blame him? No, I couldn't. We hadn't been together. Neither of us knew we would see each other again, least of all *be* together again.

"I wouldn't tell you any of this under normal circumstances, but once the media get wind of you and me, you're gonna hear it anyway. What I want you to know deep down to your bones is that you have no reason to be jealous. I belong to you. I will not stray, no matter the opportunity. You own me, heart and soul. I don't see anyone but you. I don't *want* anyone but you."

I could see it in his eyes; he meant every word he said: that I could trust him to never betray me; that I was the only woman he wanted to be with, the only woman he loved; that he wouldn't hurt me. But I had known that already or I wouldn't have let him back into my life the way I had.

That's why I said, "I know."

"You believe me?"

I nodded. He studied me for a few seconds then he covered my mouth with a hard kiss. "Thank you, baby." Another kiss, this one softer. "Now, your turn."

I froze. "My turn?"

"Yeah, tell me who in town you've dated, so I don't get blindsided in case we run into them."

I tried to push away from him and get up, but he only tightened his hold on me once more.

"Tell me, Loreley. I need to know."

I stopped pushing against him but shook my head. I didn't particularly want to share that I hadn't been with anyone; that I hadn't so much as kissed anyone. It was embarrassing and pathetic. I also didn't want him to feel any guiltier than he already did. So I stayed quiet.

He misunderstood my silence and narrowed his eyes. "Tell me."

I knew he wouldn't let this go, so I squeezed my eyes shut and whispered, "None."

Jason's body froze underneath me. Then he asked in a hoarse voice, "None?" I shook my head again. "None as in we won't run into anyone in town, or none as in there was no one at all?"

"The second," I mumbled, my eyes still firmly shut.

The next thing I knew, I was up in Jason's arms as he carried me out of the kitchen and his lips were on mine. "I know this makes me a hypocrite and a caveman, but I don't care. You just told me I was the last person you gave yourself to. Knowing that you haven't shared yourself with anyone else makes me hard as a rock and I need to be inside you again." To my surprise, he walked through the bedroom and into the bathroom where he placed my ass on the counter. Then, with his lips still on mine, his mouth devouring mine, he started to untie my robe and slid it down my shoulders.

He ended the kiss and followed the path of the robe as he froze. His eyes roamed the mirror behind me as he kept pushing down the robe all the way until it was pooled around me on the counter. Then his hands started roaming my back as his eyes stayed glued to the mirror.

"You have a tattoo," he whispered reverently. His fingers ran over every branch inked on my back. "It's a cherry tree."

I said nothing, just studied him as he gazed into the mirror and let him explore. He had taken me on my back last night, so he hadn't seen the tattoo. His fingers went higher and stopped at my new raven.

"This one's new," he said as he carefully touched it. It wasn't completely healed yet and last night's activities had made it a little sore. "You have a cherry tree and two ravens on your back." His voice was hoarse now. He looked at me with so many emotions shining in his eyes that I couldn't read him.

"The cherry tree is—"

"From the cemetery. I wanted to tell you, you picked a beautiful spot, Loreley, next to your mom where she can watch over him."

My breath hitched.

He remembered.

I had told him about how my mother had loved that spot and had often taken me there for picnics before she died.

169

He moved his hands from my tattoo, cupped my face and pulled it up so our noses were almost touching. His eyes bore into mine with an intensity that took my breath away.

"Now, I get why you would get a tattoo of a cherry tree, but why the ravens?"

At the time, Jesse's fascination with ravens had been somewhat ironic, seeing as the father he didn't know existed was the front man of the band named *The Crowes*. I had tried not to think too hard about that fact, had tried not to interpret it at all, dismissing it as a coincidence. But to be honest, it had always freaked me out a little bit, made me wonder if there was some kind of connection there, if Jesse had inherited his fascination with ravens from his father. Just like he had inherited his looks: light brown hair, always dishevelled no matter how hard I tried to get it under control; warm hazel eyes with flecks of honey in them that in the right light would shimmer golden; and always a cute and warm smile or mischievous smirk on his face. Their laugh had been the same as well and every time my son had laughed, I had been reminded of how I had enjoyed making Jason do the same, how getting that loud and full belly laugh from him at least once a day had been one of my goals in life. It was glorious, and being the reason for it had made me feel special.

I held Jason's gaze as I told him, "Jesse loved them." The intensity in his eyes grew even sharper at my words.

"Jesse loved them?"

I nodded. "He was fascinated by them."

"All this time you kept me with you," Jason's whisper was rough with emotion. "First you had me in Jesse and when he was gone, you tattooed both of us on your back." I nodded again, because it was the truth. No matter how much I had denied that fact to myself, I got the tattoo not only with Jesse in mind.

"Take off my shirt." My body jerked at the sudden change in topic. "Do it, baby," he urged me softly when I didn't move. I gripped the bottom of his shirt and lifted it up and over his head. He took it out of my hands and dropped it to the floor. Then he slowly turned around.

It took me a minute to make sense of what my eyes were seeing, but when I did, I gasped. There on his back—his whole back—was a tattoo of Loreley, The Siren, as she was sitting on the rock, combing her hair and singing. It was stunning. Her hair was golden as it blew in the wind and her face...her face looked like my face. She was me. He had me tattooed on his back portrayed as The Siren, her eyes—my eyes—teasing and seductive, beautiful and fierce. On the bottom under the rock, my name was spelled out in a beautiful filigree font. And in the back flying over her there were two ravens. My hands were shaking while they touched the marked skin on his back.

"I never let go of you either, baby. I couldn't. I carried you with me wherever I went. And, unknowingly, our son."

"When did you get this?" I asked as I kept my hands on his back.

"I started it a few months after you left. It took almost a year to finish." At his words, silent tears were running down my face. Jason had branded me on him. And he had done so only a few months after I had left. He never let me go, he never stopped loving me.

I lay a soft kiss right between his shoulder blades, right where the two birds were flying in the wind and worked my way down towards my name.

Jason groaned.

"I have waited so long for you to do that, baby. I never thought it would happen," he said in a throaty whisper.

"I love you. So much," I said with my lips against his skin.

171

The last word hadn't completely left my mouth before he turned around, cupped my head almost violently, and pulled me up to meet his mouth in a fierce and hard and deep and wet kiss.

"You have no idea what that means to me, having your mouth on my back, hearing you say you love me. It means everything, baby. *You* mean everything." Then he took my mouth again and his hands started wandering over my body, brushing, stroking, pinching.

"I want to make love to you right here, take you where I can see your tattoo in the mirror while I can look into your eyes. And I want your hands on my back the whole time, baby. I want your hands on your brand with you knowing it's there." I wanted that, too. This time, it was me who took his mouth in a fierce kiss as I wrapped my arms and legs around him, my hands on my brand on his back, touching, stroking, groping, his hands on my back doing the same.

And we made love right there on the bathroom counter. Jason's eyes didn't leave mine unless it was to take in my tattoo; my hands didn't leave his back. It was the most intense lovemaking I had ever experienced and one of the most passionate moments of my life when we reached our climax together while our gazes were locked on each other.

Twelve

LORELEY

We spent the rest of the morning in bed, cuddling, touching, and whispering to each other. We mostly talked about Jesse. Jason's eyes turned soft when I told him how much he had looked like him.

"It was hard sometimes, seeing you in Jesse every day, reminding me of what I had lost," I whispered as he was holding me in his arms. He touched my cheek and ran his fingertips along my hairline oh so softly.

"I'm here now," he whispered low, "I'm here now and I'm staying. You never have to feel that way again." Then he kissed me, a deep but soft and gentle kiss with lots of emotion. "I love hearing about our son. I will never tire of it. I want to know every story you can remember. We'll do this often, lying in bed like this, holding each other while you tell me all about him over and over again. And I'll love every second of it. But I also want us to live in the here and now, Loreley. We will remember Jesse. He will always be with us, will always be a part of our family, but I want us to live in the present. We're starting fresh. No regrets, no blame. We're moving on with Jesse in our hearts."

That was a beautiful thing to say. And it was something I

173

wanted. I wanted to move on and build a future with Jason, build a life together, a family.

So I nodded and breathed, "Okay."

Jason smiled his beautiful smile and leaned in to kiss my forehead. There he whispered against my skin, "I have a confession to make. A secret I've been carrying with me for six years now."

I couldn't help but tense a little at his words. "And what's that?"

He pulled me in a little closer and tightened his arms around me as if he thought I might bolt at hearing his secret. I tensed even more.

"Don't worry. It's something good. Or at least I hope so," he said as he read my reaction. "I just don't want you to freak or feel sad or regretful. I'm telling you this in the spirit of not living in the past but moving on. Okay?" I relaxed slightly and nodded as I waited for him to continue.

He studied my eyes for a few seconds before he said, "Six years ago, I bought you a ring. I was going to propose to you and talk you into eloping to Vegas with me before we went on tour together. That was part of the reason why I lost it that night, because with you leaving so soon, we weren't able to do that."

I had stopped breathing and my eyes had gone big with surprise. Then it hit me that if I had known, if he had asked me, there would have been a good chance I'd never have left for that internship, that I would have eloped with him and gotten married and stayed with my husband.

"Hey, no regrets. Remember?" I nodded, but I couldn't help it. Things could have turned out so much differently. There were so many ifs and should haves and could haves, it was hard not to think about it. Jason rolled onto his back and took me with him, so that I was spread out on his chest. He cupped my face in both of his hands and pulled my face close to his, so that I could see nothing but his eyes, as they were intense and lovingly on me.

"I mean it, baby. No regrets. We're here and we're together. We've both made mistakes, but we got our second chance and we're not going to waste any time this time around. I want you to wear that ring now." My eyes grew big again as his words penetrated. This time in shock.

Was he proposing to me?

"Are you asking me to marry you?"

He smiled and kissed me softly. "I know I'm gonna marry you. That's not an option. I'm saying I want you to wear my ring today. Now."

"You still have it?" I asked breathlessly.

"Of course I do. I told you I've been carrying the secret with me for six years."

Tears pooled in my eyes once more at the beauty of his confession. Jason brushed them away when they started spilling over and running down my cheeks.

"So, what do you say?"

I took a deep breath as I tried to organize my thoughts. "Don't you think we're moving a little too fast?" I could feel his body shake under mine as he laughed silently.

"You think eight years is moving too fast?" His tone was amused. I couldn't help but giggle with him. Looking at it like tha,t it was silly to think that we should wait.

"You're sure this is what you want?"

His eyes lost all the amusement and turned dead serious. "I have never been more sure about anything in my life, Loreley. We belong together. You are mine and I am yours. I want us to be a family. I want you to wear my ring and carry my name."

God, this man was so good with words. He made me feel special and loved and wanted and I could see in his eyes that he meant every word he said.

"Yes," I breathed.

"Yes?" His eyes blazed.

I nodded and repeated, "Yes."

I thought he was going to kiss me, but he didn't. Instead he leaned and reached towards the side of the bed without losing me on top of him. When I turned my head to follow his movements, I realized he was reaching for his pants. He pulled them up onto the bed and pulled out his wallet, opened it, and retrieved something from a small secret compartment before he dropped both the pants and the wallet back on the floor.

It was a ring.

He had meant it literally. He had literally carried the ring he bought for me with him in his wallet for six years.

The tears were flowing freely now and I had trouble making out Jason's face. He took my left hand from his chest and placed the ring on my third finger, then looked at it with pure happiness on his face. He placed a kiss on the ring and looked into my eyes.

"That's the most beautiful thing I've ever seen: my ring on your finger." Then he took my mouth in a fierce kiss, taking my breath away. He rolled us, so that now he was on top and broke the kiss.

"How long does it take you to plan a wedding?" He asked. I burst out laughing. Jason grinned at me. I had never seen his face this happy. His eyes were shining with bliss and joy and his grin was wide and pure and real.

"You think I'm joking," he said, amused. "I can guarantee you I'm not. I want to marry you as soon as possible." I sobered at his words and studied him. He wasn't joking.

"I don't know. How long can you manage to wait?" I asked

teasingly. His grin got wider and he leaned down for a quick peck on my mouth.

"A month. I can give you a month. That's it." He was completely serious.

"Are you crazy? I can't plan a wedding in a month. Nobody can. And you're a world famous rock star. I'm sure there are a lot of people you would want at the wedding—"

"I don't care about any of that," he interrupted me. "I'll be happy to have a small wedding with only our closest friends and your family. It's what I want actually. I don't want a big wedding, certainly no photographers and paparazzi and all that shit. Getting married is about us. It's ours. It will be one of our most intimate and personal moments and I don't want to share that with the world. They get enough of me as it is." Bitterness flickered through his eyes but it was gone so quickly that I thought I must have imagined it. "We can elope to Vegas or we can get married here in your backyard. Whatever you want, as long as it's a small wedding and it happens no later than in a month."

He was crazy, but nevertheless, I couldn't fault his way of thinking. I didn't necessarily want to share our moment with the world either. I couldn't imagine what it was like to live in the limelight like he did, but I knew for certain that it wasn't all fun and games. Three months of living in L.A. and working in the music scene had taught me that. And not being close to your family would make that even worse. Jason hadn't talked to his parents since I'd known him. I've never met them, but he told me that he never got along with them, especially with his father. According to Jason, his father had always made him feel like he wasn't good enough, like nothing he ever did came up to par, and that only got worse when Jason showed an interest in music and started playing in a band as a teenager. His father's family came from money, and Jason was expected to follow in his family's footsteps and major in business or law. But Jason wasn't interested in any of that. All he wanted was to play music. That's why he went to UT Austin, because they had a phenomenal music program and they gave him a full ride. He didn't back down even when his father threatened to disown him. It never actually came to that, but still, once Jason had moved out, he never looked back. The last time he talked to his parents was during Thanksgiving break his junior year, which ended in complete disaster. Judging by what he just said, that he wanted a small wedding with friends and *my* family, it sounded like he didn't intend to invite his parents. I was fine with that if that was what he wanted. Don't get me wrong, family was and always will be the most important part of my life, but not everyone was as blessed as I was, and with some families, it was better and healthier for everyone to go their own way. Abuse had many different forms, and as far as I was concerned, Jason had been abused by his parents by not being accepted for who he was. So I didn't question him not even giving it a thought to have them at our wedding. They didn't love him the way they should, so they weren't welcome in our lives. My family was loving and supportive and would welcome Jason with open arms, I was sure of that. They wanted me to be happy, however that came about. And marrying this man, who I had tried so hard to hate and whom I never thought I would hold in my arms again, was what would make me happy. The sooner, the better.

So I gave in with a soft smile and said, "All right. A month."

His grin grew wide when he said, "God, I love you," and pressed another kiss to my mouth.

His hands started roaming again, as did his mouth. He slid off me and turned me around so he could kiss and lick and nibble my back. My back had always been sensitive and feeling his tongue and mouth exploring every inch of it, made me moan and writhe in arousal. I was already wet but grew even wetter when his mouth reached my butt cheeks and he spread my legs with his hands on the back of my upper thighs, opening me to him. I tilted my hip to give him better access and he groaned in appreciation.

His fingers lazily played between my legs as his mouth kissed and nipped at my cheeks and his other hand kept roaming my back. It was so overwhelming it was almost too much.

"I want to bring you like this before I drive into you and make you scream my name while I fuck you from behind. Then I want to flip you over and keep fucking you until I can feel you come apart around me again while I look into your eyes and tell you how much I love you." His words alone and the anticipation they created were almost enough to bring me right then.

Jason intensified his effort between my legs and slid one thick finger inside me. He started pumping slowly while the other fingers kept teasing my clit. My hips moved in synchronization with his fingers. I needed him, wanted him inside me so desperately that I started begging.

"Please, Jace. I want you."

"You'll get me, baby. I'll give you my cock as soon as you come on my hand." He pumped harder, grinding, and moved his mouth up my back to my neck, kissing and nipping. I moaned. I was close, so very close. I could feel his body heat as he hovered above me. His erection was touching my ass and he started slowly rubbing himself against me, bringing me over the edge. I exploded around his finger as I moaned and writhed underneath him.

Before I had even come down, he was inside me, spreading me open even more with his knees. He laced his fingers with mine and pressed my hands into the mattress beside my head as

179

he thrust into me hard and relentlessly over and over again. I couldn't move. I was completely open and pinned underneath him, taking what he had to give. His mouth was still at my neck as he moaned and grunted.

"My hot little fiancée. You're so hot and wet around me, clamping down, as if your pussy can't get enough of me." It couldn't. It would never get enough of him. Jason increased his pace and at this angle, with me being unable to move and wide open, he went so deep and rubbed my front wall over and over again with such ferocity that it didn't take me long until I cried out again as I came.

The next thing I knew, I was on my back and Jason was moving inside me, slower now, shallower. I opened my eyes and found him watching me with nothing but pure and raw love in his eyes.

"Wrap yourself around me, baby. I want to feel you all around me." I did as he asked and wrapped my arms and legs tightly around him. His arms were underneath me, pulling me into him as he devoured my mouth.

"I love you," I breathed when he broke the kiss and went back to staring into my eyes, holding me captive as he answered, "I love you, too, baby. You have no idea how much." He increased his pace again and hardened his strokes. His eyes were wild with passion and love. His breathing went ragged and he started groaning and grunting with every stroke.

"I need you to come, baby. I need you to come with me." He moved inside me with an energy that was almost brutal. I loved it, loved the strength and emotion behind it. He touched his lips to mine and grunted, "Come. Come now!" And I exploded with such force that I almost blanked out as I heard and felt his release. He shouted my name and erupted inside of me, his eyes never leaving mine.

Beautiful.

After we both caught our breath, he tucked me into his side and held me close. I studied the ring that was now decorating my finger. It was vintage and simple. No over-the-top huge and ostentatious diamond, but a simple black stone surrounded by smaller diamonds. I loved it. It was gorgeous.

"You like it?" Jason asked. His voice sounded worried. I looked from the ring to his face. "Obviously, I can afford a better ring now, but I couldn't bring myself to buy a different one when I decided to come after you."

I smiled at him. "I love it. It's gorgeous. And very me." The worry left his face and his face split into a huge and relieved smile.

"I knew it was yours when I first saw it; I couldn't *not* buy it. You're right. It's you. And you're mine."

"That I am," I whispered. He lifted his head and kissed me softly and lovingly.

"We should probably get up. I still need to get my stuff before we head over to your dad's," he murmured against my lips. I loved it when he talked quietly like that. It felt intimate and beautiful.

I pouted, not ready to leave the bed and share him with anyone.

He grinned and bit my lip. "I know. I'd love nothing more than to spend all day in bed with you, but it's your birthday. You've got obligations." He kissed me again then slapped my ass playfully and sat up, pulling me up with him.

"Shower," he said and put me onto my feet by the bed, then grabbed my hand and pulled me behind him to the bathroom.

By the time we got out of the shower and my hair was dry, I had to hustle if we didn't want to be late to my dad's. I threw open the doors to my closet to quickly grab a clean pair of jeans and a shirt only to realize that I hadn't done the laundry in a while and there *was* no clean pair of jeans. I pawed through the clothes on the floor in the hopes of finding a pair that was at least passably clean but was unsuccessful. I grumbled and swore under my breath, at a loss of what to wear now, as I heard asked from behind me, "What are you doing?"

Jason stood in the door to the bedroom, leaning against the doorjamb with his arms crossed on his chest. He was smirking as his eyes ran up and down my body. Seeing as my getting-dressed-quickly mission had failed, I was still in only my underwear and bra.

"I'm trying to find clean clothes to wear," I answered in a duh-tone of voice.

Jason chuckled. "I see you still hate doing laundry." I could tell that he was inside the room now. I was still bent over, pawing through another pile of clothes on the floor. "Advice, baby. Don't stick your ass in the air like that if you don't want me to take you up on that invitation." His voice was low and filled with heat.

I straightened and threw him a mock-glare over my shoulder. We didn't have time for another round. We had to go. He was closer than I thought; so close that our bodies almost touched. His hands landed on my hip and his thumbs started stroking me there.

"We don't have time for another round. We have to go," I said with a lot less urgency as I had intended.

Jason smiled and lowered his lips to my shoulder, kissing me softly. "It's not me who's not dressed yet." He kissed me one final time before he turned me towards my closet and gave me a little push.

"Get a move on then, love." I grumbled and stomped to the closet. But inside I sighed. Jason used to call me "love" all the

182

time, and I was happy that I had that back. I had really missed it. Jason chuckled again and watched as I got dressed. I gave up my search for a clean pair of jeans and decided to wear my short jeans skirt and a loose blouse that would go great with my cowboy boots. Then I headed to the bathroom to put on some deodorant and make up. Eyeliner and mascara would be all I'd have time for. It would have to do.

I came back into the bedroom, my hands busy putting an earring in, my mind on the task of finding my favourite bracelet.

"Only you," I heard Jason say from the door. It didn't make any sense to me, so I asked, "Only me?"

"Yeah, only you," he answered, which again didn't give me anything to go on. I raised my eyes from my jewellery chest to his and saw that he was staring at me, or better, staring at my skirt.

"Only me what?" I asked when he didn't say anything else.

"Only you could look like the hot and sexy version of the girl next door slash rock star slash country girl with almost zero prep-time. That skirt looks great on you."

I blushed, pleased that he thought so.

"That what you're wearing to the bar tonight?"

"Uh...yeah."

"Fuck," Jason mumbled under his breath then he looked from my ass to my face. "If that's the case, then you're not leaving my side tonight."

I rolled my eyes. "Everyone in town has seen me in this outfit about a million times."

"That might be, but you weren't mine when they did, and I gotta make it clear to everyone who will want in your panties when they get a good look at you in that skirt that you're taken."

I giggled. "You don't think the ring on my finger will take care of that?" I watched, fascinated, as Jason's whole face

183

softened. It was like when Cal looked at Ivey. My heart skipped a beat.

"Yeah, it will." His voice was just as soft as the expression on his face. "Doesn't mean I'm gonna let you leave my side." I rolled my eyes again but smiled. Who was I to complain about that?

I turned back around and found my bracelet, put it on, and walked to Jason. His hands automatically went to my ass and he pulled me against him.

"I'm gonna have to work at some point, so I'll be behind the bar."

Jason lifted his eyebrows. "You have to work on your birthday?"

"Well, yeah. It's my bar. Bosses don't get time off." I shrugged.

"Well, boss lady, then you'll find me sitting at the other side of that bar, glaring at every man who even dares to look at your ass or long-as-shit legs."

I shook my head at him, grinning. "You do what you gotta do."

"Oh, I will." He kissed me quickly but deliciously then pulled me behind him through the house, grabbed my purse from the front table and then we were out the door and heading to his Challenger.

He stopped when he saw another car parked behind his.

"Oh, looks like Chris dropped off my car," I said at the same time he said, "Why is Chris' car parked behind mine?"

His eyes got big and round when my words penetrated. "The Shelby is yours?" He asked in surprise that bordered on shock.

"Uh...yeah."

I watched as he walked over to my girl as if in a trance and then ran his hand admiringly and adoringly along the hood. "She's a beauty," I heard him mutter under his breath. I laughed silently and shook my head.

Boys and cars. It never changed.

I got the keys out of my purse and walked to where he was standing, then dangled the keys in front of his face. He snapped out of his car-lust fog and saw the keys, then his eyes snapped to mine and he took them slowly, as if he couldn't believe his luck. His grin was so wide I thought his face might split.

"You gonna let me drive her?"

I shrugged. "Sure. If it makes you that happy."

His hand shot out and he grabbed me by the back of my neck, pulling my face to his, then crashed his lips down on mine and took them in a hard kiss.

"You have no idea how sexy that is, my hot as hell fiancée driving one of the hottest cars in the world. I would like nothing more than to bend you over that hood right now and fuck you, but we're already running late and I don't think your neighbours would enjoy the show. But don't mistake me, Loreley, I will take you on that hood eventually." He gave me another quick and hard kiss before he pulled me to the passenger side door and opened it to guide me in.

Jason liked his dirty talk and I enjoyed it immensely, but what he just said to me must have been the hottest thing anyone has ever said to anyone. I couldn't get the picture of him fucking me on my baby's hood out of my mind.

"Buckle up, baby," Jason said, his voice knowing and amused. I glanced at him as I buckled myself in. He was smug. I rolled my eyes but couldn't help but smile. He chuckled as he leaned over and kissed me once more, softer this time, lovingly. "I love this. Having you back, being with you, teasing you, making you smile. I've missed it. So much."

"Me, too," I breathed as I stared into his shining hazel eyes.

He started the car and we were on the road up to Cal's rental when his phone rang.

"Nathan, we're just on the way up to the house." Silence as Jason listened to what Nathan was saying on the other end. Then he stilled and the vibe in the car turned from happy and playful to tense in less than a second.

"What?" He almost shouted. "Shit. How bad is it?" Silence again. "You think we need security?" My eyes snapped to him. Security? "Goddamn it! Those fucking bastards!" We pulled into Cal's driveway. "Yeah, we're here now." He closed the phone and swore under his breath.

"What's going on?" I asked, worried.

"Let's talk inside." He got out and took my hand when I made it to where he was waiting for me at the front of the car. He said nothing, but I could tell that he was extremely unhappy as he led me into the house.

As soon as he saw me, Nathan pulled me into one of his tight hugs. "Hey there, beautiful," he murmured into my ear. "You look great. Everything good?"

"Yeah, everything's good."

"You think you can let go of my fiancée now?" Jason grumbled from beside us.

Nathan pulled back and looked at me in astonishment. "Your fiancée?" I held up my ring in answer. "I see," he said through a smirk and looked at Jason. "You don't let any grass grow, do you?"

"Nope. Made that mistake once. Was not gonna make it again."

"Smart. A little extreme, but smart." Nathan was still grinning. Then he sobered and asked, "So, what are we going to do about the newest drama?"

186

I looked from him to Jason who was already looking at me.

"The media got wind of me being here," he explained in an annoyed voice.

"What? How?"

"Someone recorded Jason singing to you at the bar and carrying you off last night. They sold the video and it's all over the internet," Nathan explained.

"Shit. That's not good," I muttered.

"No, it's not. It means that we can expect the paparazzi to show up in town any minute now." Jason was working himself up.

"Paparazzi in Cedar Creek?"

"Oh yeah, they'll be here. And those vultures don't consider anything too private to use to their advantage." His eyes on me were serious and wary. And concerned. Realization hit me and my heart started beating rapidly.

"Jesse," I whispered, "They're going to find out about Jesse. What are we going to do?" I asked, slightly panicked.

Jason closed in on me and pulled me against him. "I won't let that happen, baby. They're not dragging him into this."

"And how are you gonna stop it?" Nathan asked. "You know how relentless they are, Jace. They'll dig up any dirt that's not buried deep." Then a thought seemed to hit Jason and he stilled in my arms. I looked up at him and his face was ashen.

"What is it?"

He looked down at me. "Jesse's birth certificate. Am I on it?"

I nodded. "Of course you are." He gave me a small smile that didn't reach his eyes and kissed my forehead. "Thank you for that."

"Shit," Nathan swore.

"What?" I asked, confused.

"They're gonna find it and if I'm named as Jesse's father, they're gonna use it."

"But why would they even look for it? Nobody other than my family and Chris know that you're Jesse's father. Oh, and Rick."

"But what they *do* know is that I lost you six years ago and came here to claim you back. I said as much last night and it's on that video. People in town might not know that Jesse was mine but they do know that you gave birth to a son six years ago. It's not hard to connect the dots."

That was true. Shit.

"Maybe you should release a statement, set things straight and put them out there before they can twist them into lies and drag Lore and Jesse through the dirt," Nathan suggested.

"Maybe," Jason replied.

"You think they would do that? Drag Jesse and me through the dirt I mean?"

"The way I see it, this can go two ways: they either make this out to be a fairy tale of long lost lovers reunited or they make you look like a bitch who kept Jason's son from him and disappeared. Though happy stories don't sell as good as nasty ones, so I'd go with possibility number two," Nathan said.

"Fuck!" Jason swore this time. I didn't know what to say. The prospect of Jesse and me being mentioned in the gossip magazines at all was not a happy one, let alone being called a cold-hearted bitch. I didn't know if I should be angry or sad that people were capable of using other's misfortune to make money and sell stories that were based on lies.

"Loreley," Jason called my name when I was silent for a while. "Remember what we said last night." I just looked at him, not sure what exactly he meant since we had said a lot of things. "You promised not to run when things got tough. I wish we had more time before the drama started, but this is a part of my life. You promised to stick with me."

I saw the fear in his eyes clearly; the fear of losing me again. I was still standing loosely in his arms. I gave him a squeeze. "I'm not running, Jason."

He leaned his forehead to mine in relief. "You went quiet there for a second, I thought you were going to bolt."

"That's not why I went quiet. I just…I don't know how to feel about this. I don't know what to do. It makes me sad that people would take advantage of a story and twist it to make a few bucks, and it makes me unbelievably mad that there doesn't seem to be anything we can do to prevent it."

"So you didn't think it would be too much to handle? You didn't think about running?"

I shook my head. "No."

"Thank God," Jason breathed as he kissed my forehead. Then he turned to Nathan and asked, "You talk to Dana yet?"

"Yeah. She likes the idea of you giving a statement but she also knows that you most likely won't do it. She's pissed by the way. Apparently, she couldn't get a hold of you all morning."

Jason sighed. He had turned his cell phone off to be able to enjoy the morning with Loreley. He should probably give Dana a call before she totally lost it. "I don't know, man. I have never given the media anything, never confirmed or denied any rumours about me. It always seemed like the easiest way to take the wind out of their sails. But this is different." He sighed again. "What do you think?" He asked me.

"I don't know enough about the business or the media to answer that, Jason."

"Maybe not, but this is about you as much as it is about Jesse and me. I want to know what you think."

I thought about it for a few moments.

"I think I agree with you. I don't think we should say anything. Let them write what they want to write. They will anyways. And maybe if we don't feed into it, they'll move on sooner and leave us alone."

Jason smiled a proud smile at me. He gave me a quick peck then said, "Okay, then that's what we'll do. As long as we're on the same page. I can't lose you over this. Over anything."

"I'm not going anywhere, Jason. I promise." I reassured him.

"Good."

"You know it's not gonna be easy to ignore them. This is a small town where everyone knows everyone. It's not L.A., where you can hide behind your big fence and security system. They're gonna be right in our faces and all over town." That came from Nathan.

Great. That sounded like fun. Not.

"I know. I'll call Frank. Tell him to get his butt up here asap."

Nathan nodded in agreement.

"Who's Frank?"

"My bodyguard. I gave him some time off when I came here," Jason explained.

"Oh." I wasn't aware that Jason had his own private bodyguard.

"I don't have him with me all the time. Only when things are a little crazier than usual or we go on tour or to events. He lives in my guesthouse in L.A. It's just easier to have him at hand instead of hiring an agency. They send different people every time, people I don't know and don't trust. Frank is solid. He's a great bodyguard and a good friend." Okay. That made sense.

Apparently, Jason wasn't kidding when he said that we had lived completely different lives these past six years. Clearly, it

190

would take me a while to get used to everything.

"You okay with all this?"

"I guess so. I'm not the expert when it comes to security and media all that stuff, so I guess I'm gonna have to trust you on that."

"Good," Jason grinned. "Not that you have much of a choice, but I thought I'd ask," he added teasingly. Then another thought occurred to me. I touched my ring as I asked, "Should I take this off?"

"Take it off? Why the fuck would you do that?" Jason was instantly angry.

"So the paparazzi don't see it."

"And why don't you want them to see it?" Yes, he was definitely angry.

"I don't know. I wasn't sure if you wanted everyone to know just yet——" I tried to placate him, but he didn't let me finish.

"Listen to me, Loreley. I told you earlier that I want everyone to know that you're mine and I meant that. I also want everyone out there to know I'm yours. We're not hiding that we're getting married and you're definitely not taking that ring off. Not ever. Not until I slide another one underneath it next month when you take my name."

"Okay," I agreed quickly.

"Next month? Jeez, man. You really don't let any grass grow." That was Nathan. I grinned at Jason and he grinned back at me.

"Hey, dad."

"Hey, my beautiful girl. Happy Birthday!" My dad wrapped his arms around me and hugged me tightly. He gave the best hugs ever. I would never tire of them.

"And who do we have here?" He asked when he let me go and inspected Jason. Jason held his hand out for a shake and said, "Roy, it's good to see you again." My dad looked from Jason to his hand and back again. I tensed as they stared at each other, silently communicating the way men do. I was about to say something when my dad slowly lifted his hand and took Jason's.

"I have to say, if Cal and Chris hadn't filled me in this morning, this meeting would have gone a lot differently. I'm not the youngest anymore but I do own a gun and I'm not afraid to use it. You get me?" I rolled my eyes. I loved my dad and I got where he was coming from, but mentioning his gun was a little dramatic.

Jason didn't agree. "I get you. And I wholeheartedly agree." Dad's head jerked in surprise, but he was impressed, I could tell. After a few moments of contemplation, he gave Jason a chin lift to communicate that then looked at Nathan.

"And who are you?"

"Dad, that's Nathan. He's the drummer in Jason's band and an old friend from college." They shook hands.

"Please don't shoot me, sir. I've always been on Loreley's side," Nathan joked. My dad chuckled.

"Well, then, any friend of Loreley's is welcome at my house. Let's go on back. You're late as usual, so everyone is already here and enjoying a drink in the backyard."

We all went through the house and out the back door into the backyard. Everyone was lounging on the deck—the adults and Tommy— or playing in the yard—Macy's kids Lucy, Conner, and Noah, and of course Stella.

"Finally, the guest of honour graces us with her presence." Cal grumbled, though he was smiling. I stuck my tongue out at him and he started laughing.

"Hey, she's only thirty minutes late. I thought they wouldn't make it out of bed at all today," Chris teased.

"I wouldn't have if I was her," Betty said under her breath, shocking the shit out of me and everyone else but Pete and my dad. "I know you all like to think of us as asexual just because we're old and most of you think of us as your parents. But let me tell you, we might be old, but we are sexually very active, thank you very much! And look at that man. If I didn't have my own hot guy, I would jump him right now!" She pointed at Jason.

"What am I? Chopped liver?" Nathan asked through a smile.

"I hear you, man," Chris agreed.

"Please tell me my mother did not just use the words sexually and very active in the same sentence referring to herself." Cal looked at Ivey beseechingly, begging her with his eyes to tell him he had misheard. Ivey was giggling hysterically, so was Macy, and so was I. Jason said nothing. I think he might have been too stunned by Betty's words.

"Okay everyone," I said when I had recovered. "I know most of you know him already, but this is Jason and that over there is Nathan. Jason and Nathan, this is my family." I pointed at everyone and told their names. Macy went a little overboard when she hugged Jason hello, seeing as she was still bouncing up and down as she did so, but that was Macy. Larry just laughed as he pried her off of Jason and gave her a mock-glare, shaking his head.

"Good to see you set things straight with our girl here," Larry told Jason when they shook hands.

"Thanks, Larry."

"Oh my God!" Somebody screeched in my ear. I turned to see it was Macy. Of course. Who else would screech in someone's ear like that? Before I could ask her what was wrong she grabbed my hand and held it up for inspection.

"Holy Shit!"

193

"You are shitting me!"

"Oh my God!"

Shouts, excited and shocked, erupted all around us.

"Shit, man, you don't let any grass grow, do you?" Chris asked through astonished laughter.

"That's exactly what I said," Nathan stated.

"You're getting married? Don't you think that's a little fast?" Cal asked.

"Pfft. As if you waited much longer," Ivey told him chidingly.

"I did. I waited months until I proposed."

"Yeah, a full two months. Loreley and Jason have dated for over two years in college and they shared a son. Heck, if you do the math, they have dated for longer than we have. We haven't even reached our first anniversary and I'm shackled and knocked up."

"Are you complaining?" Cal glared at his wife.

Ivey's face softened. "No, baby, far from it. Just telling you to cool it and be happy for your sister." Cal's face gentled like it always did when she called him baby. He kissed her softly before he looked back at Jason and me.

"I still think it's too soon. I hope you'll have a long engagement," he said.

"I gave her a month," Jason informed him. Everyone around us broke out into loud laughter. Everyone but Cal and Jason that is.

"What's so funny?" Jason asked.

"That's exactly how much time Cal gave me to plan our wedding. Said he wouldn't wait any longer than that."

Jason grinned. Cal grinned back at him. Then Cal got up and shook Jason's hand and they clapped each other on the shoulder.

The only person who hadn't said anything about Jason and I getting married was Tommy. He was standing separated from our big group, leaning against the railing, his eyes on Jason. "Tommy?" I called his name. His eyes came to me and they warmed a little, though it didn't erase his scowl. "You okay?" I asked.

"Depends," he answered as his eyes went back to Jason.

"On what?"

"On whether he's staying this time."

I could feel Jason tense beside me, but he wisely didn't say anything and let me handle this. Jason didn't know Tommy, though he knew about his mother abandoning him when he was just a baby. I had told him all about it years ago when we shared about our families. Jason abandoning Jesse and I would hit too close to home for Tommy, as he had proven at dinner last week when he stormed off after learning who Jason was and what he had done. It was understandable that he'd need some reassurance.

"He's staying."

"You sure about that?" His eyes were still narrowed on Jason. God, I loved that boy.

"Yes, Tommy, I'm absolutely sure about that. He didn't abandon me before. It was a misunderstanding," I explained.

"Yeah, that's what dad said, too. Still, he should have tried harder."

I opened my mouth to defend Jason, but Jason beat me to it. "You're absolutely right. I should have tried harder. And because I didn't, I missed not only six years of being with the woman I love, but also being a father to my son. I'm gonna have to live with that for the rest of my life."

Tommy's eyes grew wide at Jason's confession. He was impressed and relieved. His eyes flickered to mine and I gave

195

him a small reassuring smile. Everyone around us was quiet as they watched the scene unfold before them. Then Tommy gave Jason a small quick nod.

"We good?" Jason asked.

Tommy repeated his nod. "We're good."

My God, Tommy was so much like his father it was scary sometimes.

I felt tiny arms wrap around my legs and when I looked down, I saw Noah smiling up at me. He was the quiet one of the bunch and always hung out with me. He reminded me a lot of Jesse.

"Hi, Lore," he said through his smile. "I wanna sit with you."

"You wanna sit with me, huh?" He nodded happily. "All right big guy, go find us a chair and you can sit on my lap." Without delay, Noah scuttled off in search of a chair.

Jason's arm around my shoulder pulled me in closer. "What if I want you to sit on my lap?" He whispered in my ear.

"Sorry, but Noah's got dibs. He always sits with me." I gave him a wide smile.

"I see." He nuzzled my nose with his and kissed me softly. "You've got quite the male following."

"What can I say? I'm a fun person to be around," I grinned at him.

"Can't argue with that." He returned my grin.

"I'm gonna marry Tommy when I grow up," Lucy announced from across the deck. All eyes went to her and the boy in question she was now standing next to.

Tommy chuckled a boy chuckle and said. "You can't marry me, Luce. We're practically family."

Lucy scrunched up her face, not liking his answer at all.

"You're not my brother," she stated.

"No, I'm not." Tommy answered.

"Or my cousin."

"No."

"Or my uncle."

"No."

"Then how are we family?"

Tommy shrugged. "We just are."

Lucy scrunched up her face again. Then she had a thought. "Wait! If you're family, then I can kiss you! Mommy and daddy say I can only kiss boys if they're family." Macy, Ivey, and I tried not to laugh. This wasn't the first time that Lucy was trying to get around Larry's no-kissing rule.

"Drop it, Lucy. You're not kissing anyone but your brothers and me." Larry growled.

"But you said—"

"I know what I said and now I'm saying this."

"That's not fair," she pouted and crossed her arms on her chest. "Either Tommy is family and I can kiss him or he's not and I can marry him." The three of us couldn't hold it in any longer and burst out laughing. All the men chuckled.

"She's quite the character, isn't she?" Jason asked in my ear. I couldn't answer him. I was still laughing too hard.

"There's nothing even remotely funny about this. My daughter is boy crazy at seven years old."

"I'll let you borrow my rifle when she's a teenager when it gets really interesting," my dad told him. The chuckles and laughter grew louder.

"I don't know what you're grinning about," Larry looked at Cal. "Aren't you having a girl?" Cal stopped grinning immediately and tensed, which made all the women laugh so hard tears were running down our faces.

"Yeah, man, you better hope she doesn't look like Ivey."

197

Cal shot Chris a glare.

"My little sister isn't kissing anyone. I'll make sure of that," Tommy declared.

"Bud, do the math. You'll be far away at college by the time she's Lucy's age." Tommy looked at Chris, wide-eyed, seemingly just now coming to that realization. His eyes went from Chris to his father as if asking for a solution, but Cal didn't have one since what Chris said was true.

"I have nothing, bud. Chris is right, unless you're going to University of Boulder or Denver and live at home."

"Boulder or Denver it is then," Tommy mumbled.

"Perfect! That means you can still date me when you're in college and I'm in high school!" Lucy exclaimed with her hands up in the air over her head in a 'Woot! Woot!' gesture. All the women burst out laughing again and even Tommy chuckled this time as he shook his head at Lucy in loving exasperation.

It was later in the afternoon, when I was playing in the yard with Noah and Conner with Ivey and Macy sitting close by and chatting with me, that I felt Jason's eyes. They were longing and thoughtful and a touch sad. I walked over to him and sat down in his lap.

"You okay?" I asked. I ran my hands through his hair before resting them on his shoulders. I was worried that all this would be too much too soon.

"Yeah. Just thinking," he said, his voice quiet.

"About what?"

He looked at me lovingly. "I was wondering what you looked like when you were pregnant with Jesse."

I gave him a small and sad smile. "I can show you pictures."

"I know and I want to see them. But I want to see you pregnant in real life as well. I want to see you heavy with our child. I want to touch and kiss your big belly and feel our child move inside of you."

"You will, Jace. Give us some time to settle in after we get married and we'll have more children."

Jason shook his head. "You might think I'm crazy, but I don't want to wait. And I don't think you want to either."

"What do you mean?"

"Let me ask you something." I nodded for him to go on. "Are you on the pill?"

I froze. I wasn't. I didn't need it. I was one of those few lucky women whose cycle was like clockwork. And I wasn't having sex until last night, so I hadn't needed the protection aspect of it either. It all came to me right then. Oh my God! We had sex, lots of it, and without protection!

"Yeah, baby, I see you understand what I'm getting at," Jason's voice was amused and loving, but that didn't penetrate in that moment. All I could think about was that we were playing with fire.

"I...I didn't...I didn't think..."

"I know, baby. Neither did I. Not the first time. Not until after. All the times after that, I didn't put a condom on because I didn't want to. I want you pregnant. As soon as possible."

"I...Jason, it's too soon. I can't...I don't..."

"You can and you do. It's not too soon. We've wasted too much time as it is. I want a family. And I want that with you. Only you." My heart melted at his words, but I was still skeptical. We got back together less than twenty-four hours ago, and here we were, engaged and discussing making a family.

"You sure you don't just want that because of Jesse."

He gave me a squeeze. "Yeah, I'm sure. You wanna know why?" I nodded. "You think Jesse would have been our only child if we'd never broken up?" I shook my head no. We had always planned on having at least two or three children. We would at least have two by now if not all three. "I don't think so, either. So we're not moving too fast. Actually, we're trying to catch up."

My lips twitched. He was impossible and I couldn't believe that what he was saying actually made sense in a backwards way. His face split into a wide smile as he witnessed my uncertainty melting away.

"So you agree?"

"Can we at least wait until after the wedding?"

Jason pulled me closer. "All I can tell you is that I'm not going to wear a condom. There's nothing like the feeling of sliding inside you bare, and I'm not gonna give that up now that I finally have that back."

"I guess we won't be having sex until the wedding then," I breathed, not meaning a single word I just said. Jason's smile widened even more. "Right," he murmured as he stared at my mouth. Then his lips were on mine and he kissed me long and deep and wet.

"No condoms," he said when he let me go.

"Okay." Then something occurred to me. But I didn't want to ask.

"What is it?" Jason asked when he felt me tense in his arms.

I took a deep breath. There was nothing for it. I had to ask even if I didn't want to know the answer. "Have you ever…in the past six years…without…with anyone?" I stammered. Jason's eyes warmed on me.

"No, baby, I've never had sex without a condom with anyone but you."

"Not even when you were drunk? Who knows—"

"No. Believe me. I'm not gonna deny that I was drunk every time I had sex with someone, but I was never too smashed to forget to protect myself." His eyes and voice were sincere. I believed him. My body sagged in relief and his arms around me tightened. He kissed my hair.

"I told you, Loreley, none of the others meant anything to me. It's always been you."

We sat like that for a long while, holding each other, watching our friends and family until it was time to go to the bar for my birthday bash.

Thirteen

LORELEY

Jason and Nathan weren't joking when they said the paparazzi could descent on Cedar Creek any minute. My eyes got big when we turned the corner onto Main Street and saw a blob of people with cameras around their necks camped out on the sidewalk in front of Cooper's.

"Holy shit," I whispered in awe. I stared at the crowd, wide-eyed. Both Jason and Nathan swore under their breath. Chris shared my sentiment. Jason had taken both Chris and Cal aside during the barbeque and told them about the video and what to expect, so they wouldn't be blindsided by it.

"How did they get here so fast?" I wondered.

"It's been almost a full day since the video went viral. A lot of time to get on a plane or make the drive from wherever you're based," Jason explained.

"Wow," I murmured, "That's just crazy."

"Welcome to my life," Jason muttered, annoyed.

I looked from studying the crowd to him, put my hand on his leg, and gave him a light squeeze. "Don't worry. It'll be okay. They're not allowed inside, right?"

"No. They're not allowed on the premises actually, which

202

includes the parking lot."

"Okay. Well, that's at least something. Drive around to the back. We'll go in that way. Maybe we can sneak in unseen."

Jason didn't slow the car as he drove past the paparazzi, but it was no use. Even though they didn't know my car, they spotted us almost instantly and started taking pictures and shouting out questions. I just watched, amused and disbelieving, as they started running alongside the car, holding out their cameras blindly in the hopes of getting a good shot. They followed us until Jason pulled into the back parking lot that only had a few spaces for the employees.

"Stay in the car until I come around and open your door. And keep your sunglasses on."

"I thought you said they aren't allowed in the parking lot?"

"They're not. That doesn't mean they won't come close anyways." Jason was tense with worry and irritation when he looked in the rear view mirror before he got out of the car.

I turned around in my seat to look out the back window. Jason was right. They were already on the premises and were closing in fast. Nathan got out with Jason while I waited, a little nervous. I had seen this happen as a bystander a lot of times during my three-month stint in L.A., but it was a completely different story when you were all of the sudden the focus of ten or so photographers. Even though they hadn't even reached us yet, they shouted out questions at Jason and Nathan as soon as they and Chris emerged from the car, and the frenzy got even worse when Jason opened my door and I got out.

Holy Shit!

Camera flashes erupted all around, blinding me. Now I got why Jason told me to keep my sunglasses on. Without them, I would undoubtedly go blind.

Jason threw his arm around my shoulders and pulled me

into his body protectively, while Nathan and Chris flanked us as we walked the short distance from the car to the back door. Neither of them answered any of the questions or gave the paparazzi even the slightest glance other than to glare at them when they got too close or were in the way. I tried to follow their lead but had more trouble ignoring them than I thought I would. Leaning into Jason, I put a smile on my face and pretended that being photographed and harassed like this was nothing unusual, but I wasn't sure I succeeded. Though it seemed like much longer, we were through the back door within seconds.

"You okay?" Jason stopped me and asked.

"I'm okay," I said through an amused snicker. Jason's eyes lost some of its worry and warmed on me.

"You think this is funny?"

"I think this is crazy," I corrected him. Jason grinned down at me.

"She's right. This is definitely crazy. Or insane. Though I'm sure Nick won't mind the free publicity. We'll have a full house tonight."

"Nick?" Jason asked.

"*Breaking Habit's* front man," Chris explained.

"Ah. Always happy to help."

I laughed silently.

"We should put someone on the door tonight. Just to make sure that things go smoothly."

"Agreed. We're fully staffed tonight so that shouldn't be a problem. I'll be behind the bar and—"

"Oh, no," Chris interrupted me. "You're not gonna be anywhere but drinking and having fun with your friends tonight. And rocking out on stage of course."

"The bar is going to be packed tonight, Chris. You said so

yourself. You need me," I argued. I appreciated his gesture but this was my bar and I was needed.

"No, I don't. I've got it covered. I hired two more waitresses this week while you were wallowing. We're good."

I glared at him and he smirked at me. Jason chuckled. "Told you so," he mumbled. I ignored him.

"Come on, Lore. You really gonna be mad at me because I want you to enjoy your birthday?" I guess I couldn't, but I wasn't ready to let him know that just yet, so I kept glaring at him. Chris knew I didn't mean it and blew me a kiss before he turned around and disappeared into the bar.

"Listen, baby," I looked back at Jason at hearing his serious voice. "Frank is coming tomorrow. Until then, I don't want you to go anywhere without either me or Nathan or Chris. Those fuckers can get mean and I don't want you to have to deal with that on your own."

"Is that really necessary?" I grimaced, not happy at the prospect that I wasn't allowed to go anywhere by myself.

"Humor me. At least for a few days until the worst of it dies down. You've never dealt with anything like this and it can be overwhelming."

"All right. As long as it isn't permanent," I grumbled.

"Thank you." He kissed the top of my head and we followed Chris into the bar.

When we hit the main room, we saw that Nathan had already introduced himself to the members of *Breaking Habit* and was chatting with them animatedly while he helped them finish with their set-up. We had about an hour until opening.

"Hey guys," I greeted them as we came closer to the stage. Everyone turned and smiled at me.

"Lore! Happy Birthday!" Joss shouted from behind her drum set.

"Yo! Happy Birthday," came from Noah, and another "Happy Birthday, Lore," from Jonas. Nick jumped off the stage and gave me a tight hug. It was a little awkward since Jason didn't relinquish my hand. "Happy Birthday, gorgeous," he murmured into my ear.

Nick was the lead guitarist and singer of *Breaking Habit*, an up and coming band from Boulder. They had played at *Cooper's* too many times to count over the last few years. Chris and I had become friends with all the band members: Nick, his brother Noah who played the bass, Jonas who played second guitar, and Joss who was the drummer and also Nick and Noah's little sister. They were all great, though Jonas was somewhat of a player. Joss was hilarious and a spitfire, something that was essential if you were the only female playing in a rock band with two of your band members being your overprotective big brothers. But she didn't take any shit from anyone and I liked and admired that about her. Nick had been the one who had coaxed me back into writing and playing music. He would stop by at my place or at the bar with his guitar and we would sit down and talk while we jammed just for fun. After Chris and Rick, he was one of my closest friends.

The hug lasted a little too long for Jason's taste. He squeezed my hand and pulled on it slightly. I let go of Nick and he stepped back, giving me a huge and warm smile.

"Jason, this is Nick. Nick, this is Jason."

"The fiancée," Jason added as he held out his hand. Nick's eyebrow shot up and he looked at me, surprised. Or shocked was probably a better word.

"Fiancée? Last time I checked he left you hanging. That was less than thirty-six hours ago." He sounded almost accusatory.

"That was then, this is now," Jason stated, his voice serious and a little threatening. I felt like I was caught in the middle of a pissing contest.

"We talked it out and decided not to waste any more time," I explained. Nick stared at me in disbelief and something else. Was that hurt I saw in his eyes? "I'm sorry I didn't tell you sooner, Nick, but everything happened so fast and—"

"Yeah, you can say that again." He studied me for a few moments then asked, "You still gonna play with us tonight though, right?"

"Of course."

Nick nodded at her. "Good," he said then gave Jason another look I couldn't interpret and went back to the stage.

"What the hell was that all about?" I asked as if talking to myself.

"That, love, was what you'd call a pissing contest." Jason confirmed my earlier thought.

"That's ridiculous. Nick and I are just friends; have been for almost two years now." Jason turned to me and gave me a crooked smile.

"It might be that way for you, but he definitely wants more from you than just a friendship." I shook my head in denial and confusion and looked over at the stage again to where Nick was standing with Noah.

"I don't know if I should be happy or worried that you still haven't figured out how unbelievably gorgeous you are," Jason muttered against my skin as he brushed his lips against my temple. I didn't know what to say to that so I said nothing.

Less than an hour later, the bar was starting to fill up with customers. The paparazzi were still camped outside, but so far, nobody seemed angry or upset about it. On the contrary: people seemed to be either excited or amused by it. Cal and the rest of the gang arrived about an hour after we opened. Betty and Pete were babysitting all the children tonight. My dad was here, too.

"Nothing gonna keep me from celebrating my baby girl's birthday with her," he had said when I spotted him and embraced him in a hug. "This is still your birthday party, isn't it? Or is it your engagement party now?" He was teasing me.

I rolled my eyes at him and said, "No, dad. It's still my birthday party. At least it is if you ask Chris. He won't let me work tonight."

"He better not. We pay him good money to manage the bar without your help."

We were all sitting at the bar having a drink and chatting when it was time for *Breaking Habit* to go on.

"Lore!" Chris called my name over the noise in the bar. "You mind announcing them? I've got my hands full here." He wasn't kidding. The bar was full to capacity and he hadn't been able to take a break at all.

"Sure! No problem!" I shouted back at him. I gave Jason a quick peck on the lips before I hopped off my barstool. The band was assembled at the side of the stage, waiting and ready. They all grinned at me huge, excited and hyped up to go on. I climbed the steps and walked to the front of the stage to stand in front of the microphone. Loud cheers and clapping greeted me.

"Are you guys ready to party with one of Boulder's most favourite bands?" The cheers and shouts and clapping grew so loud I had to raise my voice even though I was using a microphone. I grinned at the audience.

"All right, all right! I won't keep you waiting any longer! Put your hands together for the phenomenal and exceptionally talented band *Breaking Habit!*" I was about to leave the stage when Nick grabbed my hand and pulled me back in front of the microphone. I wasn't supposed to sing with them until after their first break, so I was a little confused as to why he would do that but didn't resist.

208

"Before we let her go, I would like us all to sing a little song for this beautiful young lady here. Or should I say middle-aged woman since she turned thirty today?" I gave Nick a mock-glare for that comment while the audience cheered and laughed. He burst out laughing.

"Okay. You guys ready?" Nick started playing the starting notes of a rock version of Happy Birthday and everyone in the bar chimed in. Then he turned the song into *Lorelei* by Styxx and everyone kept singing with him. Being in the spotlight like this made me a little uncomfortable but also very happy and grateful that I had such good friends. When the song was over, Nick drew me into another hug and kissed the top of my head. I pushed him away, laughing, and told him to get on with it already then jumped off the stage and headed back over to the bar.

Jason had his eyes on me as I walked towards him and they weren't happy at all.

Oh, dear.

Deciding to cut him off before he could start with his misplaced jealousy, I didn't stop when I reached him but walked straight into his chest and kissed him, so that he had no choice but to put his arms around me and kiss me back. He didn't disappoint. He pulled me into him so tightly and kissed me so deeply that people around us started breaking into catcalls. I pressed into him and couldn't help but groan into his mouth. I was breathless by the time he ended the kiss. His eyes were less angry, but the annoyance wasn't gone completely.

"That guy puts his mouth on you again I'm gonna kill him." Yes, he was still angry. I sighed. "I mean it, baby. I can just about take him hugging you, but his mouth on you? No. And just so you know, the same goes for your friend Rick." I popped my eyes out at him. Though, with Rick I definitely knew he

209

wanted more from me than just a friendship, so I couldn't much blame Jason for being jealous. I just hadn't known he had picked up on that.

"How would you feel if I let women, who you know want to fuck me, kiss me and hug me?" I stilled. Shit. He was right. I almost saw red just imagining it. I relented and gave him another kiss, this one soft and apologetic.

"I'm sorry."

"You need to talk to him, tell him that he has no chance in hell of stealing you from me. If you don't, I will."

"I'll talk to him. Though I still think you're wrong. He's just a really good friend. He doesn't like me that way."

"Humor me."

"Looks like I'm humoring you a lot today," I grumbled a little petulantly.

"I'll make it up to you later." His voice had gone from annoyed and angry to low and sexy. My body reacted almost instantly and clenched deep inside. I shivered. Jason read me and gave me a lascivious grin as he lightly ran his finger across my cheek to my mouth. "Later," he whispered his promise then touched his mouth softly to mine. He let me go and turned me around in his arms so that I was facing my friends again as I leaned my back against his front.

JASON

Jason hadn't been this happy and content since before Loreley had walked out on him all those years ago. He loved the feeling of holding her in his arms with her body leaning against his as she was chatting and laughing and drinking with her friends. And now that she was finally wearing the ring he had bought for her years earlier, he felt whole again. He had known that no other woman could ever fill the hole that was left behind when he lost her, and feeling her body shaking against him now as she laughed, brought that truth home. He was completely in love with her, heart and soul, and there was no way he would ever let anything or anyone come between them ever again.

Especially not another man who wanted more than just her friendship.

He could understand the feeling since he had felt exactly the same way when he met her in college and she had captured him with her mix of sweet carelessness and sassy attitude. She possessed a charm and vulnerability that made men fall in love with her instantly. And the fact that she was unaware of that power made men want her even more. That was something he knew he would have to live with for the rest of his life. But he didn't care as long as Loreley understood where he was coming from and didn't feed into their attraction once he made her aware of it.

He glanced to the stage and listened to the music. He had to give it to them, the band was really good. Nick's voice sounded phenomenal and the accuracy the whole band played with was impressive. They played like a well-oiled machine and had so much fun doing it that the audience had no chance but to love them.

"Told you they were good." Loreley's face was turned towards him, her smile big and proud. Jason couldn't help but return the smile.

"They are. They only play cover songs?"

"No, they have a whole set of originals. They always play covers first to get the crowd going, though I told them again and again they didn't need that. They're great on their own." Jason nodded and looked back to the stage. Loreley had impeccable taste in music and a great ear. If she said their original songs could hold their own, then he believed her. He was looking forward to hearing them.

He didn't have to wait long.

About fifteen minutes later, Nick introduced their next song as one of their originals and when they started back up, Jason was even more impressed. Their style was simple but brilliant, their plays and synchronicity were clean, and their lyrics were deep and soulful. Nick's voice was rough enough to be rock 'n roll and smooth enough to melt the ladies' hearts. The perfect balance. This band would definitely go places.

"See?" Loreley nudged him. Oh yeah, he definitely saw.

"You weren't kidding. They're very good." Another proud smile from Loreley. A thought occurred to him.

"You have a hand in that?"

She shrugged, but kept that proud little smile on her face. "A little." Jason had to kiss that mouth. So he did.

"You've always had a great ear."

"They remind me of you guys before you became one of the world's most famous rock stars." There was melancholy in her voice. Jason studied her. Loreley had had a hand in some of their early songs that became number one hits. Thinking about that reminded him that there was something else they had to talk about, but this wasn't the time or the place. But the melancholy in her voice told him that she missed writing. He hoped she missed doing it with him just as much as he had missed it with her.

"You miss it, don't you? Taking writing music more seriously like you used to?" It was such an integral part of who she was that he knew he was right. He could see it in her eyes. But living the life of a single mom working a full-time job must have not left her with enough time or energy to pursue that passion. Fuck. Now Jason felt even guiltier for not being there when she needed him.

She shrugged. "I do. I just got back into it these past few months actually."

"Yo, Lore!" Nick's voice boomed through the room before Jason could say anything else. Loreley's head whipped around and Jason looked up. Nick was looking at them, his face was smiling, but his eyes were glinting angrily. "Stop canoodling with your boyfriend and get your sweet ass up here!"

Jason tensed. Calling him Loreley's boyfriend instead of her fiancée had been deliberate, Jason was sure. As was calling her ass sweet. Nick was goading him.

He returned Nick's hot stare with a warning glare and kept his eyes locked to his as he turned Loreley in his arms. He only broke eye contact when he clasped her face with both hands and leaned down to kiss her. It wasn't a normal kiss.

It was carnal.

It was passionate.

It was possessive.

It was showing Nick that Loreley was and always would be his.

"You're incorrigible." Loreley knew that the kiss was another pissing contest. She shook her head at him in disbelief but couldn't quite keep the smile off her face. Jason smirked at her. Then he lifted her left hand up to his mouth and kissed the ring that decorated her finger.

"You think you can stop pissing all over me now? I'm sure he got the message. Heck, the whole bar got the message." She scowled at him. He grinned at her.

"My point." Loreley rolled her eyes, but smiled. Jason gave her a quick peck on that irresistible mouth of hers before he turned her and smacked her sweet ass that only he would ever touch in a prompt to go up there.

213

Loreley squealed and shot him a mock-glare over her shoulder, making him laugh.

God, he had missed her.

He watched as she made her way through the crowd and went up the steps onto the stage, then kept watching as she took her acoustic guitar, hooked it up, and climbed on the stool that had appeared next to the one Nick was now sitting on.

Jason had a feeling he wouldn't like what was about to happen. Nick was talking into the microphone, but his eyes were warm and smiling as they were following Loreley's movements.

"This next song has a very special place in my heart. It's new and it was created by chance during a lazy afternoon jamming session with this beautiful lady sitting next to me. I hope you'll love it just as much as I do."

Shit.

They had written a song together.

And by the looks of the set-up it was a slow and romantic song.

Jason also hadn't missed Nick's implied meaning of him and Loreley getting together regularly to jam.

He locked his jaw and ground his teeth as he crossed his arms over his chest. No, he was most definitely not going to enjoy the next five minutes.

To his surprise, he did, at the same time he didn't.

Loreley had always been something else on stage. The way her movement flowed naturally when she strummed the guitar, the way she cocked her head when she started singing, the way you could read the emotions crossing her face when she was singing. She was such a presence he could feel everyone in the room being mesmerized by her.

He wasn't the only one who was completely enthralled.

And he was proud, so very proud of her talent and passion

214

for music.

And proud that she was all his.

The part he didn't like was Nick and her singing a powerful and heartfelt song about second chances and being strong enough to move on. No, he didn't like that part at all, nor the thought that they had written it together before Jason had reclaimed her. It was almost a message, a plea from Nick to let go of the hurt and losses in her past and give him a chance. It was a beautiful song of healing. And Jason was insanely jealous that Loreley was singing it with Nick instead of him.

"She doesn't see him that way. Never has. Doesn't even have the slightest clue that he's had a thing for her for years." Chris was standing beside him. Jason didn't say anything. He kept his eyes on his woman as hers found his and she smiled a huge, brilliant smile at him, lighting up her whole face. Jason grinned back at her. Chris kept talking.

"Nick was the one who got her back to writing music. About three or four months ago, when she still hadn't picked up her guitar after Jesse's death, he started going over to her house a lot, asking her to help him out with this or that song, and never gave up until she finally relented. He's helped her a lot."

Jason ground his teeth but stayed silent. If Chris was trying to reassure him, he was doing a piss poor job of it.

Loreley had told him that morning when they were whispering to each other in bed that she hadn't touched her guitar for months after Jesse's death. She had played for him almost every day and Jesse had just started to learn playing the guitar himself. So many memories were connected to her playing that it had been too painful for her. Jason's heart had constricted at hearing her tell him all this as he imagined the pain she had been in.

She had lost her music when their son had died and he was

215

grateful that she had found it again so it could help her deal. But he wasn't grateful to learn that the person who helped her rediscover it was the one who was now singing with her on stage with love and adoration in his eyes. It might be selfish, but he wanted to be the one who gave that back to her. Writing songs together had always been theirs; knowing she had shared that with someone else, someone who clearly wanted her for himself, made jealousy curse through him, unreasonably or not. Thank fuck he got his shit together and made her his again. If he had waited much longer, it might have been too late, judging by all the admirers who seemed to be positioning to move in. Thank fuck he knew they wouldn't stand a chance. Not now.

"You gotta trust her, man. I don't know if she told you, but she hasn't been with anyone since you. Not with anyone. Not for anything."

"I know. She told me. I trust her, Chris. Implicitly. It's him I don't trust. He wants her and I have a feeling he's gonna go in for the kill. Twice he has tried to push my buttons tonight. I know she thinks of him as nothing but a good friend, so how do you think she's gonna feel when he shows her different?"

Chris thought about that for a minute. "I see what you mean."

"Yeah. As much as I don't like him simply for the fact that he's gonna try and steal my woman, I don't want her hurting over losing a friend either."

"You think he's gonna go for it?"

"Absolutely."

"Shit," Chris swore after he watched Nick for a few moments.

Jason didn't answer.

LORELEY

I was following *Breaking Habit* off the stage with only Nick behind me. We had just finished the song Nick and I had written together and the band was going on a short break. Playing that song while Jason was watching had worried me. It was a deeply emotional and heartfelt song. I was concerned he would misinterpret it and get angry or upset. But when I had looked over to where he was standing with Chris and had smiled at him, his return grin had been nothing but proud and loving.

"Lore! You have a minute?" I was about to head to the restroom to freshen up when Nick's voice stopped me.

"Sure. What's up?"

"I just...I wanted to ask you something." He stepped closer to me, so close that I could see the sheath of sweat covering the skin on his neck and arms.

"Actually, I want to show you something."

"Okay," I said, confused as to where he was going with this.

He leaned in as if to whisper something into my ear, but to my complete horror instead of heading for the ear, his mouth landed on mine and he started kissing me. Soft and gentle, almost hesitant, but still urging me to reciprocate. His body was now touching mine, his hands at my hips holding me in place. In my total and utter confusion and shock, I gasped. Nick took that as an invitation and his tongue entered my mouth. The touch of his tongue to mine was what snapped me out of my complete surprise. I pushed against his upper arms at the same time I stepped back.

"No, Nick. No," I shook my head from side to side rapidly, trying to clear it. This couldn't be happening. He must have made a mistake, got carried away in the moment or something.

Nick's face fell. "I love you Loreley. I've been in love with you for years but I knew you weren't ready for anything—"

217

"No. No, no, no, no, no. This isn't happening. You don't mean that." I was still shaking my head, my eyes wide, begging him to take back what just happened.

"I do mean it, Lore," he sounded agitated now. "I was giving you time, but I waited too long and now that asshole has moved in and—"

My back straightened instantly and I stiffened. "No, Nick. I'll stop you right there. I appreciate your concern for me, but you don't know the whole story."

"I know that he didn't want you and Jesse six years ago. He cheated on you and abandoned you. What makes you think he's gonna stick around this time?"

"I told you. You don't know the whole story, Nick. He didn't cheat on me and he didn't abandon us. He didn't know anything about Jesse. I thought he did but he didn't. It was all a misunderstanding."

"Bullshit, Lore, you're just using that as an excuse—"

"No. I am not." I was getting mad now and Nick could hear it in my voice. He stopped and looked at me, really looked at me. I'm not sure what exactly he was seeing, but his face fell even further.

"You don't feel anything for me then?" His voice had lost the desperation and urgency and sounded defeated.

I sighed, my anger gone instantly. "I do feel something for you, Nick. You're one of my closest friends and I love you. As a friend." My eyes were beseeching him. "Isn't that enough?"

Now it was him who shook his head. "I'm not sure, Lore. I don't think I can be in love with you and be your friend at the same time, knowing that you don't feel the same way about me and watching you with *him*."

"Nick, I—" I stepped closer to him and went to touch his arm, but Nick retreated from my touch.

"No, Lore. I...I'll talk to you later." Then he was gone. He walked past me and disappeared out the back door. I wanted to go after him but decided that was probably not a good idea.

Shit.

I went to the restroom to freshen up. Staring into the mirror, I hoped I hadn't just lost a friend. Nick was an important person in my life and I cared deeply about him, but not in that way. I was in love with Jason, had been since college. I finally had him back and I was happy.

"Shit," I murmured.

I decided to give Nick some time. We would figure this out. We had to.

I dried my hands and walked out the restroom door. I could hear the band starting up again when I walked into someone. Someone big and strong.

"Oh, excuse me," I said and tried to walk around the person. Not only did he not budge, but he stepped towards me, making me take a step back so as to not being pushed by his big body. It was then that I looked up.

Brad was glaring down at me.

He must have slipped through the cracks. He wasn't welcome at Cooper's anymore since last week's incident.

"Brad. What do you want? You're not allowed in here." I was annoyed. I didn't want to deal with him right now or ever again.

Brad's big body advanced on me once more in a threatening move so that I had to retreat until my back hit wall.

This was not good.

I had managed to take him by surprise last time but I knew that if he really wanted to hurt me, I didn't have a prayer. And if his body language was any indication, I had reason to worry.

I looked over his shoulder in the hopes of seeing someone

who could help me out, but we were hidden from view in the corner of the hallway that led to the restrooms.

"Nobody here to save you this time." Oh, yes, I had reason to worry. Brad's voice was a lethal hiss. He was out for revenge. His eyes were narrowed into slits and his upper body was looming over me. I wasn't short, but Brad was a huge man. I knew I was in trouble.

"Now listen, Brad—" I tried to placate him in a calm tone, but he didn't let me finish.

The left side of my face burned hot and angry and my head pounded as it ricocheted off the wall.

Holy shit!

He hit me!

Without preamble, he had full on hit me across the face. I tasted blood on my tongue as I licked my lips and I could already feel the bump that was forming at the back of my head. His hand was at my throat when we heard a voice from behind him. I would have been happy to know that someone was there to help me if the voice hadn't been Ivey's.

"Hey! Get your hands off her!"

Brad's head turned to look at her but he didn't let me go.

"Walk away," he said, his voice a dark warning.

Oh hell no, he would not touch her. Ivey had been hit enough in her life, had endured enough from her abusive father and ex-boyfriend. And she was pregnant. I would not let Brad touch her. I started to struggle and kick as I tried to pry his hand away from my throat.

"Let go of me you motherfucking asshole!"

His hand tightened and choked me. His eyes were still on Ivey when he repeated his warning. "Walk away."

Instead of listening to Brad and walking away or maybe getting someone to help, Ivey launched herself at Brad. My eyes grew wide with panic when she landed on Brad's back and started hitting and biting him.

"No, Ivey," I gasped. "Don't——" but I was too late. Brad had already thrown her off and she was sitting on her ass on the floor, her face grimaced in pain.

"No!" I tried to shout, but it came out as little more than a whisper since Brad's hand around my throat was suffocating me. Tears were pooling in my eyes as I tried in vain to breathe. Then I was on my knees and bowled over as he dropped me abruptly and I coughed as air flowed into my lungs again.

I heard a commotion and looked up to see Cal holding Brad against the wall by his throat now. He was seething. And then he was punching Brad in the face once, twice, three times and Brad's nose was bleeding.

"Tell me you didn't put your hands on my woman and my sister."

Brad was struggling to get a word out. His face was turning red. Yeah, he was a big guy but so was Cal. And Cal was hanging on to his control by a threat. It wouldn't take much for him to completely lose it. I got up off the floor and glanced at Ivey. She was still sitting on the floor a few feet away from me, her eyes wide. I had seen Cal angry, but never like this. I imagined this was what he must have looked like when Ivey was taken and beaten last fall. Or close to it.

"From what I hear your wife can take it," Brad managed to say through his choking. Ivey's body locked at the same time Cal pulled Brad's body away from the wall only to slam it right back into it.

"What the fuck is going on?"

Jason was standing at the mouth of the hall, his eyes going from Cal to me to Ivey before they shot back to me and zeroed in.

221

"Why are you bleeding?" His voice had turned from surprised to murderous in less than half a second. "And what...are those marks around your neck?" He was close to shouting, his face twisted in horror and absolute fury.

"I walked in on this asshole with his hands around Lore's neck, choking her, after he threw my wife on her ass." Cal kept his eyes on Brad as he explained to Jason.

"He hit her and tried to choke her. I jumped on his back to make him let go of her and he threw me off," Ivey chimed in. Cal moved only his eyes to glance at his wife. "I'll deal with you later," he promised her in a dark voice. Ivey opened her mouth to retort something, but Jason beat her to it.

"Get out of my way, Cal." His body was vibrating with rage and I knew if he got his hands on Brad, he would kill him. Cal didn't move but kept Brad exactly where he was: pinned against the wall, unable to move. I stepped in front of Jason and put my hands on his chest. He was so focused on Brad he didn't even glance at me.

"Jason—"

"Get the fuck out of my way, Cal," Jason repeated, completely ignoring me in my effort to calm him down.

But Cal ignored Jason and kept Brad locked against the wall. "Someone call Rick to get his ass in here. You're pressing charges. Both of you." Out of the corner of my eye I saw Ivey get up and pull out her phone. A minute later, Rick shot into the hallway, the phone still at his ear and stopped short at what he saw. Brad was still pressed against the wall by Cal. He wasn't quite choking anymore but he had trouble breathing. Jason was still seething with rage and ready to rip Brad's head off, while I still had my hands on his chest and tried to calm him down.

"Jesus fuck, Brad. How stupid can you be?" He closed his phone, opened it again, and pushed a few buttons before he put it back to his ear. "Rick here. Need you to send a car to Cooper's. Take in Brad Williams. Yeah. We're in the back hall." Then he hung up and walked to Cal and Brad.

"You can let him go now," Rick murmured to Cal as he laid a hand on his shoulder. It took Cal a few moments, but then he did as Rick asked and stepped back, but not before he gave Brad one last shove. Ivey moved into his side and Cal closed his arm around her shoulders, pulling her into him, as he watched Rick put handcuffs on Brad.

"You okay, baby?" Ivey nodded and Cal kissed her forehead. "You ever do something stupid like that again, I will spank you raw," he murmured against her skin. I didn't hear what Ivey said in return because in that moment, Jason roughly pulled me into his arms and hugged me tightly to his body.

"Fucking hell," he murmured into my hair.

"I'm okay." His arms tightened around me. One of his hands moved to the back of my head and I flinched in pain. Jason pulled back and looked at me questioningly. I didn't want to tell him but I knew this was not something he would let go.

I sighed. "My head. It hit the wall when he backhanded me."

Jason clenched his jaw so hard I could see the muscles in his cheeks jump. Then he moved his fingers tentatively through my hair until he found the bump.

"You need some ice," he rumbled roughly. Then he cupped my face and held my face up to his for closer inspection. He softly touched his thumb to my split lip then moved his fingers down to run along my neck gently. It stung a little.

"I'm taking you to the hospital." He took my hands in his and kissed my knuckles. "Let's go."

"I don't think that's necessary, Jason. Really, I'm okay now."

"No, Lore. You're not. I want you checked out and I want this on record." I opened my mouth to protest but didn't get there.

"He's right, Lore. You should get checked out, make sure you don't have a concussion. Then come to the station tomorrow morning. Bring the medical report," Rick said in a strained voice.

"We're coming with you," Cal announced. "He threw Ivey to the floor and she landed hard. I want her and the baby checked out, too." He didn't give Ivey a chance to have a say in that as he strode past us to the back door with her still tucked to his side.

"Let's go," Jason repeated. He gave Rick a chin lift, who returned it, and then we were following Cal and Ivey out the back door. Luckily, there were no paparazzi back here to take pictures of my bruised face and we made it out of the parking lot without them noticing, which probably had to do with the fact that we were all riding in Cal's truck.

"This was not how I envisioned this day to end."

We were lying in bed, my head on Jason's chest, our legs tangled under the blanket. Jason's fingers were drawing patterns on the small of my back under my shirt.

Cal had dropped us off at my house rather than driving us back to the bar. My car was still in the parking lot. We would pick it up tomorrow.

"Me neither," he replied as my fingers stroked his chest.

I didn't have a concussion, just a goose egg that the doctor told me to put ice on as often as I could during the night and the next day. My lip was all cleaned up and hadn't needed any stitches. My throat was the worst of my injuries. It was still burning and it hurt when I swallowed. The doctor had said it would be like that for the next few days and to eat soft foods until the pain was gone. He had also given me ointment for the angry red welts that decorated my skin that Jason had applied carefully after our shower a few minutes ago.

What a day. So much had happened over the past twenty-four hours it was hard to wrap my head around it all: Jason and I had forgiven each other and were back together, we had lots of make-up sex, he was moving in with me, we got engaged, had more sex, decided to start a family, and then I got beat up at my own birthday party.

"Can I ask you something?" Jason interrupted my thoughts.

"Sure," I answered.

"Shits me that I have to do this now when you're already battered and bruised, but I wanna deal with this so we can move on from it." I tensed a little at his ominous words. Then I waited for him to move on. "He make a move on you?"

I relaxed. Thinking he was talking about Brad, I told him, "Yeah, he did. A while ago. I blew him off. I wasn't nice about it. That's probably why he's been even more of a jerk than he usually is. But I never thought he would actually physically hurt me."

Jason's fingers kept caressing my back. "I could have guessed that part. But that's not what I meant. I meant did Nick make a move on you tonight?"

I tensed again, giving Jason his answer without having to say the actual words. "I knew it," he whispered harshly. His fingers had stopped and his hand was now lying flat against my back. I said nothing and waited, hoping he would let this go for now. I was too tired to deal with anything else today.

I should have known he wouldn't.

"Tell me what happened." I closed my eyes and sighed before I relented and told him how Nick had stopped me after our song and had kissed me.

225

"That fucker," Jason swore through clenched teeth.

"I made it clear that I'm not interested in him that way and that I love you." His hand at my back pushed in slightly.

"I know, baby. I'm not worried about that. And I can't blame him for falling for you."

"Then what are you worried about?" I moved my head on his chest so I could see his face. He tilted his chin down so he could do the same.

"You think of him as a friend. A good friend."

I nodded. "Yeah, I do."

"So how would you feel if he couldn't get over this, if he couldn't be your friend anymore like he used to?"

The pain of disappointment and loss ran through me and I grimaced.

"Yeah. Exactly," Jason whispered. "I don't particularly like him and as I said, I can't blame him for falling in love with you. But I can and will blame him if he makes this hard for you and hurts you. You've experienced enough loss. I don't want you to hurt." He pressed a soft kiss against my forehead as he said those lost words. I took a deep breath and planted my face in his chest.

He was such a good man.

A lot of men would be only too happy to get rid of someone who could potentially be their competition, but not Jason. He was worried that I would get hurt over this. And he was right. I would. If Nick couldn't accept Jason in my life, if our friendship wasn't enough for him, it would hurt losing him.

"He's a good guy. He'll get over it," I said with hope in my voice.

"I hope so, baby. 'Cause if he doesn't, he'll have to answer to me. And not just for putting his mouth on a woman who isn't his to kiss."

"He didn't get very far."

"Spare me the details, baby. I don't want to know. I can't guarantee to not hunt him down and hurt him if you give me a visual."

I kept my mouth shut.

"How's your head?" Jason asked after a few minutes of silence.

"Throbbing a little, but not too bad."

"Your throat?"

"Getting better."

"Good." He kissed my forehead once more. "Go to sleep."

Not long after, I did exactly that as Jason held me in his arms and his fingers had resumed drawing random patterns on my skin.

Fourteen

LORELEY

I woke up the next morning spooned by Jason. We were touching from shoulder to feet as he held me close. I could feel his breath as it brushed the skin on my neck where his face was buried. I knew he was awake, too, since his thumb was gently brushing back and forth over the knuckles of my hand he was holding.

"Good morning," I whispered sleepily.

"Morning," he returned as he placed a soft kiss right behind my ear. I shivered.

Waking up like this, cuddled and loved by Jason, was one of the best things in the world. I had missed it so much. I snuggled further into his heat and sighed contentedly. His arms tightened around me as his lips travelled from over my ear down the side of my neck.

"How are you feeling?" He whispered.

"Great," I breathed. I stretched my neck to give him better access and could feel his smile against my skin.

"Not sore?" His fingers had let go of mine and were travelling up my arm, over my shoulder, down my side until he found the edge of my shirt where they slightly caressed my bare

228

stomach. Those soft touches were driving me insane. I pushed my butt into his growing erection and moaned, asking for more. Jason laid his hand flat on my stomach and pressed in at the same time he ground his hips against me. My insides weren't the only things that fluttered at that contact and the promise it communicated. I slowly circled my hips against him and moaned again.

"Baby?" Jason asked through his chuckle.

"What?" I breathed. It was completely lost on me that he had asked me a question.

"Your head. Is it sore?"

It took me a second to focus on his question, already too lost in his touch and my desire for him to think clearly. Jason's hand on my stomach turned me so that I was on my back and he was on his side, half next to me, half on top of me. He grinned down at me as I stared up at him. His eyes ran over my face and stopped on my right cheek.

"It's bruised but it's not as bad as I thought it would be," he murmured as if speaking to himself. I took a quick inventory of my body. Both my cheek and my lip stung a little, and there was a dull distant pain at the back of my head, but it was much less than last night. My throat still felt a little scratchy, but that too, was better than I would have expected just a few hours ago. If I took it easy today and didn't talk too much or sing, I should be okay.

"I'm feeling okay. Much better than last night."

"Your head?" Jason asked again when his eyes came to mine.

"I can feel it a little if I think about it, but the throbbing is gone."

"Good." He leaned in and placed soft little kisses on the corner of my lip and my cheek, then switched direction and kissed along my neck. I hoped the bruising there wasn't too bad.

"This looks worse than your cheek. Does it hurt when I touch it?"

I shook my head. He placed more kisses there until he reached the other side, then moved up again and across my other cheek until he found my mouth. His hand was back at my stomach and was now moving with intend.

"I want to make love to my fiancée," he whispered seductively.

I wanted that, too.

I gasped and my hips twitched at the touch of light fingers over my panties. He found my clit through the fabric and pressed in gently, giving me more but not nearly enough. I pushed out against his hand, seeking more friction. He gave me what I wanted and pressed in harder and started to circle my nub. I closed my eyes and moaned again.

A second later, his hand was in my panties and his fingers were sliding through my folds.

"You're soaking wet," he growled. Then he lifted up, whipped his shirt over his head, and pulled his boxer briefs off so he was completely naked. He quickly divested me of my panties and my shirt and climbed between my legs. With his hands on my knees, he opened me wide and stared down at me.

"You're absolutely beautiful like this, spread open wide for me. I can see how wet you are." His hand grabbed his cock and he started pumping slowly, his eyes roaming my body. I couldn't help but lick my lips as I watched him pleasuring himself. I had always liked watching him when he did that. It was hot.

"God, the way you're looking at me right now...greedy, wanting me. Nothing is hotter than that."

I licked my lips again as my eyes found his. He radiated heat and hunger and the promise of desire and passion and love, and

230

I wanted all of it. I reached out with one hand and ran my nails over his chest, making him groan. His pupils dilated and his eyes turned into a dark brown. He let go of his cock and spread my legs even wider, holding them up at the back of my knees as he aligned himself with my entrance. Then with one long and smooth stroke he was inside of me, filling me. We both cried out at the pleasure of it. Jason instantly began to move with long and slow thrusts, making me feel all of him as he pulled out slowly then slammed back into me. He threw his head back and groaned. Nothing was hotter than seeing your man groaning because of you, because of how you felt around him, because of what you did. I wanted to move, to push against him, to make him go faster, but with the way he held me, I could do nothing but take what he had to give me.

And it was glorious.

"Jason," I breathed as he pushed me higher and higher.

"I feel it, baby. I feel your pussy clenching down on me. God, you feel so good."

My breaths were coming in pants. I was close. So close.

"Jason," I breathed again, desperate now, needing to come.

He started to move in earnest now, thrusting into me hard and fast over and over.

"Come on, baby. Let go. I want to feel you explode all around me!" One, two more thrusts and I cried out his name as I came. Vaguely, I heard him grunt then felt him still as Jason emptied himself inside of me with a loud groan.

When I came back down, Jason was sprawled on top of me, still breathing hard. I wrapped all four limbs around him and held him tight, burying my face in his neck the same way his was buried in mine. A few minutes later, our breaths had evened out and Jason started nibbling my neck.

"I missed waking up next to you," he echoed my thought

231

from earlier as he murmured against my sensitive skin, making me shiver once more. Unpleasant thoughts of him waking up next to other women entered my mind, but I pushed them away. It was in the past and thinking about it would do neither of us any good. Jason must have felt my body react to the thoughts though, because his head came out of my neck and he looked down at me.

"Never. I never woke up next to anyone else, Loreley. I never spent the night with anyone else. I couldn't bear the thought of being that intimate with anyone but you." My body relaxed under him. He kissed me, reassuring me. It was silly really, being jealous of the time he spent with other women when we were apart, but I couldn't help it.

Once again, Jason proved that he could read me better than anyone. "It's only ever been you, Loreley. I was broken without you. I was hollow, a shell. I knew that no woman could ever fill the hole that was left behind when I lost you, so I didn't even try. Nobody compared. Nobody will *ever* compare to what I feel for you. You're my best friend, my soul mate, my everything. I'm nothing without you." His sincere eyes bore into mine. Then he lowered his lips for a soft and loving touch and whispered there, "Only you."

"Only me," I repeated.

"Always. Forever." Another soft touch.

"Always," I whispered. "Forever."

And just like that, the jealousy was gone. Jason's heart and soul were mine. They always had been and they always would be.

Just like mine were his.

My head was feeling better, yet not quite good enough to go for a run. Since we'd had a long wait at the hospital and got home late last night, Jason and I had slept in and it was now almost ten o'clock.

Dressed in cut-off jeans shorts and my Rolling Stones t-shirt, I padded from the kitchen to the living room on my bare feet and found Jason staring at the photographs that were arranged on my mantle. I watched as he retrieved one that showed Jesse on his first Halloween. He'd only been nine months old and had looked super cute in his little cowboy outfit. Jason smiled as he touched the glass protecting the picture then put it back to inspect another one. My mantle was covered, showing pictures of Jesse and me throughout the years, sometimes the both of us, sometimes just him, sometimes with other family members or friends.

"I brought you more coffee." Jason turned at my words and reached out for the mug I was holding out to him. He took it and used his other arm to pull me into his side. Leaning into him, I took in the photographs of our son. I couldn't imagine what it must feel like for Jason to know he would only ever see Jesse in pictures.

"I have tons of pictures and videos if you want to see them."

"I want that. Very much so. I want to see everything you have and hear every story you can remember." His voice sounded wistful.

I leaned up to kiss the side of his neck then headed to the bench under the window where I stored all my photo albums and opened it. Jason followed me and sat down cross-legged on the floor when I handed him the first album with Jesse's baby pictures. I sat down beside him, our shoulders touching.

The first pictures were of me pregnant, starting probably somewhere around my fifth month in. Jason gasped when he watched my tummy grow bigger and bigger in the pictures. There were pictures of me up to a few days before delivery.

"So damn beautiful," he whispered reverently and my heart

233

skipped a beat.

He stopped when he came to the first picture that had ever been taken of our son. We were at the hospital, about an hour or so after Jesse was born, and I was smiling huge as I was holding him in my arms. I remembered that moment like it had been just yesterday. I remembered the absolute and pure bliss of seeing my baby boy for the first time, of holding him, touching him, and smelling him. He had been so beautiful I couldn't take my eyes off him and had stared at him for hours. Jason looked at the picture for a long time.

"Perfect. He was perfect." His voice sounded strangled. He touched the picture with his finger, slowly running it over his son's face over and over again as if he was stroking his cheek in wonderment. "You look so happy."

"I was. It was the most beautiful moment of my life." It was hard telling him this, knowing he wasn't there with me to experience the beauty of that moment, knowing he would never get that back. I wanted to give him something to make him feel part of what I experienced, something that he could hold on to, that was only his and mine and Jesse's. So I told him everything from the beginning, how and when I found out I was pregnant, where I had been, how I had felt; what food I had craved during pregnancy; my mood swings and crying jags; all my wishes and dreams, my worries and my anxiety; my excitement. I told him everything from what colors I had chosen for Jesse's nursery to the first outfits I had bought; from my heart melting at seeing Jesse's first smile to my heart stopping at having to take him to emergency because he had a high fever that wouldn't go down. I shared all my emotions with him as Jason turned page after page, all my joy and all my worries, my elation and exhaustion, all my memories. Because they were his just as much as they were mine and if life had been fair, Jason would have been here

234

to experience every single one of those moments with us.

We sat for hours, me mostly talking, him mostly listening, as we went through every last one of my photo albums and Jason got to know his son. There was a lot of laughter and there were a few tears. When the last page was turned and he had looked at the last photo I had ever taken of Jesse for a good long while, he closed the book and looked at me with love and gratitude and pride and joy shining in his eyes. There was still some sadness left, and I supposed there always would be when either one of us thought about our son, but the joy and happiness outweighed the heartache.

"Do you know how truly amazing you are? You have given me something I thought I would never be able to feel. You made me feel like I knew him, as if I was here with you to watch him grow and watch him experience life. Thank you for giving me my son." His voice was low and full of emotion.

Words left me as tears stung my eyes at the beauty of what he just said. I opened my mouth to say something, anything, but nothing came out. Jason smiled the most beautiful smile I had ever seen him smile right before he leaned down and kissed me softly, reverently, lovingly.

"I have videos, too," I whispered when he ended the kiss and held me there with his eyes. Jason stilled for a second then threw his head back and burst out laughing. He let himself fall onto the carpet and pulled me with him so that I was lying on top of him. It felt so glorious that warmth filled me and all I could do was watch. This was what I had lived for all those years ago, to see true happiness on Jason's face and knowing that I was responsible for it.

And now I had it back.

Jason's laughter died down to a chuckle and he kissed me again while his body was still shaking. That felt great, too.

"You could hear his voice, hear him laugh," I whispered.

The mirth left his eyes as he comprehended the meaning of my words. "I would love that." His voice was rough with emotion and yearning.

"He had your laugh," I smiled down at him. "Hearing it, knowing he was happy and knowing I was partly responsible for his happiness made everything else in my life less important. Just like with you."

"You really mean that, don't you?" Jason asked, amazed.

"I do."

"God, I love you." He did. I could see it in his eyes, could see it all over his face. He truly loved me with every single fibre of his being.

"I love you, too," I replied, overwhelmed by the love I was feeling for him.

He kissed me once more, a soft lip touch that conveyed everything I could see in his eyes.

"Let's watch our son," Jason said, his voice full of anticipation. Then he sat up and took me with him.

"It's fascinating how much he was the perfect blend of you and me."

We were still sitting on the floor, now hunched over the computer while we were watching a video of Jesse and Chris and I during a water gun fight at my dad's July 4th barbeque. Jesse and Chris had snuck up on me with their water guns—not surprising since they were always in cahoots together—and had mercilessly attacked me. But when Chris had me on the ground, Jesse had turned traitor on Chris and protected his mom. He tackled him and emptied his whole water gun in Chris' face.

Jason chuckled. "He was protective of you."

"Yeah. He was a great kid."

"The best."

"The best," I repeated.

"And we'll have lots more."

I laughed silently. "How many more are we talking?"

His eyes came from the screen to mine. "At least three."

My eyebrows shot up in surprise. "At least? What does that mean?"

"It means I liked what I saw in those pictures of you pregnant." His voice was low and full of meaning. His eyes had turned dark and promising.

Oh my.

I remember being extremely horny when I was pregnant. Not having a partner to get that type of release with had been more than frustrating. My vibrator had seen a lot of action during those months.

My eyes glazed over and I licked my lips. It had only been a few hours since we'd last had sex, but I wanted him again. It felt like my body needed to make up for lost time. And I could tell that Jason had the same need. But before either of us could do something about it, my phone rang.

I jumped and looked at the screen to see who it was.

"It's Rick," I said, puzzled. Jason's jaw tensed either at the mention of Rick or the interruption, I wasn't sure, but he gave me a small nod to answer the phone.

"Rick? What's up?"

"You forget something?" He sounded put out. I scowled.

"I don't think so."

"You forget what happened last night?"

Oh shit. I had.

I had been so wrapped up in Jason and Jesse that I had completely forgotten about going into the station to press charges.

"Ivey came down already to give her statement, but I can't

hold him much longer without yours."

Shit again. I hadn't thought about that.

My eyes darted to Jason when he made a move to get up, then went to his hand when he held it out for me. He must have heard what Rick said. I took his hand and let him pull me up.

"I'm sorry, Rick. We'll be right here. Give us ten minutes."

"All right. I'll be here. Bring coffee." Then he hung up.

"He's not happy that I forgot," I told Jason. He was pulling me towards the front door.

"He'll get over it." He sounded annoyed.

"You okay?"

Jason sighed. He stopped in front of the door and turned to me. His hands clasped my face and he leaned his head down until our foreheads touched.

"I'm fine. Just annoyed at life interrupting our moment." He kissed my nose. "I enjoyed our little family bubble." I wrapped my arms around his waist and pressed my lower body into his, keeping our foreheads connected.

"Me, too. We'll be a family soon enough and have lots more of those moments, I promise."

His lips came to mine where he murmured, "We're already a family."

My heart melted and I surrendered to his kiss.

We were at the police station. Rick had just told us that it wasn't likely that Brad would actually stay in jail for much longer.

"I reckon he'll get out on bail, so you gotta be careful, Lore."

"You telling me she's in danger from that asshole?" Jason was tense beside me. He had gotten more and more tense by the second as I gave my statement and rehashed the events from last night.

"She could be. Brad is a proud man and he's holding a grudge. If you had asked me last week, I wouldn't have believed he would seek her out with the intent to put his hands on her after what happened last week with me as a witness. It was stupid, but he has proven before that he's not necessarily the sharpest knife in the drawer. So I want her to be careful just in case."

"I'll be careful," I said at the same time Jason said, "She'll be safe. I've got my bodyguard fly in this afternoon. He'll keep an eye on her and so will I."

"Good. I'll keep an eye out, too."

Jason didn't respond.

This had the potential of turning into yet another pissing contest. I couldn't blame Jason for wanting to mark his territory so to speak, especially after what had happened last night with Nick, so I decided to not comment and stay out of it other than to squeeze Jason's hand in reassurance.

We left shortly after that.

When we stepped out of the police station, we were greeted by a couple of paparazzi.

"Remember what I said," Jason murmured into my ear, "Ignore them. Don't look at them or answer their questions. Pretend they're not here." I nodded. Jason had his arm around my shoulder as we walked down the sidewalk. It was hard not to look when I heard the shutters on their cameras click.

"I'm starving."

I turned my head and looked at Jason's profile as we kept walking. He met my eyes and grinned.

"I could cook us lunch, but we don't have any food in the house. We'd have to stop at the grocery store before we head home."

"How about I take my fiancée to lunch?"

I smiled at him, loving it when he called me his fiancée. Judging by the huge grin on his face, he loved it just as much.

"Your fiancée would love that."

"Then lunch it is." He gave me a quick peck on the lips. "Where to?"

"Have you tried the shakes at the diner yet?"

Jason shook his head, smirking. "Nope."

"Then let's go there. You'll love them. Tom's got all the flavours you could possibly imagine and you can mix and match as many as you want." Jason chuckled at my excitement and kissed me again.

"They've got all the flavours you could possibly imagine and you pick chocolate?" Jason sounded amused but not surprised.

"Double chocolate. But what can I say? I'm a sucker for anything chocolate."

"I remember," he muttered as he perused the menu.

"All right, folks, what can I get you today?" Martha was standing beside the table, pen at the ready.

"I'll have the double chocolate shake and a burger with fries."

"Ever thought of mixing it up a bit, darling? Maybe try something new?" Martha asked dryly. Jason chuckled.

"Nope," I said. "I like what I like."

"Ain't that the truth?" She murmured through a small smile then looked at Jason and waited for his order.

"I'll try the strawberry banana shake and the BLT, heavy on the B." Jason said.

"Coming right up." Martha took our menus and headed towards the counter.

"I want you to come with me this afternoon."

I frowned at him in confusion. "Come with you where?"

"To pick up Frank from the airport."

Ah. Frank, the bodyguard. "What airport?"

"He's flying into Denver. There wasn't a flight open to Boulder until tomorrow and I wanted him here as soon as possible." Denver was almost a two-hour drive away, which would make it a trip of at least four hours if it wasn't busy at the airport.

"I'd love to come with you but I've got to catch up on all the paperwork. I didn't really get much done this week." Jason didn't like that. "I'll be okay, Jason. Brad is still in jail and I'll be safe in my office. Mark is gonna be there, too. It'll be okay." Jason sighed. He still didn't like it but he was giving in.

"When do you have to leave?" I asked.

"In about an hour. I'll walk you to the bar from here. Do you mind if I take your car?" My girl was still at the bar from last night. We hadn't gotten around to picking her up yet.

I shrugged. "Sure. I don't mind." I wouldn't need it anyway.

"Promise me you'll stay inside the bar. I don't want you alone with those weasels."

I rolled my eyes. "I promise."

Jason glared at me. "I mean it, Loreley. They can be mean motherfuckers and I don't want you alone with them."

"I know. You've said that already. Though honestly, I don't know what the big deal is. Yeah, I was a little overwhelmed at first last night, but I think I can handle ignoring them when you're not around, now that I know what I'm dealing with."

"I'm not doubting you can. I don't want you to have to."

Luckily, Martha came with our milk shakes and we dropped the subject.

Fifteen

LORELEY

"Yo Lore!"

I lifted my head from the computer screen where I was finishing up the schedule for the coming week at hearing Mark's call. I had caught up on all the paperwork that had accumulated over the past week. Writing up the new schedule was the last thing on my list. Jason had been gone for almost five hours now and should be back soon. Mark appeared in the door. "Someone's here to see you."

I frowned. "Who?" I didn't have any appointments or meetings today. Mark shrugged his shoulders. "No clue. She didn't say." He turned around and headed back the way he came without saying anything else. I looked back at the screen to quickly finish the schedule and smiled to myself. Jason would be pleased. I had decided to take a little break and only schedule myself in when nobody else was available, giving me most of the week off. I couldn't wait to spend time with each other to catch up and just be together.

I printed off a copy and tacked it to the board before I switched the computer off and left the office, locking the door behind me.

When I turned into the bar, I saw Mark talking to a pretty blonde. He was leaning on his elbows on the counter and flirting his face off. I shook my head and smiled. Mark loved all women and never hesitated to make that obvious. They never admitted to it, but I knew that he and Chris had a little competition going about who could bag women the fastest. It was disgusting, but I couldn't help but be amused at how they all threw themselves at the two men even though they knew the score. This one though didn't seem to be interested in Mark's advances at all. She looked bored and annoyed as she sat on the stool in front of him and tapped her manicured fingernails against the wood of the bar. I couldn't say why but I instantly disliked her. It could be the way she was made up with her blond hair curled to perfection and her face smothered in make-up, or maybe it was the snarky and uppity expression she had on her face. Whatever it was, she seemed like an arrogant bitch.

I looked away from her and scanned the room, trying to figure out who it was that needed to see me. It was still early, especially for a Sunday, but there were a few people already milling about, chatting over a bottle of beer. Nobody seemed to be waiting for me though.

"Hey Mark, who was it you said wanted to see me?" I turned my eyes back to him and saw that the blonde was now looking at me. She was studying me from top to bottom with a sneer on her face.

What the hell was her problem?

I ignored her and fixed my eyes on Mark. He tilted his head and jerked his chin in the direction of the blonde, indicating it was she who was waiting for me. "This beautiful and charming young lady asked to speak to you." I raised my eyebrows in disbelief, not only at Mark calling her charming and a lady when anyone with eyes could see that she was anything but, but also in

243

confusion as to why she would want to talk to me. I didn't think she was looking for a job and even if she were, I would never consider hiring her. She had *bitch* written all over her and would undoubtedly cause more trouble than she was worth.

I walked behind the bar to stand beside Mark and faced her. She was still looking at me with that sneer on her face, but there was also a small smug smile tugging at the corners of her lips that I did not like.

"What can I do for you?" I asked as politely as I could, which wasn't very polite at all.

"I don't get it," she murmured as if talking to herself while she looked me up and down once more.

"You don't get what?" I really didn't like her and the way she eyed me. She met my eyes. They were filled with hatred and bitterness. I flinched involuntarily.

"I'm not really here for you. I'm here for Jason."

I stiffened at her mention of Jason. Did he know her? Had he been with her? The way she eyed me certainly made it seem like he had. She was still studying me as if she was scoping out her competition.

"If you need to speak to Jason, then why did you ask for me? Why come here?"

She shrugged her bony shoulders. "I was curious."

"Curious about what?" I prompted when she just kept looking at me down her nose without saying more. I could imagine what she was curious about, but for some twisted reason, I wanted to hear her say it.

"Curious as to why he left L.A. in such a rush. I have to say, I'm disappointed. How he can go from someone like me to someone like you in less than two weeks is beyond me."

My heart dropped and my stomach twisted. Her words confirmed it. Jason had been with this woman and the way she

244

made it sound, it had been for more than just a one-night stand. She talked and behaved like the scorned ex-girlfriend who wouldn't go down without a fight. I took a deep breath through my nose and told myself to calm down, to tamp down the jealousy that was slicing through my body like a hot vice. Jason had said that none of the women he had been with meant anything to him; that he had been in love with me this whole time. I was the only one who had ever been his girlfriend, the only one he had ever spent the night with and woken up with. And I believed him.

I lifted my chin and gave her a dismissive look. "Well, you can leave now that your curiosity is satisfied. Jason isn't here." I said through clenched teeth. I wanted this woman gone. I knew she was no threat to me. Still, knowing Jason had had sex with other women was one thing, but seeing one of them face to face and having to talk to her was another. It hurt like a bitch and was shredding me on the inside, but there was no way I was going to let her see my inner turmoil. So I locked my face into what I hoped was an impassive expression and held her eyes.

"But he'll be back, won't he?" I didn't say anything, couldn't say anything for fear of either taking a lunge and bitch slap her or letting my hurt get the better of me and let the tears I could feel at the back of my eyes come out—and I would not give her that satisfaction. "He'll be back soon enough. And I'll be waiting right here."

Oh, no.

She was *not* waiting here. And I wasn't going to watch while she threw herself at my man, which I knew without a doubt was her intention. I wouldn't be able to control myself.

"You want to talk to Jason, you can wait for him outside."

She smiled that knowing little smug smile at me that I did not like and made my stomach clench in foreboding. "You're

245

not going to kick me out." She sounded sure. Too sure.

"I'm not?" I asked sarcastically, my eyebrows raised.

"No."

"And why is that?" I really didn't want to know the answer to that but I wouldn't give her the pleasure of backing down.

Her smile widened and I stiffened further. "Because if you do, I will find someone who will be more than happy to break the story of how the famous rock god Jason Sanders got me pregnant."

My whole body locked in shock and hurt. My heart stopped beating and my stomach dropped. I couldn't breathe. The word *pregnant* was repeating itself over and over in my head, ripping me apart. I stood, unable to move or say anything, and watched as she rummaged through her purse and pulled out a piece of paper. She laid it on the bar in front of me and I knew immediately what it was.

It was proof.

An ultrasound picture.

I couldn't look at it, couldn't look at the baby that was Jason's but not mine.

I started swaying and had to put a hand out to catch the edge of the bar so I wouldn't fall. Someone grabbed my arm and said my name, but I couldn't place who it was. My mind was consumed with the knowledge that Jason was going to have a baby with someone else. The bar door opened and I immediately caught Jason's eyes as he walked in. His were smiling but turned into worried and alarmed the instant he took me in. Before I could blink, he was behind the bar and I was in his arms.

"Loreley? Baby, what's the matter?"

The arms that only a few hours ago had given me love and comfort and safety now felt constricting and suffocating, so I pushed him away and took a step back.

"What—" Jason asked, confused. I saw his blurry body step toward me as tears were running down my face.

"Well, well, well," I heard the bitch taunt. I kept my eyes on Jason. I couldn't look at the woman who was going to share her future with Jason, who was going to be bound to him for the rest of his life. I was going to lose him. As soon as he found out he was going to be a father, he would walk away from me to be with his child's mother. He had lost out on Jesse. He wouldn't make that mistake again.

Jason's head whipped around to her and I saw recognition and horror hit his face.

Oh God. It was true. He knew her.

"What are you doing here?" He sounded angry. "I told you I wouldn't talk to you unless my lawyer was present."

What?

"Well, I couldn't let you shack it up with your old flame while I carried your baby, now could I?" She sounded like Jason already knew she was pregnant.

"You fucking bitch!"

"You knew?" My voice sounded croaky and was little more than a whisper, but Jason heard me. His head whipped back to me, his eyes softening.

"Loreley, baby—"

"You already knew she was pregnant?" My voice was getting stronger, since with the realization that he had known and hadn't told me came my anger.

"Yes, I knew, but—"

"You knew and you didn't tell me?" He was coming towards me, his arms raised to hold me, but I backed up further.

"I...I can't do this," I said in a broken whisper before I turned to escape through the front door. He had known and had

247

kept it a secret from me. All that talk yesterday about wanting to see me pregnant, about wanting to start a family with me, about me being the only woman he could ever imagine having a baby with was bullshit. He was already having a baby with another woman. Why he would say all that to me and why he would even come back at all I couldn't fathom, but I couldn't think about that now. I had to get away. I ran across the bar, trying and failing in the effort to block out the images of Jason holding and loving and adoring a baby that wasn't mine. If they had a daughter, I knew he would adore her and do everything to keep his little princess happy, a princess who would look like the blonde, not like me. And if they had a son…I had to cover my mouth so I wouldn't be overcome by loud and body racking sobs. A son would be the replacement for Jesse. Feeling like this might make me a bitch, but I didn't care. It was too much to bear.

I ran for the door as fast as I could but I didn't make it. Halfway across the room, I felt a hand grip my upper arm and turn me around. A second later, my back was pushed against the wall and Jason was less than an inch away from my face. His body was pushing against mine, trapping me.

"You promised me you wouldn't run." He sounded angry and disappointed.

"You lied to me, Jason," I spit in his face. "You knew about her being pregnant and you didn't tell me."

Jason's grip on me tightened and he gave me a small shake, "Yes, I knew and didn't tell you because it's of no consequence to us."

My eyebrows shot up in shocked surprise. He couldn't be serious. How could he not think having a child with another woman was not affect us? "What? How can you say that? That's your child you're talking about. You already missed out on Jesse and—"

Another shake to shut me up. "It's not true, Loreley. There is no child. Or if there is, it sure as hell isn't mine." I stilled as his words sunk in.

"She's not pregnant? But she has proof. She has an ultrasound picture—"

"I don't know about that. What I *do* know is that if she is, it isn't mine."

"How can you be sure?" He couldn't be unless he had done a paternity test.

Jason sighed. "Because we checked into it. She came to me a few months ago, claiming she was pregnant and that it was mine. But when I started asking questions, she got all vague on me, so I dug a little deeper and found out that she has done shit like this before. Several times actually. To other musicians, movie stars, take your pick. And it's always been lies to trap them into marrying her or milking them for money. She disappeared when I threatened her with a lawyer."

Okay, that made me feel slightly better.

But there was still the issue of the ultrasound picture. She clearly had proof that she was pregnant this time and it could be Jason's.

"She has a picture, Jason, an ultrasound picture. How do you know it's not yours? You won't know for sure unless you take a test—"

"I don't need a test, baby. I'm sure." He sounded it, but I kept pushing. "How?"

"Because I slept with her six months ago. Does she look six months pregnant to you?"

I looked over Jason's shoulder to the bar where she was still sitting on her stool. Her eyes were on us and they were smug and full of glee. My eyes went down to her stomach. To her flat

249

stomach. There was no bulge, no nothing. She wore a tight skirt, so it was easy to see that there was no way she was six months along. I looked back at Jason. His eyes had stayed on me and he was still pressing me against the wall as if he was afraid I would make another dash for it.

I shook my head. "No, she doesn't look like she's six months pregnant."

"You believe me then?" I bit my bottom lip.

"You swear it's been six months since you slept with her?" Jason nodded. His eyes were serious and sincere.

"Then I believe you," I whispered.

"Good," he whispered then softly kissed my forehead. I lowered my eyes and looked at his chest. I took a deep breath and tried to relax into his body. He pulled me close, but I couldn't fully release the stiffness that had my body in its grip. How many more women would come and claim Jason had knocked them up? How many more women would try and take him away from me?

Jason tipped my chin up with his finger to catch my eyes. He studied me for a few seconds then stated firmly, "No."

"No?" I questioned, doubt clear in my voice. I knew he knew what I was thinking.

"No, Loreley. Nobody else will try and claim me as the father of their child. I told you, I've always been careful. And I haven't slept with anyone but you in months." My eyebrows hit my hairline in surprise. Jason smiled a self-deprecating smile before he brushed his lips against mine. "I'll explain later. Now, are we over this?"

I nodded. "I'm sorry. I thought...I couldn't stand the thought of—"

"I know, baby. Neither could I. I get it."

I pressed my lips against his. He accepted my apology and

kissed me back fiercely, his arms going around me and pulling me closer, which finally made me relax and accept the comforting warmth and strength of his body. When he ended the kiss, he gave me one last assessing look before he took my hand and led me back to the bar where the bitch was still sitting on her stool, now staring daggers at me. I held her eyes and narrowed mine.

"You'll be hearing from my lawyer. And prepare, bitch. I'll be making some phone calls. I'm sure I'm not the only one who would love a little revenge and shut your shit down permanently." The bitch's eyes turned panicky when Jason delivered that warning in a scathing voice. The guy standing beside her chuckled. I looked at him. He was huge and scary looking. His eyes were on Jason.

"All good?" He asked.

"Yeah. It's all good." Jason squeezed my hand. "Get that bitch out of here, Frank." Oh, so this was Frank. His eyes came to me. "Nice to finally meet you," he said.

"Hey," I greeted him on a short wave of my hand, making him chuckle again. Then his face lost all its humor and became dead serious. "I've heard a lot about you. I'm glad this motherfucker finally got his head out of his ass and I'm even more glad you took his sorry ass back." Jason chuckled as I stared at Frank. I watched as he turned and grabbed the bitch—whose name I still didn't know and didn't care to know, I just wanted her gone—by the arm and kept watching as he dragged her off the stool and out of the bar.

Jason's hand on my cheek turned me to look at him. He brushed his thumb across my cheekbone while pulling me closer to his body with the hand that was still holding mine. He let go of my hand when my body was touching his and placed his hand on my other cheek, cupping my face, while I held on to his

251

wrists. His face was tipped down to mine, his serious eyes holding mine captive.

"No more running." His voice was just as serious as his eyes. He was disappointed that I hadn't let him explain, that I had believed someone else and making assumptions. I bit my lip and nodded. He moved his face closer to mine until our noses touched. "I understand why this is hard and I get why that one got to you. Believe me, I do. Just the thought about you sharing a child with another man makes me feel violent." He closed his eyes for a second and took a deep breath before he kept talking. "Promise me, Loreley. Promise me no matter what you hear or see, no matter how hurt or angry you might be, no matter what life throws at us, promise me you come to me and let me explain. You don't run. You don't shut me out. You talk to me."

I nodded and whispered, "I'm sorry." I felt awful. I had promised him I would trust him and then went back on that promise at the first hurdle.

He kissed the top of my nose then brushed his lips against mine. "Don't be. I get it." He swallowed and gave me an apprehensive look. "Courtney's shenanigans were one of the reasons why I finally got my head out of my ass as Frank calls it and went after you."

Courtney? Who was Courtney?

Jason must have seen the confusion on my face. "The bitch I just sent packing," he explained.

Ah. That made sense.

"I panicked when she first told me she was pregnant and said it was mine. I panicked because I didn't want a child with her, or anyone, but you. You were whom I saw in my mind when she told me. You, your smile, the feel of your touch. You, becoming my wife, holding our baby, raising our children with me. I knew if I had a child with anyone else, I would lose you forever and it gutted me. I couldn't stand it. I'm not proud of it because I didn't know then she was trying to play me, but I lashed out and immediately doubted her. I didn't know then what I know now, but it didn't matter. I didn't want that child. It might make me an asshole, but I don't care. Good thing I did what I did since it became crystal clear pretty damn fast that she was lying." He paused as his eyes roamed my face, reading me. "What I'm trying to say is, her lie gave me the push I needed. I stopped drinking, stopped sleeping around, and told Frank to find out where you lived so I could go after you and get you back. And make no mistake, Loreley, I would have trampled anyone and anything in my way to get you back. You are mine. You always have been and always will be. Just like I am yours. Yours alone. You understand?"

I nodded again. "I understand." And I did. We belonged to each other. He was mine and I was his and I had to trust that everything would be okay, that we would make it through whatever life threw at us as long as we believed in each other, as long as we believed in *us*. We had forgiven each other and ourselves for what had happened and now it was time to move on together.

"Good," Jason murmured against my lips before he took them in a fierce and deep kiss. I pressed against him and responded in kind, completely losing myself in the taste and feel of him, forgetting everything else around us.

It took someone clearing his throat for us to stop devouring each other's mouths. "There a reason why a guy as big as a tank is standing outside the bar glaring at a blonde who is spitting fire and cussing him out?" It was Chris. He was here to start his shift.

"Shit," Jason swore under his breath. "Any photographers out there?"

Chris nodded. "A few. Less than last night though."

253

"That stupid bitch," Jason grumbled. Chris' eyebrows shot up in question. "You know her?" His eyes went to me and I shook my head, indicating I would tell him later.

"Yeah, I know her." Jason left it at that and Chris didn't push any further. A few moments later, Frank came back inside and stopped at our little huddle. He gave Jason a look I couldn't quite decipher other than that it was annoyed. Jason clenched his teeth and turned to me when Frank introduced himself to Chris.

"Everything okay?" I asked.

"Yeah. Frank is pissed at me. He told me months ago to shut Courtney down. Told me to not give her a chance to regroup. Looks like he was right."

"I usually am. You just choose to ignore me." Frank muttered. I saw a muscle jump in Jason's cheek at being admonished like that and couldn't help but laugh silently. He shook his head at me, but I could see the corner of his lips twitch infinitesimally.

"You ready to go?" He changed the subject.

"Yeah. I'm all done and Chris is here now so we're good to go."

"All right. Let's go." He grabbed my hand, lacing his fingers through mine, and we headed to the front door, followed by Frank. I turned and gave Chris a goodbye-wave over my shoulder, to which he responded with a chin lift and a small smile.

Outside, I saw that there was no sign of Courtney, but the photographers were still there. As soon as we exited the bar, the cameras started to click and requests about looking this way and smiling were shouted our way along with questions about who the blonde was Frank had just kicked out. Frank moved in front of us as if to shield us, and Jason swung his arm loosely over my shoulder and kissed my temple. My arm went around his hip in response and I leaned into him until it was time to let go when Jason opened the driver's side door for me and asked me to slip in the back so that Frank could sit in the front with him. I grumbled but did as I was asked. Frank chuckled and so did Jason.

"Sweet ride," Frank said when we were all in the car and driving to my dad's house. It was his turn for our weekly family dinner. "How long have you had it for?"

"My dad gave it to me for college graduation. It took him years, but he completely rebuilt it for me." Jason met my eyes in the rear view mirror.

"Nice. Sounds like you have a cool dad." Frank stated. I did. My dad was one of the best people I knew. He had always been there for me, had always been supportive even if he didn't like the choices I had made. I smiled as I remembered coming back from L.A., scared, heartbroken, and disillusioned, when he had given me the car.

"Looks like we're gonna have to go out and find a car seat that fits in the back of the Shelby," was all he had said when I had fessed up about being pregnant and alone. He had adored Jesse from the moment he laid eyes on him and hadn't been happy when after five months of living with him, we moved out of his house. But, like he always did, he had understood that that was what I'd needed. My dad was the best and I was immensely grateful and felt blessed for having him in my life.

I still had a small smile on my lips and my eyes met Jason's in the mirror again when I answered Frank. "Yeah, he's the best." Jason's eyes weren't smiling. They were contemplative. It took me a second to figure it out what he was thinking about, but when I did, my body stilled.

He was thinking of the accident, wondering what car I had

been driving if I'd had the Shelby for six years.

The accident that had killed Jesse was something we hadn't talked about. So far, I had shared as much as I possibly could in the short time we'd had about Jesse's life but I hadn't shared about his death. Even after all the therapy and grief counselling I had gone through, it was still extremely hard to even think about that day. Jason deserved to know what had happened and he deserved to hear it from me, but I wasn't sure I could do it. I looked away from him and stared out the side window.

"I...it wasn't...we weren't..." I stopped and closed my eyes, trying to bring up the strength to tell him. "We weren't in this car. The Shelby was at the garage for an oil change. I was driving dad's car." My voice sounded empty and sad and my throat was clogged. I still didn't look at Jason but kept my gaze out the side window instead. A lone tear I couldn't hold back travelled down my cheek.

The next thing I knew, Jason pulled over and stopped at the side of the road, got out of the car, pulled me out of the back, and I was in his arms. He held me tightly and kissed the top of my head as I hid my face in the crook of his neck and sniffed quietly. It had only been a year since the accident and even though I was coming to terms with Jesse's death, thinking about how it had happened brought back all the emotions I had felt that day and I had to work hard to not let them overwhelm me.

Jason didn't say anything. All he did was hold me as I got control of myself and that was exactly what I needed: just him and his arms around me holding me tight, keeping me safe and giving me comfort.

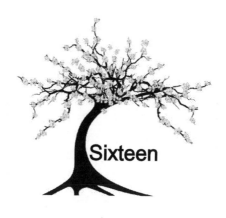

Sixteen

JASON

Jason was standing at the railing of the back deck in Roy's backyard, taking a deep pull from his beer and looking out over the trees that backed onto Roy's property. He needed a minute after the episode during the drive here.

When Loreley had calmed down enough to the point she wasn't shaking anymore, he had guided her back into the car. Frank had moved to the backseat so that Jason could hold Loreley's hand during the rest of the drive. He had needed that connection and he could tell that Loreley had needed it just as much. He had felt helpless at seeing her like that, fighting against her emotions while she was shaking in his arms, holding on for dear life. He couldn't imagine what it must have felt like to see your son die like that. Losing a child was hard enough to deal with as it was, but to actually be on the scene of the accident was something different altogether. He wanted to take away the pain Loreley was feeling, was desperate for it, and felt completely powerless knowing that he couldn't. All he could do was be there for her and hold her, be her rock, her anchor. It was something, and it felt good that he could give that to her, that she accepted it, but it was nowhere near enough. The sorrow and devastation

257

had poured off of her almost to the point where he could taste it on his tongue. It broke his heart.

And it brought back the guilt.

The guilt at not having been there for her when it happened. The guilt at knowing that for the past year, his Loreley had to deal with the anguish and grief the loss of their son had brought without having him by her side to be her rock. Yes, she'd had her family, but he couldn't help but think that his presence would have made a difference in how she would have dealt with Jesse's death. He blamed himself, and that guilt weighed heavily on his shoulders.

So he needed a minute to collect himself.

He took another deep pull of his beer. All the men were out on the deck with him: Roy, Pete, Cal, and Frank. The women and Tommy were in the kitchen getting dinner ready and setting the table, and Jason was grateful that he had a minute without Loreley. He didn't want her to feel bad for upsetting him, which she undoubtedly would. His Loreley felt deep, always had. Another reason why he couldn't imagine what the past year had been like for her.

"Jace. Take it easy, man." It was Frank. His voice was neutral, but Jason could hear the worry and warning in it. A warning about not getting carried away. He couldn't blame him. This was what he had been like whenever he felt the need to drown his sorrows during the past six years. Removed and lost in his own thoughts, a quick beer that lead to a dozen more, everything he could do to forget the face and the memories that kept haunting him. But Frank didn't need to worry. This was different. Jason wasn't drinking to get smashed because he was trying to forget. If he were a smoker, he'd be smoking a cigarette right now instead of drinking a beer to calm down his nerves. He didn't care about the alcohol or its effects. He just needed something to do with his hands while he tried to sort his raw emotions.

"It's all right, Frank," he assured him as he took the last sip and placed the empty bottle on the railing.

He could feel everyone's eyes on him, but nobody spoke as Jason leaned his elbows on the railing and buried his face in his hands. He didn't know how long exactly he stayed like that. It seemed like a long time even though it could only have been a few minutes before he lifted his head again and broke the silence. Without turning around, he made his request.

"Right here, right now I need you to tell me exactly what happened the day my son died. I need to know so I can process it and be there for Loreley. I won't ask her to tell me. It's too painful for her. I refuse to make her go through that." He knew what he was asking. Just the thought of hearing about the accident and the suffering and heartache that followed made pain slice through his body and his gut clench, but he had no choice. He had to know not only for himself but for the two of them as a couple. He needed to understand what Loreley had been through if he had any hope of helping her through it, of helping her heal to a point where she wouldn't break out in a sweat and start shaking uncontrollably whenever she thought about that day.

Another minute went by without anyone speaking. Jason turned around and took in the men that would soon be his family. Roy and Pete looked at him with immeasurable sadness in their eyes. Cal was staring at the ground, his jaw clenched and his eyes wild with emotion. He was the first to talk.

"It was bad, Jason. Seeing her like that...." he shook his head. "It was bad." Jason could hear the desolation in Cal's voice. Cal was a man's man through and through: strong, protective, respected. Watching the person he considered his

259

sister suffer had broken his heart. Jason closed his eyes and hung his head.

"What happened?" He asked.

"She had to borrow my truck that day." It was Roy who spoke this time. "And thank God she did because if she hadn't, we would have lost her, too." His voice broke on the last word. Jason looked at Loreley's father and saw grief and loss written all over his face. Loreley wasn't the only one who hadn't completely healed, if that was even possible. Each one of these men was still suffering and probably would be for the rest of their lives. Jason felt like a jackass asking them to share, but Loreley was his priority, so he couldn't let that penetrate.

Pete was the one who gave it to him, all of it, in its raw and suffocating detail.

"She was on her way to drop off Jesse at a friend's house for a birthday party. They were going to have a sleepover, camping in the backyard. Jesse had been excited for weeks." A small smile played at Pete's lips but it didn't reach his eyes. He was looking straight ahead, lost in the memory. "It happened just outside of town. An SUV t-boned her at the intersection. Tourists. Teenagers out for a drive in their daddy's car. It wasn't her fault. She had the right of way, but they ignored the stop sign and smashed right into her passenger side, the side where Jesse was sitting in the backseat." Jason closed his eyes and tried to swallow past the lump in his throat. "The truck was pushed and turned around by the force of the impact but it didn't tip over. If she had been in the Shelby…" Jason didn't want to think about what would have happened if she had been driving the Mustang. "Loreley got banged up a little, but was fine. She pulled Jesse from the car and started CPR." Now it was Pete's voice that broke and he took a second to collect himself before he continued. "Rick had to pull her off him. He was the first one on scene. He wasn't on duty that day, happened to come across the accident by coincidence. He pulled her off Jesse and continued CPR, but it was too late. He knew it but he still kept going. The medics arrived and did what they could, but Jesse was declared DOS before any of us even got there."

"She was sitting in Rick's lap, both of them covered in Jesse's blood. I will never forget the sight of that. She was crying and screaming. One second, she would huddle into his chest, crying; the next, she would try and escape his hold and get to Jesse, fighting him and screaming." Cal said in a hoarse whisper. As much as Jason disliked Rick simply for the fact that he would steal his woman if he got the chance, all those feelings disappeared and turned into instant and deep gratitude. He hated that it hadn't been him, but he was grateful to Rick that he had been there for Loreley and understood that they would always have a bond because of it.

Cal continued. "Lore still doesn't remember the details of what happened after they got hit and I hope she never does. She was in shock and her mind has suppressed the memory as a form of self-protection. We took her to the hospital, but she was released that same afternoon. She refused to stay with any of us, wouldn't hear any of it. Chris came down the next day and stayed with her. He was the only one she would talk to. Well, him and Rick actually. But nobody could get close enough to help her. Nobody could reach her. She retreated into her head, completely. She was consumed by grief. It was frustrating and heartbreaking as hell. Then one night, she started drinking and didn't stop." Cal stopped and Jason could see him close his eyes and swallow. "Chris found her. They had to pump her stomach. I don't think she tried to kill herself, but it was a damn close call. She snapped out of it. Seeing Roy in tears at the hospital was what did it, I think. Chris and I reamed her ass and she started therapy and grief counselling as soon as she was released. She got better, much better. She still has that sadness cling to her from time to time, but that's nothing compared to how she was a year ago. She's found her will to live again, and that's only intensified during the past few days." Cal's eyes were on Jason now. They were grateful and hopeful with a hint of brotherly worry.

A slight sense of relief ran through Jason. It was good to hear that he was helping, that his reappearance in her life had a healing effect on Loreley. He told himself to hold on to that feeling, to not let the images that were raging havoc in his mind, consume him. He had to be strong, had to be the rock that Loreley needed. He would grieve for his son, and Loreley would help him with that. She already was by telling him everything about Jesse, by letting him experience his life through her. And Jason thought that remembering the good times, talking about them and sharing them with him helped Loreley as well. He would do anything in his power to keep them on that path and come out stronger and even more connected to one another.

"I promise you I'll keep her safe. She's my priority and I'll do anything in my power to make sure she's happy." Three sets of serious but hopeful eyes were looking at him. He held their gazes. Then one by one the hope turned into relief. They got him.

The backdoor opened and Loreley peeked her head out. "Dinner is ready." Her eyes landed on Jason questioningly. She could feel the heavy vibe in the air. Jason smirked at her and beckoned her to come to him with a crook of his finger. The questioning eyes turned sassy and his smirk grew bigger. Jesus, he was so deep with this woman, he would never find his way out again. Not that he cared. He was happy exactly where he was. He repeated the gesture and this time, Loreley gave in and came to him, accompanied by the chuckles of the other men who were starting to get up and head inside. Once Loreley was close enough, Jason reached for her elbow and pulled her to him roughly.

"What—" she said in startled surprise, but Jason didn't give her a chance to say anything else as he crashed his mouth down on hers. He took her mouth passionately, fed on her, went as deep as he possibly could while she clung to him and let him take whatever he wanted. He slowed the kiss and nipped at her lips then rested his forehead against hers and said, "I love you so much I want to crawl inside you, get lost in you, and never find my way back out of you." Her body stilled in his arms for a split second right before she sagged into him.

"You remember," she whispered.

"Of course I do, baby. I told you. I remember everything about you, everything about us. I'll never let you go again. And I'll do whatever I have to do to make you happy. I'll do anything to see you smile, make you laugh, watch your eyes glitter with happiness." Her face split into a bright and happy smile right there for him to watch. There it was. His reason for living. He existed in this world to make this woman as happy as he possibly could and was grateful that he got his second chance. He wouldn't need a third. From now on, it was him and Loreley. And the beautiful babies they would make.

LORELEY

I was driving us home. Jason was sitting beside me in the passenger seat, Frank was sitting in the back. I had put my foot down when Jason was heading to the driver's side door, which would once again relegate me to the back seat of my baby. It had been hilarious to watch the big man as he tried to get comfortable. It was hopeless, of course, and he soon realized that, too, but it was still fun to watch him try. He hadn't stopped brooding. That was hilarious, too. And hot. His glare met my eyes in the mirror and my lips twitched in amusement. He tried to hide it, but I could see the sparkle in his eyes as he shook his head at me.

"You know, bodyguards usually drive or sit in the passenger seat. I can't protect you when I'm stuck back here."

I scoffed. "There's nothing here I need protection from."

"You think rock star over there overreacted when he called me, don't you?" I had to smile at the casual way Frank referred to his employer. Jason didn't react to it, which told me it was a regular occurrence.

"Yep," I said flippantly.

"So what're you gonna do when there are photographers at your house?"

I shrugged. "Then they'll take pictures of us getting out of the car, and more of us walking to the front door. I think they're harmless."

Frank chuckled.

"They've been good so far, but believe me, Loreley, they're anything but harmless," Jason stated earnestly. I shrugged again, but didn't answer.

We were almost at the house when it occurred to me that I didn't know where Frank was staying. I seeked out his eyes in the mirror once again. "I don't know where I'm dropping you off."

"Dropping me off?" Frank asked, confused.

"Yeah. Where am I dropping you off?"

"We're not dropping him off anywhere, baby. He's staying with us." Jason said through a chuckle.

"All night?" Frank joined Jason in his chuckle. I looked at Jason. His eyes were on me and they were glinting with amusement. And mischief.

"Yeah. All night. It's his job. You got a problem with that?" He was teasing me. It was almost a challenge. A challenge I was only too happy to accept. Our sex life had always been fun and adventurous. In college, we'd had sex in all kinds of places. I wasn't an exhibitionist, and as far as I knew, neither was Jason, but I enjoyed the thrill of having sex in unusual places. Jason had come up with interesting ways to keep me quiet so we wouldn't get discovered, and I had no doubt that that's exactly what was on his mind right now.

My gaze went back to the road when I said in the most casual tone I could muster, "Not at all."

"Good," Jason replied in his raspy sexy voice. I couldn't help but shiver and knew he saw it when I heard him chuckle but decided to ignore him. Then something else occurred to me. "Where is Frank gonna sleep?" The vibe in the car turned from playful and sexy to apprehensive.

"I'm fine with the couch," Frank said.

"I'm not gonna put you up on my couch. It's lumpy and uncomfortable."

"You mind if he sleeps in Jesse's room?" Jason asked carefully. I thought about it for a second. No, I didn't really mind. I knew Jason knew that I hadn't changed anything about Jesse's room yet, but my therapist and I had agreed that that would be the next step. I had fought her on that in the beginning but I knew it was time so I had been preparing myself to start on that. Having someone else sleep in it was as good a start as any and Jesse would get a kick out of it if he knew. There was just one problem.

"It still has Jesse's bed in it. I doubt Frank will fit."

"Shit, I hadn't thought of that."

"I'll take the couch. No biggie."

"Or we could all stay at the rental," I suggested.

I saw Jason turn his head to me. "You okay with that?" He asked, surprised.

"Yeah, it's not like we're moving into it. We can stay there until Frank goes back to—" I stopped. Frank was Jason's live-in bodyguard. Which meant he would be living with us. There was no way we would all fit into my house even if we converted Jesse's room into a guest room. It was too small and cramped with three adults. There wouldn't be any form of privacy for any of us. And it would get even more cramped if Jason and I had children sooner rather than later.

"We'll figure it out, baby. I told you not to worry. We'll make it work. We can always expand your house if you don't want to leave it. Or build a new bigger house on the same lot."

I was trying not to panic at the thought of leaving the house that held almost all of my memories of Jesse. But then I saw his face in my mind's eye. Not his five-year old face, but his face as he came to me just a few nights ago when he talked to me and assured me that everything would be all right. I could almost feel his touch on my cheek again. He had told me that he would always be with me in my heart. And as I was sitting there, driving us home, I realized that he was right. It didn't matter what house I lived in, what city I lived in. The only thing that mattered was that he would always hold a piece of my heart; that I would always love him and he would always love me.

"So you're sure you want to live here, not in L.A.?" I pulled into my driveway and shut off the engine then turned in my seat to look at Jason. His eyes were already on me and they were just as careful but reassuring as his voice had been.

"Yeah, I would prefer if we lived here. All your family is here and it's nice and quiet, far away from all the drama that's L.A. It's an easy commute if I have to be there for recordings or promotion or events. Though, I still want to take you there so you can meet everyone and I want you to travel with me whenever you can."

"I haven't been anywhere in the last six years," I mused as if talking to myself.

"You haven't?" Jason asked.

I shook my head. "No. Travelling costs money, money I didn't have. And anyways, Jesse loved camping so that's what we did every summer since he was two years old." Jason stared at me with a strange look on his face. He seemed annoyed with something but didn't say anything, so I kept talking. "I have most of next week off. I'm sure dad would cover the two shifts I have if I asked him." The annoyance left Jason's face and he smiled at me.

"Then that's a plan. We'll go tomorrow."

I smiled at him, excited all of a sudden. "Can we go to Disneyland?" I had never been. My plan had been to take Jesse this year since he would have been old and tall enough to go on more of the rides.

"You wanna go to Disneyland?" Jason was back to being amused.

"Yeah. I've never been."

"Not even when you lived there?"

I shook my head. "Nope. Motion sickness. Or general sickness." Understanding flashed over Jason's face and it turned soft. "Then we'll better get you there fats since I'm planning to keep you knocked up for the better part of the next decade."

My eyes bulged at what that statement meant. "I thought you said you wanted two or three kids."

"I do. But you gotta have at least two years in between."

"That would make it six years then."

"We'll see." Jason smirked at me.

"As interesting as the family planning session is, my legs are cramping up. You mind getting out of the car?" I had forgotten that Frank was still sitting in the back seat.

"Sorry," I gave him an apologetic smile and got out of the car so he could squeeze out of the back.

"So what's the verdict? Here or the rental?" Jason asked me as he rounded the car and stopped in front of me.

"The rental. More room," I answered.

"More privacy you mean." He was teasing me again. I raised my eyebrows and accepted the challenge.

"Fancy a dip in the hot tub?"

His smirk grew wider and sexier as he stepped closer to me until our bodies almost, but not quite, touched. "I didn't bring any swim shorts," his voice was low and seductive. Two could play that game. I leaned into him so that my breasts brushed against his chest. His eyes turned dark and carnal. "Well, then it looks like we'll be skinny dipping." Jason's body froze and I grinned. Then I slowly licked along his lower lip before I leaned back and walked to the front door where I could see Frank waiting.

"Payback's a bitch, baby," Jason growled into my ear. He had caught up with me and held my hips as he was walking behind me.

"Bring it on," I murmured back, and to my satisfaction, heard another growl as he nipped my ear lope.

Seventeen

LORELEY

Flashbacks to how different this flight was from the last time I had sat on a plane to L.A. kept running through my mind as I was staring out the window to see nothing but clouds and the bright blue sky above them.

The most obvious difference was that we were sitting in first class as opposed to me flying coach last time. I wasn't the type of woman, who needed or desired fancy and expensive things, but I had to admit, flying first class was something I could definitely get used to. So much space and legroom and the service was outstanding. Even the food tasted great, though the last time I had been so consumed with hurt and betrayal that I honestly didn't remember what the food had tasted like or if I had even eaten anything. All I had been able to think about had been how wrong I had been about Jason. I kept seeing the blond woman wrapped in her towel over and over again, and my over-imaginative mind had tortured me as it pictured Jason in bed with her. The man sitting next to me that day had asked me if I was okay when he had seen the tears running down my cheeks and had offered me a handkerchief. He was older, maybe mid-fifties, and the look in his eyes had reminded me of my dad.

269

"Man trouble, I presume?" He had asked.

I sniffed as I accepted the handkerchief to dry my face and blow my nose and nodded before I broke out into sobs again.

"Now, now," he swung an arm around my shoulders and tried to soothe me. "I know it doesn't seem like it right now, but it will get better. You'll get over him and find someone who is worthy of your love."

"How do you know we broke up?"

"Sweetheart, it's written all over your face." His eyes roamed my face and he gave me a sad smile. "I've got three daughters. My youngest just turned twenty-five, which if my eyes and intuition are correct, is about the same age as you are. Believe me, I've had to deal with my fair share of broken hearts over the years."

I nodded and kept wiping my tears.

"Now, tell me all about the jackass that broke your heart." I had to giggle a little at his swearing. Then I told him what happened, starting from the first time I had met Jason and how we had fallen in love, and ending with what I had seen yesterday morning. The more I had talked, the angrier he had become, until when I finished, his jaw was locked in a pissed off position and his eyes were hard.

"Let me tell you something, sweetheart. Men can be idiots, especially in their early twenties, but that doesn't excuse how you've been treated. I can see that you are a lovely woman with a big heart and big dreams. Don't let anyone take that away from you, no matter how much you might love him. You follow your dreams and stay true to yourself and the right man will come along and respect you and make you happy."

"You really believe that, don't you?"

He nodded. "I absolutely do. Without a doubt."

I hadn't been ready at that point to share his optimism, and to be honest, had never really gotten there until a few days ago, and he could tell. When we parted at the baggage claim, he had given me his card and told me to give him a call if I ever needed to talk to someone.

"You got friends in L.A.?"

I shook my head.

"Give me a call and I'll introduce you to my daughters. Making new friends can never hurt." Then he had left and with everything that had happened after, I had forgotten all about him until now. Bob. He had told me to call him Bob. But for the life of me I couldn't remember his last name.

"Hey, you okay?" Jason squeezed my thigh, snapping me out of the memory. "Looked like you were miles away, baby."

I looked at him and gave him a smile. "Just thinking. And remembering."

"Remembering what?"

"The last time I flew to L.A." Remorse flashed through his eyes for a second before they turned contemplative.

"Can I ask you something?"

"Sure," I said.

"You never told me about your internship or the reason why you didn't accept their job offer at the end of it."

My eyebrows went up in surprise. "How do you know about the job offer?"

"Frank found out when I told him to find you and told me about it."

"Oh," I said, not knowing what else to say. I wasn't too eager to talk about my time in L.A. and the missed opportunities.

"Will you tell me?" He took my hand in his and started to play with my fingers. I sighed. "I loved it. It was everything I had imagined it to be and more. It was exhausting. I worked fifteen

271

hours a day and loved every single minute of it. But I wasn't happy in L.A." I looked away from his face and kept my eyes on our hands. "I was...lonely. And when I found out I was pregnant and with everything that happened after, all I wanted to do was go home. I didn't see myself being a single mom and raising my child in a city like L.A. while trying to make it in the music business. It wouldn't have been fair to the baby." Jason said nothing for a few minutes and I looked back up to his face. His jaw was clenched and he had that same annoyed and angry look on his face he had when I told him about me not having been anywhere in the past six years. I assumed he was mad at himself for not having been there when I needed him, for not having been able to support me.

"It wasn't your fault. You didn't know," I said in a soft whisper. Jason shook his head and looked out the window. His jaw was still clenched.

"I'm grateful you feel that way, baby, but that doesn't change the fact that I *am* responsible for you not getting what you've worked so hard for."

"I'm happy where I am, Jason. I still get to write music and play every once in a while. Really, it's enough for me."

His eyes came back to mine and he studied me. "I can see that you're trying to make yourself believe that, but we both know that you're lying to yourself. Writing music is your passion, it's what you've always wanted to do, not managing a small town bar in the mountains somewhere in Colorado."

I straightened my spine in offense, but Jason's hand cupped my cheek before I could say anything. "I'm not being condescending. I know you love the bar and you're great at what you do. But you're not passionate about it and we both know it. Don't lie to me because you don't want me to feel bad."

I sighed in exasperation, pissed off that he knew me so well, but said nothing. Jason's lips twitched at my stubbornness. "I want to get back to how it used to be. I want you to start writing songs with me again."

I gasped, shocked by his request. I had found closure with that part of my life, content with writing just for me and working with small bands like *Breaking Habit*. Yes, I missed it to some degree, but never would I have imagined that Jason would ask me to write with him again. Back then, we had been a great team and had written lots of songs together, but that had been so long ago and quite frankly, I hadn't listened to any of his music. It had been too painful. I knew about them of course—you would have to live under a rock to not know about at least his number one hits—and I had been so angry in the beginning that it was our songs that made the band so famous, but I had never intently listened to any of the new ones.

"Loreley? What do you think?" Jason asked at a squeeze of my hand.

I shrugged. "I'm not sure."

"Let me ask you this: how many songs have you written in the past six years?"

I shrugged again. "I don't know. Lots."

"Give me a ballpark number. Ten? Twenty? Fifty? A hundred?"

"Somewhere around fifty I guess. Why?"

"Because, baby, you were a single mom who managed a bar full time and still found time to write somewhere around fifty songs. It's your passion. It's what you're meant to do."

"Jason," I sighed, confused and a little annoyed. "Two days ago you told me you want us to start having babies, the same day you told me I'd have a month to plan our wedding. If you get your way, we'll have a baby within the year." The joy on Jason's face at hearing my words took my breath away and I

273

smiled back at him. "And I wasn't lying. I enjoy managing the bar. I'm not sure I want to give that up."

Jason gave in, if only slightly. "Promise me something then. Show me your songs and come to the studio with me while we're in L.A. My studio, the one in my basement, and play with me." I could give him that, even though I could see through his plan, knew where he was going. The thought of playing with him again after all these years excited me and gave me butterflies. I wasn't against writing music per se, I had been doing it most of my life, and Jason was right. It was my passion. But I wasn't sure I wanted to pursue it as a career anymore. Especially if he planned on keeping me knocked up for the next decade.

"Fine. I'll show you my stuff and I'll play with you, but don't think I don't know exactly what you're doing."

Jason grinned his wide grin, telling me he knew that I knew but wasn't the least bit ashamed. He brushed his lips softly against mine and whispered, "Thank you, baby. I can't wait." His eyes shone with excitement as he gave me another soft kiss. "But first, hot tub." My eyes grew big and I shuddered.

We'd had to postpone our hot tub session the night before, since Nathan had already been in it. To my surprise he had been alone. I was sure there were more than enough willing women in town who would have gladly joined him, but when we walked outside onto the back deck, he had sat there alone staring into the distance while he was sipping his beer and listening to music. Nathan had always been the most level-headed of Jason's band members. He knew how to enjoy himself and got around, but he wasn't a player like the other ones had been, or at least he wasn't as obvious about it as let's say Murphy. He was honest but charming and sweet, and always treated every woman with nothing but respect. He even dated a few times back then and when he did, he never strayed. He was a good man and I had always thought that some woman would be lucky someday to snatch him up. Still, it was surprising that he was sitting in the hot tub by himself since I knew he wasn't tied to anyone.

"Yo," Jason had greeted him. "You almost done?"

"Done?"

"With the hot tub."

Nathan glanced at me standing next to Jason, then at our firmly clasped hands, then his eyes went back to Jason and he grinned knowingly. "Nope. Just got in, but feel free to join me."

"Fine with me," I muttered, but Jason looked at me and shook his head.

"I wasn't joking, baby. I didn't bring my shorts." My eyebrows went up in surprise.

"Neither did I," Nathan murmured. I burst out laughing. Jason growled. "Easy, man. I was kidding. See?" He stood up and showed us the proof that he was indeed wearing shorts, then sat back down and grinned at a glaring Jason. "Nothing against a little flirting. You know I'd never poach."

"We're going to L.A. tomorrow. You coming?" Jason stopped glaring but his voice still showed his displeasure.

"You're going to L.A.? Why?"

"To show Loreley around and introduce her to everyone. And she wants to go to Disneyland."

Now it was Nathan who laughed. "Disneyland, huh?"

"Yup," I answered, smiling.

"As much as I'd enjoy watching Lore meet Dana, I'm gonna pass. I just got here and I have to say I quite like it. Think I'll stick around for a while."

Dana? Who the hell was Dana?

I raised my eyebrows again at Jason, this time in question. He squeezed my hand in his and answered, "She's our manager." That explained who she was but not why Nathan would find me meeting her so interesting. So I prompted, "And?"

"And nothing." My eyebrows went higher and if I'd have both my hands free, I would have crossed them over my chest.

"She's got a thing for Jason," Nathan explained.

I cocked my head to the side. "One of your conquests?" I asked, a little irritated that Jason wouldn't fess up. I realized I would probably run into a lot of women he had been with, as proven earlier today, and it would make it a lot easier if I at least knew in advance if we were going to meet one of them instead of going in blind. I tried to pull my hand out of his, but his tightened and he pulled me closer.

"No. I've never touched her." Jason reassured me in a low voice.

"And therein lies the problem," Nathan muttered. "Though, it was probably the smart thing to do. I think she's the clingy kind. She wouldn't have just let you drop her. And then things would have gotten really awkward."

Jason turned his glare back on and stared Nathan down. "Thanks for clarifying that."

"Just keeping it real, my friend," He said and winked at me.

Jason pulled me behind him as he turned and walked us to his bedroom without saying anything else.

"Jason," I called his name when I closed the door behind us.

"What?" I could tell he was still upset.

"I need you to tell me when you know we're going to run into someone you've been with. I don't like being blindsided."

"I told you I've never touched Dana."

"Okay, but if you know we're going to see one of them, please tell me, so I know what I'm dealing with." He was sitting on the bed, taking his shoes off with his eyes on me while I was still standing by the door. He got up and walked to me then cupped my face in his hands. "I'll tell you. I promise." I could see the remorse in his eyes, remorse for having slept around and for me having to deal with it now. I could also see that he understood my request and would keep his promise even though he didn't like telling me any details about that part of his past. He leaned his forehead against mine and sighed deeply before he leaned back and kissed me, softly at first, then harder and deeper.

"I was looking forward to the hot tub with you all wet and naked for me. Since that's out, I'm gonna make love to you in that big bed right over there." He was walking backwards, leading us towards said bed while he was talking against my lips. His hands let go of my face and started undressing me slowly but determinedly. My hands followed his lead and did the same to him. We were naked in less than a minute and, just as promised, Jason proceeded to make slow and intense love to me.

"As soon as we get to my house, I want you naked in that tub, baby." I wasn't going to decline but couldn't help but cock an eyebrow at him teasingly. "You telling me you've lived in L.A. for almost six years and you don't own any swim shorts at all?"

Jason chuckled but ignored my question. "Naked, baby," was all he said before he leaned in and devoured my mouth until all I could think about was him and his mouth on mine.

His house was exactly what I thought a big celebrity's house would look like: huge windows everywhere, letting in the bright Californian sun; sleek white marble floors; a gourmet kitchen— also white; rooms that were so big they made you feel a little lost. I bet I would get an echo if I shouted, that's how big and empty and clean cut the rooms were. Coming in the front door, I could see the big double glass doors at the other end of the room that led out to the deck and backyard. Just a few steps outside those doors there was an infinity pool that made you think it was part of the ocean beneath you. We were up in the hills and from here had an amazing view of the Pacific.

The house was impressive.

And utterly cold.

I hated it and couldn't imagine why Jason was living here. It was nothing like him. So sleek and clean and white it gave me goose bumps. There were no personal touches anywhere, no pictures, no nothing.

It was depressing.

"You hate it, don't you?" Jason asked. I couldn't read the tone of his voice so I schooled my features to neutral and tried my best to give him a smile. He had wanted to bring me here to share his life with me and I shouldn't be so judgemental.

"It's a great house," I managed to sound impressed if nothing else.

Jason threw his head back and burst out laughing. It was a sight to see and I watched like I always did. His body was still shaking with silent laughter when he walked over to where I was standing by the back doors and laid his hands on my hips.

"Baby, you're a terrible liar." He murmured against my forehead.

I looked up at him through my eyelashes with what I hoped was an apologetic expression, making him chuckle once more. "You don't have to spare my feelings. Tell me what you think."

"I...uhm...it's quite something," I stalled.

"Spit it out, honey," Jason said through his smile.

I sighed. He wanted to hear the truth? Well, I was nothing if not straightforward. "It's awful. Yes, I hate it. It's cold and impersonal. Lonely. It makes me want to run screaming. Why do you live here?"

"Well, if I'm correct, I don't really live here anymore. I've never really thought about it before, but now that you're here, my vibrant and sassy and full of life fiancée, it's crystal clear to me why I chose this house."

"And that would be?" I asked when he didn't continue and stared out the window as if lost in thought. It pained me to imagine Jason living here, by himself, with nothing and nobody to comfort him. His gaze came back to mine.

"Don't you see it? This house, this life that I've been living, has been empty without you here with me. I was nothing but a shell, just like this house." His words made my heart ache for him. "Do you remember how we used to dream about the house we would buy once we could afford it?" He seemed to wait for my answer so I nodded and he continued. "This house is nothing like that. You're right. It's cold and impersonal. It makes you feel lonely. I didn't realize I was doing it when I bought it, but it's as far away as possible from the house you and I imagined living in together. Don't you see? If I couldn't have you, I didn't want what we'd dreamed about without you."

My heart melted as did my body and I leaned into him. Jason's arms slid around my hips and held me to him as his mouth brushed the top of my hair. "We'll sell this one and buy a house we both love, a cottage maybe, down by the beach, yellow, with a big wrap-around porch where we can sit and enjoy the view and listen to the waves crash on the sand while our kids are inside sleeping." That was exactly what we'd always talked about: a small cozy house right on the beach with a big porch to lounge on. And I had wanted it to be yellow. Jason really did remember everything. I melted into him even more.

"Okay," I breathed into his neck, overwhelmed by the love that was coursing through me.

"It might take a while to find exactly what we want. Most of the houses down there are massive and look nothing like what

279

we've dreamed about, but we'll keep looking until we find it."

"Okay," I breathed again.

"And keep in mind that we'll need a space for Frank. Not to mention, all the babies I plan on giving you, so it might turn out to be a little bigger than we planned."

Another "okay," came out of my mouth. I sounded like a complete idiot, but I couldn't bring myself to say anything more.

"I know we won't be staying here year round, but I want us to have exactly what we want for when we're in L.A." I said nothing this time. "You're very complacent. What happened to my little firecracker?" Jason asked in a soft and teasing voice.

I shrugged. "I just can't believe we're standing here, talking about our future and our dream house like that. I can't believe it's all real."

"Believe it, baby. It's real. And nobody and nothing will ever take it away from us again. I won't let them." I leaned my head back to find his mouth and kissed him with everything I had. It was deep and passionate at the same time it was loving and cherishing. It was everything.

Jason pulled his mouth away from mine and we both breathed heavily. "You. Naked. In the hot tub. Right now." I shivered at his words as a soft moan escaped my lips, making Jason take my mouth again with a growl.

"I love you, Loreley. So much it hurts." He gripped the edge of my shirt, pulled it up and over my head, and let it fall to the floor. Then his hands were at the button of my jeans. I stood there, breathing hard, as he undressed me, then watched as he undressed himself. When we were both naked, he lifted me up into his arms, and I wrapped my legs around his waist and my arms around his neck. Neither of us said anything as we stared into each other's eyes in complete understanding.

This was it.

This was us.

This was what we were supposed to be.

Together.

And it felt absolutely beautiful.

I could feel his erection pulse between my legs as he walked us onto the deck and into the hot tub. As soon as we were submerged to our chests, he crushed his mouth down on mine in a searing hot kiss. All I could do was let him as he explored every inch of my mouth with his hot tongue. His hands were roaming my body. They were everywhere, touching me, gripping me, massaging me, pushing me higher and higher. I gripped his hair and held on as I gave myself over to him completely. His mouth released mine and moved down my neck over my collarbone down to my nipples. He licked and nipped and bit, making me writhe in his arms, rubbing against him. I needed him inside me so desperately that I started begging.

"Please, baby, I need you."

"You'll get me. Let me play first." I moaned, not sure I would be able to hold on as he kept torturing me, bringing me to the brink then backing off, over and over again, until finally, I could feel the tip of him pressing against my entrance. I braced for it, wanted it, needed it, but nothing happened. I opened my eyes and found his on me.

"Say my name," he growled, his teeth clenched. His body was shaking with the effort of holding back.

"Jason," I breathed, my voice needy and begging.

"Say you love me."

"I love you."

"Say you need me."

"I need you."

"Say that you're mine."

I gripped his hair and pulled his face close to mine. "I'm

281

yours. Forever." He groaned and slammed into me with one swift thrust. Our eyes stayed connected as he moved, slowly pulling out of me, then slamming back in so forcefully it bordered on pain, the good kind of pain. I moaned as I moved with him, urging him to go faster, to thrust deeper. He gave in and let go, his thrusts becoming irregular and uncontrolled. I closed my eyes in bliss.

"Eyes, baby. I want to see you." My eyes snapped open to his. They were burning with fire and passion and a love so deep it almost hurt looking. My breath hitched and he went even faster, his hard cock touching every sensitive spot inside me. I was close to coming.

"I feel it. You feel so good, baby." His mouth took mine again, but our eyes stayed open and connected. His hand on my breast tweaked my nipple at the same time the thumb of his other hand pressed my clit, pushing me over the edge. I heard his groan as I exploded around him and felt it when his cock swelled inside me and he came with me.

When we came down, we were both breathing hard. We kept holding on to each other and staring into each other's eyes and waiting for our breathing to even out.

"Marry me," Jason said to my surprise.

I giggled. "I already said yes."

Jason grinned. "So you did." He brushed his lips against mine and murmured, "I mean right now, today." I stilled in his arms and searched his eyes. He was completely serious.

"Today?" I almost screeched.

Jason tightened his grip around me. "Today." His voice held no doubt. He didn't want to wait any longer. He wanted to get married now.

"How?" I asked, dumbfounded.

"You want a big wedding?" I shook my head. I had hoped

we could have a small wedding, maybe in my dad's backyard, with only our closest friends and family.

"Me neither," he said. "We could get married here, on the beach, just you and me." That sounded perfect, so perfect I almost gave in.

"But what about my dad? And Chris and Cal and everyone else?"

"We can have another ceremony for them when we get back to Colorado. But I want you to be mine now. I don't want to wait any longer."

"I'm already yours."

"I want you to have my name, to wear my ring for everyone to see. I ache for it, Loreley. Please, say yes." He nibbled my lips as he said this. I wanted that, too, for him to wear my ring. And I wanted to carry his name, be his completely.

"Yes," I whispered against his lips and he stilled.

"Yes? You're gonna marry me today?" His eyes shone with pure happiness. I nodded and he crushed me against him, squeezing me so tightly it was hard to breathe.

"Thank you, baby. You have no idea how happy you make me."

"I do have an idea," I said, "because you make me just as happy." His lips took mine again in a soft and loving kiss.

"All right, as much as I would love to spend all day with you wrapped around me naked and wet, I've got a few phone calls to make, very-soon-to-be Mrs. Sanders." My heart jumped in joy and excitement at hearing him calling me that, telling me I'd made the right decision. He stood up with me still wrapped around him and walked out of the hot tub then put me on my feet and reached for a towel. He wrapped me up in it before he reached for another one for himself and wrapped that around his waist, then grabbed my hand and led me into the house.

I heard noises as soon as we crossed the threshold, and so did Jason. He changed directions and walked to where the noises were coming from. "Good, Maggie's here. I can introduce you."

"Maggie?" I asked, not accusingly, but appalled. He was going to introduce me to someone while I was wearing nothing but a towel?

"Maggie. She's my assistant. You'll like her. And she'll be thrilled to finally meet you."

"Jason, I'm naked under this towel!" He really had to pull me behind him now since I was resisting and trying to pull my hand from his. He smirked at me over his shoulder. "I know." I glared at him and he chuckled. We drew closer and I could hear voices now. One of them was Frank's, the other a woman's I didn't recognize but assumed was Maggie. Then she laughed and I couldn't help but smile at hearing that laugh, it was so great and genuine. Then we entered what looked like an office on the other end of the house and I saw her at the same time she saw me. Her face split into an even bigger smile than was already on her face and she leaped towards me and grabbed me in a big hug, surprising me. She was so enthusiastic that I had to wrap my arms around her and take a step back to prevent us from going down. When I looked up, I saw both men grinning at us. Frank was shaking his head.

"I'm so happy to finally meet you!" Maggie released me and jumped up and down in excitement, clapping her hands. She reminded me of Macy.

"It's nice to meet you, too, though I would have preferred to wear clothes while I did." I send another glare in Jason's direction, but his grin didn't falter. I made sure that my towel was still safely attached and hiked it up a little so it didn't show any more than it should. Maggie gazed first at my appearance then at Jason's then she grinned in delight.

"So, you're Maggie," I broke the, for me, awkward silence and tried to act as if I wasn't half-naked.

"Yep. I'm Maggie. The hot shot's personal assistant. I do everything and anything he needs or doesn't want to do himself and don't get paid nearly enough for it." She stated promptly and hilariously, making me snicker. I had a feeling Maggie and I would get along, no problem. She had an attitude, the good kind, along with a lot of energy, and I bet she didn't take anyone's shit, not even Jason's, and I liked that.

Now that she had released me, Jason claimed me back with an arm around my waist. "You need to get on your phone and do your magic. You've got a wedding to plan," he told Maggie.

"A wedding? Yay!" She screeched again as she clapped her hands before she got down to business and took out her phone. "Okay. I need specifics. When, where, who needs to be invited?"

"This afternoon, the beach, and no one. It's just gonna be the two of us. And keep it on the down low. I don't want the press to get wind of it." Frank burst out laughing. "Jeez, man, you don't let any grass grow, do you?" I giggled since that wasn't the first time we'd heard that.

Maggie's eyes bulged out of her head. "You're kidding."

"Nope," Jason stated proudly. I wasn't sure if he was answering Frank or Maggie, but it didn't matter. Maggie's eyes came to me. "Please tell me you won't let him steamroll you like that."

I shrugged. "I want to be married to him. We've wasted enough time. So why wait?" Jason squeezed my waist and kissed my temple. Maggie watched us for a few moments before she shrugged and said, "Can't argue with that," as she unlocked her phone and started to scroll through it. I had assumed by the way she had greeted me and by what both Jason and her had said about finally meeting me that she knew our story and her words confirmed it.

"And call Robert, too. I'm sure he has some forms for me to sign before we get married. There're a few things Loreley and I have to discuss with him."

"Already on it," Maggie muttered with the phone at her ear as she wandered away from us towards the living room.

"Who's Robert?" I asked.

"My lawyer."

"And what do we have to discuss with him?"

"Lots of things, but what I really want him to look into is what it would take to change Jesse's last name." Tears instantly came to my eyes and my lower lip trembled.

"Hey. None of that. As of this afternoon, you'll be carrying my name for the rest of your life and Jesse was our son. I want him to have the same name we do." All I could do was stare at him. God, I loved this man.

"Are you okay with that?" His thumb was caressing my cheekbone as he looked into my eyes questioningly. Was I okay with that? How could I not be? It was one of the most beautiful things I had ever heard.

"Of course I am. It's beautiful. Thank you." Relief and gratitude flashed through Jason's eyes and he kissed my forehead lovingly.

"All right you. Let's get dressed. First stop, Robert; then dress shopping, then rings, and then I have a surprise for you."

"A surprise?" I wasn't a big fan of surprises but I could tell by the gleam in his eyes that I would like this one.

"Yup. Let's go." He took my hand again and as he led me out of the office I saw Frank's gaze on us. It was warm, happy, and relieved. He was happy for us. That meant a lot since it seemed like Frank was one of the few close friends Jason had aside from the band. Frank and Maggie. I gave him a small smile over my shoulder and he winked at me. Holy heck! That guy was hot in general, but when he smiled like that and winked I doubted any woman's panties didn't disintegrate on the spot. Good thing I wasn't wearing any. And good thing Jason hadn't noticed. Or so I thought.

"You done drooling?" Jason asked over his shoulder, a smile playing around his lips. I tried to school my features even though I knew he had seen. "What's that, honey?"

Jason chuckled low. "Nice try. It's okay. I'm not jealous. I know Frank would never go there just like I know that neither would you."

That was news to me. He had always been the jealous type.

"But yesterday with Nathan—"

"That was different," he interrupted me. "Nathan has always liked you and I know for a fact that he would have gone after you if I hadn't gotten there first. With Frank, I know it would never happen. Besides you, he's probably the only person I trust completely and undoubtedly. It also doesn't hurt that I know he's got his eyes set on someone else." I scowled at his words.

"Who?" I asked, instantly curious.

Jason shook his head. "Nope. Not my secret to share. But I'm sure you'll figure it out for yourself."

Hmm, I would have to keep my eyes open for sure. I was dying to know who Frank had his eyes on and why he hadn't done anything about it. But there was something else Jason said that bugged me.

"Frank is the only person you trust one hundred percent?" I didn't like the thought of that. That meant he really had been all alone these past six years, and it made my heart hurt for him.

"And you."

"What about the band?"

"I trust the band, mostly. They're like my brothers, but things haven't been smooth in a long time. I hardly ever talk to any of them but Nathan when we're not working or on tour." There was sadness in his eyes. Sadness and regret.

"Why?" I asked. Back then they had all been really close.

We were in Jason's bathroom now and he unwrapped the towel from me and pulled me into the shower. He positioned me under the spray and reached for the shampoo.

"I wasn't lying when I told you that I was miserable without you. I missed you and deep down I always blamed myself for what happened and I took it out on them. They understood and put up with my shit for a while. But you can only take so much crap from someone and eventually they stopped doing that. I don't blame them. I was a miserable fucker." He squeezed shampoo in his hand and massaged it into my hair. It felt divine and I closed my eyes for a moment. Jason rinsed my hair and then started on my body.

"Sorry, I don't have conditioner," he murmured.

"That's okay," I assured him. "Do you think you can fix it?"

"Your hair?"

"No, the band."

Jason sighed heavily. "I hope so. I've got a lot to make up for. I didn't realize just how much until this last tour. Murphy won't even talk to me."

"I'm sorry, baby."

"It's okay. I'm happy now that I've got you back and I'll work on Murphy and Dex. They'll come around." Dex was the fourth member of their band. He was almost as bad as Murphy, but just like Murphy, deep down he was a good and loyal guy. I hoped Jason was right and he would be able to fix what had been broken. It couldn't be fun to work with people who wouldn't even talk to you unless they had to, especially since they had been your friends before all the craziness of stardom had started.

"Let me know if there's anything I can do to help."

"You're already doing it, Loreley. I was miserable because you weren't a part of my life. Now you are and you always will be, so there's no longer a reason for me to be miserable." He was done washing my body and moved me out of spray so he could turn into it. I grabbed the shampoo this time and started to wash his hair.

"I'm glad. But that's not what I meant. I want to help."

"I know you do and I don't doubt you will. I just don't know yet exactly what I'm gonna do. We'll have to play it by ear I guess."

"All right. As long as you'll let me help when the time comes." I rinsed his hair thoroughly and smiled at his groan.

"So, Frank is the only one who's allowed to flirt with me or tease without any retribution?" I brought us back to our original topic.

"Yes," he stated seriously. There he was, my possessive tyrant. I smiled at him. "You're mine and no one is allowed to look at you for too long. Flirting is out of the question. Touching I don't even want to think about." He sounded disgruntled now. My smile grew bigger. "You're enjoying this, aren't you?" *Just a little, maybe.* I shrugged.

"So, does the same apply to me?" I asked.

"What do you mean?"

"Do I get to defend what's mine?" I had finished washing his body and he turned off the water before his arms went around my waist and pulled me into him.

"Absolutely," he said through his grin.

"You sure about that? You know I can be hell on wheels when riled. That hasn't changed."

289

"Oh, I'm sure. And I sincerely hope that hasn't changed. It's hot," he growled in a low voice and nipped my bottom lip. My body was getting excited again and so was his. I could feel his arousal pressed against my stomach.

"I want to take you again, but we don't have time," he said against my mouth before he took it in a fiery kiss.

"We can be fast," I tried to persuade him. I snaked my hand down his stomach, grabbed his already rock hard cock, and started to pump. He groaned into my mouth and pressed me against the side of the shower stall at the same time he turned me. I lost hold of his cock and braced both hands against the glass.

"Fast," Jason breathed and was inside me only a second later. Then he showed me what fast really meant.

Eighteen

LORELEY

"Mr. Sanders is here to see you," the sugary sweet voice of the secretary said into the intercom. Her eyes didn't move from Jason the whole time. We were at his lawyer's office. It was swanky with deep brown leather furniture and a mix of contemporary and modern art on the walls. Swanky, but somewhat cozy and homey. The secretary—Rose, as the sign on her desk told me—didn't seem to mind that I was standing right there, my hand in Jason's, as her googly eyes roamed all over his body. I took a step forward and leaned my hip against her desk.

"Hi, Rose," I said in a voice that was just as sweet. The smile on my face was over the top fake, but she didn't seem to notice when her eyes finally came to me. I felt Jason's questioning eyes on me but ignored him. My focus was on the bitch who thought she could look her fill of my man and pretend I wasn't even in the room, or better, didn't exist. "Excuse my fiancée's rudeness. I'm Loreley. It's so nice to meet you." My voice was dripping with sarcasm. At the word fiancée, her eyes snapped down to the ring on my finger, then to Jason, then back to me. This time when she looked at me, there was no pretense of friendliness. Disdain and jealousy were written all over her. If

I hadn't known she wasn't one of Jason's one-night stands—I was sure he would have told me before we walked into the office—the contempt and bitterness on her face would have fooled me to believe she was. I dropped the smile from my face and glared at her as I leaned in closer across the desk. I didn't have to say another word for her to understand that I meant business.

"Loreley," Jason said in an amused voice behind me.

"Yes, honey?" I kept my glare on Rose, but my voice was soft, making her glare intensify, which of course, brought my smile back, but this time it was smug. With a hand on my elbow he turned me towards him, effectively breaking my eye contact with Rose. He cupped one side of my face and laid a big wet one on me, right there in front of her, which I thought was awesome. "Hot," he murmured against my lips, gave my bottom lip one a quick nip, then leaned back and turned to face the door that was opening behind the desk.

"Jason," someone said in a deep voice. "It's good to see you. Maggie tells me we've got a lot of things to talk about."

"Robert," Jason greeted him with a chin lift. "Yes, we do." He gave me a proud smile and I turned around to meet Robert—and was surprised that I already knew him. I cocked my head as he stopped mid-stride and took me in.

"It can't be," he murmured under his breath, then a huge smile flashed across his face and he closed the distance between us. Instead of shaking my hand like I thought he would, he wrapped me into a big and fatherly hug. "It's you, isn't it?" he asked when he leaned back, clutching my upper arms. I nodded. "See? I told you you'd get over him and find someone worthy one day." He looked extremely pleased.

I giggled and shook my head at him. "Not quite."

His eyebrows scrunched up in confusion and he looked at

Jason then back at me. "What do you mean? Are you not Jason's Loreley?"

"I am. See, Jason is the guy I told you about, the one I thought broke my heart."

His eyes narrowed on Jason but he spoke to me. "Are you telling me that Jason is the asshole who threw you away all those years ago?" His voice was hard and shocked. I was shocked, too, at his surprising outburst.

"Can someone tell me what the hell is going on? How do you two know each other?" Jason sounded irritated. He laid his arm around my waist and pulled me into his side. Robert—or Bob as I knew him—let go of my arms, if reluctantly. His narrowed eyes were still on Jason.

"I met this young lady on a flight from Austin to L.A. six years ago. We were sitting beside each other. She was heartbroken and in tears, because she had caught her boyfriend cheating on her." His words were accusatory as he fired them at Jason. I was still too shocked to say anything, to defend Jason and explain. I hadn't expected a man who I hardly knew to come to my defense like this, from one of his important clients who he'd known for years no less. Then Bob's eyes went wide in understanding. He knew. Bob knew about Jesse.

Before he could say anything else, I snapped out of my stupor and said, "I'll explain, but do you think we can take this someplace else?" I could feel Rose watching us with interest and I bet she was soaking up every ounce of information she could get. I didn't feel comfortable with her knowing anything about Jason and my personal life. Who knew what she would do with that information?

Bob lifted his arm in a gesture for us to walk into his office and we did. We all sat down at the table that was set up with sandwiches and drinks for lunch, and I explained what had

293

happened. I wouldn't have thought that I would ever explain Jason's and my story to anyone outside my closest friends and family, especially not Jason's lawyer, but I somehow felt obligated to. Bob had been kind to me. He had worried about me and had tried to help me when I had been at, what I thought then, my lowest point. Deep emotions, easily readable, flitted across his face as he listened carefully to every single word I said: shock, anger, disbelief, sadness, grief, then joy, happiness, and relief.

"I cannot tell you how glad I am that your story has a happy ending. I've thought about you often over the years, Loreley, and if I'd had your name or phone number, I would have checked up on you."

"Thank you, Bob. I'm sorry I never called. So much happened so fast—"

His hand came up and he interrupted me. "No need to explain. I'm just grateful that everything got cleared up and you're happy, even though I'm sorry it took so long." He gave me a warm and fatherly look. "And you," his eyes turned to Jason, who hadn't said a word this whole time. "I'm sorry I jumped to conclusions out there. I know you're a good man and I should have known better."

Jason nodded at him. "No harm done. Believe me, you're not the only one who's blamed me for what's happened." My head whipped around, not at his words, since they were true, but at the tone he said them in.

"Stop." I ordered. "Don't do this." Jason clenched his jaw but said nothing. "You demanded I forgive myself. Well, guess what? I demand you forgive yourself, too. If there's one thing I have learned in therapy it's that you can't turn back time and change things. What happened, happened, and there's absolutely nothing either of us can do about it. We were both young and did what we thought was right. I won't let you blame yourself for one more second. Let it go." There was no doubt in my voice that I would follow through on my silent threat.

Jason's jaw had unclenched and he was smirking at me. "All right, baby. I'll let it go."

I narrowed my eyes at him. "Promise?"

"Promise." He squeezed my knee in assurance.

"Good," I said and looked back at Bob.

"She doesn't give an inch, does she?" He was amused but seemed proud at the same time.

"Not when it's about something that's important to her," Jason confirmed through a smile.

"It's good you have a woman who keeps you on your toes."

"She certainly does that," Jason muttered on another squeeze. I raised an eyebrow at him and he chuckled.

"Now, let's get down to business. Maggie gave me a list of things you need and I've added a few points myself. First off, I think congratulations are in order. Your marriage certificate will be ready in a few hours. It would normally take a few days at least, but I pulled some strings. So you're good to go on that front."

"Thank you, Robert, I appreciate it."

"Now, don't be offended, but I have to ask this as your lawyer. Have you thought about a pre-nup?"

"No pre-nup," Jason answered instantly. I looked at him. "Are you sure? I'll sign anything you want."

"You thinking of leaving me?" Now it was him who cocked an eyebrow at me.

"No," I replied immediately.

He turned back to Bob and said, "No pre-nup."

"All right. We've put a rush in with the bank as well. Your new bank and credit cards should be here within a day,

Loreley."

"My new bank and credit cards?"

"What's mine is yours, literally and legally, in a few hours." Jason said.

"Jason, I don't need—"

"No, Loreley, I'm not discussing this. I know you don't need all the blitz and bling, but there's no way you're fighting me on this. I've let it go once. I'm not going to do that again."

"What do you mean, you've let it go once?" I was confused. I couldn't remember a single time where he had offered to pay for something and I didn't let him. Having grown up with alpha men all around me, I had always understood that that was part of who he was.

Jason sighed. "I wasn't going to bring this up since it's a moot point now, but it's been bugging me. Loreley, why did you return the royalty money I sent you?"

Huh? Now I was even more confused. "What royalty money?"

"The money I sent you when we got our record deal. You wrote most of the songs on that album with me, and I sent you a cheque for the royalties. Twice." He was annoyed.

"I never got a cheque."

"Loreley—" I could tell he was getting angry now. But so was I, so I cut him off. "I swear, Jason, I never got a cheque from you. I was trying to get a hold of you, but never got a response. Don't you think that if I'd gotten that cheque from you, I would have somehow followed that trail to get an address or a phone number or something? I don't know if I would have taken the money from you. I was mad and heartbroken and wanted to hate you, but I would have tried harder if I'd had anything to go on." At the end of my rant my voice was almost a shout. Jason was taken aback by my sudden outburst.

296

"You never got it?"

"No. I didn't." I snapped.

"That something I need to look into?" Bob asked, interrupting our stare down.

"I don't know yet. Maybe. Probably." Jason sounded pre-occupied and lost in thought. Then he turned his eyes back on me and apologized. "I'm sorry, baby. I could have handled that better."

"So you believe me?"

"Of course I do." He picked up my hand and kissed my knuckles. "Forgive me."

"All right," Bob said, getting back to business. "You'll let me know if you need me to dig a little deeper. Let's move on for now. You wanted to know about changing your son's name." Jason's attention snapped back to Bob, as did mine. "It's not a problem. As long as your name is on the birth certificate and the mother agrees, which I assume she does, it shouldn't take all that long. All I need is a copy of the birth certificate and both your signatures on the bottom of this form." He passed a form across the table and Jason stared at it. It was a request for a name change and looked pretty straightforward to me. But Jason didn't move to sign it. He just kept staring at it.

"Honey," I asked. "You okay?" My bad mood from a few seconds ago was forgotten.

"Yeah," his whisper was hoarse. He cleared his throat, but still didn't move. I slowly pulled the form to me, picked up a pen, and signed it. Jason followed my every move.

"Here, your turn." I moved the form back to him and saw his hand shaking as he picked up a pen. "Jesse Sanders," he whispered again, reverently this time. I had known this meant a lot to him, but until now I hadn't realized just how much.

"Jesse Sanders," I repeated, my voice shaky. I watched with

tears in my eyes as Jason signed the form and handed it back to Bob. Then he grabbed my hand under the table and gave me the biggest and most loving smile I had ever seen on his face.

"There are a few other matters we need to discuss in the near future, Jason. As requested, I've looked into the Courtney situation and I need to give you an update on that. And your new contract with the record company is coming up, but we'll discuss those things at another time. I'm sure you've got lots to do this afternoon, so I'll let you go."

We all got up and Bob moved around the table to embrace me in another hug. "I'm so very happy for you two."

"Thank you. For everything."

"Any time, dear. And now that I know how to contact you, you'll have to come and meet my daughters."

"I would love to."

Jason and Bob shook hands and we left the office. Rose was still sitting at her desk, but neither Jason nor I paid her any attention.

"So, what's next?" I asked when we were sitting in the back of the SUV again and Frank was driving us through the city.

"Maggie is meeting you so you can find a dress. I'll go and get the rings and your surprise and I'll meet you at the house in two hours."

"I don't get to pick out my own wedding band?" I asked.

"No. I'm a man. That's my job." His voice was resolute.

"Is it now?" I muttered under my breath, knowing by his tone that there wouldn't be any room for me to argue. Jason was a man and as such he had a strict set of rules as to what was the man's job and what was the woman's job. He didn't mean it in a sexist way, that for example the woman was only relegated to housework or any such nonsense. No, he had a code that he thought any man should follow and respect, as should the woman who belonged to him. He reminded me of Cal in that sense. He was of the mindset that a man should always take care of his woman, as in hold the door for her, pay when they went out to dinner or whenever they were together really, drive when they were both in the car—though that one I knew would be a point of dissension on a regular basis since I loved driving my girl—make sure she was safe and protected and taken care of at all times. Men like Cal and Jason were providers and as their woman you'd be advised to never undermine them in that way. I hadn't expected Jason to choose our wedding rings by himself without me having a say, but I trusted him and knew that he would make the right choice. He had good taste, as proven by the engagement ring that was sitting on my finger. And it was kind of romantic if you thought about it.

"Yes. Don't worry. I've got it covered."

"All right," I gave in. That earned me an approving smile and a quick kiss.

Frank pulled over and stopped in front of a fancy looking store. It was a bridal shop and Maggie was waiting for me on the sidewalk, grinning and waving.

"In only a few hours you'll be Mrs. Sanders for real. Now go find me a dress that I can't wait to rip off of you." Jason kissed me again, softly this time. I giggled against his lips and he gently pushed me towards the door that Frank was holding open for me.

"See you later," I said over my shoulder as I got out of the car and went to meet an overexcited Maggie.

"Later, Mrs. Sanders," I heard before the car door was closed and the SUV disappeared into traffic again.

A little over two hours later, Maggie parked her car in front of Jason's garage. We had gone to three bridal stores only to go back to the first one and buy the first dress I had tried on. I had known pretty much from the second I had seen myself in the mirror that it was the one, but Maggie insisted I try on more. And more. And more. She had been so excited about everything and had chatted constantly that I didn't have the heart to tell her no. And I'd had fun. I wasn't really into fashion, especially not dresses, but even I had to admit that it was fun dressing up in gown after gown after gown. In the end, I had stuck to my guns though and had chosen the dress that was the most me. It was a simple flowy chiffon strapless A-line dress with a lace trimmed sweetheart neckline and a twisted empire front with tiny gold beading. It was gorgeous and I was absolutely in love with it. It was long enough to cover my feet—I had opted out of shoes and would go barefoot, it was a beach wedding after all—and the first layer had a slit that went all the way up my legs in the front. The back had a short sweep train. The dress was simple but beautiful: the perfect dress for a beach wedding. And compared to the other prices I had seen that day, this one had been a steal. I had decided that I would keep my hair down. It was wavy naturally and would look great with the simple vintage tiara-like band and the matching earrings we had found. I couldn't wait for Jason to see me in it.

"Great, the Wicked Witch of the West is here. Prepare yourself for a bitch attack," Maggie muttered under her breath. I looked around and saw another car parked off to the side of the driveway, closer to the front door.

"Who's the Wicked Witch of the West?"

"Dana." Ah. Dana. After what Nathan had told me, I wasn't looking forward to meeting her, especially not today, but since she was here and inside the house it looked like I wouldn't have a choice.

"Any advice?" I asked Maggie. Maggie had been Jason's assistant for a few years now and must have had countless encounters with Dana during that time. I liked Maggie. We clicked and it wouldn't hurt to hear how she thought I should handle the woman that had a thing for my man and worked closely with him. She was going to be a part of Jason's work life if I liked it or not and I needed some inside advice. Maggie looked at me out of the corner of her eyes and bit her bottom lip, hesitating.

"I know she's got a thing for Jason. Nathan told me." I informed her.

"Oh, good. I didn't want to be the one to break it to you," she said, seemingly relieved. "She'll try to rile you up, get a reaction out of you, at least when Jason's not looking. Don't let her, it just gives her more ammunition." I nodded, understanding.

"Is she gonna throw herself at Jason in front of me?"

"I don't think so. She's never too obvious about it, but there's no doubt that she thinks Jason will come around and want her. It's like she's waiting in the shadows for him to be ready to settle down or something. She won't be happy to see you here and she'll be even unhappier when she sees the way Jason looks at you." Great. I wasn't sure if I could succeed in not letting her rile me up if she thought she had a claim to what was mine.

"Don't worry. I'll try my best to be your buffer. She hates me and vice versa, so it's no skin off my nose if she comes after me." Maggie stated.

"Why hasn't Jason fired her if she is such a hateful person?"

Maggie shrugged. "She's one of the best in the business and has a lot of contacts. And it's not like they are super close. I probably see and talk to her more often than he does. And when he does, he seems to tolerate her at best. I don't think he even likes her as a person, but he feels loyal to her since she was the

301

one who initially discovered them."

Okay, that made sense. And why wouldn't you want to work with one of the best managers in the business, even if she was kind of a bitch?

Holding my dress up high in its bag so it wouldn't touch the ground, I carried it through the front door and stopped at hearing Jason's angry voice.

"Get off me, Dana. And put your fucking clothes on. What the fuck do you think you're doing?"

I heard Maggie say something beside me but I was too focussed on getting to the kitchen where I thought the voices were coming from to pay any attention to her. I rounded the corner and saw her. Her back was to me and she was leaning into Jason, her hands on his chest.

And all she was wearing was lingerie and high heels.

If I hadn't known any better, I'd have thought I was in a bad movie. Really? That was her play? She thought Jason would want her if she came here in nothing but sexy underwear and slutty high heels and threw herself at him? It was the cliché of all clichés and I would have laughed if I wasn't so unbelievably mad.

"Get your slutty hands off of him." I was seething. Just yesterday, another woman had tried to break us apart. I could deal with the googly eyes and the come hither looks, but this was crossing the line by at least a mile.

Both their eyes came to me: Jason's panicked, Dana's smug. She had the gumption to lean her tits against his chest, but almost fell flat on her face a second later when Jason pushed her off and came towards me, his hands up in a placatory gesture, panic still written all over his face.

"I swear to God, Loreley, this is not what it looks like." He stopped two feet away from me, unsure.

"What are you doing?" I snapped at him accusatorially.

"I swear I wasn't doing anything. She got here not five minutes ago and—"

"That's not what I meant," I waved him off impatiently. "I mean, what are you doing over there?"

"Over there?" He repeated, not understanding.

"Yeah, over there. I need you over here." His whole body sagged in relief and he closed the distance between us and wrapped his arms around me. I leaned into his embrace. "You believe me," he whispered against my temple as he brushed it with his lips. "Of course I do. I would have even if I hadn't heard you tell her off when we came in."

He leaned back and gave me a look that said he didn't quite believe me. I gave him a stern look. "I would have."

"Baby, that was quite the scene you just walked in on. Don't get me wrong, I'm not complaining, but it looked bad."

"Yes, it did. But I trust you. I admit I didn't a week ago, not like this. Maybe not even yesterday when that bitch came to the bar. But that has changed. I know you wouldn't throw away what we have for some random pussy. I wouldn't marry you today if I didn't."

"You're marrying her today? Are you out of your mind?" Dana screeched, bringing both our attention back to her. Dang it, I had forgotten she was here. Jason stood beside me with his arm around my shoulders.

"Not that it's any of your fucking business, but yes, we're getting married today." His voice was back to being hard and angry.

"None of my fucking business? I'm your manager. Anything you do is my business," she sneered. "I'm the one who has to put out the fires when you get drunk and fuck your way through a volleyball team of women."

303

"Watch it, Dana," Jason growled menacingly. His body next to mine was strung tight with anger. "And put your fucking clothes on."

"Why? I seem to remember you enjoyed it more than enough the last time you saw me like this."

"You fucking bitch. Don't make it sound like I've ever seen you with your clothes off. I never wanted to and now that I have I wish I hadn't. Go play your games somewhere else. I'm not interested." His voice was dripping with disgust. Dana flinched.

I'd had enough of this show. "All right. That's enough. You've tried to make him want you and failed miserably. We've got things to do. Get dressed and then get lost. And don't come back. You're fired." I told her.

"You can't fire me! I don't work for you, you slutty little gold-digging bitch!"

"Dana—"

"Fine. You're right. I can't fire you. Jason?" I didn't look at him but kept my eyes on her instead. I wanted her to see that I was the one who would always have the upper hand when it came to Jason.

"You're fired. Get out," he said without a second's hesitation.

"What?" She screeched. "You're firing me because your little slut is afraid of a little competition?"

"You don't get it, Dana," I said, bored now. "There *is* no competition. Jason is mine. He always has been and he always will be. Stop. You're embarrassing yourself."

Her eyes narrowed on me. "He wasn't yours six years ago, now was he? Six years ago, you watched him being all over someone else and that was all it took for you to scamper. Not even sharing a child with him made you stick around."

Both Jason and I froze at her words. I gasped and stopped

304

breathing. Then it came to me.

Oh my God.

Dana was the woman from the concert. The one who had told me to not ever get involved with a musician since they could never keep it in their pants anyway. She had stood beside me backstage all those years ago when I had seen Jason with that other woman. She had asked me my name and I had told her, too shocked to wonder why she wanted to know. She must have seen something on my face that night that made her curious. It all made sense now. She had known exactly who I was, had known that I was pregnant. Because she was the one who had intercepted my messages and made sure Jason never got them. Which meant that she was responsible for Jason not knowing about Jesse.

A red haze of fury covered my vision.

That motherfucking bitch.

JASON

"What did you just say?" Jason's voice was soft but menacing. He couldn't believe what he'd just heard.

"Nothing," Dana had frozen at the same time he and Loreley had. Her eyes were big and round with alarm. She must have realized that she'd just signed her own death certificate and was trying to save herself by pretending to be nonchalant. But it was too late. Jason had heard and understood. Everything was crystal clear to him now. And it took everything in him to not punch Dana in the face.

She had known about Loreley being pregnant.

She had gotten the messages and emails Loreley had sent to tell him about their baby.

And she had kept them from him

That motherfucking bitch.

Jason felt Loreley's arms go around him, one around his back, the other around his front, trying to hold him back. She knew that he was moments away from snapping.

"You knew, didn't you?" His voice was so cold he didn't recognize it himself.

"I don't know what you're talking about." Dana said impassively as she went to her clothes and started to put them back on. At least that was something.

"You knew. You knew about Loreley and you knew about the baby." She said nothing. "Tell me, did you get a good laugh behind my back for all these years?" His voice was still dangerously soft, while his body begged him to let loose and go after the person who was responsible for this whole mess. It didn't care that she was a woman. All it wanted was to pummel into her, to let go and let the anger that was boiling inside him get his own back. "Tell me!" He shouted, making Loreley flinch in his arms. He gave her waist a small squeeze in apology but didn't take his eyes from Dana. She was dressed now and seemed intent on getting out of here as fast as possible.

Jason moved out of Loreley's embrace and blocked her. "Oh no, you're not going anywhere until you tell me." Then something occurred to him. If Dana had known back then who Loreley was, she had known about her when he tried to send her the cheque for the royalty money. Back then he didn't have a PA, so everything had gone through her. "You never sent the money, did you?" He watched as Dana's body froze once more. He had her now and she knew it. If she had sent the money, there would be a paper trail somewhere, proof that she had issued the cheque and it hadn't been cashed or had been sent back.

"You motherfucking bitch!" He yelled into her face, beyond

306

furious. "I'm gonna nail you on his. You're going down. No matter what I have to do, you're going down and you're staying down. I'm suing your ass with everything I can until you have nothing." It wasn't a threat. He wasn't going to hesitate in making her pay for what she'd done. And when he was done with her she'd hope she'd never met him.

"Jason, I was just trying to protect you—" she pleaded.

"Protect me from what? From getting to know my son? From being with the woman I love?" He roared, making Dana flinch again. He knew he should back off but if he moved now, away from her wouldn't be the direction his body would go.

"She and the baby were going to ruin your career. If I hadn't—"

"Get out of my house!" Jason thundered. His heart was beating fast and he knew his face was red with absolute fury. If he heard another word out of that cunt's mouth, he would not be held responsible for his actions. "Now!" Dana's eyes went even bigger than they already were. She turned on the spot and ran out the front door.

Run, bitch. Run while you still can.

He listened to Dana's car start and its tires screech as she sped out of his driveway and took that moment to try and compose himself.

But Loreley was having none of that.

Her arms were going around his waist from behind and he felt her rest her head against his back, trying to soothe him with her touch. He let her and gave into it like he always did. He needed her touch, needed her love right now more than anything. Someone he had trusted for years, since the very beginning, had committed the worst kind of betrayal imaginable. And for what? For the off chance that he would take her to bed?

He rested his hands on Loreley's and hung his head as he

307

sighed deeply.

"Are you okay?" Loreley asked. The concern for him was evident in her voice, but he could also hear shock and a whole lot of anger there. He could only imagine how much it had taken for her to not pummel Dana herself.

"I will be," he answered as he turned in her arms and wound his own around her tightly. She lifted her head and looked up at him. "I'm sorry, Jason." She was pushing her own anger away so she could comfort him. It took a good woman to see what her man needed and give it to him when he needed it, and Jason was unbelievably grateful that Loreley was his. She knew how much Dana's betrayal hurt him and moved to make him feel better, despite what she might be feeling herself in that moment. Jason returned the favour and touched her forehead with his in a gesture of comfort and intimacy.

"Nothing for you to be sorry about. I've believed her lies for six years. Never even thought to second guess anything she told me." He kissed the tip of her nose, then tucked her cheek to his chest, right over his heart and gently rubbed her back to soothe both her and him.

"Wow. I've always hated her, but even I never expected her to be capable of anything like this." Jason's eyes moved to Maggie, who stood at the opening that led from the hallway into the living room. She looked just as shell shocked as Jason felt. A dress bag was hanging over her arm, making Jason remember. He leaned back, making Loreley do the same in his arms, and looked at her.

"Baby, I've got to call Robert and fill him in on what just happened. I want no time wasted on that shit, so I gotta do that right away. You go on up and start the shower. I'll be with you in a few minutes. Maggie arranged for a hairdresser to come to the house in half an hour. She does make-up, too, so we gotta hustle."

"You sure you still want to get married today? We just got another big bomb dropped on us. We need to digest it and—" Jason stopped her from saying more. He moved his hands from her back to the sides of her face and leaned in close enough that all she could see were his eyes.

And they were dead serious.

"Listen to me, Loreley. I've been in love with you for over eight years. I've wanted to marry you for almost as long. Nobody and nothing will mess with us getting married today. You are the most important part of my life. I love you and I won't wait another second to make you mine. You've said yes and you can't change your mind. I won't let you."

"I wasn't going to change my mind about marrying you. I just thought we could use some time to let it all sink in, like, maybe a day or so." Jason grinned, but shook his head. God, he loved this woman.

"I appreciate the thought, but the answer is no. If we change our plans she wins and I won't give her that. The only people who come out winners in all this are you and I. Together. Forever." He kissed her lips softly. "Now go and start the shower and I'll be right behind you."

"Okay," she breathed against his lips that were still touching hers. He loved that he had the power to make her go completely complacent for him. His Loreley had sass and a lot of it, which he loved and wouldn't want to live without. But he also loved it when she was like this, soft and caring and compliant in his arms, ready to give him what he needed, trusting him that he would take care of her and everything else. He loved it, because he knew she didn't give that to anyone else besides her father and maybe Chris, but that was different. He knew that no other man who wasn't her father or whom she loved like a brother had ever received that gift. It was a gift that wasn't given lightly and he knew he would always cherish it and keep it close to his heart.

Nineteen

LORELEY

I could hear the waves crashing against the sand as soon as Frank opened the door of the SUV and helped me out. I looked up and gasped. Frank smirked at me knowingly. Hundreds, no, thousands of twinkle lights were decorating the trees around us. We seemed to be in a quiet and secluded little alcove just above the beach. If I squinted, I could see the ocean through the branches. It wasn't quite dusk yet and the glimmering lights made the place seem magical.

"What is this place?" I wondered in awe. I had never seen anything like it.

Frank's smirk turned into a grin. "It's just a spot that Jason and I discovered one day when we were driving around. He likes to come here when things get too much for him."

"It's beautiful."

He chuckled. "It is, though the lights make it all the more so." I couldn't believe that Jason had pulled this off with practically no time at all. It was the most romantic spot I had ever been to and I couldn't have imagined any better place to get married. It was perfect.

"Does he come here often?" Frank started walking me

towards an opening in the trees and bushes. I could see a small path that led to the beach beyond.

"Every couple of weeks or so. More often during the past few months."

"Why is that?"

"He was thinking about you, girl. He missed you terribly. One night about five months ago he asked me to drive him here after a show he'd had downtown. He was miserable. He's a broody guy, but that night, he was at his worst. I had never seen him like that. We sat down on the beach and he started talking about you. How much he loved you, how much he missed you, how much he wanted you back. From that night on he stopped drinking and sleeping around."

"Five months? Why didn't he come back to me sooner?" I wasn't being accusatory. I was genuinely curious.

"He was afraid you wouldn't take him back. See, it took a lot for Jason to talk about you, to tell someone else how he felt about you. We're men. We don't share our feelings with each other. Ever. Not like that." Frank stopped me at the beginning of the path and took my hands in his. "He was afraid that once he admitted to himself that you were the only person who could make him happy and he did something about it, you would reject him. A lot of time had passed, a lot of things had happened. He didn't even know then if you were married to another man. So I started looking into it, found out that you weren't married and lived in your hometown in Colorado."

His eyes were telling me something. Something that he seemed to want me to figure out. "You knew about Jesse, didn't you?"

He nodded. "I did."

"But Jason didn't." He shook his head. "Why didn't you tell him?"

"Because I don't think he would have gone after you if he had known. He would have either blamed himself and stayed away from you or blamed you and stayed away from you. He had to find out on his own, he had to hear it from you." Another chuckle. "Maybe not quite as brutally and bluntly as how it went down, but this was the only way." I understood what he was saying and I agreed with it.

"Jason never suspected that you were keeping things from him?"

"No. When he asked me to find you, I told him I already had. I told him the basics, that you were single and lived in Cedar Creek, worked at your dad's bar. He believed that's all I knew, that I hadn't dug any deeper than that."

"What if he ever finds out?"

"He won't." His answer came instantly. His eyes again were telling me something he wouldn't say out loud, but I could read him clearly. He would deny it. He did what he had to do and gave Jason what he had needed, had nudged him in the right direction, protecting him from himself at the same time.

"You're quite the matchmaker, aren't you?" I said through a smile.

"You didn't need me to match make. From what Jason told me, I knew that you were an outstanding woman. I knew you'd probably give him a run for his money, and you haven't disappointed, but I hoped that you would find it in you to forgive him."

"That's a lot of faith you had in a person you didn't even know."

"Sometimes having faith is all anyone can do."

I leaned up on my tiptoes and kissed his cheek. "Thank you, Frank, for being such a good friend to Jason and for watching his back."

He smiled. "You're welcome, sweetheart. Now go and marry that sorry ass already."

I giggled and did as I was told. I let go of Frank's hands and carefully walked down the path so as not to get my dress stuck on any of the branches. Maggie had told me to wear flip flops. I had given her a questioning look then, but now I knew why.

I pushed the last low-hanging branch out of my way and saw him. He was standing with his back to me, his hands in his pockets, his feet spread wide, looking out over the ocean where the sun was about to disappear into the water. He was so beautiful he took my breath away.

As if he felt my eyes on him—though he had probably heard me come down the path, it was impossible to walk quietly when you were wearing flip flops—he turned and smiled at me. Then one hand came out of his pocket and he crooked his finger at me. I'd usually have something to say about that, but not now. Now, it was all I could do not to run to him and throw myself into his waiting arms.

I stepped out of my flip flops and walked towards him on my bare feet. He was wearing a pair of loose linen pants and a white flowy linen shirt with its sleeves rolled up that matched my dress perfectly in style and tone. I was sure Maggie had something to do with that and smiled to myself at how perfect this all had turned out in only a few hours. As I got closer, I could see the tattoo on his left forearm. It was brand new, only a few hours old. Jesse's name was written on the inside of his arm in beautiful script. It had been the surprise he had talked about earlier today. He had joined me in the shower after he had called Bob and had just stood there and looked at me. Then he had lifted his arm to brush the hair out of my face and I had seen it. Neither of us had said anything. We didn't need to. We just looked into each other's eyes lovingly and in complete

314

understanding.

This was it.

This was us.

The way we would be forever.

As soon as I was within reach, his hands went to my face and he cupped my cheeks.

"You are the most beautiful woman I have ever seen." His whisper was hoarse and full of emotion. "And you're all mine."

"You're not too shabby yourself." He grinned down at me then kissed me so softly and reverently that my heart skipped a beat. I grabbed his wrists and held on as I kissed him back. He ended the kiss and leaned back without letting go of my face. "You ready?" He asked in a soft voice.

"Always," I answered just as softly. Then, with one last soft brush of his lips, he turned me so we were facing a man I hadn't seen standing only a few feet from us.

"We're ready," Jason announced. He took my hand in his and laced our fingers together. I leaned into his side and rested my head against his shoulder.

And that's how we got married on a secluded beach in California at sunset: just the two of us, holding hands, and leaning against each other as we listened and exchanged our vows and rings, completely in love with each other.

And we wouldn't know it then, but that night when we made love over and over again until we were both happy and sated and completely exhausted, we created the most beautiful thing a couple in love can create: an addition to our family.

JASON

Jason had been awake for an hour, but he couldn't make himself leave the comfort and contentedness of holding his wife to his side.

His wife.

He let his fingers trail random patterns on the skin of Loreley's back as he remembered the past week. Just a week ago, he could have never dreamed to be here with her like this: happy, content, and secure. And married. He grinned to himself.

A week ago, he had felt betrayed and hurt in the knowledge that Loreley had kept his son from him. He was grieving for the loss of the son he had never known and wallowing in self-pity and guilt. He had almost given up on the hope that he could ever be this happy. Now, his life was completely changed. He got his Loreley back only four days ago, but these four days had by far been the happiest of his life.

Now she was his wife.

Loreley stirred in his arms, snuggling deeper into him in her sleep. He brushed his lips against the top of her head and resumed drawing random patterns on her skin. He wanted to stay like this forever. Unfortunately, they had an agenda for the day, something that he hadn't told Loreley about. It would be another surprise. He hadn't been sure if he'd be able to pull it off, but Maggie as well as Robert had worked their magic and had come through for him. He couldn't wait to show her. He just hoped that she wouldn't be upset.

"Good morning, husband," Loreley's whisper brought him out of his thoughts, her words making his heart beat faster. He would never get tired of hearing her call him that.

"Good morning, wife," he whispered back. Then he did what he'd been itching to do for the past hour. He rolled into her so that she was on her back and he covered her body with his, his weight pressing her into the mattress.

"Took you long enough," he teased her while nibbling her bottom lip.

"Why didn't you wake me?"

His fingers brushed through the hair at her temple as his eyes roamed her face. "You looked too beautiful snuggled into my side, so peaceful. I couldn't bring myself to disturb you."

Jason couldn't help himself. He needed his mouth on her, needed to feel her soft skin on his lips. So he gave into the urge and covered her face with soft kisses. When he was done with her face, he moved on to her neck, then to her collarbone and to her shoulder, from her shoulder down to her chest where he brushed his nose against her nipple, then flicked it before he took it in his mouth and sucked.

"You could have gotten up and made breakfast," Loreley said through a quiet moan that made his cock go from half-mast to hard as a rock in less than a second. He let go of her nipple with a plop and soothed it with soft strokes of his tongue.

"You hungry?" He asked while he moved his mouth across her chest to her other breast. Loreley helped him and arched into his mouth.

"Starving." She grabbed his hair with both fists and tugged, making him groan. He loved it when she got rough with him. He loved making love to her any way she would let him, but teasing her to the point where she would get rough and take what she wanted, what she needed, making her lose control, turned him on big time. He ground his cock into her softness, satisfied with her response when she lifted her pelvis against him, urging for more. He didn't hesitate and ground in again.

"Sorry to disappoint."

"Huh?" She asked. She had lost track of their conversation. Jason smiled to himself. He let go of her nipple and leaned back.

Grinning, he said, "I apologize for not fulfilling my husbandly duties and bringing my wife breakfast in bed. But there was no way I was going to leave her in our bed on our first morning as husband and wife without making love to said wife first."

"You're forgiven," she replied instantly then lifted her head and pressed her mouth against his firmly. Her lips opened for him and he dove in hungrily as they once more got lost in each other.

LORELEY

"You know we can only get married once, right?" Frank was pulling up at exactly the same spot he had last night. It looked different in the morning light, less magical, and of course, there were no twinkle lights now, but it was still unbelievably beautiful.

Jason grinned at me and said, "Technically, we can have as many ceremonies as we want." He was sitting beside me in the back of the SUV. I was leaning against his side with one of his arms around my shoulders. He used one hand to play with my fingers, or mostly with the rings there, and the other to play with my hair. I felt content and happy. I was in total and complete bliss.

At his words, I turned my head from looking out the window to looking up at him. "We're having another ceremony?" I asked, surprised and confused. Why were we having another ceremony? We did get married last night, didn't we? We said the vows and signed the papers and everything.

Jason's eyes roamed my face and he burst out laughing at the thoughts he could probably read there. "Don't worry, baby. Everything was legit last night. You're my wife and I'm your husband. And no, we're not having another ceremony."

"Then what are we doing here?"

"That, my love, is a surprise." I scrunched up my face,

making Jason chuckle and kiss my nose. "Don't worry. It's a good one. At least I hope it is." That sounded a little ominous. I didn't have a chance to reply since my phone started ringing again. I checked the screen. My dad. It was the third time he had called this morning. Add four calls from Chris and two from Cal to that, and my phone had practically been ringing off the hook all morning.

"You gonna get that?"

"I'll call him back later," I said as I hit the button that would send the call to voicemail.

"Are you avoiding talking to your dad?" I could hear amusement in his voice as well as a hint of disapproval and maybe disappointment.

I shrugged my shoulders. "I don't know how to tell him. I don't want him to be disappointed or mad at me that he wasn't there when his only daughter got married."

"That why you haven't answered any of Chris' and Cal's calls either? Because you think they'll be mad?" I nodded. My eyes were still on my phone, avoiding making contact with his. This was a tricky situation. I was a grown woman and didn't need anyone's permission to marry the man I loved, but on the other hand, I had been through so much this past year and all my friends and family at home had done everything they could to get me to a place where I could do more than just exist, to get me back to life. I didn't regret getting married to Jason last night. Not one single bit. But I felt a little guilty that we hadn't let anyone share that moment with us.

It was completely silent in the car. Frank must have gotten out at some point since he wasn't sitting behind the wheel. I hadn't even noticed. I moved my eyes back to Jason and saw that his jaw was clenched. He had stopped playing with my fingers and my hair and was tense beside me as he looked out

319

the side window.

"What is it?" I asked, worried by the sudden change.

He didn't turn his head when he said, "Do you regret we didn't wait?" His voice sounded sad and hurt, making my heart drop. I hadn't considered that my hesitancy to tell my family we had gotten married would hurt him. I realized now that I should have thought about that. I scrambled out of my seat and onto his lap. I cupped his face with my hands so he had no choice but to look at me.

"Don't you think for one second that I regret getting married to you last night; I don't. I love you and I love the fact that you are my husband. I wouldn't change it for the world. That's not it. And I don't think any of my family will be mad that we got married. I'm just a little worried that they'll be disappointed we didn't share our moment with them. They're my family and they've been there for me whenever I needed them. No questions asked. I'm worried that they think I didn't want them at my wedding."

Relief flooded Jason's eyes at hearing my words and he snaked his arms around my waist, pulling me flush with his body. Our noses were touching when he spoke. "Baby, they know."

Now it was me who got tense. "They know?"

Jason nodded. "I called your dad as soon as you agreed yesterday and asked him for permission."

My eyebrows flew up in disbelief. "You asked my dad for permission?"

He nodded again. "I did."

Wow. I couldn't believe it. Jason had asked my father for his permission to marry me without him there. I was completely blown away by the thought that the man who never defended his actions to anyone, who didn't care if people liked him or not or agreed with his actions, who was a man's man who didn't appreciate unwanted advice, had put all that aside for me. Because that's the reason he had done it.

For me.

He knew my family meant a lot to me and he wanted to make sure I had their support in this even if I didn't know it. I thought I couldn't have loved him any more than I already did, but as that realization hit me, I fell that much more.

"Thank you," I breathed against his mouth before I took it in a no-holds-barred kiss. He not only joined me too happily, but took over and turned the kiss into a full on make out session. We were like teenagers, making out hot and heavy in the back seat of the car. But all too soon, Jason broke the kiss and we were both breathing heavily. "Jesus, woman."

I smiled, knowing that it took everything right now for him not to take me right here. I had snapped his control. I loved that I could do that.

"You'd be advised to wipe that sexy little smile off your face, baby, unless you want to get fucked on the backseat," he said in that sexy growl of his. My smile grew bigger.

"Fuck, woman," he groaned and hid his face in my neck where he took a few deep breaths. I giggled happily. "Your family and friends are planning a party for us as we speak. That Macy is not someone I want to mess with, so I had to promise to bring you back as soon as possible. We only have today and tomorrow and then we're heading back."

"You talked to Macy?" I asked, surprised. When had he done all this without me knowing? Apart from our separate shopping expeditions we had been together practically every second.

"No. She talked to me. I just listened. That woman is a ball buster." I giggled again. He wasn't wrong. Macy was a handful, but she was the most caring and loyal friend one could wish for.

Jason's face came out of my neck. "I'm not joking. That woman is scary as hell. I feel bad for Larry."

I started laughing. Larry was only too happy with where he was. He didn't need Jason's sympathy. "Don't worry, I'll protect you."

"I had to make a deal with her to get her off my back and stop her from calling me."

"What deal?" My body was still shaking with silent laughter.

"Backstage tickets to any of our concerts for life." My laughter turned from silent to loud out laughing. That sounded like Macy. God, I loved my friend.

"So you gonna answer your phone now and stop worrying?" Jason asked when I calmed down.

"Yeah, I'm gonna answer my phone now."

"And stop worrying."

"And stop worrying," I agreed. "Thank you, honey. I love you."

"I love you, too. More than you'll ever know." He gave me a soft and gentle kiss. "Though I'm a little miffed that you didn't say anything yesterday. I could have eased that worry and guilt."

"I didn't even think about it that much yesterday. I wanted to be married to you and was too excited to think about much else."

"All right, you're forgiven. Now, climb off me. Your surprise is waiting." I had forgotten all about the surprise and where we were. Jason opened the door on his side, and I climbed off his lap, meeting a grinning-from-ear-to-ear-and-shaking-his-head-at-us Frank. As soon as Jason got out behind me, he took my hand and led me down the same path I had taken last night. This time when I made it out the other end, there was a folding table set up with papers all over it and a man leaning on his outstretched arm, studying them.

"What's going on?" I asked.

Jason squeezed my hand and gave me a hesitant look. "Can you keep an open mind?" His voice was just as hesitant as his look.

What the hell was going on?

The guy behind the table must have heard our approach. He lifted his eyes and straightened up. "Mr. and Mrs. Sanders! Nice to meet you on this beautiful morning!" My heart gave a little happy jump at hearing someone address me as Mrs. Sanders. Jason gave me a big smirk, apparently sharing my feelings.

The man rounded the table and shook first Jason's hand then mine and introduced himself as Dan Hopkins. He was a little taller than Jason with wide shoulders, and muscular arms. You could definitely tell that he worked out. His blue eyes were smiling at us and his blond curly hair was blowing in the breeze. He was very good looking, and if he weren't wearing nice suit pants with a button down short sleeved shirt, I would have pegged him for the typical laid back and happy surfer dude.

"I apologize in advance for not having the drawings anywhere near done. My team and I started on it as soon as we received the signed contract yesterday, but unfortunately, it will take a couple of weeks until we have everything narrowed down enough to start."

Drawings? Contract? What was this guy talking about?

"No worries, Dan. I knew we wouldn't have anything solid today. I just wanted to give my wife an idea."

Dan nodded and gave me a wide smile. "Well, I hope you'll like what we've come up with so far. Take a look." He waved towards the papers on the table and I looked at them for the first time. It took me a minute to make sense of what I was seeing, but once my brain made sense of it, I gasped.

They were house plans; footprints of a beautiful beach house. It had two stories, both what seemed to look like big and open with huge windows. I could see an enormous living room, an office, and a kitchen on the main floor, and four big bedrooms, a what seemed to be a flex room, and a loft on the second floor. Then there was the basement with a music studio and another office. And last but not least, the plan of the backyard with a swimming pool, a hot tub, and a guesthouse. In the top corner of the plans someone had pinned photographs of different houses, all with a beach house style theme, and in the opposite corner more photographs, this one of the beach we were standing on from all kinds of different positions and angles.

"What do you think?" Jason asked me, his voice soft and apprehensive.

What did I think? I couldn't think long enough to think anything. All I could do was feel, and what I felt was an overwhelming love for the man standing beside me.

Jason was building us a house here on this beach.

The beach we had said our vows on.

And he wasn't building just any old house.

No.

He was building the house we had always dreamed about.

My heart overflowed and tears welled up in the eyes I couldn't tear away from the drawings.

"Baby?" Jason prompted when I didn't say anything. I sniffled and felt Jason's hand on my cheek turning my head to face him. "Those better be happy tears."

"They are," I whispered through the tears that were now running down my cheeks. Jason used his thumb to brush them away, again and again, until he gave up.

"Why are you crying?"

"Because I can't believe how beautiful you are. You make me so happy."

Jason's face softened and he kissed the top of my nose. "When did you do all this?" I asked him.

"Remember we talked about how we might have to look for a long while until we find the exact house we want?" I nodded. It had only been yesterday. "It gave me an idea. Why waste time looking when we can just build exactly what we want? The house we've always dreamed about? The only thing we'd need would be a lot to build on. This place is special to me. Not only because it's where you became my wife, but because this is where I finally admitted to myself that I wanted you back and would do anything in my power to make that happen. It's the only place where I actually let myself think about you in depth, where I regretted having let you go. And it's the place where I found you again in my heart and in my soul. So I set Robert and Maggie on it, and they tracked down the owner of the land. I made him an offer he couldn't refuse and signed the papers that same afternoon. It's ours, and it will have our dream house on it in less than a year's time."

He was killing me. His words were so beautiful the tears were coming in full force now, and I was sobbing in his arms. When I was done, Jason kissed my wet cheeks.

"You ready to go over the plans?" I nodded and wiped the rest of the tears away with the back of my hand before we both turned back to Dan and discussed every little detail we could think of.

"We'll get on this right away and make the necessary changes. We should have a more final plan by the end of next week. We'll also apply for all the necessary permits now so we don't lose time once we're ready to start building," Dan informed us when we had finished.

"Thank you, Dan. We appreciate it. If you need anything, you have our numbers."

"I'll give you a call if we come across anything we need your input on," Dan confirmed and we parted.

"All good?" Frank asked when we reached him where he had been standing at the edge of the trees this whole time.

"It's great!" I squealed, earning a grin from him. "You'll be happy to hear that you'll have a nice cozy guest house to live in once the house is done."

"I'm glad to hear it," he said through his grin. Then he looked at Jason. "Santa Monica?" Jason agreed with a chin lift and we both followed Frank up the path back to the car. I assumed we were going to Santa Monica to stop at a restaurant for a bite to eat so I didn't ask. Not ten minutes later, we stopped in front of what looked like a hotel. It was on the smaller side for L.A. standards, and cute, more like a boutique hotel, but still looked sophisticated and sexy. It was right on the beach, close to the Santa Monica Pier, and had a somewhat Spanish flair to it.

Instead of turning towards the restaurant, Jason walked us to the check-in counter and handed over his credit card after we were welcomed. "Last surprise for this trip, baby. We don't have time for a honeymoon, but I wanted to give you something to remember. I know you hate my house, so I booked us into the honeymoon suite for two nights until we have to go back to Colorado Thursday morning."

"We're staying here?" I looked around, amazed. I had never stayed in a swanky place like this. Tons of comfortable and expensive looking couches and chairs were spread throughout the lobby, creating several separate seating areas. There was one with a wood-burning fireplace surrounded by a mirrored wall and a piano in the corner where a pianist was playing soft background music. The ceilings were high and decorated with mouldings and gold and brown wallpaper and chandeliers that created soft and warm lighting. Believe it or not, there were even a few palm trees in pots. It was swanky, yes, but somehow it also felt very cozy, as if you could cuddle up with a good book and a blanket on one of the couches and enjoy an afternoon of reading. I could only imagine what the guest rooms would look like and got giddy with excitement.

And I was not disappointed.

When we entered the suite, the first thing I saw was the beach through the large circle top windows. There were so many windows that there was no room for artwork and it felt like you were actually *on* the beach. A chair and two big couches with lots of fluffy pillows were placed in front of the wood-burning fireplace that was surrounded by built-in shelves filled with books. The high ceilings and the soft lighting continued from the lobby and made the room feel grand but homey. There was another small sitting area facing the biggest window with the view of the pier. An opening in the wall lead to the bedroom that hosted the biggest four-poster bed I had ever seen. It was made up with a white comforter and white sheets and lots and lots of decorative pillows. A chaise lounge at the end of the bed and another seating area by the window completed the room. It was absolutely magnificent and I was in awe. I didn't dare look at the bathroom for the risk of being overwhelmed by all this luxury.

I flopped onto the bed backwards and stared at the intricate ceiling.

"You like it?" Jason propped himself on his elbows so he was hovering above me.

"I love it. It's mind-blowing. But you didn't have to do this. We could have stayed at your house." I knew what simple rooms cost in L.A. hotels, and this one was far from simple, so I was aware that it probably cost a fortune. I wasn't used to spending

327

money like this and was a little uncomfortable with it.

"Get that out of your head right now," Jason once again proved his ability of reading me only too well. "We could stay here for the rest of our lives and still not have spent all our money." My eyes grew wide. "Relax, Loreley. I pay a high price by being in the limelight the way I am and even though it guts me, you're going to have no choice but be in the limelight with me. You haven't seen yet what having your life written and lied about in the magazines can do, and I'll do anything I have to do to make up for that part of our lives. I don't care how much money it costs. I want us to have this before the news of us being married leaks. We deserve it. We haven't had this and I need it. And I know you need it, too. Just you and I locked in this room for two days, room service and nothing but our naked bodies to explore. No outside distractions. No phones. No TV. Just us."

The way he said it, it sounded absolutely fantastic. To show him this, I gripped the edge of his shirt and pushed it up until he lifted his arms and I could take it off. Then I roamed my hands over the skin on his back and wrapped my legs around his hip.

"Naked for two days, huh?" I tilted my hip up and ground into him, feeling his erection growing against me.

"For two days and two nights," he murmured against the skin of my neck where he was nibbling and licking and biting languorously.

"That sounds perfect," I sighed and the next second, my shirt was gone and Jason's hands were working to take my jeans off. I followed suit and undid the buttons of his and less than a minute later, we were both naked and breathing heavily as we explored and loved every inch of each other.

And we stayed like this for two whole days and nights with only short breaks to nap and eat: naked and hot, touching, exploring, giving, taking, loving.

It was the best honeymoon ever.

Twenty

LORELEY

Two days later, we had to leave our little bubble of happiness and privacy and were thrown back into reality as soon as we checked out of the hotel. Neither of us had checked our phones or watched TV or been on the internet for forty-eight hours so we didn't know that someone had leaked the news of our wedding to the media.

We were blinded by flashes as we walked out of the hotel and Frank had to cut a way for us to get through the paparazzi to the SUV that was parked out front. Jason had his arm around my shoulders and I was tugged into his side. Question after question and taunt after taunt was shouted at us, calling me a gold digger, calling Jason a man-whore who got duped, telling me not to get too comfortable since everyone knew Jason got around. Some of the things they said were shocking and hurtful, but I tried to ignore their words and block them out in my effort to get to the safety of the car.

That was, until I heard Jesse's name.

That started a whole different wave of questions and insults, the worst calling me a negligent mother who killed her son.

I flinched and Jason swore under his breath. He started

330

walking faster and told Frank to hurry the fuck up and get us to the car. I was shaking by the time we were sitting in the backseat.

"Those fucking bastards," Jason swore, making me flinch again. I was huddled in his arms, too shocked to do anything else but stare at the back of the front seat. "Baby, are you okay?" I shook my head, telling him that, no, I was most definitely not okay. "What the hell was that?" I whispered. "How do they know about Jesse?"

"I don't know. I'm so sorry, baby." Jason kissed my temple and stroked my arm soothingly. He pulled out his phone with his other hand, turned it on and called Maggie.

"Maggie, what the fuck? What the hell is going on?" He snarled at her. I was sitting so close I could hear her response.

"I know. Don't get me started. I've been trying to contain this for the past day."

"You didn't think to warn me what we'd be walking into?" He was mad as hell.

"You had your phone turned off, Jason, and you told me not to contact you under any circumstances. All I did was follow your orders, so keep your pants on. I've been doing my best here and I don't like being snarled at," she snapped back at him.

Jason sighed as he leaned his head against the headrest and closed his eyes. "Fuck, Maggie. They called Loreley a negligent mother who killed her own son!" Jason's body was shaking with fury.

"Shit! How is she?" Maggie asked.

"What do you think? She's sitting in my arms right now, shaking and staring at nothing. Fuck!"

I turned my head and snuggled in deeper as I hid my face in his neck. His arm around me tightened.

"I'm sorry to say that that isn't all they know, Jason. As soon as I put one fire out, there's already another one blazing. They know things that *I* didn't even know. And they have pictures."

"Pictures? What pictures?"

"Of you. With other women. Backstage. Drunk. You name it, they have it."

"What the fuck? How?"

"I'm not sure, but I have an idea. Some of the pictures I've seen can only come from someone who is or works close to you and has done so for a long time. It wasn't me or Frank or any of the band, so it could have only been someone who worked on the team during the tours or..."

"Or who, Maggie?"

"Dana. I think Dana is doing this."

Jason pulled in a breath "That fucking bitch!" he exploded then kissed my temple in apology. But he didn't need to. My shock was turning into rage.

How dare she?

How dare she take something so personal and traumatic and turn it into something to exploit like that?

What a fucking bitch!

I straightened in Jason's arms and looked at him. His head came around and he met my eyes, fury meeting fury.

"Call Robert. I want everything he's got on this and I want him to sue her ass with anything he can come up with."

"Already on it. He's just as furious as you are and he's assured me he'll do whatever he can. You heading to the airport?" Maggie asked.

"Yeah, we are." Jason's eyes were still locked on mine as he kept talking to Maggie.

"Good. I booked you into First Class and made sure you get the special treatment."

"Thanks, Maggie."

"Don't let them get to her, Jason."

"I won't. Gotta let you go. I'll call you when we land." Then he hung up, his eyes still on mine. "You're mad," he said.

"Oh, I'm mad. I don't think I've ever been this mad in my whole life." Even my voice was vibrating with anger.

"That mad, huh? At me?"

I ignored that stupid question and went on. "I'm gonna rip that bitch's head off. Who does something like that? And for what? Because you wouldn't fuck her? I hate women like that, who think they can lay claim to something that isn't theirs, who twist the truths and turn them into something that fits their needs. I fucking *hate* them!"

"Calm down, baby."

"I'm not gonna fucking calm down, Jason! She's gone too far and she's gonna pay for it!"

"Yes, she is. I'll make sure of it. Believe me, you're not the only one who wants to rip her head off, but we gotta be smart about this. Let Robert do his job."

I clenched my teeth and glared at him. No way would I back off or calm down. If I ever saw that woman again, I was going to bitch-slap the shit out of her. I was hoping I would get that chance.

"We gotta talk about something else. There'll be paparazzi at the airport and I assume in Denver and Cedar Creek as well. The story has festered for a day now, which means they'll be like vultures."

I nodded, understanding.

Jason kept talking. "Maggie called ahead for the special treatment. That means we'll be checked in right away and escorted to the First Class lounge where we'll have our privacy. No reporters, no paparazzi, other then when we get out of the car, but Frank will be there to open the door for us and get us

333

through the crowd."

I nodded again, telling him I could handle it. Nothing could be worse than what they had already thrown at us.

"There are pictures."

"I heard," I said through clenched teeth, not liking the thought of that.

"Pictures of me, drunk. With other women."

"I heard that, too."

"I don't want you to look at them."

"Oh, believe me, I don't want to."

"That means no internet, no magazines, no TV reports, no nothing." He seemed anxious. Did he think I was going to run for the hills and leave him over this?

"I'm not leaving you, Jason. You should know better," I said, offended. He gave me a soft kiss on the lips. "I know, baby. Thank you for that. I'm just trying to protect you. Seeing me like that would hurt you and I don't want you hurt. If there were pictures of you out there with other men, I don't know what I'd do."

I softened towards him and leaned my forehead against his. I sighed. "I know. I promise not to look at anything." Another soft brush against my lips.

"Thank you."

"I'm still gonna kick that bitch's ass when I see her again." Most of the fire had left me at his soft words and pleas, though I was still mad."

Jason chuckled. "You saying I won't be able to stop you?"

"Damn straight you won't."

"Don't worry. If we get the chance, I not only won't try to stop you, but I'll damn well cheer you on."

"Same here," we heard Frank murmur from the front seat, making me giggle and Jason chuckle.

334

We pulled up in front of Cooper's. I could only see two people with cameras waiting.

The situation at the airport in L.A. and Denver hadn't been anywhere near as bad as the one in front of the hotel. There were less paparazzi around and Frank did a great job of cutting a path for us so we could get into the terminal quickly. The airport staff checked us in and we were escorted to the lounge within five minutes. It was early afternoon, but as soon as we boarded, we cuddled into our seats and fell asleep since we had to make up for the lack of sleep of the past few days. Not that I was complaining.

We slept through the whole flight. When we landed in Denver, there were even less paparazzi, maybe a handful, and they weren't half as bad as the ones in L.A. had been. Must be that Colorado friendliness and courtesy that every Coloradan was proud to possess. I was relieved that we had escaped the worst and could now hunker down in the mountains and wait for Bob to do his thing and the worst to blow over.

"Why are we at the bar? I thought we were going home?" Jason got out of the car and walked around the back to open mine.

"I told you they'd be throwing us a party as soon as we got back."

"The party is today?"

"Yup. Right now to be precise." He gave me a quick kiss then laced our fingers and walked us to the front door.

"Ready?" He asked before he opened it. I nodded. "Ready." I was excited to see all my family and friends and celebrate with them.

Jason opened the door and we were greeted with loud shouts of "Congratulations!" and "Welcome Home!" It felt amazing to know that everyone was so happy for us. I saw my

335

dad, Cal, Betty, and Pete stand in the front with big smiles on their faces. My dad opened his arms and I flew into them like I always did, as if I was still four years old. His arms wrapped around me tightly as he crushed me to his big body and pressed a kiss to the top of my head.

"I'm so happy for you, my sweet baby girl." His voice broke a little on the last two words, his relief telling me how worried he'd still been about me.

"Thanks, daddy." He squeezed me once more then handed me over to Betty, who swayed me back and forth in her arms.

"I'm proud of you, Lola Girl. And your mom would be, too. And Jesse. So proud of you for making it through, for fighting and not giving up."

"Thank you, Betty."

Next was Pete, who, as usual, didn't say anything, but expressed his feelings with a tight hug. As soon as Pete released me, I was attacked by my two best girlfriends. In pure Macy-fashion, she was jumping up and down with her arms around my neck while she squealed into my ear. Ivey was a little more reserved in her enthusiasm, though she had no choice but to bounce with us.

"How was it? I want to hear everything! In detail! With pictures!" Ivey and I and everyone standing within a ten feet radius burst out laughing, knowing exactly what she was referring to.

"I don't kiss and tell," I said through my laughter.

"Boo. You're boring. Just like Ivey," she pouted. "Everything about the wedding then. And L.A. And the house Jason is building for you." Jeez, Jason hadn't been kidding. Was there anything this woman didn't know already?

"You think I could get a turn with my sister before you ladies start yappin'?" Ivey gave her husband a scowl but didn't object when Cal pulled me out of their embrace and threw his own arms around me. He didn't say anything as he held me.

"You mad at me?" I asked.

"I'm not gonna lie. Would have loved to see my little sister get married. But I got over it. Most important thing is that you're happy and I can see that you are. You're practically glowing, squirt." I laughed into his shoulder at him calling me the nickname I had hated for so many years. "With Chris though, you might have your work cut out for you."

I leaned back and studied his face. It had turned serious and apologetic as he was looking at someone standing behind me. I let go of Cal's shoulders and turned around. Chris was standing in front of me, his arms crossed over his chest and a scowl on his face. He was the only one in the room who didn't look happy to see me. I threw my arms around his neck, taking him by surprise. He had to take a step back to soften the impact. His hands landed on my waist but his arms didn't close around me. I didn't let go and hugged him tighter.

"Please don't be mad at me," I whispered into his ear. "I couldn't stand it. Please, Chris."

He sighed a heavy sigh then gave in and hugged me back.

"I'm sorry," I said as I kept clinging to him.

He sighed again. "I can never stay mad at you for long. It kinda pisses me off." I giggled, happy in the knowledge that I was forgiven.

I leaned back and grinned at him smugly. "How can I make it up to you?"

He shrugged. "I don't know. This is a big one so you better come up with something good." My grin widened and I kissed his cheek. "Love you, Chris."

"Love you, too. You think you can call off your husband? I kinda need all my limbs attached to my body." I looked behind me and saw Jason standing close, glaring at Chris, waiting in the wings to rescue and defend me it looked like.

"It's okay, honey. I'm forgiven," I reassured him on a smile as I beckoned him to come over.

"You'd better be," I heard him murmur as he reclaimed me and pulled me into his side.

"Relax, Sanders. It's all good. As long as you can keep her as happy as she looks right now." Jason nuzzled my neck. "That's the plan," he said. Chris slapped Jason's shoulder, which in guy code meant "We're moving on."

The music started and the party began. For the next hour, I was hugged and kissed and hugged some more as everyone who had come congratulated us. Jason didn't leave my side once. He kept my hand clasped in his, which made the hugging part a little awkward at times, but he wouldn't let go even after I gave him a look.

"I'll share you with your family and close friends, but that's it." And that's all he had to say about that. I didn't think it was worth throwing a fit over, and everyone thought it was sweet, so I let it go. This time.

Until Rick was standing in front of us.

I felt Jason stiffen beside me as he tried to pull me closer to him. "Jason," I said warningly.

"I get it, Sanders. She's taken. Don't worry. I won't try anything." Jason stopped pulling at my hand but still refused to let go when I leaned in and hugged Rick. I rolled my eyes. We'd have to work on his possessive streak.

"I'm happy for you, sweetheart," Rick whispered into my ear.

"You are?" I asked disbelievingly.

"Of course I am. How could I not be? Look at you. I've never seen you this happy." Wow. Rick really was a good guy. I hoped someone would come and sweep him off his feet soon. We separated and I gave him a grateful smile. He smiled back at me then turned his eyes to Jason.

"I'll admit I wanted what you have, but I'm her friend first and I'm happy for her. I wouldn't do anything to destroy that friendship so wipe that glare off your face, Sanders."

I elbowed Jason in the ribs, earning a scowl. "Stop it," I said, my voice low and full of meaning. I was about to pull my hand out of his for real this time, done with his theatrics, when he gave in with a sigh. Then he shocked both me and Rick.

"I wanted to thank you, Rick. For being there for Loreley when I wasn't. I know what you did. All of it. So, thank you. I owe you." I stood there, my eyes wide and my mouth open as I stared at my husband holding his hand out for Rick to shake. This was huge and it made me unbelievably proud that he could put his possessiveness aside and be the man I knew him to be towards a man he didn't like all that much.

I looked from Jason to Rick and saw that Rick, too, was shocked. Then I watched as he took Jason's hand and they shook. And that was it. They understood each other. They might never become best buds, but they respected each other enough to let go of the rivalry. Rick gave me another smile then turned and headed back to the bar.

"I want to jump you right this second," I said when Rick was out of earshot.

"Yeah?" Jason rested his hands on my hips and leaned in for a kiss.

"Oh yeah," I confirmed right before I laid a hot and wet one on him. Catcalls erupted all around us, but I couldn't care less. I was lost in my husband and the happiness and love we shared.

339

Twenty-One

LORELEY

The party was in full swing and I was a little tipsy when I realized I needed to use the washroom. As he had most of the night, Jason was standing behind me with one arm around my waist, his hand resting on my opposite waist, as he chatted and laughed with everyone. At the moment, we were standing with Nathan, who, upon seeing us, had scooped me up and twirled me around, whooping and laughing, Jason had received a man hug with lots of hard and painful looking pats on the back and an "About time, my man."

I took his hand in preparation to extricate myself from Jason's arms and felt his chin on my shoulder. "Where're you going?"

"Restroom," I answered. He kissed my temple and let me go.

I looked into the mirror as I was washing my hands. Many people had mentioned tonight how happy and glowing I looked. And I could see it, too. The sadness that had lived in me and hovered above me like a constant dark cloud was gone. My eyes were wide and glittering with a certain sparkle, my cheeks were flushed, and the corners of my mouth were turned up in a small

340

happy smile. Having lost Jesse the way I had when I had would always make me sad to some degree, but now, instead of focusing on that sadness and pain and letting it control me, I concentrated on all the good and happy memories and was grateful that I had those to share with his father. It was almost like talking about our son the way we had had brought him back to me, but in a different way. Even though I was heartbroken that I would never be able to hold him again, I knew that his spirit would always be with me, Jesse would always live on within us; he would never be forgotten. He was a part of both Jason and I, and I was unbelievably grateful that I had had the fortune of knowing him and sharing a part of my life with him. I knew wherever he was he was happy and with my mom, and that was enough for me.

I dried my hands and left the restroom, but before I could make it back into the main room of the bar, I felt a hand on my upper arm pulling me towards the back of the hall. First I thought it was Jason, wanting some alone time in my office, but then the stale scent of an unwashed body mixed with beer breath reached my nose and it hit me that this wasn't Jason or anyone I would want near me. By the time my brain clicked and told me to do something, the man had me almost out the back door. I started to panic and struggled as I tried to hold on to the doorframe to stop him from taking me outside where he would do only God knows what to me but it was no use. My body was yanked viciously by an arm around my waist, making my fingers lose hold, and my fingernails bent the wrong way.

"Don't start, bitch. You know I don't have any trouble knocking you out cold. You're coming with me, one way or another." His mouth was right at my ear as he held my body, my back flush to his chest. His breath smelled foul and rank and his voice was hoarse, but I had no doubt who he was.

341

Brad.

I thought he was still in jail.

"What are you doing, Brad?" I tried to sound stern but knew I failed by his low and pleased laugh.

"You think I would let you get away with what you did? With humiliating me? The whole town has shunned me. I lost my job because I got arrested and have assault charges against me. All that is your fault. And you're gonna pay."

"What are you going to do to me?" I couldn't help but let my fear seep into my voice. I knew I didn't stand a chance. Brad was a big guy and the way he held me right now, effortlessly, without giving me a chance to even move, I knew that all I could do was stall and hope that someone would see us before he hauled me off.

"Oh, I'm gonna do lots of things to you. And not all of them will be fun for you, but that doesn't matter. I enjoy a little fight before I get what I want." I knew what that meant. Disgust churned in my stomach and I gagged. I started struggling again, but he had my arms wrapped around my own stomach as he carried me across the dark parking lot, making them useless. I kicked my legs but that didn't help, either. "I'm gonna take you to a place where nobody will find you and I'm not gonna let you go until you gave me what I've wanted for over a decade. When I'm done with you, your world famous husband can pay up if he still wants you. We'll see who the loser is then." I started screaming as loudly as I could in the hopes that someone would hear me. Brad had to let go with one hand to clamp it over my mouth and that gave me enough leverage to free one of my arms. I gripped his ear and twisted harshly.

"Aaargh!" Brad howled and let me go. "You fucking bitch!"

I ran, ran as fast as I could.

He tackled me to the ground and landed on top of me,

making me hit my chin against the pavement and knocking the wind out of me. Then I was on my back and he was sitting on my stomach. A sharp impact on my temple made me see stars for a second before I could focus on him again.

I heard voices far away, and running footsteps.

Then I heard a roar and felt another impact in the same spot as before. I groaned and tried to hold on to my consciousness. My eyes felt heavy and everything was out of focus. I could feel that Brad was trying to lift me up, but he must have tripped and fallen, because I was back on my back on the pavement.

Then I felt nothing but a sharp pain in my head. I didn't know where he was, if he was still on top of me, or if he was carrying me. My body felt numb and heavy and my head was pounding so hard I could feel it in the back of my eyes.

The last thing I heard before the blackness took me was Jason's roar of "Loreley!", but he sounded too far away. I knew he would never get to me in time.

JASON

Jason was craning his neck to look at the hallway that led to the restrooms. Loreley had been gone for a long while now and his gut was telling him that something was wrong. He tried to find Frank in the crowd that surrounded him, cursing himself for not having him on duty tonight. But this was a party and as Loreley had told him over and over again, there was nothing she needed protection from here. They were surrounded by friends and family. Still, he couldn't shake the feeling of foreboding as he scanned the crowd and finally made eye contact with his good friend and bodyguard. Frank knew immediately that something was up and came over, leaving the girl he'd been

343

talking to in the middle of the conversation without a second glance.

"What's wrong?" His voice was alert and his eyes were scanning, looking for something out of place. He was in bodyguard mode.

"I don't know. Loreley went to the restroom a while ago and hasn't come back. I've got a bad feeling."

"I'll go check it out." Jason followed him. They checked the hallway and both restrooms, but she wasn't in either. Jason strode to the office door, thinking and hoping that maybe she was in there. The door was locked, and when he knocked and called her name, he got no answer.

"I'm gonna sweep the floor. Maybe she just got stuck talking to someone." They shared a look and Jason could tell that Frank didn't believe his own words. There was a tightness on his face that told him that Frank felt it, too. Something was wrong. Panic hit his gut when he followed Frank back into the bar and they both started searching for her in the crowd.

Then he heard his name called from the front door. "Mr. Jason! Mr. Jason!" Jason turned his head and saw one of the photographers he had seen outside earlier wave his arms at him. He was short and was wearing black slacks and a button down shirt that was tucked into his pants. Jason had seen him before and this guy was actually the only paparazzo he had never hated. He was always polite and asked before he could take his picture, never said a rude word to him and always had a small smile on his face. He didn't now though. He looked panicked.

"Mr. Jason! You need to come! Quickly!" He said in his heavily accented English. The bad feeling in his gut got heavier and he followed the man outside. He could feel Frank right on his heels. The picture that greeted him when he got outside and they turned the corner made his blood boil.

344

There was Loreley, lying on the ground, covered in blood, groaning. And Brad was trying to drag her up and carry her off. Frank was already running towards Brad and tackled him, dislodging Loreley from his arms as he did so.

"Loreley!" Jason shouted and fell to his knees beside her on the ground. There was blood everywhere. On her temple, on her lip, and when he lifted her into his arms, he saw there was blood on the back of her head as well.

"No, no, no, no, no! Baby, wake up! Loreley, wake up!" He kept shouting at her, willing her to open her beautiful eyes for him, but she didn't move. "Call an ambulance! Somebody call an ambulance!" He roared. He could hear running footsteps and shouts heading his way but he didn't take his eyes off his wife. "Wake up! Loreley!"

"Let me take a look." A guy was kneeling beside him, gently taking her out of his arms and lowering her back to the ground. Jason remembered meeting him inside. He couldn't remember his name but he did remember his occupation: he was an EMT.

Jason watched anxiously as he checked Loreley's vitals, took her pulse, checked her eyes and inspected her wounds. There was so much blood.

He tore his eyes away from his wife's injured body and found Brad. Frank had him in a restraint on the ground, his arms behind his back held up high, a knee in his back. Jason could see that Frank was speaking to him but couldn't make out what he was saying. As if in a trance, he got up and walked over to where they were on the ground only a few feet away. Red-hot fury was blazing through him. He didn't know what he was going to do once he reached them, but he knew he wouldn't be able to control himself once he started.

"Don't be stupid." Jason felt a hand in his chest holding him back from advancing on the scumbag who had hurt his wife. He looked up to see Rick in front of him. "Don't be stupid," he repeated. Jason said nothing as he glared at Rick.

"I'm taking him in. A car is already on the way."

"Why the fuck was he out in the first place? And why the fuck did nobody tell us?" Jason roared in his face.

Rick shook his head. "I don't know. It was my day off and nobody informed me that he had been released," Rick didn't sound happy to admit. He sounded furious.

"I want him to pay for what he's done. Everything you've got, and make sure it sticks this time. Or I swear to God, if he gets out again, I will hunt him down and I will not stop until I've had my revenge."

Rick ground his teeth. "You have my word." They stared at each other for long moments before Jason turned around and went back to his wife. The ambulance had arrived and two EMTs were lifting Loreley onto a stretcher. Cal and Chris were standing close, both with murderous and worried looks on their faces. Ivey was huddled into Cal, crying. Jason walked right to the stretcher and took Loreley's limp hand in his. She was still unconscious and seeing her like that tore at Jason's heart.

"Tell me she'll be okay." He didn't make eye contact with any of the EMTs, but they knew he was talking to them.

"We'll be able to tell you more once we've done some tests, but she is stable for now. She has sustained a severe trauma to her head and that comes with some risks, but her eyes look good and we're optimistic. I assume you're coming with us?"

Jason nodded absentmindedly, still stuck on the words *severe trauma*. He wasn't about to leave her and let them take her from him. There was no way he would leave her side even for a second. She was his reason to breathe, his reason for existing. She had to be okay.

He didn't let go of her hand as they loaded her into the back of the ambulance and he climbed in with her. He never let go of her hand as they drove to the hospital, he never let go until he absolutely had to when they took her in for tests, and even then they had to pry his hand off of hers.

LORELEY

I woke up with the worst headache I had ever experienced. It was so bad that I wanted to fall back into unconsciousness. I knew by the smell that assaulted my nose that I was in a hospital. I opened my eyes a crack. The brightness of the lights blinded me, shooting sharp pains through my head, making the throbbing pain even worse. I closed my eyes again and groaned.

Whose bright idea was it to put blinding ceiling lights in hospital rooms anyway? Whoever it was, he should get fired.

I felt pressure in my hand right before I heard a soft voice calling my name. "Loreley? Baby, you awake?"

It was Jason.

I turned my head towards his voice and groaned again at the pain that movement caused.

"You can hear me, can't you?" I wanted to nod to tell him that, yes, I could hear him, but was afraid it would hurt too much. I opted instead for giving his hand a slight squeeze.

"You can hear me," Jason semi-repeated. He sounded tired and relieved. How long had I been out? "Please, baby, try and open your eyes for me. Let me see those beautiful green eyes of yours." I wanted to see him, too. So badly. I tried and pried my eyes open another crack. My eyelids were heavy, but I won the fight and managed to keep them open long enough to focus on Jason. He looked unbelievably tired. His eyes were red-rimmed, had black circles under them, and he looked like he hadn't shaved in a few days.

"Hey," he whispered softly. "Welcome back." I saw him reach for something and assumed he was calling a nurse. I was grateful. The pain was so bad I needed them to give me something.

"Hey," I croaked. My tongue was dry and thick and my throat felt like someone had shoved barbed wire down it.

"You want some water?"

"Yes, please," I replied on a whisper, my voice sounding raspy and weak.

Jason reached for something and came back with a cup of water that had a straw in it. He held it to my mouth and helped me with the straw. I took a tiny sip and flinched when the water hit my throat as I swallowed.

"Easy, baby. Small sips." I took another one and this time it hurt a little less.

"What happened?" I asked when I was done.

Jason put the cup back on the tray. "You don't remember?" I thought about the last thing I remembered. We were at a party at the bar. Our party. I went to the restroom and then…Brad. It all came back to me in an instant. "Brad. He grabbed me when I came out of the restroom."

Jason nodded. His eyes had turned angry in hearing Brad's name but his face remained soft. "He was going to take me somewhere and …" I didn't want to say out loud what Brad had planned to do to me. I didn't need to. It looked like Jason knew only too well. His eyes turned darker. I kept talking. "I fought him and he hit me. That's all I remember. He must have knocked me out."

Jason's hand came up and stroked my cheek gently. "He did knock you out. And you hit your head on the cement when he dropped you when Frank tackled him. You have a small crack in your skull, but all your tests came back clean."

"He cracked my skull?" That made sense. My head did feel like it was split open right down the middle. Jason nodded solemnly. "Where is he? Did they get him?" He nodded again. "He's in jail and has been refused bail. You're safe." That was good news. I sighed and closed my eyes, exhausted.

The door opened and a nurse walked into the room. "Hey there. How are we feeling today?"

"My head hurts," I said with my eyes still closed.

"I bet it does. I'll give you something for it as soon as the doctor has had a good look at you."

"Okay," I said, grateful.

She made me open my eyes again and checked and prodded what felt like everywhere before she left and said she'd be back with the doctor.

"How long have I been out?" I asked Jason when the nurse had left.

"Almost two days," Jason answered, his voice heavy and tired.

"Two days?" Wow. No wonder he looked like crap.

"Two very long days. The longest days of my life." I tried to lift my hand. I needed to touch him. My arm was so heavy it took all the strength I had to put my hand to his cheek, but I succeeded. We both sighed at the contact. Jason grabbed my hand with his and pushed it against his skin as he nuzzled into it. "You scared the shit out of me, Loreley. If you hadn't made it…"

"Shh," I soothed him. "I'll be okay. You said it yourself. All my tests came back clean."

"I know." He closed his eyes and kissed my palm.

"You need some sleep."

"I'll sleep when you're back home and lying beside me." I smiled to myself. It might be selfish, but I didn't want him to leave and I was grateful that he didn't want to leave my side either.

Then the doctor came in and examined me thoroughly.

"You'll have a headache for a couple of weeks, but everything else looks fine. Your vitals are stable and your memory seems good. Give it a couple of days and take it easy and you can go home."

"Okay. Thank you, doctor." He smiled at me, nodded at Jason, and left the room. The nurse came back and gave me my pain medication, making me pass out in less than a minute.

It went on like this for the next two days, me in and out of consciousness, but more alert and in less pain every time I woke up. My family visited me and talked to me whenever I was awake. Jason never left my side. He grabbed a shower in my room while I was asleep and promised me he would eat something and at least catch some shut-eye with me, but he never left.

It was the day I was finally being released. Betty had gone to my house and brought me some clothes and everything I needed to take a shower. Jason refused to let any of the nurses help me, so it was he who not only helped me in and out of the shower, but who hopped in with me and washed my body. There was no hanky-panky going on, that would have to wait for a little while until my head stopped pounding. He washed me gently and with a purpose and held me to his naked chest when I asked him to. I needed the contact and so did he. We stood like that for a good long while, until he turned off the water and dried first me, and then himself. Then he carefully brushed my wet hair before he helped me dress and sat me in the chair to wait for him while he sorted himself.

As Jason had promised me, Brad had not been released and was waiting for his trial at the Colorado State Penitentiary.

Robert had called just that morning, informing us that it had been Dana who had paid bail for Brad. If you asked me, she was one fucked-up bitch to say the least. Who does shit like that? Scorned woman or not, the extremes she had gone to were just plain insane. Jason had gone ballistic and if it hadn't been for the fact the he wouldn't leave my side I think he would have hunted her down himself. As far as Robert could tell, Maggie had been right in her guess and it was also her who was feeding the media with all the garbage that had been published, though since my hospitalization, the tone of what had been said had changed dramatically. The few paparazzi that had been outside the bar that night, had seen enough to testify; with the pictures they took as evidence. The only one who hadn't taken any pictures was the man who had gone inside the bar to get Jason. His name was Ajay Chowdhury. The others had run with the story, and let me tell you, it was no fun seeing those pictures of me in the news. Those people had no scruples. But it changed how the public saw me from then on. I wasn't the gold digger and child killer they had called me at first. I was the victim of a vicious attack, who had almost been killed on top of having endured the trauma of having lost her child just a year ago. So that was at least something. In his gratitude for getting to him that night, Jason had promised Ajay an exclusive interview with the both of us once I was feeling up to it.

Jason was going to sue Dana, not for posting bail, since she couldn't be sued for that, but for releasing information that she garnered while she worked for him. It was a little tricky to get the proof on that, but Robert was optimistic that he could get his hands on something they could use in court. He promised us that she wouldn't dare show her face ever again once he was done with her. I still wanted to bitch-slap the shit out of her, but unfortunately, it looked like I'd never get the chance.

We signed the papers and Jason took me home. Well, to Cal's rental. Jason was a little paranoid about my safety right now, and I couldn't blame him.

"I want us to stay close to Frank and there isn't enough room at your house." I didn't fight him on it. It's what he needed. I understood. I was okay with it for now, but we couldn't stay here forever.

"I've paid the rent for the next few months, baby. Don't worry about it." We were lying on the lounge chair on the back deck, Jason on his back, me on my side snuggled into him. I had been released almost two weeks ago now and felt better every day.

"That's not it, Jason. As much as I love this house it's not ours. It's not home."

Jason sighed, frustrated. This wasn't the first time I had brought it up and he was getting annoyed with me. "You said you understood. Your house is too small, especially if it turns out that you're pregnant. And I can't make it safe enough for our family without some major renovations. I don't want to leave you right now to deal with any of that, so it's gonna have to wait."

My hand went to my flat stomach. I was late, but the doctors had said my body might skip a period because of the trauma and stress it had endured. I wasn't worried yet. Not that I would be worried if I was pregnant. I was actually hoping I was.

Jason's hand joined mine on my stomach and he smiled a proud and loving smile at me. He was smug. I shook my head at him, smiling, before went back to the topic at hand. "Then buy us a new house."

His eyebrows shot up in surprise. He had thought I wouldn't want to leave the house I had raised Jesse in, nor did I like him spending that kind of money. But that didn't matter to me anymore. The memories would always stay with me, no matter where we lived. And I'd have to get used to us being rich at some point. "You're okay with me buying you a new house?"

"Us. You'd be buying *us* a new house. You and me. And possibly our new baby. And Frank of course." I smirked at him teasingly. I expected him to hug me or kiss me, but to my surprise, Jason got up and pulled me up with him. "What are you doing?"

"We're going to look at houses," he said in a duh-like fashion as he walked us inside.

"What? Now?"

"Of course now. My wife wants a home and she's not arguing with me about spending too much money on it, so I better seize the moment and buy her one."

"You're insane," I whined.

He stopped and pulled me into his embrace. "I'm insanely in love with you," he said, melting my heart. "Now, get your pretty tush in gear and stop whining." He kissed the tip of my nose and pushed me towards the stairs, telling me to get dressed in something else than short-short pajama pants and a tank top, another point of discord we'd had over the past week. He thought they were too short for company, but they were the most comfortable clothes I had. I got my way and kept them on while we were in the house, even when we had visitors, but when we left, I had to put on something that covered me up a little more. Little did he know I'd never leave the house dressed in my pajamas anyway, so I was pretty smug about my victory.

I came back down dressed in my short jeans skirt, a loose fitting beige t-shirt with a longhorn printed on it, and my flip flops.

"Ugh," Jason groaned when he saw me. I grinned at him

353

and threw him a kiss. "How's your head?" He asked as he walked slowly towards me. His voice was low and sexy and very suggestive.

"Good," I answered, a little breathlessly. Jason hadn't touched me since I'd been released from the hospital. Not like that at least and I missed him. The doctor had given us the okay during my last check-up two days ago, but Jason had still been hesitant. He didn't want to hurt me.

"Just good?" He had reached me now and stroked his finger down the side of my face, stopping at my bottom lip.

"Great. It's great," I breathed against his finger. Jason removed it and replaced it with his mouth. I sagged into him and groaned. He saw it for the invitation it was and went deep, consuming me. He ended the kiss and rested his forehead against mine, both of us breathing hard.

"I miss you, baby."

"Then take me upstairs," I whispered, resulting in a chuckle from Jason.

"House first. I gotta make sure my wife and baby are taken care of. But you're mine for the rest of the afternoon. No visitors. Just you and me. Naked. Pretend we're back in Santa Monica."

I liked that. A lot.

"Deal," I said. Then he kissed the tip of my nose again and we went house hunting.

Epilogue

LORELEY

"I can't believe it took you almost eight years to bring me here." We were standing in front of the entrance to Disneyland.

It had turned out that Jason had gotten me pregnant during our wedding night. Two months after the attack and my subsequent hospital stay, my period was still a no-show, so I had taken a test and it had been positive. Jason and I had been over the moon and couldn't wait to welcome our new baby into the family. We both had been a little worried at first that something might have happened to the baby because of the attack and all the stress it caused me, but my pregnancy had gone smoothly and there hadn't been any issues whatsoever.

It hadn't taken us long to find a house we liked, less than twenty-four hours to be exact. We had looked at three different ones that first afternoon and had bought the second one we'd looked at. It was perfect. Funnily enough, it was one of Cal's builds. We moved in two weeks later and still lived there now during the school year. All our long weekends and holidays were spent in our house in California. Sometimes we brought the family along, sometimes it was just Jason, me, and the kids. And every year on our wedding anniversary, Jason and I came out

355

here alone and spent three days at the hotel we had been to for our honeymoon. He had wanted to take me somewhere exotic, somewhere I had always wanted to go, but going back to what I thought of as our place every year was all I wanted. So he made it happen and never suggested anything different again. At least not for our anniversary.

"Mom, let's go already!" Our oldest, Samantha, whined at me. She was seven and was bouncing up and down in anticipation, pulling at her daddy's hand. Jason grinned down at her proudly. On his hip sat Lola, our five-year-old. She was a complete daddy's girl, they both were, but Lola wouldn't leave her daddy's side. She had been like that from the second she was born. Opening her eyes wide only hours later and smiling for her daddy. It had been a sight to see.

"Mommy, am I allowed on the big rides?" Ash was our youngest. He was three years old, and just like Lola was Jason's, Ash was mine. His full name was Christopher Ash Raymond, but everyone called him Ash, mostly to avoid confusion. I remember the day we had introduced him to our family and friends like it was only yesterday.

"Christopher? You're naming your son after me?" Chris had tears in his eyes. He was looking down at the bundle in his arms and couldn't seem to tear his eyes away from him. He loved our girls and spent as much time with them as he could. He and his wife Charly were expecting their second. Our kids and Ivey and Cal's kids were all close in age and were practically growing up together like brothers and sisters.

"Yeah. Didn't you say I had to come up with something big to make it up to you for not having you at my wedding?" Jason chuckled beside me and Chris' eyes shot to mine. "I didn't mean—" me bursting into laughter at the panic in his eyes stopped him and he realized I had been teasing.

I grinned to myself, remembering. Chris and Ash were best buddies, just like Jesse and Chris had been. Ash adored his daddy and was a total momma's boy but he had a special bond with Chris that nobody could miss.

"No, baby. You have to be taller to be allowed on the big rides. Mommy will take you on the kid rides. Maybe daddy will take us more often now and soon enough you'll be allowed on the big rides with mommy."

"Okay," he complied and snuggled into my side.

"I wouldn't count on it," Jason muttered under his breath as we walked towards the entrance. I whipped my head around at his words, shooting him a glare. "You agreed that we were done."

"I agreed to no such thing." He showed no remorse as he smirked at me.

"You didn't argue."

"That doesn't mean I agreed. I say we try for one more."

"Pfft. Try. We don't need to try. As soon as I go off the pill...boom...pregnant. We probably don't even have to have sex." I scoffed. Jason burst out laughing, but he knew damn well that I was right. It had been like that with all our kids. Pregnant within the first week. It was ridiculous really.

"Well, baby, enjoy the shit out of this day. There won't be another visit to Disneyland in the near future."

"What do you mean? I'm not pregnant."

"Not yet." The sure way he said that made me narrow my eyes at him. "What have you done?" I asked.

"Nothing really. Just disposed of your pills this morning." My eyes went big with shock.

"You did not!"

"I did, too."

"You...you...I don't even know what to call you!" Damn it!

357

If I didn't get replacement pills today I ran the risk of being pregnant already. I was in the middle of my cycle, which meant missing a pill was so not a good idea. That rat bastard!

"Baby." Jason's voice was mollifying. "I love you and I love the family we've made. How can you be mad that I want more of what makes us both so happy?"

"I'm not mad about that. I'm mad about how you went about it. Tricking me into getting pregnant. That's so low."

"You wouldn't yield so I took the matter in my own hands." Yield? I thought my head was about to explode! He on the other hand grinned at me almost nonchalantly about being such an ass.

"Well, if you had given me the courtesy of discussing it like adults instead of demanding that I go off the pill and pout like a little boy when I didn't *yield*, I might have agreed. Now I'm afraid I won't be able to accommodate certain needs you might have later today. Or the rest of the month."

"That's not gonna happen, baby, and we both know it."

"Then you'll have to use—"

"That's also not gonna happen. I want nothing between you and me and neither do you."

"Arrgh." I stopped myself from stomping my foot and embarrassing myself by looking like a teenager throwing a fit. Then I took a deep breath and since I knew this would be the only way to resolve this, I decided to compromise and threw him a bone. "Two months. Give me two months. I want to enjoy this summer without being sick all the time."

"Two months?" He asked. "You promise?" I nodded. "You gotta say the words, baby."

I gave in. "I promise."

"Good. You've got a deal. We're trying as soon as the summer is over." He kissed me. "Oh, and by the way, you'll find your pills exactly where you left them last night."

"You...you..." I stuttered. "You tricked me? You didn't throw them out?" He shook his head, grinning at me. "Nope."

"I can't believe you just did that."

"Baby, you're gorgeous always, but you're over the top soul wrenchingly gorgeous when you're pregnant. I'm not ready to be done with that. I'm not ready to let go. And we make the most beautiful babies in the world. Don't be mad."

As always, the way he had with words melted my heart. I knew they weren't just words. He meant every single one of them and proved that he did every single minute of every single day. Our need for each other hadn't diminished over the years. It was the opposite. We did everything together, went everywhere together, and took our kids whenever possible. They even came on tour with the band, at least before Samantha had started school two years ago. Now we had to work a little harder on the schedule to make things work smoothly, but it was worth it. Whenever there was an event I couldn't attend and he had to go alone, we were both miserable and couldn't wait to be back in each other's arms.

"You're gonna run out of spots to tattoo our kids' names," I grumbled against his lips, but he knew that I had given in. Just like he had with Jesse's name, he had all our kids' names tattooed on his body: the girls' on his chest above his heart, the boys' on his forearms.

Jason chuckled. "Don't worry. I'll find room. I love you, Loreley."

"I love you, too."

"Now let's go have some fun."

"Yay!!!" All our kids screamed at the same time. They had been waiting patiently for their parents to finish bickering. They were used to it. I giggled against Jason's mouth and whispered,

"Yay!"

Exactly one year later, we welcomed Carter Dylan Sanders into our family.

The End.

Enjoy other works by Julia Goda

Bent Not Broken (Cedar Creek #1)

Life has taught Ivey Jones early on that with trust come pain and betrayal. Out of survival she has created walls around her to keep anyone from getting too close. Though she lives in her dream house in the Rocky Mountains and loves being the owner of the town's quirky little bookstore Serendipity, her life is narrow and governed by strict rules that she never deviates from...until Cal Bennett enters her life.

For the past nine years Calvin "Cal" Bennett has stayed away from Ivey, thinking she deserved better than to be saddled with a single dad who has never been good at relationships. Until a few chance encounters show him what he's been missing and he can't stay away any longer.

Little does he know he's got a fight on his hands that he might not be equipped to win. Shadows from Ivey's past lurk in the dark, ready to strike and bring her low once and for all. But Cal swears he will do whatever it takes to break through that wall of steel to win Ivey's heart and keep her safe.

~

Now available on Amazon, iBooks, Kobo, Barnes & Boble

About the Author

Julia Goda has been writing stories in her head since she can remember. Much to her teachers' dismay, given the task of writing a short essay she would always come back with way too long and detailed stories. Many discussions (she has always been somewhat of a smart-aleck) and bad grades were the result, so that for most of her life she thought she couldn't write worth a damn and pursued other careers. But the dream of being an author wouldn't be ignored and kept lingering. With a little help from her fantastic husband, who gave her the necessary kick in the behind, she was finally brave enough to start writing her first novel. Since then she has enjoyed giving herself over to her stories and making them come to live.

Her novels jump genres and touch on all kinds of different topics, but the things she tries to focus on no matter what are romance, strong women, and a good sense of humor.

Now, when she is not in her writing cave, spinning the tales that have been prodding her or editing, she enjoys reading, drinking coffee, eating good food, and listening to rock music.

Julia Goda has lived in Germany, Virginia, and Colorado (where she fell in love with Boulder and the Rocky Mountains). Her current home is Southern Alberta, Canada, where she lives close enough to the Rockies with her husband and chocolate lab to enjoy the beauty and excitement that is mountain living.

Connect with Julia Goda:

www.juliagoda.net
www.facebook.com/juliagodaauthor
Amazon: https://www.amazon.com/author/juliagoda
Google: www.google.com/+JuliaGoda
Goodreads: https://www.goodreads.com/author/Julia_Goda
Twitter: julia_goda